Love A Dark Rider

As they stood there oddly frozen in time, her slim body barely brushing against the whipcord leanness of his, she told herself that it was only fright that made her blood race, that it was fear that made her lower limbs tremble. But in her heart, she knew she lied. With widening eyes she watched the anger fade from his features and the sudden sensual twist to his bottom lip made her mouth go dry.

Then he was kissing her again, half savage, almost violent kisses that made the fire in her belly flare hotter. It was only when his lips began their burning descent once more that full sanity returned. And, with a soft half moan, half sob, she tore herself out of his arms and bolted from the room as if the very hounds of hell were on her heels.

SHIRLEE BUSBEE

"ONE OF THE BEST LOVED
ROMANCE AUTHORS"
Romantic Times

"SHE JUST KEEPS GETTING BETTER
WITH EACH NEW BOOK SHE WRITES"
Affaire de Coeur

SHIRLEE BUSBEE

Love A Dark Rider

AVON BOOKS ◆ NEW YORK

LOVE A DARK RIDER is an original publication of Avon Books. This work has never before appeared in book form. This work is a novel. Any similarity to actual persons or events is purely coincidental.

AVON BOOKS
A division of
The Hearst Corporation
1350 Avenue of the Americas
New York, New York 10019

This book is dedicated, with my very great affection, to my "boys"—although now that they're all over twenty-one, perhaps I should say, to my "young men"!

ALEX POPE, who has actually read and admitted, under duress, naturally, that he enjoyed *The Spanish Rose*, and who is forever linked in my mind with bone meal and Ranunculus—yes, Alex, it *is* an ugly tuber! and,

RICK SPENCE, who was gone in a flash, but who very kindly found me,

BRYAN "MOOSE" MCFADIN, undoubtedly one of the best "manure movers of America," and who *hasn't* read one of my books yet, despite the fact that I listen faithfully to all the tapes of *his* musical efforts! and,

HOWARD BUSBEE, who is *still*, after thirty years, the man of my dreams.

PROLOGUE

TWININGS
APRIL 1860

*Fortune is not satisfied
with inflicting one calamity.*

MAXIM 274
—PUBLILIUS SYRUS

1

Sara dreamed of the Dark Rider for the first time the night her father, Matthew Rawlings, was killed in a saloon gunfight. After the initial hubbub had died down and she had been kindly escorted to the privacy of her room in the boardinghouse where Matthew had procured cheap lodgings the previous day, she had lain on the lumpy cot and stared blindly in the direction of the ceiling. Grieving and stunned, she had been unable even to think; she could only lie there in the darkness, dry-eyed and numb, not able to believe the tragedy that had overtaken her so suddenly. Eventually she must have fallen asleep, and it was then, in her hour of deepest grief, that the Dark Rider had come to her. . . .

The surroundings were always a blur to Sara, but if she could not place where she was, she knew that she was in grave danger, that she was going to die. In the dream, she didn't know how she was going to die, only that she *would* die if help did not arrive soon. She wasn't afraid of dying in her dreamworld, but she was aware of a strong sensation of regret, of great sadness, a feeling that if she had done something differently, if she had made another choice, life—perhaps even a long and happy life—would have been her fate, instead of this lonely death. And it was then, when all hope was gone, that *he* appeared!

3

One moment the horizon before her was an empty and desolate blue; the next, on a slight rise, a dark rider would suddenly materialize. His face was always in shadow, his black, broad-brimmed hat pulled low across his features, his tall, lean body effortlessly controlling the movements of his horse. She never saw his features clearly, yet she knew with every fiber of her being that she loved him and that, because of him, she would not die—her beloved Dark Rider would save her.

For Sara, even in her dream, time stopped as the Dark Rider remained motionless on that slight rise, his gaze sweeping the distance, those keen eyes searching desperately for her. And then suddenly that piercing gaze would find her, and with a wild flurry of motion, his horse would explode into action and the next second she would be in his embrace, his strong arms cradling her near his thunderously beating heart, his warm mouth trailing sweet, oh-so-sweet kisses across her face, his husky voice murmuring the words she most wanted to hear. In that precious second, locked securely in his arms, she knew that she would always be safe, that never again would she be alone . . . for her Dark Rider loved her. . . .

From the grimy, rain-streaked window of her cheerless little room in the attic of the boardinghouse, Sara could just make out the small cemetery and the bare earthen mound that marked her father's two-month-old grave. Matthew Rawlings' final resting place was not one that Sara would have chosen for him, but then, in all of her nearly seventeen years of life, it had seemed that *she* had seldom had any choice but to follow willy-nilly where fate, or more specifically, her father, had led her. And while her father had loved her, his only child, he had not led her down a path strewn with rose petals!

Her thoughts as bleak as the rain-soaked Texas land-scape before her, Sara turned away from the window. With her father dead and her meager livelihood solely dependent these days upon the uncertain kindness of Mrs. Sanders, the owner of the boardinghouse where she and her father had been staying when he was killed, she had to start planning beyond her most immediate needs. Sara had never thought a great deal about her future, as the desperate need to concentrate on where her and her father's next meal was coming from and where they would lay their heads at night had taken up nearly all of her waking thoughts these past four years. But it hadn't always been so, she thought wistfully, gingerly seating herself on the rickety cot that served as her bed.

No, it hadn't always been so. She could vaguely remember her mother, the lovely, sweet-scented Rose-mary, who had died when Sara had been barely three years old. She had been too young then to understand what the death of his adored wife had done to her father. Now she knew that it had turned him from a genial, sober, hard-working planter into a reckless gambler who drank too much and took too many needless risks. She could hardly remember a time when her father had not been as foolhardy and drunk as he had been on the day he was killed. Much clearer were her memories of their former home, the stately house and plantation, Mockingbird Hill, which had been situated outside Natchez, Mississippi.

Sara glanced around the seedy confines of her tiny room, an ironic smile curving her bottom lip. How very different her surroundings were these days! Had it been over four years since her father had finally gambled away everything he had owned? Over four years since that ter-rible night when he had come home and awakened her in her silk-draped bed to tell her that they had to leave? That *everything*—the elegant home and its rich furnish-ings, the broad acres of cotton, the numerous slaves, the stable filled with its fine blooded stock—had been lost on the turn of a card?

Bewildered and confused by what had happened, when Sara had gotten over the first of her shock she had tried to view their stunning change in circumstances as an adventure. But as the days had passed, she had learned bitterly that it wasn't very adventuresome to have your former friends pretend not to see you on the street, nor was it an adventure to share your lumpy bed with fleas and vermin and to spend your evenings rubbing shoulders with often unclean, foul-mouthed rascals in smoke-filled, drink-scented saloons while your father attempted to regain his lost fortune the only way he knew how—by gambling.

Word of his appalling loss had spread almost instantly among his friends, and though there were those who sympathized, who kindly offered assistance, most turned their well-clad backs on him. Stiff-necked pride and sheer bullheadedness forbade him to accept the kindness of his friends, and so he had been reduced to gambling where he could, hoarding only enough money from his winnings for his and Sara's most basic needs.

They had not stayed long in the Natchez area, the shame of his circumstances driving them away. Leaving Natchez by riverboat, Sara and Matthew had become vagabonds, never staying very long in any one place, Matthew constantly in search of the next game, the next win that would repair his fortune, Sara dragged willy-nilly along behind him.

Sara adapted—she had no other choice—but she never got used to those times when her father had done especially badly at the tables and they had had to depart like thieves in the night, leaving unpaid, irate creditors behind them. As she had grown older, she had begun to supplement their earnings by cooking and cleaning in the various boardinghouses and places where they lodged. It was a far cry from the gracious life she had once lived, but at least, she told herself gratefully, it kept her out of the gaming hells and disreputable saloons that her father frequented—and away from the increasingly lascivious and sexually speculative gazes of the men with whom her father gambled.

It was Sara's maturing face and body that had brought them to Texas. One day it had suddenly dawned on Matthew that his beloved daughter was not a little girl anymore and that her slim, gently curved form and increasingly lovely face was going to create an unpleasant situation for them sooner or later. There had already been a few unsavory incidents that only his timely interference had prevented from getting out of hand. He had brooded over this problem for several weeks and then a notion had occurred to him: for Sara's sake, he would finally swallow his damnable pride and write to his only other relative, a distant cousin named Sam Cantrell. Sam had always been a kind, charitable man, and as boys, before Sam and his father, Andy, had left for Texas nearly forty years ago to join Stephen Austin's new colony, they had been very close. Since then their contact had been sporadic at best, but perhaps Sam would help Matthew and Sara.

They had waited anxiously for an answer and the day Sam Cantrell's letter had arrived, expressing warm assurances that he would do anything he could for both Matthew and Sara, Matthew had held Sara to him and wept. They had left immediately for San Felipe, Texas, the town nearest to the Cantrell plantation, Magnolia Grove.

They did not travel by the most direct route; earning money the only way Matthew knew how, he and Sara had slowly gambled their way in a circuitous route toward San Felipe. Matthew's luck had never been very good and it had finally run out when they had reached this unnamed, tiny settlement on the Texas side of the Sabine River. They had procured the room in which Sara now sat, Sara cooking and cleaning for Mrs. Sanders in exchange for their keep. That taken care of, Matthew had immediately wandered over to the small, shabby saloon across the street in search of a game of cards, hoping to increase the small amount of money he had kept aside for gambling. He had done very well that first night. So well, in fact, that he had decided they would stay another night and he would try his luck again.

And it was on that night, two months ago, that luck had turned her back on Matthew Rawlings for the last time. He had lost everything and, too drunk to choose his words with care, had accused the winner of cheating. Guns were reached for, shots rang out and the next instant, Matthew Rawlings lay dead on the floor.

Sara got up from her cot and moved around the room restlessly. She had loved her father, she grieved for him, but she tried not to dwell on the fact that a stronger man, a man of more moral fiber, wouldn't have let the death of his wife, no matter how beloved, drive him to the lengths to which Matthew had gone. Guilt smote her every time that thought crossed her mind, but mingled with the guilt was anger that her father had been so wrapped up in his own grief and despair that he had cared so little for her that she was now left alone and destitute and at the mercy of utter strangers.

Suddenly she buried her face in her hands. What was she to do? It had been weeks since she had written to Sam Cantrell explaining Matthew's death, and she had heard nothing. Had Sam Cantrell changed his mind? Was she truly alone in the world? Possessed of nothing but the clothes she wore? What was going to happen to her?

"Sara! Sara, get yourself down here right now! There's chores to be done!"

Jerked from her painful contemplation of a decidedly bleak future by Mrs. Sanders' bellow from below, Sara hastily scrubbed away any signs of tears and hurried from the room.

Mrs. Sanders was built on formidable lines. She was as tall as most men and her massive bulk would have made three of Sara. A widow of some years, she ran the boardinghouse, while her two husky sons operated the saloon where Matthew had died and the blacksmith shop, which was next to the boardinghouse. Mrs. Sanders was not *un*kind, but she was a practical woman, and though she didn't object to helping Sara during her moment of need and getting a hard, willing worker in the process, she certainly did not intend for Sara to make her life with the Sanders family. It had not escaped her attention that during the past few weeks, her elder son, Nate, had begun to hang around while Sara did chores.

Her manner toward Sara had cooled noticeably, and when Sara stepped into the well-scrubbed kitchen at the rear of the house, the older woman's eyes were chilly and her voice was brisk as she said, "There you are! You had better see to the pigs and make certain there is plenty of wood before we start dinner."

Nate Sanders was sitting at the rough pine table, drinking coffee, and at his mother's words, he said eagerly, "I'll help you, Sara. I can chop the wood while you feed the pigs."

Mrs. Sanders' already thin lips thinned even more. "No, you won't!" she declared testily. "I'm not letting her stay in a perfectly good room and eat at our table just because I'm a God-fearing, Christian woman—she needs to earn her keep. Besides," she added triumphantly, "since it appears you have nothing better to do, I need you to pick up some sacks of corn and beans from the dry goods store for me. Run along, Sara!"

Her red flannel petticoat and cheap broadcloth skirts flowing behind her, Sara fled, as much because she did not want to irritate her employer as because she did not want Nate Sanders' attentions. Too often of late, she had caught him staring at her small bosom and narrow waist and she hadn't liked the expression in his hazel eyes. Heedless of the rain pouring down, she grabbed the heavy bucket of slop that sat on the wooden back porch and struggled with it over to the pigpen.

Sara was not a big girl. Nearly seventeen, she was just a little above average height, but her slenderness and fine bones and delicate features made her seem taller and far more fragile than she actually was. Her long honey-gold hair was arranged today in a neat cornet of braids around her head, and despite her worn green gown and present occupation, there was an elegant air about her.

Certainly the gentleman who had just put his horse away in the stable at the rear of the house thought so. He watched quietly as she strained to lift the cumbersome bucket high enough to clear the fence of the pigpen. On the other side, in front of a battered wooden trough, a dozen partially grown pigs snorted and squealed and lunged through the mud toward her. Only the stoutness of the trough and the fence saved her from being trampled. With grim determination, Sara finally managed to tip the bucket, the slop falling into the trough below, and pandemonium exploded as the pigs fought for the choicest scraps.

The rain began to lessen, but Sara was already soaked to the skin, and it was only as she turned and started to dash for the house that she noticed the tall gentleman standing by the stable. She recognized that he *was* a gentleman from the stylish cut and fine material of his greatcoat and the buff riding gloves that adorned his hands. Beneath his wide-brimmed, low-crowned hat,

Sara could see that his cheeks were cleanly shaved and his silver-flecked brown mustache was neatly trimmed. He was a handsome man, his features even and nicely arranged, and he appeared to be in his mid-forties, about her father's age. This was clearly no scruffy stranger seeking momentary haven from the rain, and Sara's heart began to pound in hopeful anticipation. Could it be?

As she stood there staring at him with anxious expectancy, the man smiled and approached her. "I would have known you anywhere, my dear!" he said warmly. "Even in these unfortunate surroundings, your resemblance to Matthew is unmistakable." Extending his hand, his amber-gold eyes bright with emotion, he took Sara's fingers in his and added, "You must be Sara, and I am Samuel Cantrell, your father's cousin."

Despite her best intentions to maintain a stout facade, the strain of the past few months suddenly proved to have been too great and Sara's eyes filled with tears. An instant later she found herself cradled in Sam Cantrell's comforting arms as she sobbed uncontrollably against his chest.

"There, there, my child," he soothed softly, one hand tenderly stroking her rain-wet hair. "You are safe now. Don't you worry about a thing. My wife, Margaret, and I have discussed your unfortunate situation at length and we have decided that you shall live with us at Magnolia Grove as our dear little cousin. Margaret is expecting our first child and she will need a great deal of help. We can help each other . . . you will be much comfort and companionship to my wife and later the baby. Believe me, my child, you never have to worry about the future again—we shall take care of you. It is what Matthew wanted and since unhappily he is no longer able to provide for you, it will be my great pleasure to do so. Come, now, wipe those tears away."

With every wonderful word that Sam uttered, Sara sobbed even harder, barely able to believe that her lonely struggle was at an end. Valiantly trying to stem the tears, she gulped and wiped her eyes. "I-I-I'm s-s-sorry! I'm not usually such a water pot!"

Sam smiled down at her, patting her shoulder. "You have had a great deal on your young shoulders these past few months. It is only natural that you should cry. But your anxieties will soon be a thing of the past, so won't you please give me a smile?"

Sara's lovely mouth curved into a tremulous smile, her emerald eyes glowing softly between her tear-spiked black lashes as she stared up into Sam's gentle features. "You're very kind," she managed to say. "I will enjoy looking after the baby and I promise that I shall never be a burden to you or make you regret your generosity to me."

"I'm sure you won't, child. But come along now; we must get you inside and out of this weather."

Suddenly becoming aware again of her surroundings and the drizzle which was falling on them, Sara gave an embarrassed little laugh. "Oh, sir! I am sorry! Do come quickly. Mrs. Sanders has hot coffee on the stove and the house will be warm."

Mrs. Sanders was delighted that a solution to the dilemma Sara's continued presence in her boardinghouse was causing had finally appeared in the form of Mr. Sam Cantrell. It took her but a second to size Sam up and place him in the wealthy-planter class. From that moment on, especially once he had explained that he wanted her best room for himself for the night and that in the morning, before he and Sara left, he would settle whatever debts Sara and Matthew had incurred, Sam's slightest wish became Mrs. Sanders' most desired task.

Sara watched in astonishment as Mrs. Sanders hovered and fussed over Sam. Artfully disposing of his dripping greatcoat, Mrs. Sanders whisked Sam to a comfortable chair by the fire in the best parlor. Mere seconds later, Sam was sipping some fine corn whisky from her private store. Beaming at him, she gushed, "My good sir! You have no idea how happy I am that you have arrived to take care of this poor young woman." Smiling mistily in Sara's direction, for Sara had followed them into the parlor, Mrs. Sanders went on. "Of course, I shall miss her dreadfully. Why, I have grown so fond of her these past weeks that she is like a daughter to me."

Incredulously Sara stared at Mrs. Sanders, hardly daring to believe what she was hearing! Mrs. Sanders considered her as a daughter? Hiding her merriment at the thought, Sara kept her expression demure as she listened to the tale that Mrs. Sanders spun for Sam—a tale that bore little resemblance to reality!

It wasn't until the next morning, however, as she and Sam rode away from Mrs. Sanders' boardinghouse, that Sara was able to tell him the truth. Her sweet face very earnest, she exclaimed, "Sir! You should not have paid her for my keep these past two months. It was agreed that I would work for her and that she would provide me with room and board. You owed her nothing for my care and certainly you should not have been asked to pay for two months' use of one of the better rooms—*my* room was in the attic!"

Sam smiled at her. "I'm aware of what Mrs. Sanders was about, my dear. It just seemed easier to pay her what she wanted and for us to be on our way without a fuss."

A tiny frown between her brows, Sara stared at Sam's kind features. It occurred to her that Sam would always take the easy way out—that he avoided confrontation at all costs, even to his own detriment. Guilt smote her. How did she dare to criticize such a wonderful man! Sam had been overwhelmingly good to her in the exceedingly brief time she had known him; the new pink gingham gown and dark green cloak she wore and the straw bonnet with its cherry silk ribbon tied in a bow beneath her chin, as well as various other things that Sam had insisted were necessary for her, had all been purchased by him this morning from the dry goods store. He had even bought her the horse she rode, a sweet-going little chestnut mare. While she was thrilled with all her new belongings, she was vaguely uneasy.

Glancing across at him, she asked anxiously, "Are you certain that your wife will not mind all the money you have spent on me?"

"My dear child! Don't give it a thought! Margaret won't mind in the least. She is a kind young woman and I'm sure that you two will deal wonderfully together." A twinkle in his amber-gold eyes, Sam added lightly, "I am a wealthy man, although if Abraham Lincoln is elected President this November and frees all my slaves, I shall be considerably *less* wealthy! But that aside, what I spent on you this morning would not even begin to pay for one of my Margaret's gowns."

Slightly relieved, Sara said earnestly, "I promise that I will work very hard for you, sir. I *swear* I will never be a burden to you or your wife!"

"Sara, Sara, how you run on! Child, you are not coming to my household to be a servant! You are the daughter of a cousin of whom I have only the fondest memories. You are coming to my home, if not as my daughter, certainly as a valued and respected member of my family."

Sara felt tears flood her eyes and throat. Face averted to hide her strong emotion, she replied huskily, "Thank you. I will try never to cause you to regret your kindness to me."

It took Sam and Sara nearly three weeks of continuous riding to reach Magnolia Grove, and during that time they came to know each other very well. Sara had been embarrassed at first to travel with a man who was not her father, but as Sam had explained reasonably, "Sara, I am your guardian now. Your father entrusted your care to me—you are my ward. Besides," he added with a teasing glint in his eyes, "I am nearly forty-five years old, just a few years away from being old enough to be your grandfather! Won't you try to think of me as your father?"

Sara had sent him a tear-filled smile. "I shall try, and I don't think that it will be very hard to do."

Sam had patted her fondly on the shoulder and they had continued on their way, every day the affectionate bond between them growing. Sam heard about the happy days at Mockingbird Hill and the terrible time that had followed Matthew's loss of his fortune, while Sara listened wide-eyed to the tragic story of Sam's first wife, the lovely Madelina Alvarez, the mother of his only living child, his twenty-seven-year-old son, Yancy. A wistful smile on his finely chiseled mouth, Sam had said, "We were so in love and so young, about your age, and when our fathers would hear nothing of a marriage between us, we defied them, ran away and married anyway. But except for brief moments, we were not ever truly happy. . . ." He had sighed, a faraway look in his eyes. "Her father, Don Armando, was a proud Spanish aristocrat and mine was equally proud—proud to have been among some of the first settlers to heed Stephen Austin's call to settle in Texas. Don Armando was furious at the idea of his only child, an heiress to a vast rancho at that, marrying a 'gringo,' and Andy was equally furious that *his* only child had set his heart on a 'greaser'—even though the Alvarez family could trace their pure Spanish blood back to the conquistadors." Sam's lips had curved wryly. "Not a pleasant situation, but eventually Don Armando got over his fury at our marriage, and once Yancy was born he forgave us, but my father, Andy, never forgave me, never even accepted Yancy as his grandson. Quite frankly, he hated Madelina. Andy couldn't accept our marriage and made life miserable for both Madelina and Yancy. I should have done something about the situation, I admit, but I, well, I just wasn't strong enough, I guess, to stand up to him."

Sara had stared at his gentle, handsome features, realizing suddenly that though Sam Cantrell was a kind, generous man, he was also a weak man, and her earlier impression that he would always take the easy way out crystallized into a certainty. It didn't lessen the powerful affection she had learned so quickly to feel for him, but knowledge of his unwillingness to face adversity, whatever its forms, made her uneasy. Suppose Margaret *really* didn't want her at Magnolia Grove? Would Sam defy his wife?

There were few places that took in travelers on their long journey southward, and so most nights they camped out along the way. It was during those April nights, the scent of spring in the air as they sat at their cheery campfire after supper, that Sam talked of his family and Magnolia Grove. By the time they made camp that last night before reaching Sam's home, Sara was quite familiar with Magnolia Grove and its inhabitants. She was puzzled about one thing, however, and that final evening she couldn't help asking carefully, "You don't mention your son, Yancy, very often. Isn't he at Magnolia Grove?"

An odd expression that Sara couldn't define crossed Sam's face. Guilt? Remorse? Sorrow? Perhaps all three. Not meeting Sara's gaze, he poked at the fire and after a moment of silence said, "Yancy and I were never close. During the first years, when Andy was so violently outspoken about my marriage to Madelina, he and his mother lived mostly with Don Armando at his hacienda at Rancho del Sol, so I saw him infrequently. After Don Armando died from a bull goring when Yancy was seven, Madelina couldn't bear to live at the hacienda, so they came and lived with me." Sam stared off into the distance, his thoughts obviously unhappy. "Yancy was devastated by Armando's death and it didn't help that Andy could not abide the sight of him." Sam's expression became very bleak and his voice thickened with deep emotion. "Madelina died less than a year later of a fever and Yancy was totally bewildered. He didn't understand why he couldn't live at Rancho del Sol, or why his mother had seemed to abandon him. It was difficult for him to adjust to Magnolia Grove after having lived his life predominantly in the easygoing Spanish household at del Sol, and Andy's always yelling or cuffing the boy made life bitterly unhappy for him."

Unable to help herself, Sara burst out, "But why didn't you . . ." Realizing what she had said, her face flamed and she looked down at her hands in her lap.

"You're right," Sam eventually replied. "I should have protected the boy better than I did, but I was busy running the plantation—we grow cotton—and I just assumed that Andy would finally get used to the boy. Andy never did 'get used to' him, and as Yancy grew older he blamed me, rightfully so, for not having interceded."

"But once your father died and it was just you and Yancy, didn't things get better?" Sara asked quietly.

Sam shook his head. "We didn't have much time together. My father died when Yancy was almost seventeen and the next year, nearly ten years ago now, Yancy went off to school in the East—Harvard. He didn't return until over four years later and then there was . . ."

"Yes? There was . . . ?"

Looking guilt-stricken and miserable, Sam muttered, "And then there was Margaret. . . ." He glanced across the fire at Sara's earnest features and hesitated for a moment before saying gruffly, "Margaret Small and her widowed sister, Ann Brown, came from the East with Yancy. . . . Margaret was barely twenty years old then and she was Yancy's bride-to-be, his fiancée, and may God forgive me—I stole her from him and married her myself!"

❧ 2

Sara stared wide-eyed at Sam. "You married your son's fiancée!" she exclaimed in shocked tones.

Sam would not meet her gaze. His voice thick, he muttered, "You—no one—can understand how it was. I was lonely, and Margaret was—*is*—a beautiful, fragile young woman. Yancy was making her unhappy; he was determined to live at Rancho del Sol after they were wed, and poor Margaret hated the very sight of the place." Sam's gaze swung back to Sara. His eyes pleading for her understanding, he said softly, "Margaret is a gently reared young woman. She grew up in Connecticut and had no conception of Texas—of its vastness, its *wildness*—and Rancho del Sol . . ." Sams's lips twisted disparagingly. "The hacienda had stood almost deserted for over fourteen years, ever since Armando had died, and it was in great need of repair. The place is situated in untamed, dangerous country, far from any other settlement, in the middle of countless acres of chaparral, where only wild Spanish longhorns, wolves and rattlesnakes live. Del Sol was far different from anything that Margaret had ever seen before—she had believed that they were going to live at Magnolia Grove—she later confessed to me that she had fallen in love with my home at her first sight of it. The San Felipe area, too, was more what she was used to. It is civilized, there are lovely

19

homes scattered about and the countryside is extremely appealing, dotted with broad acres of cotton, and in the uncultivated sections there is the lush, almost tropical growth one finds in this part of Texas." Sam grimaced. "Rancho del Sol is very nearly the opposite. It was far too hostile and foreign for someone of Margaret's gentle sensibilities to endure—she simply could not cope with the idea of living in such a savage, isolated place."

Her face troubled, Sara couldn't help asking, "But if she loved your son?"

Sam sighed. "It wasn't just the place. During the weeks since Yancy had brought Margaret to Magnolia Grove, I had grown very fond of her—I *thought* my feelings were based on a father's love for the girl his son would marry and her sweet attitude toward me had evolved because one day I would be her father-in-law." Tiredly he ran a hand down his face and continued unhappily. "I could tell that something was very wrong when we had all come back from that initial visit to del Sol, and one evening I asked her about it. She admitted with great reluctance and many tears that Yancy had changed, that he was not the same young man with whom she had fallen in love back east, that she feared she had agreed to marry a man she no longer loved. I found myself deeply touched by her plight and I tried to soothe what I felt certain were merely bridal nerves. I teased her a little and convinced her that once Yancy had made all of the improvements to del Sol he intended to complete before they married and he took her there to live, she would find the place much more to her liking. But even though she agreed with me, I could tell that things were not going well between them." Sam sighed heavily. "It didn't help that Yancy had no time for her anxieties. He seemed obsessed with restoring Rancho del Sol, and despite Margaret's pitiful entreaties to the contrary, he left within the week to return to the hacienda to oversee the work that had to be done, leaving Margaret and Ann in my care at Magnolia Grove."

Sara didn't much like the sound of Yancy Cantrell. If Sam's words were to be believed, Yancy seemed to her to have been cold and insensitive to Margaret's understandable reservations. But that still didn't excuse . . .

Though she was dying to hear the rest of Sam's story, Sara was also acutely uncomfortable with the situation; after all, despite the growing fondness she had for Sam and the undeniable bond that had sprung up so swiftly between them, all of this was old history and really none of her business. It was obvious that it pained Sam to talk of it and her soft heart went out to him. Her eyes full of sympathy, she said gently, "You don't have to tell me any more if you don't want to."

Sam smiled bitterly. "I would prefer *never* to talk of it again, but if you are to live in my house and if you are to understand why my Margaret acts as she does, you need to know what happened. Besides," he added grimly, "if I don't tell you now of the scandal, I'm sure that some well-meaning old tabby will take tremendous delight in telling you only the tawdriest details—for your own good, of course!"

Looking across the fire at her, Sam shook his head disgustedly and confessed dryly, "I'm afraid that none of us come out of this story with much dignity or integrity—certainly Margaret and I have much to live down. It wasn't that I meant to fall in love with her or that she meant to love me—it just happened. We married six years ago this September." Sam sighed and added bleakly, "Yancy didn't learn of what had happened until he returned to Magnolia Grove almost two months after our marriage—cowardly, I had put off writing to him—I felt reading the news of our marriage in a letter would only add to the cruelty of the situation." Sam sighed. "Perhaps I was wrong; perhaps it would have been kinder to have let him know as soon as the deed was done. At any rate, he came back eager to claim his bride, and as long as I live, I will never forget the expression on his face when he learned that *his* bride was actually *my* wife!" Sam looked terrible, his eyes full of misery. "He has yet to fully forgive me and I doubt that I blame him."

Even knowing that Sam had been wrong, that there had been little or no excuse for his actions, Sara felt her heart bleed for him. It was obvious from the signs of suffering on his handsome face that even though he loved Margaret, he bitterly regretted the estrangement from his only son. As Sam continued to stare broodingly at the dancing red-and-yellow flames of the fire, Sara ventured softly, "And you have not seen or heard from him since?"

Sam smiled without amusement. "Seldom. This last year, he has shown some sign of being willing, albeit reluctantly, to make peace between us. Not, however, with Margaret—I sometimes feel that he despises her most of all. I have prevailed upon him to visit with me on the rare occasion and twice I have been to del Sol to attempt to heal the breach between us."

An encouraging smile curving her lips, Sara murmured, "Perhaps, in time, things will be better between you." An uneasy thought occurred to her. "Does he know that Margaret is going to have a baby?"

Sam nodded. "I hesitated to write and tell him of Margaret's pregnancy, but I didn't want him to think that I was trying to hide anything from him. He took it rather well, replying merely that he hoped that I would be happy being a father again at my age." Trying for a light note, Sam grinned sheepishly and said, "I am more of an age to be having grandchildren than children!"

Her face serious, Sara replied earnestly, "Oh, but, sir! You look very well for your age."

A genuine laugh escaped Sam. Affection clear in his gaze, he said warmly, "You're a nice young woman, Sara Rawlings. I hope that you will be happy at Magnolia Grove—despite all its past unhappiness."

"Oh, I hope so, too!" Sara declared ardently.

Certainly the first sight of the gracious mansion, late the next afternoon, filled her with delight. The thought that this beautiful house with its wide verandas and soaring white columns was to be her home had Sara wondering if she were dreaming. As she and Sam rode their horses down the long, oak-lined carriageway, seeing the wisps of the gray-green Spanish moss clinging to the massive tree limbs which nearly met overhead, she was reminded vividly of Mockingbird Hill and tears stung her eyes. There was much about the area to make her think of her lost home—the broad green fields of new cotton, the oak and magnolia trees and the abundance of wild-grape vines and honeysuckle which seemed to grow everywhere. Now, if only Margaret was as kind and welcoming as Sam had indicated she would be. . . .

Suddenly very nervous, Sara became aware of her less than pristine pink gingham gown and the untidy tendrils of honey-gold hair that had escaped from the neat cornet of braids she habitually wore. Anxiously she straightened her straw hat and, her eyes huge in her face, dismounted from her mare. Then following Sam's lead, she quietly handed the reins to one of the little black boys who had run out from behind the house. Her stomach full of butterflies, she walked with Sam up the three broad steps which led to the veranda. A pair of wide, dark green doors with elegant fan-shaped windows above them marked the entrance to the house, and with an encouraging smile, Sam flung open one door and ushered Sara inside.

The inside of the house was every bit as grand as the outside, and stepping forward, Sara found herself standing in a spacious hallway, the floor a diamond pattern of pale rose and white marble. A huge crystal chandelier hung high above and a graceful staircase soared upward to the next floor. Everywhere she looked, Sara saw signs of wealth, and the memory of her own home came back even stronger—so had it been at Mockingbird Hill.

They had barely stepped inside when Sara became aware of raised, angry voices. Several doors opened off the hallway and it was embarrassingly apparent that behind one of those doors a violent argument was in progress.

A frown between his brows, Sam paused, but giving Sara a reassuring smile, he had taken a step forward when the door to their right suddenly burst open. To say who was the most surprised, the tall young man scowling darkly as he stood frozen in the doorway or Sam and Sara, would have been impossible.

Despite his unwelcoming expression, the young man was undeniably the handsomest man Sara had ever seen in her young life. He wore a full-sleeved white shirt, a scarlet silk sash tied flamboyantly around his waist and slim-fitting nankeen trousers which clung to his long, sleekly muscled legs, but it was his face that held Sara's undivided attention and she could not seem to tear her fascinated gaze away from his strikingly handsome features. Handsome and dangerous, she thought giddily, her eyes taking in the bright glitter of his thick-lashed amber-gold eyes and the reckless curve to his firm mouth, the upper lip thinly chiseled and the bottom one sensually full. Ruffled black hair framed his lean features; his complexion was Spanish-dark and he had the haughty aquiline nose often seen in portraits of the conquistadors. He bore little resemblance to Sam, except for those heavy-browed, amber-gold eyes, but it was obvious that he and Sam shared the same steel-honed physique. This man's height was perhaps an inch or two above Sam's six feet and his shoulders were broader, but Sara had no doubt that she was staring at Sam's son, Yancy Cantrell.

Yancy recovered himself first, and a sardonic smile slashing across his dark face, he said, "The next time I come to visit, I shall make certain that you are in residence *before* I leave del Sol! It is indeed fortunate that you have finally arrived home, *mi padre*—another day here at Magnolia Grove with only your charming wife for company, and I might have been driven to murder!"

Consternation on his features, Sam replied, "Yancy! Don't tell me that you and Margaret have been arguing again. In her condition . . ."

If anything, Yancy's sardonic smile widened. "Believe me, sir, despite her condition, Margaret is capable of *anything*!" As if becoming aware for the first time of Sara standing slightly behind Sam, Yancy flicked his gaze over her slight form. "And what have we here?" he drawled mockingly. "Your latest act of atonement?"

"Stop that this instant!" Sam ordered sharply. "Sara is a mere child, certainly not a worthy opponent for you. Her father died recently. He was a distant cousin of mine, and now she is my ward. You will treat her with all the respect and decorum due any member of my family."

"Oh. And, of course, your *family* is so deserving of this respect, *sí*?"

A woman's voice suddenly rang out from behind Yancy. "Who is it? Who are you talking to?"

Yancy bowed with insulting exaggeration and stepped out into the hallway. "Why, only your beloved husband and his, ah, ward, I believe he called her."

"Sam? Sam is home?" came the breathless reply, and a second later a vision of butter-yellow curls and limpid blue eyes, gowned in a delectable creation of pale blue silk and delicate lace, came surging into the doorway. Due to the style of the day—steel-hooped skirts with voluminous petticoats and tightly laced corsets—Margaret's pregnancy did not yet show very much; except for a slightly thickened waist, which no amount of lacing could conceal, and a certain excessive fullness to her already impressive bosom, Margaret Cantrell was the very picture of feminine beauty.

Sam had not exaggerated when he had claimed that Margaret was lovely. She was indeed, possessing wide, fulsomely lashed eyes, a daintily shaped little nose, a rosy Cupid's-bow mouth and a naturally voluptuous form. Sara wasn't surprised that both Sam and Yancy had fallen in love with her. Youthful admiration in her gaze, embarrassingly conscious of her own lack of curves and the soiled state of her gingham gown, Sara stared hopefully at Margaret's beautiful face. This woman was Sam's wife, and if Margaret did not like her . . .

It took one glance of those cool blue eyes to tell Sara that she would find no welcome here, that and the sudden petulant curve of her mouth. "Oh, you brought her with you, after all," Margaret said flatly.

Sam began to make soothing noises, but it was Yancy who drawled, "One hears how impending motherhood brings out all that is gentle and maternal in a woman . . . obviously, such is not true in your case, is it, dear stepmama?"

Margaret's hands clenched into fists and her blue eyes sparkled with temper. "I've had about all of you that I can stand!" Margaret cried. "Go back to your miserable rancho with its snakes and cattle. I don't ever want you to come to my house again!"

"Magnolia Grove isn't yours *yet*, sweet stepmama—for all your plotting!" Yancy replied furiously, the glitter in his amber-gold eyes decidedly unpleasant.

"*Yancy*! *Margaret*! Stop this at once!" Sam commanded angrily. He threw a harassed glance around and noticed that the butler, a tall, distinguished mulatto in pristine white-and-claret garb, had come upon the scene. Sam looked back at the two combatants and said hastily, "This is no place to have such a discussion! Let us retire to the library, where we can talk in private." Glancing over to the silent butler, Sam smiled slightly and said, "Hello, Bartholomew! As you can see, I have returned. Will you please tell Tansy and ask her to prepare some of those potato dumplings that I like for supper? Oh, and see to it that the Rose Room is prepared for my ward, Miss Sara Rawlings. She will be making her home with us from now on, and I want you and the staff to extend her every courtesy."

"Of course, sir. It shall be done." Bowing, Bartholomew turned and disappeared.

His expression that of a harried rabbit, Sam looked once again at Yancy and Margaret. "To the library, please!"

Sara thought that she might have been handed over to Bartholomew. In fact, she wished most heartily that she *had* been, but such was not the case. Herding the other two in front of him, Sam clasped her hand and dragged her along behind him. "It is unfortunate that this is your introduction to my home," he muttered, "but since you are going to live here, you might as well see what you are getting yourself into!"

Sara had no choice but to follow in Sam's wake. As she hurried behind him, she had the uneasy feeling that this was not the first time Margaret and Yancy had clashed or that Sam had tried to act as mediator between them.

After reaching the library—a handsome room of generous proportions, with row upon row of book-lined shelves covering every bit of wall space not taken up with tall, ruby damask-draped windows, Sam released her hand. As he walked over to his massive cherry-wood desk, which was set at one end of the room, Sara was able to retreat to a shadowed corner and hope that better sense had prevailed upon Yancy and Margaret.

Her hopes were not realized. Sam had barely taken his place behind the desk when Margaret burst out, "Order him gone from here! I am *your* wife, the mother of your unborn child, and I tell you that I cannot *bear* to have him in my home one instant longer!"

"It wouldn't *be* your home," Yancy shot back, "if it hadn't been for my misguided misunderstanding of your character."

"Oh! How can you say such a wicked thing!" Her eyes filling with tears, Margaret glanced beseechingly at Sam. "Are you going to just stand there and let him talk to me that way? I thought you loved me!"

Throwing his son a warning glance, Sam said placatingly, "Margaret, of course I love you! Now, don't distress yourself, my dear—Yancy doesn't mean a word of it—it is only his temper speaking."

"But I do mean every word I say," Yancy retorted unrepentantly, a black scowl on his face.

An unwilling observer to the ugly scene before her, Sara was filled with pity for Sam. He was like a bone between two snarling dogs—two snarling dogs whom he loved dearly.

Ignoring Yancy's comment, peeking up at her husband from behind the heavily laced handkerchief that had miraculously appeared in her hand, Margaret murmured, "Oh, Sam! You know how much he torments me and makes me so unhappy. And in my condition . . ."

"Such wonderful theatrics, dear stepmama!" Yancy interposed with sudden amusement. "Did you ever consider, I mean beyond marrying a wealthy man, gaining your fortune on the stage?"

Over her handkerchief, Margaret glared at him, but before she could reply, Sam said tiredly, "Please! Could we cease the hostilities for a moment?"

Yancy hesitated, and Sara, despite herself, had the distinct impression that he had just noticed how very tired Sam looked and realized that his father had just returned from a long, arduous journey. His gaze softened marginally and he contented himself with merely saying, "*Dios*! How you can believe her when she twists everything to suit her own purpose is beyond me!"

"And am I twisting things when I say that not five minutes ago you threatened to kill me?" Margaret asked sweetly, a triumphant smile on her bow-shaped mouth.

Alarm on his face, Sam glanced in horror at his son. "Did you?"

Yancy's lips twisted derisively. "*Sí*! I told her that there was no way that she or any brat of hers would ever own one inch of Alvarez land—that I would kill her first!"

Despite his concern for the threat to his wife's life, Sam looked thoroughly confused. "But what is this? Margaret has no claim to any of your land."

Margaret asked gently, "But, Sam, darling, have you forgotten Casa Paloma? The thousand acres of land that Don Armando gave you and Madelina when Yancy was born?"

Bewilderment obvious on his handsome features, Sam replied, "Of course I haven't forgotten it! But what does Casa Paloma have to do with you? And what does Casa Paloma have to do with Yancy's professed desire to kill you?"

"Oh, dearest, you *have* forgotten, haven't you?" Margaret said sadly. "Or were you only teasing me?" She looked bravely resigned. "I suppose it will always be so— my child forced to take second place to Madelina's. . . ."

With every word Margaret had spoken, Sam appeared even more confused and alarmed, while Yancy's face had darkened.

There was a menacing silence, the room filled with a terrible tenseness, the very air seeming to crackle with the threat of violence, and Sara fairly jumped when Yancy suddenly exploded. Bending forward, he slammed one clenched fist against the fine wood of his father's desk. "*Por Dios*! I refuse to take part in this charade any longer and watch her lead you around like some tame bull. Did you or did you not promise her that you would give her child Casa Paloma?"

Stricken, Sam stared from one intent face to the other. Weakly, he muttered, "I never promised . . . exactly. I may have said something to the effect that I hoped . . . perhaps one day . . . that you and my unborn child might live in harmony together." He darted an apologetic glance at Margaret. "But, my dear, how you could take that to mean . . . It has always been my intention that Yancy would one day inherit Casa Paloma—it has belonged to his mother's family for generations."

Margaret's blue eyes filled with tears and she sent Sam a look of gentle reproach. "I understand. Yancy's wishes must, of course, always come first with you! It doesn't matter that my child is to be denied his birthright or that I am to be subjected to this sort of horrible confrontation in my delicate condition."

Sam was obviously torn, and after casting a despairing glance at Yancy, he looked at his wife helplessly. "Margaret, my dear, please don't distress yourself this way. It is not good for you, you know that."

A pitiful sob drifted on the air and hastily Sam added, "If it means that much to you, sweetheart, we'll discuss it more thoroughly at a later date. Perhaps some compromise can be achieved."

Margaret came around the desk and threw her arms

around Sam's neck. "Oh, darling, I knew you would not deny me!" She kissed him on the cheek. "What a dreadful wife I am, darling! You are no doubt exhausted from your journey, and here I am scrabbling with your excessively irritating son. You stay here and settle things with Yancy, and I shall go and see that a hot bath is prepared for you."

Before Sam could stop her or request that she take Sara with her, Margaret skipped gaily out of the room. There was an uncomfortable silence and then Yancy growled from between gritted teeth, "There is nothing to *settle*! You may leave her and her child everything you possess—your money, your slaves, Magnolia Grove, the plantation, the house—everything except Casa Paloma." He paused, obviously fighting his temper, and then continued with dangerous calm. "Casa Paloma is Alvarez land—as you damn well know, it sits right in the middle of my rancho—I will *not* have her or her brat claiming one inch of it." His amber-gold eyes glittering fiercely, he bent nearer his father and snarled softly, "I'll kill her first!"

∞ 3

I gnoring Sam's shocked expostulation, Yancy strode
swiftly from the library, the door slamming loudly
behind him. For a long moment Sam said nothing; then,
turning to Sara, he said ruefully, "Welcome to Magnolia
Grove, my dear. You have just seen us at our worst, and
I hope that we have not given you a distaste for your
new home."

Sara muttered uncertainly, "They are very, very *dramatic*, are they not?"

Sam chuckled. "Yes, I suppose you could say that!
But come, now—let us see if the room Bartholomew
has prepared for you is to your satisfaction."

The room was everything that Sara could have wished
for, and again she was reminded of Mockingbird Hill.
Not that this room duplicated hers at her former home,
but it was definitely as spacious and richly furnished.
The walls were hung with pale rose silk, light green
draperies of some diaphanous material floated at the
narrow windows, and the floor was covered with a fine
Axminster carpet in shades of cream, green and rose. A
tall mahogany armoire had been set against one wall; a
marble-topped washstand stood near it. On another wall
a gilt-edged mirror had been placed above a daintily
inlaid satinwood dressing table with a velvet-covered
stool in front of it, and overshadowing all was the bed,

an enormous four-poster swathed in rose-shaded silk bed hangings.

Her face alight with pleasure, Sara turned to Sam. "Oh, Mr. Cantrell! It is beautiful!"

Sam smiled indulgently. "Thank you, my dear! Now, don't worry about trying to change for supper—we'll fill that armoire with fancy gowns and fripperies in no time at all. Just acquaint yourself with your new room and refresh yourself. In a half hour or so, Bartholomew will come and escort you to the dining room."

It wasn't Bartholomew, however, who came to escort Sara to the dining room that evening. Answering the brisk knock, Sara opened the door to be confronted by an expensively gowned woman who could be none other than Margaret's sister, Ann.

The elder of the two sisters by five years, Ann closely resembled Margaret. In fact, she appeared to be a paler version of Margaret: her hair a slightly less striking shade of gold, her eyes a lighter blue, her shape a trifle less voluptuous and her features just missing the incredible beauty that Margaret possessed. She was undoubtedly an attractive woman, and except when in Margaret's company, she would outshine any other female present.

Ann stood in the hall, one silk-slippered foot tapping impatiently on the floor, her alabaster shoulders and bosom rising proudly from a low-cut evening gown of fine ruby silk, the yards and yards of material of the voluminous skirt flowing gracefully over the hoop she wore underneath. Her blond hair was arranged in two bunches of long ringlets on either side of her head, and the expression in her blue eyes was only slightly less cold than Margaret's had been earlier.

Ann's dismissing gaze ran up and down Sara's small, slim form. "So you're Sam's latest little act of charity. I swear that man has the softest heart of anyone I've ever known! It's a good thing he has Margaret to stop *most* people from taking blatant advantage of him!"

Though feeling distinctly shabby and humble, Sara met Ann's eyes defiantly and asked, "But don't *you* live here, too? Aren't you also dependent upon Mr. Cantrell?"

Ann smiled thinly. "Thank God, not any longer! I remarried over four years ago, to a man *much* more wealthy than poor Sam—my husband, Mr. Shelldrake, and I only came to dine this evening. Although the way it began to rain when we arrived, we may be forced to stay the night."

Somehow Sara got through the evening, enduring being virtually ignored by the two sisters. However, Sam and Mr. Shelldrake, a bluff, blondly handsome gentleman of about thirty-five years of age, tried gently to draw her out and make her feel welcome. The butler, Bartholomew, also seemed to look with favor upon her as he moved in elegant silence around the table, deftly serving and removing the various plates and tureens. Frequently she caught his friendly dark eyes on her and once he even winked at her—which, unfortunately, Margaret saw.

Margaret's lips tightened, and not even waiting for Bartholomew to leave the room, she said abruptly to Sam, "I've been thinking darling, that perhaps we ought to get an English butler."

At Sam's look of astonishment, she went on airily. "I mean, Bartholomew does very well and I know that he is your father's by-blow and that you feel a certain family loyalty to him, but he *really* doesn't have the polish one would wish for in one's butler. I mean, even if your poor, misguided father did have him trained and educated in England, he isn't really *English*, is he?"

Bartholomew stiffened, and from where she sat, Sara could see the angry flush that stained his dark cheeks. Feeling sorry and embarrassed for him, she focused on her Baccarat crystal glass, writhing inwardly at Margaret's blatant cruelty.

A pained smile on his face, Sam said quietly, "Margaret, I don't believe that this is the time to discuss such things."

Margaret grimaced. "Oh, Sam, darling! Sometimes you are so stuffy. Very well, we'll talk about it later. But I really think that you should find him some other duties—he does have a certain family resemblance, you know, and I find his presence a distressing reminder of your father's lamentable predilection for consorting with the prettier female slaves. Even if he is your half brother, couldn't you find some other position for him . . . perhaps in the fields? After all, he *is* only a slave."

Sam sent an anguished look in Bartholomew's direction and muttered, "Margaret! Please!"

"Oh, very well! We won't talk about it right now. But, Sam, dear, I do so *very* much want a *proper* English butler!"

There was an awkward silence and then Margaret began to prattle to Ann about a new gown she was ordering from New York, and the moment passed.

Sara found the meal interminable, but it helped that Yancy's dark, incendiary personality was not present at the long mahogany table, and if it had not been for Margaret's barely disguised animosity and Ann's cool indifference, she might have enjoyed herself. Certainly Sam and Thomas Shelldrake tried to make her feel comfortable, and while Margaret and Ann were clever enough not to say or do anything *overtly* hostile, Sara knew, with a sinking sensation in the pit of her stomach, that it was highly unlikely that she would be allowed to remain at Magnolia Grove—no matter *how* kind Sam was to her.

As the evening progressed and Sara watched Margaret—resplendent in a fabulous sapphire silk gown, her golden curls framing her patrician features—effortlessly enchanting the gentlemen and conversing gaily with her sister while coldly ignoring Sara as she sat quietly in the corner, her spirits dipped lower and lower. She'd had such hopes, she thought miserably as she gazed at Margaret's lovely countenance, such dreams that she and Margaret would forge as strong a bond as she and Sam had and that they would become as fond of each other equally as quickly, but it was not to be. Margaret didn't want her here; every word, every glance, every action made that cruelly clear.

Realizing that she was here tonight only on Margaret's sufferance and that there was no need to dwell wistfully on how happy she might have been to live here, Sara rose to her feet when there was a break in the conversation and said politely, "If you all do not mind, I should like to retire to my room. Will you excuse me?"

"Oh, here, now!" exclaimed Thomas Shelldrake protestingly. "Don't run away like that, child. It is far too early." He smiled at her, his brown eyes crinkling at the corners. "Ann and I live only a few miles from here, but we are not often at Magnolia Grove—stay and let us get to know you better before you disappear on us."

Margaret quickly said, "If she wants to go to bed, we must let her." She sent her brother-in-law a coy glance. "After all, what does she know of adult conversation?" Looking across at Sara, her expression anything but cordial, she added, "I understand that Bartholomew mistakenly put you in the Rose Room. You may sleep there tonight, but tomorrow I'm afraid we shall have to see about finding you more suitable quarters on the third floor. Run along now and find something to amuse yourself."

Feeling even more dejected, for she had a very good idea what Margaret would consider "suitable" quarters for her, Sara swallowed the lump that rose in her throat and pasted a brave smile on her mouth. She had taken just one step toward the door when Sam said quietly, "There was no mistake about her room. *I* chose it for her."

Margaret looked petulant. "Oh, darling! Don't tell me you're going to upset the running of my house. You *know* I wanted to redo that room!"

Sam smiled uneasily. "Well, no, I didn't." He glanced warmly at Sara. "Don't worry, my dear, we'll find you a nice room—I won't let you be banished to the attic."

Making some sort of reply and bidding the others good night, Sara fled. Battered by Margaret's and, to a lesser extent, Ann's cruel treatment, she was suddenly awash in tears and didn't see Yancy coming down the stairs until she blundered smack into him. Her first intimation of his presence was when her cheek came into contact with his hard chest and his strong hands closed tightly around her upper arms.

Yancy's blunt expletive rent the air as he found his arms suddenly full of soft young woman, and in startled misery Sara glanced up into his dark, chiseled features, her breath catching painfully in her throat as she came under the full force of his eagle-gold eyes.

Feeling as if she had been branded by that fierce gaze, Sara could not move her eyes from his face, and as they stood there frozen at the bottom of the stairs, she became shockingly aware of him in a way that she had never been of any man in her life. He was hard and warm and smelled of leather and tobacco, and as the minutes passed, she was conscious of some new, astonishing emotion unfurling within her.

For a long, breathless moment Yancy stared down into her tear-drenched eyes, finding himself drowning in their green depths. She was supple and joltingly sweet in his arms, and when his stunned gaze finally traveled over her shocked face, he was uneasily aware that he had never seen any young woman quite so beguilingly enchanting in his entire life. Guessing the cause of her distress, his gaze softened and he said gruffly, "I see that Margaret must have been sharpening her claws on you."

Unbearably conscious of him, her skin tingling in the strangest way, Sara said, "Yes, I mean, no."

An engaging smile quirked the corners of his fascinating mouth and he teased, "Which is it? Yes or no?"

Sara took a deep breath, wishing he would release her, wishing uneasily that his very nearness wasn't quite so distracting. Remembering her manners, she said primly, "Your stepmother has been most kind to me."

Yancy laughed outright. "Margaret? Surely you jest!"

Mesmerized by the difference laughter made on his striking features, Sara remained mute, her bemused gaze taking in the teasing glint in his amber-gold eyes, the attractive dimple that creased one lean cheek and the good-natured smile that crooked his lips.

As he stared down at the tears drying on her pale cheeks, Yancy's laughter faded, and with an odd note in his voice, he inquired, "If not Margaret, then who was so unkind to make you cry? Shall I make them regret it?"

Sara shook her head slowly, her gaze clinging to his dark face, her breathing suddenly racing out of control at the expression that leaped into those brilliant gold eyes. She knew she should do something to break this queer spell, but she could not; she could only stand there, completely unaware of her own irresistibility, unaware of the way her spiky-lashed emerald eyes glowed so mysteriously in the light of the chandelier, or of the sweet curve of her creamy cheek, or even of the provocative shape and fullness of her lips.

But Yancy was very aware of them and, his voice thick, he muttered, "Well, *chica*, since there are no villains for me to slay, perhaps I shall have to kiss your tears away. . . ."

Sara froze as his lips gently touched the tearstains on her cheeks; her breathing seemed suspended as he dropped warm, tender kisses on her face, his lips unerringly sliding downward to the inviting softness of her mouth. When his lips finally settled on hers, there was a roaring in her head and she was positive that she was going to faint . . . or that there was nothing more exciting in this world than having Yancy Cantrell kiss her.

Sara never remembered putting her arms around his neck or pressing ardently against him—it seemed the most natural thing in the world that she should be in his arms—and he muttered, "Open your mouth, *querida* . . . let me . . . let me . . ." Caught up in emotions she had never before experienced, she had no idea of denying him, her lips parting eagerly for him, and when Yancy's hot, questing tongue surged within her mouth, she shuddered, the sensations that exploded through her making her sway in his arms.

How long they would have remained locked passionately together or how the embrace would have eventually ended, neither could have guessed, for the sound of tinkling laughter behind them broke them apart like a pair of scalded cats.

"Oh, my dear!" Margaret exclaimed with malicious amusement. "When I said to amuse yourself, Sara, I didn't mean for you to test your charms on Yancy."

Buffeted by powerful emotions and sensations that had been totally foreign to her until the moment Yancy had taken her into his arms, Sara stared blankly at Margaret. She was hardly even aware when Yancy shoved her behind him and blocked her from Margaret's malevolent gaze.

Dimly she heard Yancy say tightly, "Leave her alone, Margaret! She's an innocent—if you want to vent your spleen, try to do it on someone who is more up to your weight and skill."

Margaret's lovely eyes narrowed. "Oh, my! Don't tell me you've been fooled by her air of innocence, too!" She smiled nastily. "You Cantrell men! So noble, so ready to protect the downtrodden! You're a softheaded fool, just like your father!"

"I think," Yancy said in even tones, "that you've said just about enough!"

A glitter of excitement in her eyes, Margaret came nearer to the stairs. "And if I decide I haven't? What are you going to do about it?"

Her scattered senses returning, Sara became very aware of the tenseness of Yancy's big body, and she feared that Margaret would provoke him to violence. When he took a threatening step toward his tormentor, Sara couldn't stop herself from intervening. She clutched at his arm and said, "Don't! Don't let her provoke you this way."

"Oh, pooh!" Margaret said mockingly. "I'm not afraid of Yancy! And as for you, I believe I told you to *run along*!"

Sara hesitated, not wishing to leave Yancy to face the unpleasant scene with Margaret, yet she had little choice. Reluctantly she retreated up the stairs, her attention riveted on the pair in the hallway.

"Your bitchery is showing, sweet stepmama," Yancy drawled. "Does Sara's youth and innocence make you envious? Are you afraid that her charms will attract my father?"

"Why, you ill-bred mongrel! Your father adores me! I can make him do anything I want!" Margaret smiled slyly. "Even give me Casa Paloma. . . ."

"*Por Dios*!" Yancy snarled. "I *will* kill you!"

In one fluid motion he crossed to where Margaret stood, his dark hand closing savagely around her arm, and he shook her violently. Margaret only laughed and purred, "You don't really hate me, you still want me— that's why you can't keep your hands off me."

"You delude yourself. For years the *only* reason I have wanted my hands on you is to wrap them around your neck and squeeze the life out of you!"

Margaret swayed even nearer to him, her mouth only inches from his. "You're lying! You want me!"

With a muttered curse, Yancy flung her from him and disappeared toward the back of the house, nearly knocking down the slim young man who was coming from the opposite direction. At the sight of the other man, Margaret snapped, "Hyrum! What are doing you here this time of night?"

From Sara's vantage point in the shadows near the top of the stairs, she could see that the newcomer was a man about thirty years old, neatly garbed in a light brown frock coat and brown trousers. He was pleasantly handsome, his even features attractively arranged, and his hair was very fair and wavy. Catching his balance from Yancy's violent passage, he looked at Margaret and said quietly, "I was working late tonight. There are several items I want to discuss with Mr. Cantrell, and since I heard that he has returned, I thought I would get everything in order for tomorrow morning."

"Oh! You were working. How boring!"

He smiled slightly. "Well, yes. Since I am your husband's overseer, that is what he pays me to do."

Margaret ran her hand familiarly over the lapel of his coat. "How very dull! Don't you *ever* forget your duties?" She smiled seductively, her body lightly brushing against his. Trailing her fingers upward to teasingly caress his jaw, she murmured, "Dear, sweet, *noble* Hyrum, if you would only put away your scruples and forget that I am

Sam's wife, I'm sure I would find you so much more interesting . . . and you could spend your evenings with me. . . ." Her mouth brazenly grazed his and she added huskily, "Doing something far more exciting than poring over tedious business papers!"

Neither party was aware of Sara watching them from the stairs, and she smothered a shocked gasp at Margaret's boldness.

Hyrum's mouth tightened. Stiffly he said, "And do you think that your *husband* would appreciate my efforts?"

Margaret straightened, a nasty gleam in her eyes. "Such outrage! Strange, how the fact that Ann has a husband hasn't seemed to stop you from mooning over her!"

Flushing, Hyrum said tautly, "You're turning your sister's many kindnesses to me into something vile! I have only the highest respect for Mrs. Shelldrake—thank God she is *nothing* like you!"

Margaret laughed. "She is far more like me than anyone can ever guess, and you're a fool if you believe differently!"

Hyrum merely said, "Perhaps. If there is nothing else, madam, I must be on my way. If you will excuse me?"

"But suppose I don't want to excuse you?" Margaret purred. "Suppose I want you to escort me for a walk around the grounds?"

"If that's what you wish, of course I shall be happy to keep you company," Hyrum replied tightly.

"Hmm, always the polite employee, aren't you?" Margaret asked with an edge to her voice. "I wonder how Sam would react if I were to hint that you have been making unwelcome advances toward me."

"That's a damned lie!"

"Well, yes . . . but I wonder which one of us Sam would believe."

Hyrum's fists clenched. "Yancy is right to call you a witch! It is no wonder he hates you!"

"I would suggest that if you don't want to lose your very well-paid position at Magnolia Grove, you not speak to me in such a disrespectful way!" Margaret smiled tauntingly. "After all, I just might decide that it was time my husband hired a new overseer . . . I might anyway. . . ."

His voice full of suppressed anger, Hyrum growled, "Someday you're going to go too far—I only hope I'm around when that time comes! It is a miracle that no one has tried to teach you a lesson before now—at this moment, I could gladly do it myself!"

Suddenly tired of baiting Hyrum, Margaret ordered abruptly, "Oh, go away! Your threats don't worry me— they're only boring, just as you are!"

Hyrum mastered his anger and, bowing stiffly, said, "Whatever you say, madam."

Margaret coolly watched him go out one of the wide front doors and then, a pleased smile on her lips, she disappeared in the direction that Yancy had taken.

It was only when the hall was empty that Sara was able to force herself to go to her room. Her thoughts were spinning dizzyingly in her head as she undressed and crawled into the welcoming softness of the fine feather bed. Half an hour later, she was still tossing and turning in her bed, and after deciding not to fight it any longer, she got up and wandered over to a pair of French doors which opened onto a small balcony. Stepping outside, she breathed in the warm magnolia-scented air of the night, letting the tension knotted inside her evaporate. After several moments, feeling more at ease, she started to turn away, when she became aware of the conversation going on below her.

She immediately recognized Ann's and Margaret's voices, and believing that she had learned far more about the mistress of Magnolia Grove than she had ever wanted to know, and not wanting to eavesdrop, she took a step back toward her room. But Ann's shocking words came to her clearly, and against her will, she lingered.

"Tom thinks the baby you carry is his. Is it?" Ann asked bluntly.

There was silence for a second and then Margaret's tinkling laugh rang out. "Oh, dear! How did you find out about that? Did guilt consume him and he told you?"

"Yes, he did tell me—weeks ago—of your affair. I can't deny I was hurt, but he swore it was over and we'd manage to put it behind us. He was distraught when he came to me with the news that you had told him the baby might be his—I told him I would talk to you about it." Ann's voice had taken on a brittle tone.

"Are you envious?" Margaret purred. "Do you wish you were the one pregnant?"

"Is it his child?" Ann repeated.

Ashamed of herself, yet listening intently on the balcony above the two women, Sara could almost see the malicious smile that curved Margaret's mouth. "It's possible, but then . . . ."

"Sometimes," Ann hissed viciously, "I actually pray that Yancy does kill you! And there are times when I think I shall save him the trouble!"

"Oh, Ann, don't let *us* fight! I know you were angry when I snapped Sam up from underneath your nose, but you have Tom now, and he is younger and far richer than Sam, and just as handsome. As for the other, you don't love Tom, you only married him for his money, so why be angry with me?"

"Because," Ann said thickly, "he's my *husband*! And anything that happens to him ultimately affects me and my position. I don't care that you had an affair—that's over with now and he's no longer so blindly infatuated with you that he can't see you for what you are. Your pregnancy concerns him; he fears the child might really be his and that Sam will find out." Ann paused and Sara could imagine her trying to get her emotions in check. "If it comes out that it is Tom's child when you carry, it will ruin everything. You know that he is favored to be the next judge in Austin County, and if your affair and his possible paternity of your child were to come out, the gossip and scandal would be insurmountable. He'd be ruined." An odd note in her tone, Ann continued. "He will do *anything* to gain that judgeship—I'm warning you, don't ruin it for him."

"Oh, pooh! This conversation bores me! Now, let's rejoin the gentlemen."

The voices faded, but the ugly words she had overheard lingered, and as Sara walked to her bed she deliberately pushed their implications from her mind. Serves me right for eavesdropping, she thought sourly as she lay back down. Lying there in the darkness, she took even, deep breaths, trying to focus on something other than Sam's undoubtedly wicked wife. After a while a sleepy smile crossed her face as the image of Yancy's dark features suddenly obliterated everything else in her mind. Moments later, she was sound asleep.

As was her custom, Sara woke early. For several long minutes she lay in bed, savoring its comfort, but then she recalled all that had happened yesterday, and she sighed. No use getting too comfortable, my girl, she thought resignedly. If Margaret has anything to do with it, you'll not sleep another night in such luxury.

To her pleasure, she found upon arising that someone had already entered her room and placed a silver tray with piping-hot coffee in a silver pot and a basket of warm raisin-filled buns on a table near her bed. Ignoring the temptation of food until after she had completed her morning ablutions, Sara bit into the golden-brown bun and sipped the coffee several moments later. Deliberately she did not let herself think about yesterday or last night. Her repast finished, Sara took one last look at herself in the mirror, shook out the skirts of her travel-stained pink gingham gown, gave her tidy cornet a final touch and ventured from the room.

Despite the hour, the house seemed unusually silent as Sara made her way downstairs. Upon reaching the entry hall, she stopped, not quite certain where she should go from there. Deciding not to be caught someplace that Margaret would no doubt find objectionable—and Margaret was bound to find her presence *any*where in the house objectionable—she opted to take a stroll around the grounds.

It was a lovely late-April morning. The sun was shining goldly and the sky was a bright, blinding blue with just a puffy white cloud or two drifting across its endless expanse. Sara walked aimlessly through the gardens and across the lawns. Spying a romantically designed gazebo some distance from the house, she wandered in that direction.

With an effort she continued to keep her thoughts away from the traumatic events of yesterday. She was grimly determined to simply enjoy these few brief moments. As she approached the white, lattice-worked gazebo, she reminded herself that there was no reason to run down the road to meet trouble. Perhaps things would work out, after all—maybe during the night Margaret had suffered a change of heart. . . .

She entered the gazebo, where sunlight streamed in between the gaps of the latticework. An iron-scrolled white table stood in the middle of the eight-sided room, and a wide, comfortable bench had been built against the outer walls; large cushions in gay colors of yellow and blue were scattered across it. Looking around in appreciation, at first Sara thought the heap of sapphire silk sprawled on the floor on the other side of the table was a pillow that had fallen from the bench.

Rounding the table with the intention of picking up the

pillow, she froze as the full impact of what she was seeing hit her. It was not a pillow which lay on the floor—
no pillow ever had hair that color of butter-yellow, or
had ever possessed that porcelain complexion. . . .

Gripped by incredulous horror, Sara stared dumbly at
the form before her. There was no mistaking that it was
Margaret Cantrell who lay lifelessly at her feet, Margaret
of the limpid blue eyes, still garbed in the rich sapphire
silk gown she had worn the night before, Margaret with
a fine Spanish dagger driven through her heart. . . .

PART ONE

TIME OF TURMOIL
APRIL 1867

My mind is troubled, like a fountain stirr'd.
And I myself see not the bottom of it.

TROILUS AND CRESSIDA
—WILLIAM SHAKESPEARE

4

Another rainy April morning, Sara thought idly as she stood at one of the tall windows of the Rose Room, and here I am looking once more at the grave of a man who was most dear to me. . . .

Her mouth twisted ruefully. In the small family cemetery which was situated on a slight rise a short distance from the house, Sam Cantrell's grave lay between those of his two vastly different wives, Madelina and Margaret. Sara still wasn't certain she had done the right thing by burying him there. Ann, of course, even now, seven years after Margaret had died, was outwardly ever loyal to her dead sister and had insisted that that was where Sam would have wanted to rest eternally, but Sara wasn't so certain. During the strained and horrible days and months following Margaret's murder, Sam *must* have realized that she was not the sweet wife he had convinced himself she was, and even though he had never said a word of disparagement about her in all the years that followed, Sara had often wondered what he felt in the deepest reaches of his heart.

For a moment her mind drifted back to that horrible morning so many years ago when she had stared down in horrified disbelief at Margaret's body. She never remembered how long she had stood there, her heart beating in thick, terrified strokes, but eventually she must have torn herself away from the gazebo and stumbled to the house. . . .

Breathless, frightened and shocked, Sara burst through the double front doors, startling Sam, who was just crossing the hall. He took one look at the terrified expression on her face and demanded anxiously, "What is it, my dear? What has frightened you so?"

"Margaret's dead!" she blurted out hysterically, too agitated to think of any kinder way to break the appalling news. "She's dead, I tell you—I saw her! Murdered in the gazebo!"

Sam stood there in the middle of the elegant marble-floored hallway as if turned to stone, and Sara bit back a sob. Rushing across to him and grasping his arm, she shook him violently. "Didn't you hear me—she's dead! Someone murdered her!"

"Who's been murdered?" Yancy asked carelessly, having just entered the hall from the library in time to hear Sara's last words. Unaware of the gravity of the situation, he added sarcastically, "Dare I hope that it is my sweet stepmama?"

Recovering some of her wits, Sara stared at his handsome face with revulsion, the memory of that silver dagger in Margaret's breast very clear. "Yes!" she retorted sharply. "It *is* your stepmama—someone killed Margaret with a *Spanish* dagger!"

Yancy's indolent air vanished. "*Por Dios*! You're serious!" His amber-gold eyes intent, he snapped, "Where?"

"In the gazebo, behind the house."

Sara had barely spoken the words before Yancy was striding toward the door, but catching sight of Sam's frozen features for the first time, he stopped and crossed quickly to his father's side. Putting a comforting hand on Sam's shoulder, he muttered, "Father, I'm sorry. This must be horrible for you." When Sam remained silent and unmoving, Yancy bent nearer, concern on his dark face, and asked softly, "Are you all right?"

Sam seemed to shake himself, and meeting Yancy's worried gaze, he attempted a reassuring smile, but it failed lamentably. Dazedly he murmured, "Yes, yes, of course I'm all right—it is just that it is such a shock. Margaret dead! Murdered! I cannot believe it!"

Yancy's mouth tightened and Sara was confident that he had no trouble believing that someone had murdered Margaret. But his voice was gentle as he said to his father, "Stay here. I shall see for myself the truth of the matter."

A healthy sense of outrage seized Sara. "It *is* true! I saw her!" she said heatedly.

Sam patted her arm absently. "I'm sure it is, child. Yancy didn't mean to cast doubt on what you've said." Recovering some of his shattered composure, he took a deep, steadying breath and squared his shoulders. His voice stronger, he said to Yancy, "I will come with you."

Their eyes met over Sara's head. "I think you should come with us, too, Sara," Sam added. "I don't wish to alarm the household until I have observed the scene myself."

Reluctantly Sara accompanied the two men, not relishing a return to the gazebo, but then, she didn't want to remain at the house either.

When the two men entered the gazebo, Sara didn't need Yancy's curt command to wait outside to keep her from following them inside. A shudder went through her slender form at the very idea of looking at Margaret's body again.

It seemed to Sara that the two men were in the gazebo for an inordinate amount of time; from where she stood, she could hear the faint murmur of their voices and she wondered hysterically what they were finding to talk about for so long. Finally they came out, their expressions shuttered.

A strained smile on his face, Sam walked over to her and placed his hand warmly on her arm. "Sara," he began carefully, "are you certain that you saw a dagger?"

Sara looked at him incredulously. "Of course I saw a dagger! It is sticking up from her breast." She darted an accusatory glance at Yancy. "A Spanish one! I don't lie!" Sudden suspicion occurred to her. "Why do you ask? Didn't you see it?"

Sam shook his head slowly. "It's true what you said— Margaret is dead, and from the looks of it, she was stabbed, but there is no sign of a weapon . . . Yancy and I found no Spanish dagger."

"But it was there, I tell you! *I saw it!*"

"I'm sure you *thought* you saw a dagger, but in the horror of the moment . . ." Sam paused. "Perhaps you were mistaken?"

Sara stared thunderstruck up into his grave face, hardly daring to believe what she was hearing. Sam's eyes were full of shock and sorrow, yet she thought she also detected an odd sort of pleading in his gaze as the seconds spun out and they stared at each other. A knot suddenly formed in her chest. With an effort she dropped her eyes from his, a dreadful thought occurring to her. *Sam wanted her to lie*! He wanted her to pretend that she had not seen the dagger! And there could be only one reason for that, she reflected bitterly. *Yancy*! Sam must know or suspect that Yancy had killed Margaret, and despite his grief, he wanted to save his son.

Sara risked a quick, resentful glance at Yancy's stony face. He stood a short distance behind his father, his arms folded across his chest. Was it only last night that he had held her in his arms and kissed her with such passion? But other memories crowded into her mind, too, memories of Yancy and Margaret together, of his twice-repeated threat to kill his stepmother; ugly memories of the exchange between Margaret and Hyrum after Yancy had stalked away; and the unpleasant remembrance of the conversation she had overheard between Ann and Margaret. . . . So many people had reasons to hate and fear Margaret, and it was obvious that Margaret had been a depraved woman, but had she deserved to be murdered?

Sara bit her lip, her honey-gold head bowed as she stared sightlessly at the ground. What was she to do? Insist upon telling of the dagger? For just a moment she considered that she *had* been mistaken, that in those first moments of sheer terror she *had* imagined the dagger. But I didn't imagine it, she admitted wretchedly to herself. *I saw it*!

Again she looked at the heartrending expression on Sam's face and the knot in her chest became almost unbearable. He was such a good man. Could she hurt him this way? Knowing the answer to that question, Sara dropped her gaze once more and muttered, "If it is not there, I must have imagined it."

Sam's breath came out in a rush. "My dear child! This has been a dreadful ordeal for you—it is no wonder that you imagined such a thing."

Sara could not bear to look at him, afraid that her sudden resolve to protect Yancy, and thereby protect Sam, might falter. "Yes," she replied dully, "it *has* been an ordeal and I'd rather not talk about it anymore, if you please?"

"Certainly! Certainly!" Sam agreed hastily, his hand tightening on her slender shoulder. A note of entreaty in his voice, he added, "And, of course, when the authorities question you, when *anyone* questions you, you won't mention the dagger you imagined you saw, will you?"

Her emerald eyes full of resentment, Sara glared over at Yancy's dark, shuttered face. "Of course not," she said flatly. "I will not mention the *Spanish* dagger—to anyone!"

It was the sound of Bartholomew's voice, calling her name, which broke Sara's unpleasant reverie, and with a last look at the three graves under the wide, spreading pecan tree, she turned away and called out, "Here I am, Bartholomew. I was just resting in my room."

A faint frown on his face, Bartholomew was waiting for Sara at the top of the staircase. At the sight of him, Sara felt a rush of affection for him, remembering with a smile how considerate he had always been to her, even in those first, traumatic days following the discovery of Margaret's body. He had been a friend then and had proved his friendship time and again throughout the long, terrible years of the war that had ripped the country apart.

Bartholomew had changed little over the intervening seven years, his café-au-lait skin as unlined as it had been the day Sara had arrived at Magnolia Grove, and except for a faint touch of silver at his temples, there was little about him that showed the passage of time. Oh, but there was *so* much that had changed during these past years, Sara thought wistfully as she accompanied him down the wide, curving staircase.

Everywhere one looked, the changes the years had wrought were obvious. Magnolia Grove was still *structurally* imposing, but it had been stripped of everything of value, which had been sold to raise money for the rebel war effort. The marble flooring in the formerly grand entry hall had been ripped up and sold; the crystal chandeliers throughout the house had been taken down and sold, as had the fine carpets, furniture, china and silverware. Outside the house the changes were just as dramatic. The dark green paint around the doors and windows was now faded and blistered by the punishing Texas sun; the lawn and gardens were unkempt; the stables, which had housed numerous blooded stock, stood mostly empty; the broad acres which had once brimmed with cotton lay barren and fallow, as there were neither any slaves to work the fields nor any money to buy seed or hire the former slaves. The few freed slaves who did consent to work for their former masters could not be depended upon. After a day's or a week's work they would disappear with coins jingling in their pockets, leaving the soil half planted or half the harvest still standing in the fields to rot.

The situation was not unique to Texas; all over the South, the story was the same—ruined homes and idle plantations and little hope of ever regaining what had been lost. The War between the States had utterly destroyed the once powerful plantation aristocracy, and although Texas had not suffered the ravages of the Union Army as had the other states of the Confederacy, it was still as beaten and destitute as the rest of the South. There had not been any great battles or major engagements fought in Texas during the "late unpleasantness," and so the inhabitants had been spared the tragedy of having their homes and plantations burned and looted, but that was little consolation—without compunction, Texans had stripped themselves of everything of value in their fervid support of the Confederate cause. The majority of the inhabitants had been fiercely committed to the rebellion and Texas had given more men, more money, more of everything to the Confederacy than any other state in the South with the exception of Virginia, and now it was reaping the bitter cost of that folly.

Defeated, bankrupt and humiliated, despite the promise of readmission to the Union and the amnesty offered the late rebels, Texas had to suffer the further ignominy of being placed under martial law and its citizens had to endure the sight of the hated, blue-coated Union troops swaggering proudly all across their lands. Matters were not helped by the fact that the Union military held itself above the law, the wishes and commands of the Yankee hierarchy overriding even the civil courts and the laws of Texas. Texas was a conquered territory, and the United States Congress, President Johnson and the Union troops treated it as such.

Walking down the staircase at Magnolia Grove with Bartholomew at her side, Sara wondered again, as she had so often, in the two years since President Lincoln's death, if the South would have been treated so harshly if he had not been assassinated that night at Ford's Theater by John Wilkes Booth. Her mouth twisted. Who knew?

Bartholomew interrupted her thoughts. "The lawyer's here again. He wants to see you."

Shaking off her useless speculations, she asked Bartholomew, "Did he say what he wanted? Do you think he's finally managed to locate Yancy?"

Bartholomew shook his head, a sardonic smile on his wide lips. "Since when has Mr. Sam's lawyer ever wasted time conversing with an upstart black?"

Sara's lips thinned. "He wasn't rude?"

"No more so than usual!"

"You know," Sara began in a scolding tone, "Mr. Henderson wouldn't be so brusque with you if you didn't adopt that obnoxiously superior attitude whenever he comes to call." She shook a finger at him. "You do it on purpose, you know you do! You puff up, look down your nose at him and speak with an English accent that would do a duke proud."

Reaching the bottom of the staircase, Bartholomew grinned at her. "I'se doan know what y'all is talkin' 'bout!" he drawled innocently. "Why, I'se jest a pore niggar! Doan mean to be uppity."

"Oh, stop being so provocative!" Sara said crossly. "Which room did you put him in?"

A wry grimace crossed Bartholomew's face. "The only room that is still presentable," he replied in his normal voice, "the master's office."

The door to the library flew open and Sara and Bartholomew both turned in that direction. Ann Shelldrake stood there, the expression on her face one of extreme displeasure.

The years had treated Ann kindly, her hair still just as blond, her blue eyes just as bright and her porcelain skin still as firm and lovely at thirty-eight as it had been seven years earlier. She was wearing a black silk gown that was several seasons old, but in spite of its age, it had obviously been a fashionable, expensive garment.

Sara remembered it well—Ann had bought it for Margaret's funeral and had worn it all during the mourning time for her sister. These days Ann wore black for Sam Cantrell, that kindhearted, generous man who had opened up his home and willingly shared his dwindling resources with her and her husband when their plantation had been sold for back taxes last year. There was another reason that Sam had been so generous to Tom Shelldrake. Tom's left arm had been crippled during the early days of the war, when he had intercepted a bullet meant for Sam. Sam had been convinced that Tom had saved his life, and there was nothing he wouldn't have done for his friend—even if it meant putting up with Tom's demanding wife, among other things! While full of pity for Tom, Sara disliked Ann's arrogant manners and thoroughly distrusted the woman, but she hadn't the heart to ask them to leave—yet!

Glaring across at Bartholomew, who remained by Sara's side, Ann snapped, "Where have you been? I told you that Mr. Thomas and I wanted some coffee."

Bartholomew looked haughty. "I think you forget that

it is *Sara* who pays my wages—not you!"

Ann rolled her eyes and complained disgustedly, "Oh, God! *Nothing* is the same since the war! It seems that everywhere I go, even in my own home, I am accosted by uppity servants!"

Bartholomew and Sara exchanged glances; catching sight of the twinkle in Bartholomew's dark eyes, Sara had to choke back a strong urge to giggle. Keeping her features composed, she went over to Ann and purposefully distracted the other woman. "Did you know that Mr. Henderson has come to call? He is waiting for me in Sam's old office."

Ann's expression changed immediately. "Has he found Yancy?" she demanded. "Do you think that at last we will be able to settle Sam's estate and make some improvements in this wretched place?"

Bartholomew snorted, but Sara stopped the rude comment he was about to make by sending him a severe glance and saying sweetly, "Bartholomew, would you please prepare a tray of refreshments for Mrs. Shelldrake and her husband, and one for me and Mr. Henderson?"

Bartholomew grimaced, recognizing from Sara's tone that she wasn't going to let him bait Ann Shelldrake any further. Aware that Ann was watching him, he gave Sara a deep, respectful bow. "As you wish, madam. I shall see to it *immediately*!"

Watching him stride away, Ann gritted her teeth together. "I wish to God that Margaret had been able to send him to the fields before she died! Maybe feeling the lash of the overseer's whip would have taught him some respect for his betters!"

"I doubt it!" Sara replied tartly. "Whether a butler or a field hand, Bartholomew is a very proud, intelligent man, and if your sister had been able to convince Sam to send him to work in the cotton fields, which was high-

ly unlikely, I'm sure that within six months it would have
been Bartholomew who was the overseer wielding the
whip and not Hyrum Burnell! Now, if you will excuse
me, I must go see Mr. Henderson."

A stout, florid gentleman of some fifty years of age,
Mr. Henderson was pacing impatiently up and down the
scrap of worn carpet that lay on the floor in front of the
battered old oak desk that had replaced the elegantly
carved walnut one that had been sold in support of
the Confederate cause. Mr. Henderson was frowning,
but at the sight of Sara crossing the room toward him,
his frown vanished and a benevolent smile crossed his
face.

There was much about Sara to make most men smile.
At twenty-four years of age, she had finally lived up to
the promise of startling beauty that had been hers at seventeen. Like Ann, she was wearing a once fine gown
of black silk, and like Ann's, hers had also been purchased because of Margaret's death and was worn now
in mourning for Sam Cantrell; but there the similarity
ended. While Ann's gown gave her an air of matron-
liness, Sara's black gown seemed to intensify her very
youth and the lovely fragility of her features. The somber
color of the garment only emphasized the creamy matte
texture of her fine skin and called attention to the delicate
curve of her chin and her high cheekbones. Her honey-
gold hair, still worn neatly in a cornet of braids, seemed
brighter and more golden against the black material, and
her slender arched brows and long lashes which framed
her bright emerald eyes were equally as dark as the
ebony gown. An innocently beguiling smile, a smile
that had been known to make more than one man think
he had been struck by lightning, curved her generously
shaped mouth and her voice was warm as she said, "Mr.
Henderson! I hope that you have not been waiting long."

Standing far too close, he ardently clasped her slim hand in one of his and patted it enthusiastically. "When a man waits for a woman as lovely as you, time has no meaning," he said gallantly.

"Why, Mr. Henderson! What a lovely thing to say!" Sara murmured and lowered her lids demurely. "It is no wonder that *Mrs.* Henderson is such a happy wife—and after all these years." Dulcetly she asked, "How many years is it, now, that you have been married to that excellent wife of yours?"

Loosening his grip on her hand, he muttered sheepishly, "Eh! Near on thirty years." His smile faded.

Deftly putting some distance between them, Sara asked, "Was there something in particular that you wanted to see me about?"

Mr. Henderson's smile returned. "My dear!" he exclaimed happily. "I have excellent news for you— I have just received word that my messenger has located Yancy at Fort Cobb on the Washita River in Indian Territory. When informed of his father's death, Yancy immediately resigned his commission from the Union Army and is, even as we speak, on his way here. He could arrive within the next few days."

Only by the greatest effort was Sara able to keep her own smile from slipping. This was what she wanted, what they all had been waiting for—but now that Yancy's return was imminent, she was suddenly full of doubts and, quite frankly, terrified!

In those days immediately following the discovery of Margaret's body, there had been much vociferous speculation in the neighborhood about the probable murderer. Yancy Cantrell was at the top of nearly everyone's lists of suspects, but beyond his well-known hatred of his stepmother and his threats to kill her, there was no proof. The authorities would have very much liked to charge him in Margaret's death, but fortunately for

Yancy, he had an excellent, if highly suspicious, alibi—he had spent the night discussing business in the library with his father—they had not parted until dawn was streaking across the skies, and Sam was willing to testify to that fact. No one really believed that Sam was telling the truth; almost unanimously, the community decided that Sam was just doing the natural thing by protecting his only child. But since Margaret had had a knack for making enemies and had been universally disliked, whereas Sam was a highly respected, long-standing member of the neighborhood and most people remembered Yancy as a bewildered, motherless little boy, no one was willing to press the issue. The plain and simple truth of the matter was that there were a lot of people who had a motive for killing Margaret Cantrell! Yancy might have been favored as the killer, but his father's alibi, as well as the fact that there had been nothing more substantial than gossip and innuendo to tie him to the crime, forced the authorities to cast about for other suspects. For a while, the Cantrell butler, Bartholomew Anderson, had come under close scrutiny, as had Hyrum Burnell, the overseer; there had even been, for a short time, the wild and titillatingly scandalous theory that Ann Shelldrake or her husband, Thomas, could have done the ghastly deed, and it had also been whispered that Sam Cantrell might have stabbed Margaret himself! Even Sara had not escaped without having had her name bandied about as a possible suspect, and she could still remember going to bed at night wondering if she would be charged with murder the next morning!

Margaret Cantrell's death had caused an orgy of gossip and malicious speculation in the San Felipe area, and the notoriety the family had endured hadn't abated when the local authorities had finally been compelled to give up their investigation without having found a murderer. It was months before the worst of the gossip had died down and the sheriff or one of his deputies had ceased skulking around the grounds of Magnolia Grove looking for evidence.

Yancy had not stayed at Magnolia Grove after his stepmother had been buried, and Sara had been uncomfortably aware in the days before Margaret's funeral that there had been an increasingly strained air between father and son. Once, to her dismay, she had inadvertently interrupted a terrible argument between them. Sam had wanted Yancy to stay, but Yancy had been adamant about leaving. His departure for Rancho del Sol within a day of the funeral had intensified the gossip and suspicion.

The anxious days and months following Margaret's death were not remembered by Sara with any fondness, and over the years she had laid the sole blame for the tragedy that had beset Sam squarely on Yancy's broad shoulders. Most days she was firmly convinced that Yancy had murdered Margaret; almost as bad, he had coerced his father into lying for him and had cravenly made her an accomplice to his crime by using her affection for Sam to keep her mouth shut about the Spanish dagger! And, having accomplished all of this, he had then coolly ridden away, never to step foot on Magnolia Grove again.

And now, Sara thought with a fresh rush of indignation, she was to share Sam's estate with the same man who had attempted to seduce her—how else could she satisfactorily explain that shocking incident on the stairs her first night at Magnolia Grove and her less than maidenly response to his kiss? Without a doubt, Yancy was a cruel-hearted blackguard who, after Margaret's death, had simply abandoned his father. Ignored him completely. A man who had refused to answer or even acknowledge any of the beseeching letters Sam had sent him as he lay dying.

Sara didn't begrudge Yancy one penny of his father's estate, but she found it highly galling that all of Sam's earthly belongings were to be divided between her and an unprincipled villain who had in all likelihood murdered his stepmother, turned his back on his father and proved himself a traitor to Texas by joining the Union Army!

But it wasn't those sins that made Sara dread Yancy's return. What filled her with stark terror was Yancy's no-doubt murderous reaction when he discovered that *she* was now his stepmother, the widow of his father, and that Sam had left her Casa Paloma.

5

Despite the turmoil within her breast, Sara got through the rest of the day. She tried very hard not to think about Yancy's arrival. As a matter of fact, she tried very hard not to think about Yancy at all, which was difficult because Ann couldn't seem to stop talking about him and speculating about what would happen when he arrived at Magnolia Grove.

By the time she retired to bed that evening, Sara had an excruciatingly painful headache. Restlessly she tossed and turned in her bed, the throbbing in her temples nearly making her cry aloud with the pain.

Lying there awake, attempting to think of something more tranquil than her probable demise once Yancy did return, Sara stared blindly at the ceiling, wondering at the vagaries of fate.

An ironic smile touched her lips. How very different everything had worked out than what she had imagined when she had first met Sam Cantrell! Who could have known that his wife would be murdered? Who could have known that, almost a year to the day later, Fort Sumter in South Carolina would be fired upon and that the country would be convulsed by a long and deadly civil war? Or that Sam, deeply concerned about what would happen to her while he was gone fighting for the South, would convince her, much against her will, to marry him? How could she have known that he would return home from the war a ruined and dying man?

Even now, six years after the event, it seemed incredible to her that she had allowed Sam to talk her into marrying him. She had not loved him in *that* way, and he had made it clear at the outset that he did not intend for the marriage to be anything but one of convenience and that he had no intention of ever consummating the union. The marriage would be solely to ensure that she would be taken care of if something should happen to him, and Sam had assured her that they would have it annulled when the war was over.

At eighteen, Sara had been full of girlish dreams, and she squirmed uneasily when she remembered that quite a few of those dreams had involved Yancy Cantrell! Certainly at that age she'd entertained no thoughts of marrying the father of the man who haunted her most private thoughts, a distant relative to whom she was inordinately grateful for all the kindness he had shown her. In fact, it was that gratefulness to Sam that in the end made her go along with his wishes for a marriage of convenience.

The next afternoon, with a disapproving Ann and Thomas Shelldrake looking on, Sara had married Sam. Two days later, he had left for Virginia, and his bride had not seen him again for almost four years, when he had come home a shattered man to die.

Giving up all pretense of sleep, Sara got out of bed and, since the rain had stopped hours earlier, wandered out onto the balcony. A mirthless smile curved her lips. Seven years ago, she had stood on this very balcony and overheard that distasteful conversation between Ann and Margaret; even now she sometimes wondered if she was wrong to suspect Yancy of killing Margaret. Ann and Thomas Shelldrake had had as good a motive as anyone!

Disgustedly she jerked her thoughts away from useless speculation, returning her concentration to more recent events—in particular, Sam's condition when he had finally returned home from the war two years ago. He had come home to die; that was obvious from the moment he had been unloaded from the rickety wagon which had delivered him.

Sara thought it ironic that Sam should have managed to escape unscathed all the years of the war, only to be horribly wounded at Sayler's Creek, one of the last battles of the Civil War. His horse had been shot out from underneath him and he had sustained many wounds; because of the severity of his injuries, both his legs had been amputated above the knees, and with pieces of shrapnel still buried in other parts of his body, he had returned to Magnolia Grove, a pitiful shadow of the man he had been. Despite the grievous wounds to his body, his spirit would not die. He managed to live for eighteen more months before finally succumbing. He had never mentioned annulling their marriage and Sara had never pressed the issue, as she had not wanted to upset him during the precious little time he had.

Sara's eyes filled with tears. He had been so gallant, so full of life despite his infirmities, and though he had been dead for six months, she still found it hard to believe that he was gone.

Her lips tightened. Sam had been such an innately *good* man and he had certainly deserved better than a wife like Margaret and a son like Yancy! Her opinion of Yancy Cantrell had never been high, but his actions while his father lay dying were reprehensible!

He could have at least answered *one* of Sam's letters, Sara thought bitterly. But he hadn't. At first Sam had excused him by speculating that the letters hadn't reached him, and grudgingly Sara conceded that perhaps that *might* be true. In the beginning, they had sent the

letters to del Sol, and had not known for months that
Yancy had joined the Union Army at the outbreak of
the war and was no longer at the rancho. Sam had written then to the Department of the Army, seeking word
of his son, but still there had been no response. In fact,
it wasn't until Mr. Henderson's visit today that there
had been any definite word of his whereabouts—and if
Mr. Henderson hadn't sent someone to *personally* find
Yancy and inform him of his father's death, it was likely
that Yancy still wouldn't know that Sam had died . . . or
that I am his stepmama, Sara thought nervously.

The throbbing in her temples suddenly spiked painfully and she left the balcony and went back to her
room. After shrugging into a worn green velvet robe,
she decided to go downstairs. Familiarly making her
way in the dark to Sam's office, she entered and, after
quietly shutting the door, quickly lit a lamp. Opening
the bottom drawer of Sam's desk, she found the bottle
of brandy he kept there—strictly for "medicinal" pur-
poses, he had told her often with a twinkle in his eyes.
A wry smile crossed her features. It had been at Sam's
gentle prodding that she had learned of the remarkably
relaxing propensities of brandy, and it seemed only fit-
ting that she should drink it in his office, where they had
spent so many happy, tranquil hours together before his
death. Pouring herself a healthy dose of the amber liquor in one of the thick glasses which she retrieved from
the same drawer as the brandy, she settled back in Sam's
black leather chair and slowly sipped her drink.

As the minutes passed and the burning warmth of
the brandy flowed smoothly through her tense body,
she could feel a gradual lessening of the apprehension
that had beset her from the moment she had learned that
Yancy was indeed on his way to Magnolia Grove. He
wasn't, she acknowledged uneasily, going to be very
happy with the situation.

No doubt there were many sins of which Yancy Cantrell was guilty, but she didn't honestly believe that he had been overly mercenary. He *probably* didn't care that Sam had left her a half interest in Magnolia Grove, or that Sam had willed her the tidy sum which had been safely squirreled away in a bank account in New York that Sam had opened before the war. Casa Paloma, however, was an entirely different story. Casa Paloma had been Alvarez land for generations and Yancy had made it brutally clear that he would stop at nothing to ensure that it *stayed* Alvarez land! He was going to be blazingly furious when he learned the peculiar circumstances of her ownership. For reasons which were clear only to himself, Sam hadn't *exactly* left Casa Paloma to her outright. Casa Paloma was hers to do with as she wished, for her life-time, but title to the land was actually held in trust *for the heirs of her body*—her children!

Sara took a big gulp of the brandy. Her children! What could Sam have been thinking of! An uncertain giggle broke from her. She'd been married, been a bride and was now a widow, but she had never been a real wife, and had never, ever been in a position to conceive a child! And Sam had left Casa Paloma to her children! It was insane!

Well, one thing Sam had ensured by his puzzling will—she needn't *really* worry that Yancy would mur-der her for Casa Paloma—if she died without issue, Bartholomew and Tansy were to inherit the rancho. There was no way that Yancy could ever get his hands on it unless he was willing to commit wholesale murder. Of course, there was one other way. . . .

Yancy could never regain Casa Paloma unless . . . She swallowed painfully. Casa Paloma was lost to anyone of Alvarez blood unless she were to bear Yancy's child!

Merciful heavens! Was that why Sam had set up his will in such an incomprehensible manner? Had he been hoping that she and Yancy would marry and have children? That Yancy would be so driven to keep Casa Paloma in the family that he would make certain that any children she had were his? But it would never work, she thought feverishly. Yancy could already be married—or what if she fell in love and married someone else?

Another, even more unsettling thought crossed her mind. She'd been thinking of marriage in connection with children, but in order to have children, one didn't *need* to be married. She took another gulp of her brandy, the most shocking and horrifying ideas galloping through her brain. Suppose Yancy kidnapped her and kept her in isolation until he had accomplished his nefarious deed?

A curious shiver went through her as she imagined what it would be like to be his prisoner, her body his to use as he desired. . . . A heated flush encompassed her and the memory of Yancy's mouth on hers, the texture and warmth of it, came flooding back. Almost as if it had happened only seconds ago, she could recall the taste of him on her tongue, the sensation of her breasts crushed against his chest, and all the wild emotions she had felt then came rushing to life again. To her shamed horror, she realized that the idea of having Yancy Cantrell work his will on her, even if for all the wrong reasons, wasn't as repugnant and distasteful as it should have been.

Her hand shaking slightly, she carefully set down her empty glass. Balefully, she glared at it. It was the brandy. It was the liquor that was filling her head with such nonsensical notions. Sam had never intended for her and Yancy to have children together. Never once had he even hinted at such an idea. He'd *married* her, for heaven's sake! Her eyes narrowed. And, of course, she would *never* allow herself to be used as a broodmare—no matter how attractive the stallion. Remembering Yancy's all-too-seductive kiss, she trembled. At least, she hoped she never would!

Bathed in the soft glow of the lamplight, Sara sat there for a long time, willing herself to relax, to concentrate on something less disturbing than the implications of Sam's will and Yancy's imminent arrival. It was damned difficult, but eventually she turned her thoughts to more practical matters, such as her eventual removal from Magnolia Grove.

Sara was positive that Yancy would want to sell the plantation, and since she had neither the desire nor the wherewithal even to attempt to buy out his half of the property, she had concluded that someday soon, she and the others would move to Casa Paloma. Her chin took on a stubborn cast. For her lifetime, Casa Paloma was hers, and with the money in New York and her half of the proceeds from the sale of Magnolia Grove, she was confident that she and the others could make a pleasant, if not luxurious, life at the rancho raising cattle and fine horses.

Sara had no regrets about leaving Magnolia Grove behind. The house held very few happy memories for her, and with Sam gone, there was nothing to tie her to the place. She would be glad to put the past behind her and not have constant painful reminders of all that had gone on before. She was looking forward to moving to Casa Paloma, oddly excited at the prospect of new, never-before-seen horizons and the thrilling adventures she was certain awaited her there.

She'd been sitting in Sam's office for some time, wrapped in her thoughts, the silence of the house gently cocooning her, when she suddenly became aware of a sound—stealthy footsteps coming down the hallway. . . .

Frozen, she listened, her heart beating in thick, uncomfortable strokes as the furtive sound came nearer, and her breath literally stopped when the steps halted outside the door to Sam's office. Wide-eyed, she stared mesmerized as the crystal doorknob slowly turned.

Unconsciously, her fingers closed around the heavy glass. It wasn't much of a weapon, but if she threw it and if her aim were good enough . . .

The door opened and a tall, masculine figure stood there in the darkness. Sara had a brief impression of a wide-brimmed hat pulled low across his face and menacingly broad shoulders covered by a muddy, dark greatcoat in the second before she flung the glass in his direction with all her might. As the glass flew across the room, she snatched up the half-full bottle of brandy and a second glass, armed and ready to sling more missiles, should it be necessary. It never occurred to her to scream for help.

Sara's aim had been strong and true, and there was a muffled curse as her weapon struck with bruising force high on the intruder's right cheekbone. Her small bosom heaving, her militant stance behind the desk making it clear she intended to fight, she waited tensely for his next move. It surprised her. His hand moving faster than Sara's eyes could follow it, she suddenly found herself looking down the blue barrel of a Colt revolver.

"Drop them," he said quietly, "or I'll have to put a bullet through that soft, pretty hide of yours."

The remembered sound of his deep voice reverberating through her skull, Sara dazedly obeyed. When the glass and the bottle were safely placed on top of the desk, his cool amber-gold eyes never leaving hers, he picked up the glass from the floor where it had fallen and walked further into the room. Slamming the door behind him with a deft twist of his foot, he came over to stand in front of Sara. With only the desk between them, he carefully set down the glass and appreciatively regarded the unexpectedly erotic picture she presented.

The lamplight increased the golden glow of her unbound hair, the shiny mass flowing in gentle waves over one shoulder and down one breast, and he was aware of a powerful urge to reach out and grasp those honey-colored strands to see if they were as silky as they looked. Her eyes were wide and very green as she stared back at him, her dark lashes and brows contrasting vividly with the paleness of her skin, but it was her mouth, her generously curved, enticingly pink mouth, that held his attention for a long moment. Wrenching his gaze away from the tempting promise of her lips, he let it travel indolently downward, noting with unconscious admiration the way the worn emerald-green robe clung to her slender body, and he found himself wondering just what she wore underneath it. . . .

The silence spun out as they regarded each other, and then, as if he had seen enough, he reholstered the pistol and seated himself in one of the old leather chairs in front of the desk. He tipped back his hat and with insulting familiarity put his boots on one corner of the desk, crossing his feet as he did so.

"I didn't expect you to be happy with my return . . ." Yancy Cantrell drawled softly, "but, dear little stepmama, was it necessary to greet me with such violence?"

His words broke the spell that had held her motionless. Ashamed of her reaction to his return, ashamed of the way her heart was pounding in her breast and of the crazy curl of excitement that was twisting in her belly, she glared at him and retorted tartly, "If you hadn't been creeping through the house like a thief, I wouldn't have reacted as I did. You frightened me!"

He touched his cheekbone where the glass had hit him and in the lamplight she could see a faint smear of blood. "I frightened you!" he muttered disbelievingly. "Well, lady, I can't exactly say that you didn't give me a start! As for creeping in like a thief—you forget this was once my home, and since it was late, I didn't want to disturb the household with my arrival." An unpleasant gleam in his eyes, he added, "If this is my reward for trying to be considerate, I can promise you I won't make that mistake again!"

Feeling chagrined and as if she had been just a little mean-spirited, Sara grimaced and muttered, "I apologize. But you *did* frighten me and I reacted before I realized that it was you. I'm sorry."

"Are you? I wonder. You'll forgive me if I harbor some doubt!"

Her lips tightened, but refusing to be baited, she asked quietly, "Could I get you something? Are you hungry?"

For a moment his eyes slid down her slender form and Sara's pulse leaped, but then he shook his head and smiled lazily. "I'm hungry, all right, but I reckon I can wait a while to satiate my appetite." He paused, watching with undisguised interest the blush that spread across her cheeks, and then said, "But in the meantime, I wouldn't say no to a shot of that brandy you were going to throw at me."

Wishing she'd thrown the brandy at him when she'd had the chance, Sara jerkily poured him a generous shot in the other glass. He leaned forward and handed her the glass she had thrown at him. "Pour yourself one—I hate to drink alone."

Deciding that she was probably going to need it, she didn't argue with him. When she had settled uncertainly once more in her chair, she looked warily across at him.

The years had changed him. Yancy Cantrell had always been a handsome man, but there was something about him now that was more than just mere handsomeness. It was as if the years had hardened him, obliterated any hint of softness to his features. There was a new grimness to his face that hadn't been there before, a grimness that intensified the chiseled boldness of his cheeks and jaw and reminded Sara uneasily that in all probability she was sitting here quietly alone with Margaret's murderer. She shivered suddenly, but despite all the reasons that she should get up and rush from the room, she could not take her eyes off his dark Spanish face. The slightly cruel cast to his lips seemed more pronounced than she remembered, and the aquiline shape of his nose increased the inherently haughty expression on his face, but it was the open cynicism that she saw in his eyes that made Sara move restively in her chair.

For something to do, she took a healthy gulp of her brandy and promptly choked on the fiery liquor. Recovering herself, aware her cheeks were flaming with embarrassment, she glanced across at him. He was staring at her, something in his gaze making her instantly wary and *very* nervous. "What is it?" she demanded, unable to bear his scrutiny a moment longer. "Why are you staring at me?"

He shrugged and took a sip of his brandy. "You've grown up. My memory of you was of all big green eyes and a gentle mouth that should have smiled more than it did."

That he had remembered her at all pleased Sara far more than it should have, and to compensate for that fact, she snapped, "There hasn't been a great deal to smile about these past years!"

"Oh, I wouldn't say that," he replied lightly. "After all, you've done rather well for yourself, haven't you?"

Sara had thought that she had become impervious to cynical comments about her marriage to Sam, but Yancy's words pricked her. Her eyes bright with suppressed temper, she asked tightly, "And just what do you mean by that?"

He smiled nastily. "Why, just that the last time I saw you, you were this little waif my father had decided to rescue from a, ah, fate worse than death, and now you're the mistress of Magnolia Grove. Quite a change in your social and financial position, don't you agree?"

The headache Sara had managed to overcome suddenly came roaring back. Her temples throbbing, she said grittily, "I don't think that you are in any position to judge me!" She rose to her feet and swept majestically around the desk. "Since you are so familiar with the house, I'm sure that you will be able to make yourself comfortable. If you'll excuse me, I'll leave you now—there doesn't seem to be very much for us to discuss."

She started for the door, but Yancy rose in an indolently deceptive movement and closed his hand around her upper arm before Sara had taken two steps. He jerked her around to face him and, his eyes glittering angrily, he said softly, "Don't ever walk away from me again! And I'll decide whether we have something to discuss!"

Her heart pounding, Sara stared up into his hard, dark face. They were only inches apart, and this close to him, she could smell the scent of horses and leather on his skin and feel the heat of his body radiating against hers.

As they stood there oddly frozen in time, her slim body barely brushing against the whipcord leanness of his, she told herself that it was fright that was making her blood race in her veins, that it was fear that made her lower limbs tremble, but in her heart she knew she lied . . . and that Yancy was as aware of her as she was of him. With widening eyes she watched the anger fade from his features and the sudden sensual twist to his bottom lip made her mouth go dry.

Sara made a halfhearted attempt to escape, but Yancy only pulled her into his arms. His breath warm and brandy-scented against her mouth, he muttered, "Ah, hell, *chica*, we might as well get this over with—God knows I've dreamed of it often." And then he kissed her.

It was like before, like the first time he had kissed her, only more acute and more powerful, as if the intervening years had deepened and intensified the emotion and the feelings that were within them. His mouth was warm and hard on hers, his big body crushed against hers, and he made no allowances for any resistance on her part. He simply took, his lips moving hungrily across hers, a low growl coming from deep within his throat when his tongue found the sweet, moist heat in her mouth. Feverish excitement welled up within Sara and helplessly she let him have his way, the shockingly pleasurable sensation of having her mouth invaded by his questing tongue making her dizzy. She swayed in his embrace and his arms tightened, forcing her even closer to his muscled body, making no attempt to hide from her the extent of his arousal. Her arms crept around his neck, her hands tingling to feel his crisp black hair between her fingers, and impatiently she pushed off his hat. Sighing with delight, she caressed his dark head, her slender form pressed ardently against him. His lips slid from her mouth to her throat and Sara retained just enough sanity to let out a little choked cry of protest when she felt his mouth slide lower, his hand pushing aside the fabric of her robe.

He muttered something and then he was kissing her again, half-savage, almost violent kisses that made the fire in her belly flare hotter. He kissed her many times, and it was only when his lips began their burning descent once more and she felt his hands move and tighten on her buttocks that full sanity returned. With a soft half moan, half sob, she tore herself out of his arms and bolted from the room as if the very hounds of hell were on her heels.

6

Sara dreamed of the Dark Rider that night for the first time in years. The dream was the same as always, her feelings of distress and danger were as strong as always, but for one brief instant she was aware of a tantalizing hint of recognition as she stared at the silhouette of the Dark Rider on the horizon. Even in her sleep she was conscious that there was something familiar about him. . . .

Her heart beating furiously, she woke up. For a few disoriented moments she lay there in bed and then her mouth twisted with disgust. Wonderful! Not only had she humiliated herself with Yancy tonight, but now she was trying to incorporate him into her dreams. Folly!

Sleep proved impossible after that and with aching eyes she watched the first pink-and-gold streaks of dawn creep into her room. She had curled up in a faded rose silk-covered chair near her balcony for the rest of the night, her unseeing gaze staring at nothing.

The dream forgotten, over and over again the appalling scene in Sam's office played through her mind and she wondered sickly what sort of a lewd, unprincipled creature she was. How *could* she have allowed Yancy to kiss her that way? Worse, how could she have *liked* it?

Tiredly she rubbed her eyes. Merciful heavens! How was she going to face him? Certainly, by her actions last

79

night she couldn't have risen in his estimation, and if she had wanted to prove to him that she was a little strumpet, ready to throw herself into the arms of the first available man, she couldn't have chosen a better method! And telling herself that he was no better—after all, *he* had been the one who had kissed her—didn't help in the least! What was the matter with her? She believed that he had *murdered* his previous stepmother—and what did she do but melt in his arms!

Disgusted with herself and furious with him for being able to destroy whatever common sense she possessed, Sara eventually got up and began to prepare unenthusiastically for the day. A gentle tap on the door startled her and she glanced around as Tansy entered the room, carrying a china pitcher of warm water.

"Oh! You're awake—I thought you'd still be asleep at this hour," Tansy murmured in her soft, lilting voice as she crossed the room and set the pitcher on a wooden washstand.

Like Bartholomew, Tansy was a mulatto, her skin a lovely shade of dark honey and her eyes a brilliant hazel. She was a striking woman, having been endowed with the best traits of the two races that had created her. She was tall and lissome and moved with a graceful sway that Sara secretly envied—that and her lush curves. Tansy had no idea who her father had been, but she and her mother had been purchased by old Andy Cantrell on a trip he had made to New Orleans over twenty years ago, when she had been fourteen. Bartholomew had been a young man of twenty-two at the time, but even then they had been attracted to each other, and no one had been surprised three years later when Bartholomew had asked permission to have Tansy as his woman. It was a happy union except, to their great sorrow, they had never been blessed with children.

Sam had freed Bartholomew and Tansy long before he had left to fight in the war, and Sara had been inordinately grateful that both of them had remained at Magnolia Grove. Her relationship with them had always been warm, and in those first trying months after Sam had left to join General Lee, she didn't know what she would have done without Bartholomew and Tansy. There was little that happened at Magnolia Grove that the loyal couple didn't know about and there was even less that they didn't know about Sara—they treated her like a much-loved younger sibling and scolded and cosseted her outrageously, depending upon the situation.

Since there was no point in dissembling, Sara asked, "Did you know that Yancy returned last night?"

Tansy smiled, her even teeth flashing whitely. "Indeed I do! He's in my kitchen right now filling himself with biscuits and hot coffee while that man of mine dotes on his every word!" There was much affection in Tansy's tones and a knot formed in Sara's stomach.

She had always counted on Bartholomew and Tansy as her most trusted allies and often, even after the war, she had thought of their situation as the three of them against the world. Yancy's presence was undoubtedly going to change all that.

Seeing Sara's grimace and realizing that she wasn't thrilled by the news, Tansy frowned, and as Sara poured the water into a bowl and began to wash her face, Tansy demanded, "Now, why do you look like you just swallowed a lemon? Aren't you happy that the young master has come home?"

"He's not your master!" Sara muttered. "You're free, remember?"

Tansy laughed. "Old habits die hard—I suspect he'll always be the young master to us, even when we are all very old. But you still didn't answer my question. Aren't you pleased he's home?"

Her ablutions finished, Sara turned away and pawed through her limited wardrobe. There really wasn't much choice—she was still in mourning for Sam. With a sigh, she pulled out a black gown very similar to the one she had worn yesterday.

Laying the garment on the bed, she glanced over at Tansy. "Doesn't it bother you that he probably killed Margaret? Or that he cruelly ignored Sam? Even when Sam was dying?"

Tansy's face closed up and she said, "That hussy deserved killing! As for ignoring Master Sam—they were never close, and how do you know all those letters Master Sam wrote ever got to him? Maybe there *is* a reason he didn't reply—have you thought of that?"

Sara *had* often wondered if Yancy had received Sam's letters, but she wasn't in any mood to make excuses for him. Stubbornly she said, "That might be true, but why didn't he come and see his father before the war? And whether or not Margaret deserved to be killed isn't the point—it wasn't up to Yancy to make that decision!"

Arms akimbo, a militant light in her hazel eyes, Tansy regarded Sara from across the room. "Are you so certain he killed her? He wasn't the only one who hated her. *I* was never very fond of her myself! Nor were a half-dozen other people I could name!"

Sara couldn't argue with her. Everything that Tansy said was true, and while Sara had been *almost* positive that Yancy was the culprit, she had always had a tiny niggle of doubt. But whether that had been because she didn't want Yancy to have committed such a dastardly act or because there was some real cause for doubt, she had never been certain. She wasn't, however, going to discuss it with Tansy; it was very obvious where Tansy's loyalties lay, and the knot in Sara's stomach tightened even more.

Deliberately changing the subject, she asked quietly, "Would you send Peggy up with a tray for me? I think I'll have breakfast in my room this morning."

Tansy's expression was troubled. "Did you and Master Yancy have a fight last night? He said he'd seen you. What happened between you two to make you hide out here in your room like a scared rabbit?"

A spot of color burning each cheek, Sara said sharply, "*Nothing* happened! And I'm *not* hiding!"

Tansy grinned. "Then if you're not hiding, I suggest you come down to the kitchen like you usually do and join us for breakfast."

Sara sighed with exasperation. She was never certain how it happened, but Tansy and Bartholomew had a sneaky way of twisting things around, so that she generally ended up doing what they wanted. She glared at Tansy, but Tansy only winked at her and strolled toward the door.

Over her shoulder, Tansy murmured, "Now, you just get yourself dressed and come on down like you always do. Don't be getting on your high horse for no reason."

A reluctant laugh came from Sara. "Oh, go away. I'll be down shortly."

Sara wasn't laughing some twenty minutes later as she made her way down the stairs and began to walk toward the kitchen, which was a small, detached building at the rear of the main house. The knowledge that she would be seeing Yancy again in a matter of minutes had her palms perspiring and her heart beating in funny little erratic movements, and she wished that those passionate moments in his arms last night had never happened.

Crossing the short distance that separated the kitchen from the house, she nervously pushed back a strand of unruly hair that had refused to remain braided when she had fixed her hair in its usual tidy cornet on top of her head. Just outside the door to the kitchen, she paused and took a deep breath. She was *not* going to let him rattle her! This was *her* home and she was mistress of Magnolia Grove! A determined smile on her mouth, she pushed open the door and walked in.

To her intense disappointment, the kitchen was empty except for Peggy and Tansy. Feeling deflated after she had geared herself up to confront Yancy, she walked over to the scrubbed pine table and took her usual place at one side near the end.

Almost from the day that Sam had left to fight for the Confederate cause, Sara had abandoned eating in the spacious dining room, having felt rather lonely and silly eating in solitary grandeur. For a while she had taken her meals in the smaller, more inviting morning room, but as the war had raged on, she had gradually drifted to the kitchen.

Bartholomew had been openly outraged the first time he had caught her there, sipping coffee and talking comfortably with Tansy, but in time he had grown accustomed to it. At Magnolia Grove there was little of the rigid protocol that had once been the rule, and for quite a few years now, they had all lived together in a rather small, closed democratic society.

Sara grimaced. Except, of course, things had changed once Sam had come home, and even more so when the Shelldrakes had come to live with them. Ann Shelldrake had been thoroughly affronted at the very idea that she would have to take her meals in the kitchen like common folks. She had badgered Sam unmercifully, until he had spent some of their precious resources on a decent table and chairs, which had been installed in the once grand dining room at Magnolia Grove. The Shelldrakes ate their meals there, while, except for supper, Sara continued to eat in the kitchen. She was comfortable there and it also gave her an excuse to be relieved from the tedium of Ann's complaints.

Reflectively Sara sipped the strong, hot coffee Peggy had set in front of her, wondering just what the future held. Obviously things were going to change again and she wasn't so certain that she was going to be happy with those changes.

"Did you want me to fry you some eggs and some ham?" Peggy asked softly, standing in front of the big black iron stove.

Peggy was Tansy's sixteen-year-old half sister and they shared the same tall, lithe shape and finely honed features, although Peggy's skin was the rich, dark shade of chocolate and her eyes were as black as the night. Their mother had died three years ago and Tansy had taken to mothering Peggy almost unmercifully, but Peggy was a cheerful, amiable girl and for the most part she bore it with goodwill. Sara liked her immensely and she was grateful, too, that Peggy had chosen to throw her lot in with Bartholomew and Tansy and had remained at Magnolia Grove. With the granting of their freedom, except for one old rheumy-eyed black man and his woman who helped tend the garden and the stables, all the other slaves had gone to seek their fortunes elsewhere.

Sara smiled at Peggy and said, "No, you don't have to cook me anything. This coffee will do just fine."

Pouring herself a cup of coffee, Peggy joined Sara at the table and said slyly, "Mmm-um, isn't that Mr. Yancy a handsome gent! Why, he's just about the handsomest man I ever saw!"

Tansy snorted and looked up from the bread she was kneading on the wooden counter nearby. "You just put those kinds of thoughts out of your head! I surely don't want you to get any ideas about him!"

A sullen look came over Peggy's features and she muttered, "And I surely don't want you telling me what to do!"

Sara had just opened her mouth to head off the argument that was brewing when the door to the kitchen flew open and Yancy and Bartholomew walked inside. Something exciting and dynamic entered the room with Yancy, and Sara thought it unfair that he should appear so virile and robust after she had spent a sleepless night. Obviously he hadn't! In a loose-fitting white shirt and buckskin breeches and boots, his hair falling in glossy black waves nearly to his broad shoulders and his Spanish-dark skin radiating vitality, he was the picture of health and vigor. He was also, she decided waspishly, far too attractive for his own good, and it took only one glance at Yancy's handsome face for her mind to go curiously blank and her heart to begin to behave in a most unseemly fashion.

Flustered, she quickly swallowed some coffee as she frantically tried to get her thoughts in order, but she'd forgotten how hot the coffee was and promptly scalded her tongue—which, from the smile on Yancy's face, she suspected he knew. Her mouth burning, her emotions in an uproar, she set her cup down with a bang.

"Good morning," she said with studied politeness. "Did you sleep well?"

Yancy poured himself some coffee, sat down across from her, then asked bluntly over the rim of his cup, "Do you really care?"

Sara could feel a flush start up her face, and hanging on to her temper with an effort, she said tightly, "I'm trying to be polite!"

Yancy smiled, a smile that didn't reach his eyes. "I think," he said softly, "that you and I are long past the stage where we have to be so formal with each other, don't you?"

Uncomfortably aware of the interested onlookers, Sara made one more attempt. "That may be, but there is no reason for us to be rude to each other."

Yancy flicked up one heavy brow. "Oh, is that what you were last night? Rude?"

"What the devil did you expect?" she burst out, exasperated. "You disappear for years; your father *begged* you to come to him as he lay dying, but you couldn't be bothered! You *finally* show up here without warning in the dead of night and you think I should have fallen on you in gratitude?"

Yancy's mouth twitched and Sara had the unnerving impression that he found her amusing. Her teeth gritted together, she snarled, "Don't you *dare* humor me!"

Yancy took another sip of his coffee before saying meekly, "My, how you do run on, dear stepmama! And *such* a temper!" He glanced across at Bartholomew. "You didn't tell me," he said lightly, "that she had a witch's tongue! Whatever happened to that sweet, innocent waif my father brought home?"

Suppressing a strong urge to throw her hot coffee in his face, Sara rose grandly to her feet. Looking disdainfully down her delightful little nose, she snapped, "When you are through with your coffee, if we are to rub shoulders comfortably for the time we will both be here at Magnolia Grove, I think we should continue this discussion privately in Sam's office."

A slow, sensuous smile spread across Yancy's face, a mocking light dancing in his eyes. "Believe me, *chica*, there is nothing I'd like better than to continue in Sam's office."

Sara flushed hotly, well aware that he was referring to what had happened between them last night and *not* to the matter at hand! Damn him! Her chin high, she said, "Fine! I shall expect you there in a few moments."

She meant to sweep regally from the room, but as she turned, the kitchen door opened once more and Hyrum Burnell entered. There was an odd moment of silence as the former overseer took in the scene before him.

Hyrum had followed Sam to war, fighting valiantly at his side, but unlike Sam, had come home unscathed. There was no longer anything for him to oversee at Magnolia Grove, but there was work aplenty for him to do and Sam had promised him continued employment, even in spite of their changed circumstances. When Sam died, Sara had continued to follow Sam's wishes—frankly glad to have Hyrum's help. He was loyal and had always been very polite and most pleasant to her, and though she kept him at a distance, she had begun to suspect that he had amorous thoughts about her. .

Despite her concern about his feelings for her, Sara had made plans for him to follow her to Casa Paloma— she was going to need all the help she could get in her new endeavors, and why not Hyrum? He had proved to be hard-working and dependable, and as long as he didn't step over the invisible line she kept between them, Sara was confident that he would be invaluable at Casa Paloma.

It was apparent from the curt nod Hyrum finally sent in Yancy's direction that he was already aware of Yancy's return, and from the set of his jaw it was also apparent that he wasn't precisely cheered about it either. Looking at Sara, Hyrum tugged politely at the brim of his hat and murmured, "Morning, missus. Thought you'd like to know that old Noah and me plan to plant that field of corn today. After we get that done, did you want us to start plowing up the north forty?"

As Hyrum had started speaking, Yancy had gotten up and lazily walked over to stand just behind Sara. To her surprise, he rested one hand familiarly on her shoulder and she had the uneasy sensation that he was somehow staking a claim on her, sending some sort of primitive male message to Hyrum. Forestalling her reply, Yancy said smoothly to Hyrum, "My memory must be playing tricks on me, Hyrum, but I could swear that when I spoke to you earlier this morning, I distinctly said I wanted you to start going through the storage sheds and getting rid of everything that isn't usable anymore. Was I wrong?"

A pugnacious cast to his mouth, Hyrum replied, "I take my orders from Mistress Sara—not from the likes of you!"

Yancy's hand tightened on Sara's shoulder, keeping her where she was when she would have moved away from him. Everyone seemed to be waiting to see how she would handle this confrontation, and cursing Yancy for putting her in this position, she said quietly to Hyrum, "Since Yancy has already given you your orders for the day, I suggest that you do as he says." Then, coolly throwing off Yancy's hand, she whirled around to face him. "And I would appreciate it if you would please discuss it with me first before you issue orders to my employees!"

Yancy observed her angry expression for a long moment; then, taking hold of her upper arm, he said silkily, "I think it's time that you and I had that private discussion, don't you?"

Not giving her a chance to agree, he half marched, half dragged her from the kitchen. In an angry, simmering silence they made their way the short distance to the main house. Flinging off Yancy's hold on her arm once they were inside, Sara headed for Sam's office, a dozen scathing remarks she intended to hurl at him buzzing around in her brain.

Positioning herself behind the desk, she glowered at Yancy as he closed the door behind them and strolled indolently over to one of the chairs in front of the desk. Just as he had done last night, he settled back comfortably in the chair, propped his booted feet on the corner of the desk and crossed his ankles. Idly, as if he had all the time in the world, he found a thin black cheroot, and only after he had it lit to his satisfaction and a narrow stream of blue smoke wafted near his dark head did he speak.

"I suppose," he said slowly, "that I should be thankful you didn't countermand my orders out of sheer pigheadedness."

"Sheer pigheadedness!" Sara gasped in fury. "How dare you! In case you forget, for nearly the last six years I have run Magnolia Grove *by myself*! Hyrum Burnell is *my* employee! We may be forced to share Sam's estate, but I will not have you coming in here disrupting my household and ordering about the people working for me—is that understood?"

He regarded her impassively across the width of the desk, the expression in his amber-gold eyes hard to define. "Since you brought it up, perhaps before we go any further with this little conversation, you would be good enough to explain to me the *exact* terms of Sam's will. All I know is what I learned from the all-too-brief letter that Henderson sent to me: Sam had died, you were his widow and I was one of the main heirs to his estate." His mouth tightened. "You might also want to explain why the Shelldrakes are living here. The last I heard, Tom Shelldrake was a wealthy man—far wealthier than Sam, if memory serves me."

Sara's mouth suddenly went dry as the awful knowledge occurred to her—*Yancy didn't know the full terms of Sam's will*! Fright mixing with anger now, she stared uneasily over at him, but, determined not to be browbeaten, she asked nastily, "Didn't Bartholomew tell you? Since you two seemed to have discussed *me*, I wonder that he didn't also tell you about Tom and Ann."

"The Shelldrakes didn't interest me at the time," he replied sharply. "You did!"

Sara's heart dropped clear to her feet at his words and she tried to ignore the sudden fuzziness in her head. "I don't see why," she muttered.

"Don't you, sweetheart?" Yancy drawled derisively. "Didn't you think I'd be interested in the young woman my father married? A woman *almost* young enough to be his granddaughter? A seemingly innocent little waif, without family or fortune, who took blatant advantage of a tragic set of circumstances? Didn't you think I'd be just a bit interested in her?" His voice had grown harsher with every word he spoke and his eyes were narrowed as he stared at her through the blue haze of his cheroot's smoke. Her stricken silence seemed to enrage him further. He stood up, tossing the cheroot in the brass spittoon near his chair; placing his hands on either side of the desk, he leaned forward until his dark face was only inches from hers. "Didn't you think I'd be interested in this clever woman who insinuated herself into my father's home and who managed to make certain that she figured largely in the dispersal of my father's estate? A woman, my own father's widow, who just last night let me kiss and fondle her? Didn't you think it would be reasonable that I'd want to learn everything I could about such an opportunistic, conniving little creature?"

Mutely Sara stared back at him, her eyes very big and green in her white face, the inky blackness of her gown making her look extremely young and vulnerable. His words and the fury behind them nearly devastated her. She had known all along that Yancy would take the worst possible view of her marriage to Sam, but somehow she hadn't expected it to hurt so badly. Many people assumed that she had married Sam for his fortune, and though that had hurt deeply, she had borne their scandalized looks and sly malice with fortitude. But this, *this* was far more painful than anything she had imagined!

To her utter horror, she felt her eyes start to swim with tears, but she was determined not to let him see how his words had wounded her. Her jaw tightened and she said doggedly, "You could have asked me—I would have explained everything to you. You didn't have to go sneaking around and questioning my servants!"

"I didn't," he said through gritted teeth, "go sneaking around! You seem to forget that while you have lived here for the past six or seven years, *I* grew up here—and as for questioning your servants . . ." He stopped and swore softly under his breath. Looking at her with open dislike, he said, "Bartholomew is my *uncle*, for God's sake! Even if his mother was black and he was born on the wrong side of the blanket!" His mouth twisted. "You might say that Bartholomew and I share not only the same blood but the same heritage—we are both considered half-breeds, and believe me, sweetheart, that makes a bond which few people can understand!"

Feeling as if somehow he had turned the tables on her and *she* were the one at fault, she said defensively, "That may be true, but you had no right to start issuing orders to Hyrum—or to make unfounded assumptions about me!"

"Is that so?" he replied softly and, to Sara's relief, slowly sank back into his seat.

Her head held at an imperious angle, she nodded curtly. "Yes, that's so!"

"Then suppose you explain to me where I went wrong. . . . Aren't you very young to have been Sam's wife? And did I misunderstand the situation, but weren't you penniless and without family when he rescued you and brought you here to Magnolia Grove? Was I wrong about that?" Yancy spit the words out like bullets and, daggers in his eyes, he accused softly, "And didn't you marry him? And didn't you inherit a large share of his estate? Tell me, Sara, where did I go wrong?"

"Those are the bare facts," she said tautly. "But it wasn't the way you're making it sound! I loved Sam! I didn't want his blasted money! He was good to me, he cared for me and protected me, and I would never have done anything to hurt him or take advantage of him! I loved him!"

An expression that made Sara suddenly breathless and frightened at the same time crossed his dark face. "You loved him!" he said furiously. "You loved him! Well, if you loved him so damned much, if you're such a grieving little widow, tell me why you turn to fire in my arms when I touch you! Tell me that!"

Sara swallowed, deeply agitated by the course of the conversation. Even if she wanted to, there was no way she could explain to him, to herself or to anyone else why he affected her as he did, and she said the first thing that came to mind. "It was the brandy!" Seeing the sardonic smile that curved his lips, she stammered, "A-a-and the lateness of the hour! You s-s-startled me!"

Something gleamed in the depths of his golden-brown eyes and he sprang up from his chair and came around the desk in one lithe move. Grasping her upper arms and pulling her next to him, he drawled, "Let's just see the truth of that, shall we, *chica*? You've had no brandy, it is broad daylight and you can't say that I've popped up unexpectedly in front of you."

Sara could smell of the not-unpleasant scent of tobacco on his breath mingling with the coffee he had drunk earlier, and in that instant before his mouth closed warmly on hers, it seemed the most intoxicating aroma in the world. The touch of his lips on hers, the firm heat of his mouth as he kissed her leisurely, were nothing like the other kisses they had shared, but the effect was the same: she could feel her breathing suddenly becoming suspended and the pounding of her poor, silly heart beating in the same wild, sweet tempo of her blood. His hands tightened and he dragged her closer, deepening the kiss as he did so, his tongue demanding and finding entrance into her mouth. She moaned softly, half entreaty, half delight as he stroked his tongue coaxingly against hers, tempting her further into the heady web of desire he was weaving around them. Sara could feel herself slipping, could feel the world beginning to spin violently out of control when he groaned deep in his throat and his hands caught her head, holding her where he wanted her while he drank greedily of her sweetness.

Her carnal senses in an uproar, she was dizzily aware that if she didn't stop him, if she didn't do something immediately, in a precious few seconds it would be too late . . . and he would have proof that everything he had said of her was true. . . . That thought exploded through her brain and with a sob she wrenched her mouth from his, breaking the hold of his hands on her head. Her lips crimson and swollen from his kiss, she looked despairingly at him. His breathing was faintly labored and his eyes were full of the powerful desire that had so swiftly seized them both.

For a long moment they stood there staring at each other, and then his mouth slanted into a grim smile. "Well, I think we've just proved the lie of your words, haven't we, sweetheart?"

Sara slapped him. She couldn't help it. His words enraged her so much that before she even thought about it, before she even knew she was going to do it, her hand had already shot out and smartly connected with his cheek.

In guilty satisfaction she stared at the imprint of her palm burning redly on his dark face, but the expression in his eyes made her take several prudent steps away from him. "You deserved that!" she muttered. "You've done nothing but insult me and try to take advantage of me since the moment you arrived."

Thoughtfully, he touched his skin where her hand had landed, and to her astonishment, he nodded slowly. "I suppose that's one way my actions could be construed," he said dryly. To her further bafflement, he turned and reseated himself in his previous position. As if the moment of passion had never been, he folded his arms over his broad chest and said quietly, "Tell me about the Shelldrakes. Why are they living here?"

Unsettled by the sudden change in Yancy, Sara walked back to the desk and fiddled for a moment with a few papers that were lying on top, trying to gather her flustered thoughts. "It was the war," she said finally. "Although it wasn't *just* the war. Like most Texans, Tom supported it fully and stripped himself to provide funds for it—that and several bad investments left him almost destitute by the time Lee surrendered at Appomattox." Sara lifted her gaze and looked at Yancy. "He was wounded, did you know? He saved Sam's life by risking his own. His left arm is virtually useless and he has found it hard to deal with his infirmity." Her eyes darkened for a moment, memories of Sam's broken body crowding into her mind. Dear God! If only Sam had come home with nothing more than a useless arm . . .

The door to the office was suddenly flung open and Ann Shelldrake surged inside. "Does he know? Have you told him?" she demanded.

Yancy looked slowly from one woman to the other, his golden gaze moving from the guilty expression on Sara's face to Ann's malicious one. His eyes narrowed and in a cold, deadly voice he asked, "What? What hasn't she told me?"

Ann smiled with satisfaction. "Why, only the fact that Sam left *her* Casa Paloma!"

7

There was an awful silence in Sam's office as the seconds slowly spun out. Yancy's hard gaze locked onto Sara's tense features, he asked icily, "Would you care to tell me what in hell she's talking about?"

"Oh, you needn't badger Sara about it," Ann said airily, coming further into the room and seating herself comfortably in the chair next to Yancy's. "She doesn't like to talk about it, but apart from some small bequests to Bartholomew and Tansy and a few others, Sara gets everything . . . except, of course, your half of Magnolia Grove." Ann sent a sly glance in Sara's direction. "For a little nobody, she did very well for herself, wouldn't you agree?"

Never taking his eyes off Sara's increasingly strained features, Yancy agreed silkily, "Oh, yes, I'd say that she did damn well for herself! But tell me, does the will specifically state that she is to have Casa Paloma?"

"Certainly!" Ann said sweetly. "Of course, there *are* some rather peculiar conditions set forth." She smiled like the cat that got the cream. "Shall I tell you what they are?"

Fighting free of the terrible paralysis that had beset her the instant Ann had entered the room, Sara exclaimed hotly, "*That's enough*, Ann! Yancy can learn the full terms of Sam's will from Mr. Henderson, anytime he wants to." Forcing herself to meet his cold gaze, she added tightly, "Since you seem so interested in the contents, I suggest that you ride into San Felipe this afternoon and see Mr. Henderson. He will explain everything to you."

Yancy smiled wolfishly at her. "But I would much rather have Ann explain it to me. After all, she is right here and most eager to tell me *every*thing!"

Wishing desperately that she'd had more time to prepare herself for this moment, cursing Ann's untimely arrival and just generally wishing she were anywhere but right here, Sara took a deep breath and said with commendable calm, "There is no reason to bother Ann. I can tell you the contents of your father's will myself."

"But, darling," Ann cooed, "it is no bother at all!"

Sara's soft mouth hardened. "I'm sure it isn't, but since this is technically none of your business, I would appreciate it if you would allow Yancy and me to finish our conversation in private."

Ann pouted, but she didn't pursue the matter. She rose gracefully from her chair, her black silk skirts rustling about her feet. "Well, since you feel that way about it, darling, I have no other choice." Slanting a provocative look at Yancy, she murmured, "You and I shall have a nice little chat later on—I have so *much* to tell you!"

Sara nearly stamped her foot with vexation at the older woman's provoking tactics, and not for the first time, she considered firmly telling Ann and her husband that they would have to make other living arrangements. Ann was too much like Margaret for anyone's good. Watching Ann complacently make her way from the room, Sara knew she had made a very bad mistake in consenting, even tacitly, to the Shelldrakes' accompanying her when she began her new life at Casa Paloma, and that if she was wise, she would immediately take steps to undo the damage she had so foolishly done to herself. But that was a problem she could deal with later. At the moment, she had a far more volatile situation to face, and bracing her slender shoulders, she looked squarely at Yancy.

Yancy, too, had been watching Ann, and it was only when the door had shut quietly behind her that he glanced back at Sara. His expression inscrutable, he said, "Tell me again how the Shelldrakes ended up here."

Glad to postpone the inevitable, Sara shrugged. "You know your father—Tom was a dear friend of his, and when he lost his plantation, it seemed only natural for Sam to offer them a place to stay, especially since Tom had been gravely wounded protecting your father during the war."

"A place to stay, *sí*, but I don't think my father, despite his sometimes ridiculous generosity, intended for them to be his dependents forever," Yancy commented dryly.

Sara's gaze dropped and she grimaced. "Probably not! I'm sure he would have eventually come up with some way for Tom to reclaim a certain amount of independence, but . . ."

"But Sam died," Yancy said coolly, "and you inherited everything."

"Not everything!" Sara replied, stung, glaring across at him. "He left *you* half of Magnolia Grove!"

"I don't give a *damn* about Magnolia Grove! I don't give a damn about anything of Sam's except Casa Paloma! And you know it!" He gave a bitter laugh. "Hell, everyone knows it—isn't that why I killed Margaret, to keep her from getting it?" His face hard and set, his amber-gold eyes glittering fiercely, he said harshly, "And if I didn't want her to have it, I sure as the devil don't want *you* squatting right in the middle of my rancho either! Now, tell me: what will it take for you to let it go?" He leaned forward, his expression intent, and offered bluntly, "I'll sign away any interest in Magnolia Grove if you'll grant me Casa Paloma." When Sara only stared mutely back at him, he tried a different tack and said more softly, "Casa Paloma is Alvarez land; it always has been. Sara, my great-grandfather settled that land, and it means nothing to you. It is wild and untamed and no place for someone like you—you have no use for it. I'm asking you—no, I'm pleading with you—to be reasonable. I'm willing to give you my share of Magnolia Grove for the place. It's probably a fair trade, considering the condition of Casa Paloma." He waited for several minutes and when Sara still remained silent, his mouth thinned angrily and he growled, "*Por Dios*! Since that's not enough, I will pay you a good price for it—in gold. Surely *that* will satisfy your greedy little soul!"

Sara was already shaking her head before he had finished speaking. Quaking inside, she muttered, "It's not mine to give you."

His eyes narrowed. "Oh, and what do you mean by that? Either he left it to you or he didn't. Which is it?"

Sara took a deep, fortifying breath and said in a rush, "Sam left it to my children, and—and if I don't have any children, then Casa Paloma is to pass on to Bartholomew and Tansy."

Braced for an explosion, she stared defiantly across the desk at him. His expression one of ludicrous astonishment, he slowly leaned back in his chair. Like a man having been dealt a stunning blow, he bent his head and dazedly rubbed his forehead. "Your children!" he muttered under his breath. "Casa Paloma is to go to *your* children!"

Encouraged by his reaction—at least he wasn't throttling her—Sara admitted gingerly, "I was as surprised as you are when Mr. Henderson read me the will." She bit her lip, waiting for him to say something. He didn't.

There was a curious stillness about his long body, and with every passing second, Sara was uneasily aware that he was turning the implications of Sam's will over and over in his mind. To her shame, the image of herself big with his child slid slyly into her thoughts and to banish it, she hurried into speech. "I'm sorry that this has been such a shock for you—it was for me, too, when I first learned of it." She nervously cleared her throat and added, "I'll just leave you alone for now. I'm sure you have a lot to think about."

He raised his head at that and the expression in his eyes froze her where she stood. "*Válgame Dios*!" he muttered with quiet fury. "Behind those angelic features of yours, you're even more clever than Margaret was! *She* was willing to settle for what she could get from my father, but you, you want it all, don't you?"

Angered at his coupling of her name with Margaret's, Sara glared at him, but she was also puzzled by part of his statement. "What do you mean by 'more clever than Margaret'?" she demanded.

"Why, only that you must have very cleverly manipulated Sam for him to have put a provision like *that* in his will! And he must have been utterly besotted with you even to conceive of you bearing my children! If you were *my* wife, even if I were dying, I would not be able to tolerate the thought of you giving birth to another man's children." Yancy laughed, but it was an ugly sound and there was no mirth in it. "What is it, I wonder, about your enchanting little face that makes normal men act like fools? You almost fooled me, too, did you know that?"

Sara shook her head, hardly comprehending what he was saying, too stunned by his horrible interpretation of the facts to defend herself. She was like Margaret? She had manipulated Sam?

Like a wide-eyed doe mesmerized by the approach of the stalking tiger, she stared as he rose swiftly from his chair and came around the desk to stand in front of her.

Insultingly, his gaze traveled assessingly up and down her slim body.

"I've probably seen," he began silkily, "better candidates to be the mother of my children, but Sam, thanks to your self-serving intervention, seems to have limited my choice." The fury underlining his words terrified Sara, but she seemed unable to move. Even when he touched her, when he reached out for her and jerked her roughly up against him, she remained immobile.

His breath was warm and smoky against her cheek as his lips moved with surprising gentleness over her skin. "Do you want to know the real irony of the situation, *amiga*?" he asked in an oddly tortured tone, the fury still evident, but muted by the stronger emotions that flowed through him. "The real irony of this entire situation, *querida*, is that you haunted me as no other woman ever has, not even Margaret. I couldn't get the memory of your big green eyes or the sweetness of your mouth out of my mind. When I left here, I took your beguiling little image with me—I even almost came back for you, but I told myself that you were too young, too innocent for me." His hands slid to her throat. "Can you imagine what I felt when I learned that you had married Sam? When I discovered that I had totally misjudged you? The chagrin? The fury at my foolishness? Do you even begin to understand my bitter disillusionment when I learned so painfully that the sweet guise you project so effortlessly is a lie and that you had tricked me into seeing you as something you weren't?" His fingers tightened imperceptibly and Sara knew a moment of fear. "I could have killed you!" he snarled softly. "You appeared to be so guileless, so sweet and gentle . . . you made me dream of things I had given up hoping for and yet underneath . . . underneath, you were every bit as black and corrupt and calculating as Margaret!"

His eyes were locked on her mouth when he finished speaking and then he smothered a curse under his breath, and as if he could not help himself, his mouth lowered to hers and his teeth nipped half tenderly, half painfully at her bottom lip. He lifted his head and starred derisively down into her upturned face. "It shames me to admit it," he muttered, "but even believing you as iniquitous and cunning as Margaret— I *still* wanted you! I hated you then, cursed your soul and damned you to hell!" He smiled without humor. "And now I find that through your own cold-blooded manipulations, you have bound us together in an unholy union—my children, born of your body, for the lands of my ancestors." He kissed her fully then, his hands cupping her face, his mouth taking hers with a swift brutality.

The touch of his mouth on hers shattered the paralysis which had gripped her, and with a soft moan Sara fought to escape from the fierceness of his kiss. Despite her struggles, he held her fast for several seconds, his lips and tongue taking what he wanted. Only when her hands clamped tightly around his wrists and she tugged with all her might did he lift his head and stare down into her appalled, angry green eyes.

"You're blaming me for something I didn't do and you're attributing ugly, wicked motives to me that I never had!" Sara exclaimed vehemently, her lips stinging from his savage kiss.

"Am I?" he asked harshly. "Somehow I don't think so! The facts are plain: you married Sam for what you could get and, not satisfied with that, you concocted a scheme which would force me into an alliance with you . . . and with me comes all the wealth and vastness of Rancho del Sol, as well as the silver mines in Mexico." He gave a rough bark of laughter. "I suppose that these days I am a *much* better catch than Sam. Even Margaret might been have been tempted, considering the condition of Magnolia Grove! As for you . . ." He sent her a look full of contemptuous hostility. "You found as clever a way as I have ever seen to make certain that you could get your avaricious little claws on everything—why else would Sam have left Casa Paloma to you as he did?"

Sara stared at him, visibly shaken and deeply dismayed that he could believe her capable of such villainy—that he could take the facts and twist them into something so ugly and unrecognizable. Unhappily, she began, "You don't understand . . ."

"What don't I understand? That you saw an opportunity and took it?" he demanded grimly.

"It wasn't that way at all!" she replied sharply, her temper rising.

"Then perhaps you can explain it to me—particularly why Sam left Casa Paloma tied up in such a ridiculous fashion!"

"I don't know!" Sara cried with exasperation, jerking free of him. "I don't know what was in his mind those last days! He was dying! I certainty didn't pester him about the contents of his *will*! I had no idea how he had left things until Mr. Henderson read the will aloud."

Yancy snorted. "I'm sure you appeared very prettily astonished when you learned of your good fortune. Margaret probably couldn't have given a better performance!"

"Don't equate me with Margaret!" Sara snapped, her green eyes flashing. "And since you're so busy impugning my honor, what about yours? Whatever disgusting motives you may attribute to me, at least I didn't *murder* anyone!"

There was a tense moment, and Sara suddenly feared that she had gone too far. But then Yancy seemed to relax and, his arms folded across his chest, he stared at her, one eyebrow roguishly cocked. "You really believe that I murdered Margaret?" he asked bluntly.

His reaction startled her, and as some of her anger began to ebb, she regarded him uneasily. Yancy had always seemed the most likely suspect, and then there was the matter of the Spanish dagger. . . . He certainly didn't look like a murderer, she thought inconsequently. Her accusation seemed to amuse him, rather than enrage or insult him, and that confused her and gave her pause. "Didn't you?" she finally asked.

His smile widened and he replied, "Do you know that you are the first person to actually accuse me face-to-face or dare to ask me if I did the vile deed?"

Sara's eyes searched his, seeking some clue to what was going on behind that brilliant golden gaze. "You had the best reason—the most to gain from Margaret's death."

"Did I? Or was I just the handiest? *Por Dios!* Did it never occur to you that someone might have used my open hatred of her and that last argument of mine with her to cover his own tracks?"

That this was a very foolhardy conversation to be having with a possible murderer suddenly occurred to Sara, along with another startling notion: if she really believed that Yancy had murdered Margaret, why wasn't she frightened of him? He did frighten her, of course, at times, but not for any reasons connected with Margaret's death; it was his effect upon her that made her wary of him—*not* because she feared that he would kill her! If she truly believed him a killer, why had she *never* felt as if she were in physical danger from him? Why didn't she even now fear for her own life? Unsettled by the train of her thoughts, she murmured, "But the dagger was there. I saw it! A Spanish dagger!"

"And, of course," Yancy said dryly, "I'm the only person who could have owned a *Spanish* dagger!"

Sara flushed at the sarcastic inflection in his voice and moved restlessly away from him. Confused by the nagging idea that perhaps she had been wrong all these years, that it was possible—no, probable, if her instincts were right—that Yancy hadn't killed Margaret, she abruptly left the unsettling subject of that long-ago murder and returned doggedly to the matter at hand. Facing him defiantly, her chin held high, her hands clenched tightly at her sides, she said coldly, "I'm sorry that you are unhappy about the contents of your father's will, but there is nothing I can do about it. I'm sorry, too, that you have chosen to take the blackest, most despicable view of my marriage to Sam and distort it into something that bears absolutely no resemblance to what actually occurred." She took a deep breath and plunged on. "Mr. Henderson has indicated that it will be very hard to find a buyer for Magnolia Grove. If this is so, and I pray that it is *not*, you will just have to force yourself to put up with my wicked presence." She paused and sent him a dark look. "Of course, you could just sign the necessary papers and leave within a matter of days."

He hadn't changed his position, and with a smile that she didn't like at all, he drawled softly, "Ah, *chica*, I think you have forgotten about Casa Paloma. . . ."

Sara's heart gave a funny lurch in her breast, but she said stoutly, "I haven't forgotten about Casa Paloma. When the sale of Magnolia Grove is finally complete, and I hope that Mr. Henderson is wrong about finding a buyer for the place, I intend to take up residence there! And even if Magnolia Grove doesn't sell for months, I plan to leave for Casa Paloma just as soon as the estate is settled." She flashed him a challenging look. "Now that you're here, that shouldn't take too long! It is my fervent hope that by no later than the end of June I shall be living in my new home at Casa Paloma."

His mouth tightened, but to her surprise, there was no furious outburst. "And what," he asked dryly, "do you intend to *do* at Casa Paloma? It will take a great deal of money, probably the whole of your share from Magnolia Grove, to bring the house into any state of habitability—remember, it has been vacant and untended for thirty years or more. What will you live on once you have squandered all your ready cash?"

"I won't be *squandering* it! But even if it does take all of the money from Magnolia Grove to make Casa Paloma comfortable, there is still the money that Sam had placed in the bank in New York. It is a sizable sum. I will have that money to live on and will use it for the most basic repairs to the house. Once Magnolia Grove is sold, I shall begin—" She stopped abruptly, suddenly realizing that there was no earthly reason to tell Yancy Cantrell *all* of her plans.

"Begin?" he prodded with a quizzical expression, his eyes fixed intently on her face.

"Nothing!" she said hurriedly. "And I think this conversation has gone on long enough!" She flashed him a bitter smile. "You will, of course, I am sure, make yourself at home here, but I would prefer to have as little to do with you as possible. The house is rather large and I think that if we both try, we should manage, for the time you are here, to avoid each other! We have nothing more to say to each other!"

"Ah, but you're wrong, sweetheart," he replied coolly. "As long as you have Casa Paloma, I'm not going to be far from your side." A spark leaped into his eyes and he said huskily, "You see, since you arranged it that way, I have every intention of making certain that any children you may have are *my* children! And that, my little dove, means that not only am I never going to be far from your side, but that I have every intention of having you in my bed! We shall, I think, make beautiful children!"

Transfixed, Sara stared at him, a mixture of anger and excitement battling for supremacy within her. Anger won, and her eyes sparkling with temper, she snapped, "How *dare* you! Do you really believe that I shall just tamely go along with your outrageous plans?"

"What?" he asked innocently. "Don't you think we shall make beautiful children? Do you think they'd be homely?"

"Whether they would be beautiful or homely isn't the point! If there would *be* any children is the topic under discussion."

Yancy looked wounded. "You don't want to make sweet little babies with me?"

Sara smothered a decidedly unladylike curse and glared at him, ignoring the mocking gleam dancing in his golden eyes. Walking toward her, Yancy cupped her cheek almost tenderly and brushed a teasing kiss across her lips. His mouth inches from hers, he murmured, "Believe me, *chica*, there is nothing I would like better than attempting to make a child with you . . . in fact, I'm looking forward to it!"

"I wouldn't look *too* forward to it," Sara said sweetly. "Life can be just full of unexpected disappointments— even for someone like you!"

Yancy grinned at her. "You think so?" he asked quizzically.

"I'd wager everything I own on it!"

"Well, we'll just have to wait and see what the future holds," he murmured as he walked away. "Won't we, sweetheart?"

It was several minutes after he had left before Sara was able to compose herself. Thinking crossly that she had never met a more conceited, *infuriating* man in her life, she crossed to the desk and sank into a chair.

She sat there fuming for several moments, her thoughts very black and not the least kindly disposed toward

Yancy Cantrell! Dwelling on his arrogant, despicable assumptions about her, and on the nasty fates she'd like to arrange for him, banished the worst of her angry dismay over the entire situation. It was only then that she allowed herself to consider those bittersweet moments when he had confessed that he had carried the memory of her away with him . . . that he had even contemplated, however briefly, returning for her. . . . For a second she let herself drift in a warm, hazy dream, picturing herself, at seventeen, protectively cradled in Yancy's strong arms as he spurred his horse and they galloped away to Rancho del Sol. . . .

She gave herself a shake and pulled a face. That was the sort of girlish stuff she had given up on long ago—or should have! Fairy tales! And besides, she reminded herself sourly, whatever softer emotions Yancy might once have nourished for her, her marriage to Sam and Sam's utterly impossible will had managed to thoroughly destroy.

She shook herself and began to think about the immediate future—just getting through the next few days with Yancy in the house was going to be a fiendish experience. He had bluntly admitted that he hated her and damned her soul to hell, and she didn't think he was going to change his mind about her any time soon!

Then it occurred to her that, except for all his expressed hatred of her, he seemed to have a very hard time keeping his hands off her. When she thought about it, she realized that he took every opportunity to hold her in his arms and that while he might profess to hate her, he was also mightily attracted to her. . . . She smiled unhappily. Even though he was *physically* attracted to her, it didn't mean he liked anything else about her.

Sara sighed. Well! She certainly didn't need to be sitting here mooning over things that could never be. There was work to be done!

It was difficult, but for the next several hours she managed to keep her mind away from tantalizing and disruptive speculations about Yancy Cantrell. The sudden rumble of her stomach, however, reminded her that it was long past noon and that she was very hungry. With relief she left off sorting through Sam's papers—something she'd been avoiding doing for months—and prepared to leave the office. She was actually reaching for the doorknob when the door opened.

Yancy and Mr. Henderson stood in the doorway and Sara stared at them in surprise. Mr. Henderson beamed at her and said, "Good day, my dear! I trust you will excuse my bursting in on you like this, but Yancy came to see me this morning with a marvelous solution and he insisted that I come back with him to tell you."

Wordlessly Sara indicated for the two men to come into the room. Yancy lounged with his usual negligence in one of the chairs in front of the desk. Mr. Henderson waited until Sara was seated behind the desk and then, fairly rubbing his hands together with delight, he said, "We have decided on a price for Magnolia Grove—one we think you will concede is more than adequate—and Yancy has agreed to immediately buy out your share of the plantation!" Mr. Henderson beamed at her again. "There is now no need to worry about finding a buyer—within a matter of days the sale and the settlement of Sam's estate can be completed. Isn't that wonderful?"

It *was* wonderful news, but it also made Sara terribly uneasy. Why was Yancy doing this? She looked at him, but his expression was enigmatic as he stared steadily back at her.

Feeling something was expected of her, she said reluctantly, "That is indeed wonderful news, Mr. Henderson. I just didn't expect . . ." She glanced nervously back at Yancy. "I know you will want to take possession right away, but it will take me a few weeks to vacate the premises."

Yancy nodded. "Of course. I understand perfectly. We can leave whenever you're ready."

"We?" Sara repeated weakly.

"Oh, yes!" Mr. Henderson said happily. "That's the best part—you are going to stay at Rancho del Sol until the repairs are completed at Paloma! Yancy explained it all to me on our ride out here!"

8

How Sara kept a civil tongue in her mouth during the next several harrowing moments, she never knew. With growing fury she listened to Mr. Henderson's innocent prattling about how *marvelous* it was that Yancy had returned and had so generously provided a solution to the situation. Unconscious of the angry currents swirling about the room, Mr. Henderson droned on and on, exclaiming again and again how wonderfully everything had worked out, how *pleased* Sam would be that Yancy was doing the right thing by offering Sara the hospitality of his home and how *comforted* Sara must be to know that she now had a man to watch over her and protect her from the cares of the world. Why, it was just *splendid*! She bore it as long as she could, all the while hotly aware of Yancy watching her closely, a smile of grim amusement on his dark face. Finally she'd had enough and gently but firmly urged Mr. Henderson into taking his leave.

Yancy rose with indolent grace to accompany the lawyer to the door and Sara said sweetly, "After you have seen Mr. Henderson on his way, would you please return here?" Her eyes glittered fiercely at him and despite her best efforts, she couldn't help the sharp edge that crept into her voice as she said, "After all, we have *so* much to discuss!"

Yancy smiled mockingly at her. "Perhaps later, *chica*—since we will be leaving for del Sol just as soon as things can be arranged, there is much that I must see to."

Fully aware of Mr. Henderson watching them benignly, Sara bit back the wrathful words that choked her throat and got out tightly, "I think it would be best if we discussed it first."

There was a slight commotion in the doorway and Ann breezed in. "Oh, Mr. Henderson! It is you! Peggy said that someone had come to call, but she didn't know who it was." Smiling sunnily at the lawyer, she purred, "Do you have some news for us?"

Of course, Mr. Henderson had to divulge all, and he had barely finished speaking when, after a swift, comprehensive glance at Yancy and Sara, Ann exclaimed, "Why, how absolutely divine! I have wanted to visit del Sol for simply *years*—especially since the last time I saw the place it was in *such* shambles." She flashed Yancy an affable look. "Sam spoke often over the years of all the excellent improvements you have made there. It is so generous of you to have all of us stay with you while Casa Paloma is made habitable. My husband and I cannot thank you enough for coming up with such a superb solution! We all have been dreading the move to Casa Paloma, not knowing what we would find."

Yancy's face was the picture of incredulous dismay, and when he opened his mouth, clearly intending to bluntly disabuse her of the notion that his invitation included the Shelldrakes, Ann rushed on. "Oh, I just know that this move will be a much-needed tonic for poor Tom. I'm sure that once he is no longer deviled with worries about the uncertainty of the future, he will improve dramatically. You are so kind to us, Yancy— Sam would be proud of you! It is just too, too touching the way our little family helps one another." She brushed a kiss on Yancy's cheek and murmured, "You must excuse me—I simply have to tell Tom the exciting news!"

She disappeared in a whirl of rustling black skirts, and like a man hit by a cannonball, Yancy stared dazedly after her. It was Mr. Henderson's enthusiastically pumping his hand and telling him what a magnificent fellow he was to watch over his extended family this way that brought him out of his trance. He threw a distinctly harassed glance at Sara, and taking pity on him—after all, too well did she know how adept Ann was at manipulating things to her advantage—she guided the voluble Mr. Henderson toward the front door.

With the lawyer happily on his way to town to spread the fascinating news that young Yancy wasn't such a bad sort—in spite of the rumors about him—Sara slowly turned to look at Yancy. A mocking smile curving her rosy mouth, she said with a certain amount of understandable malice, "Perhaps *that* explains why the Shelldrakes are still living at Magnolia Grove!"

The animosity between them gone for the moment, Yancy grinned ruefully. "She is very like Margaret in getting her own way, isn't she?"

"Very!" Sara agreed dryly.

Bartholomew appeared just then and said to Sara in a scolding voice, "Here you are! I have been looking all over for you! It is long past noon and Tansy says that you are to come right now and eat some of the nice chicken and dumplings she has especially prepared for you."

Sara was used to Bartholomew's faintly bossy manner, but she wished that he hadn't chosen this moment to display it. Flushing slightly and feeling as if she were suddenly twelve years old, she said meekly, "Mr. Henderson delayed me. I will come right away." Glancing at Yancy, she scowled at the amusement dancing in his eyes. "And as for you," she began grimly, "don't congratulate yourself too soon on how clever you have been! Just as soon as I have eaten, I want to see you in Sam's office. We *still* have a great deal to discuss."

Yancy rubbed his chin thoughtfully. "Well, sweetheart, it's like I told you—I'm afraid that I'll be busy this afternoon." He smiled kindly at her. "But don't worry, I'm sure we'll find some time to talk." He turned and started to walk down the hall.

Sara watched him go, her emotions in a raging turmoil. She wasn't certain how he had done it, but in less than twenty-four hours it seemed as if he had effortlessly wrested control of her very life from her. It was intolerable! Somehow she had to regain what she had lost, and there was no time like the present! Fear as much as rage fueling her words, she called after him, "Don't you *dare* walk away from me! I'm not through talking to you! And I would remind you that Magnolia Grove is not yours yet—I have to agree to the sale, no matter how generous your offer!"

Yancy glanced back at her, the expression in his golden-brown eyes hard to define. "Are you telling me," he said with soft menace, "that you *aren't* going to accept my offer?"

"No, it isn't that! I will gladly accept your offer for Magnolia Grove—I'll be happier than you could ever know to be rid of it," Sara said coolly, and deciding that since he'd left her no alternative she might as well get it over with, she added bluntly, "But I'm afraid that my living at del Sol is out of the question!"

Something dangerous slid into his eyes and as he took a step in her direction, Sara was conscious of a sensation of great peril. It was Bartholomew's delicate cough that stopped Yancy's advance, and somewhat apologetically, Bartholomew murmured, "I think that this discussion should be continued in a more private place . . . and after

Sara has eaten." He looked meaningfully at Yancy, and Yancy relaxed slightly and shrugged indifferently.

For once Sara was glad of Bartholomew's protective intervention, and sweeping grandly past Yancy, she said airily, "Actually, there *is* nothing further to discuss! I shan't be going to del Sol and that's final!"

Yancy caught her arm and spun her around. "I had hoped to do this pleasantly, but you're not going to give me any choice, are you, *chica*?"

Despite her inward trepidation, Sara's chin came up. "You mean we were going to do things *your* way and that as long as I spinelessly went along with them, it would be pleasant—for *you*!" Her small bosom heaving from sudden, deep emotion, she snapped, "I am *not* going to del Sol—I'm going to Casa Paloma and you can't stop me!"

His mouth thinned and he hung on to his temper with a visible effort. "You shouldn't toss about that kind of challenge, sweetheart . . . and when you twist the tiger's tail, you'd better be damned ready for what comes afterward!"

He flung her arm away from him and stalked down the hall. Obviously disturbed by the exchange, Sara nervously rubbed her hands on the front of her black skirts.

"You know," Bartholomew began conversationally, "Yancy is used to arranging events to suit himself. Sometimes he does things without thinking of the consequences, but it has been my observation in the past that when it is *diplomatically* pointed out to him that he might have been too hasty . . . or high-handed in his plans, he usually will reconsider." He shot Sara an oblique look. "I should tell you also that one sure way to have him dig in his heels and obstinately refuse to budge is to hurl a challenge at his head the way you did just now."

"Well, that's just too bad!" Sara retorted. "I'm not about to just let him barge right in and start rearranging my life to suit him! Besides, since he feels the way he does about me, I can't imagine why he wants me at del Sol. Whatever he might say to the contrary, it wasn't *kindness* that prompted him to make the invitation! And now, if you don't mind, I'm going to the kitchen to eat that excellent meal you said Tansy has waiting for me."

In the mysterious ways of extended households, the news of Yancy's offer to buy Sara's share of Magnolia Grove and the proposed removal to del Sol had already spread to all the interested inhabitants. While she ate her meltingly tender dumplings and tasty chicken, Sara had to listen to the excited chatter of Peggy, Tansy, Noah and his wife, Mercy, who also happened to be in the kitchen as they exclaimed over the news. Inwardly seething, Sara kept her own thoughts to herself; until she had settled things with Yancy, there was no use telling the others that she'd eat sand and spit out bullets before she'd go to del Sol! The food stuck in her throat, and after calming the worst of her hunger, she pushed her half-full plate away, ignoring Tansy's vocal dismay at how little she had eaten and fled the kitchen.

Afraid that she would be ambushed by either Tom or Ann if she returned to the house, she decided to take a stroll along the small creek that ran behind the kitchen. It was pleasant here, the shady oaks and magnolia trees creating a cool haven from the almost tropical heat of the April sun. She took several steadying breaths, and with her thoughts dwelling on what had occurred this morning and what it all meant to her immediate future, she wandered aimlessly along the gently burbling creek.

Sara was so lost in her own musings that she didn't realize how far she had walked until a faint, ominous rustling in a thicket of blackberry bushes startled her. Despite the various plantations scattered about this part of southeastern Texas, there were countless acres of wilderness, only the land cleared for planting and the areas near buildings and barns in any way considered tamed. Somewhat uneasily, Sara glanced around; seeing the tangle of honeysuckle, blackberries and wild grape that festooned the thickly crowded trees, and with visions of rattlesnakes, bears and cougars spilling into her brain, she decided that she had better head back to more civilized areas.

There was another rustle, closer this time, and a shiver snaked down her spine. She spun around, her steps quickening as she walked swiftly back the way she had come. Almost at a run, she rounded a slight curve and stopped abruptly when she saw Hyrum, a frown on his face, coming toward her. His expression bleak, he hurriedly approached her and asked bluntly, "Is it true? Yancy is buying you out and you are moving to del Sol?"

Sara was so glad to see him that she didn't take offense at his manner. "No, I'm not going to del Sol! That's just a silly notion that Yancy has—and just how very silly it is, he will soon learn."

Hyrum's handsome features relaxed slightly. "I'm afraid that my motives in coming to you are totally self-serving—I was fearful that you would be letting me go."

"Hyrum, don't worry! I have promised you that when we go to Casa Paloma, you will go with us." She smiled at him. "Haven't we discussed that you are to help me in the breeding program? That you will be my foreman?"

"If Yancy will let you," he said bitterly. "He hates me and will stop at nothing until he has driven me away."

Sara sighed. She was in no mood to soothe Hyrum's worries and she wasn't about to get into a discussion about Yancy Cantrell! "I wouldn't worry about what

Yancy thinks," she said lightly. "Yancy will not be running Casa Paloma, *I* will!"

"I repeat, *if* he lets you! He swore he'd kill Margaret before he'd let her have Casa Paloma." Startling Sara, Hyrum suddenly grabbed her hand and clasped it tightly between his. Staring fervently at her, he muttered, "Look what happened to Margaret—he killed her! Do you really think he will just tamely let you take over Casa Paloma? And if he manages to spirit you away to del Sol, what chance do you think you will have?" His grip on her hand became almost painful. "You must not trust him, no matter how charming and kind he may seem. I don't want you hurt by him and . . . and . . ." Before Sara's horrified gaze, he dropped to his knees in front of her and began pressing frantic kisses onto the hand he held. "Sara, Sara, you must know how I feel about you!" he exclaimed passionately, his eyes lifted to hers. "I've tried to hide my feelings—I know it is too soon after Sam died, but Yancy's presence compels me to speak now!" He took a deep breath and said in a rush, "I've always loved you—practically from the first—marry me! Let me stand between you and Yancy Cantrell!"

"Oh, Hyrum!" Sara said distressfully, trying to untangle her hand from his and wishing heartily that she could instantly disappear in a puff of smoke. "Oh, don't . . . Oh, please, you don't know what you're saying! You're upset right now, but I'm sure if you think things over, you'll realize that . . ."

Nothing was going to stop Hyrum, not even the fact that his lady-love seemed distinctly unenthusiastic about his proposal. Rising from his knees, he embraced Sara. "I know it is too much to hope that you will love me as I love you, but, Sara, *darling*, give me a chance!"

He pressed his mouth ardently to hers and Sara had never been so uncomfortable or embarrassed in her life.

As his mouth groped for hers, a shudder of repugnance went through her. She wanted and needed Hyrum's help to implement her plans for Casa Paloma, but not at this price! She didn't want to hurt his feelings, but she also wasn't about to be subjected to his unwanted and uninvited advances! She began to struggle in his arms, turning her face aside so that his seeking lips only grazed her cheek and trying with a minimum of fuss to disengage herself from his embrace.

To Yancy, approaching from the same direction Hyrum had taken, the situation looked far different; with something that resembled a feral growl, in two swift strides, he fairly leaped upon the entwined pair and ripped them apart. With one powerful movement he sent Hyrum flying to the ground, knocking the breath from him. One hand firmly wrapped itself around Sara's wrist, and a revolver suddenly appeared in the other— the long blue barrel aimed at the stunned Hyrum.

Hyrum glared at Yancy and rose slowly to his feet. Fists clenched at his sides, he asked harshly, "Why don't we ask Sara how she feels about me touching her?"

For one terrible moment Sara thought that Yancy would shoot Hyrum where he stood, and desperate to avert a terrible tragedy, she said sharply, "Stop it—both of you! I am not a bone to be fought over by a pair of surly dogs!" Sending Hyrum a speaking glance, she said in a calmer tone of voice, "It's all right. I can handle this myself." She smiled shakily. "Please, Hyrum, don't cause any trouble—go back to the house."

It was obvious he didn't like it, but after taking a considering look at the gun in Yancy's hand, Hyrum nodded curtly and said tightly, "We'll talk later."

"I doubt it!" Yancy retorted in a clipped tone.

"We'll just see about that, won't we?" Hyrum threw back challengingly, an ugly look in his eyes. "Perhaps you'd like to drop that gun, and we can see just how bold you really are!"

"Hyrum! *Please!*" Sara cried in an anguished voice. "Go."

Ignoring Yancy, Hyrum looked intently at Sara. "Only because you ask it of me," he said softly and turned and walked away.

Held prisoner by Yancy's unyielding clasp, Sara watched him go, envying Hyrum his escape. Somehow she didn't think she'd be let off so easily. Although, she thought with a frown, what she had done to arouse such behavior on Yancy's part was inconceivable! Her initial astonishment at what had happened faded and a strong sense of injustice welled up through her. Whether or not she wanted to be kissed by Hyrum wasn't any of Yancy Cantrell's business, and he'd had no right to burst upon them like that. As the seconds passed, she became thoroughly enraged, and finally managing to free her wrist, she unconsciously rubbed it where Yancy's savage grip had bruised the soft skin. Her green eyes snapping with temper, she demanded hotly, "And just what the devil do you think you are doing? How dare you treat Hyrum that way!"

Yancy's fierce gaze swept back to her, and instinctively Sara took a step away from the fury she saw glittering in the depths of his eyes. There was something so deadly in his expression that for a moment she wondered uneasily if her instincts had played her false and that she would be wise to fear for her life.

Some of what she was thinking must have shown on her face, because in the next instant the worst of the terrible rage had left his features. Slowly reholstering his pistol, he said quietly, "You know, if I were you, I'd be more worried about myself than Hyrum!"

"Why?" Sara countered bravely. "I've done nothing wrong! But you! You're the one who burst in on us and threatened Hyrum. How do you explain *your* actions?"

Yancy took her firmly by one arm and began to lead her back toward the house. "Let's just say that I was protecting my interests, shall we?"

"Protecting your interests!" Sara exclaimed furiously. "And what do you mean by that?"

Yancy slanted her a mocking look. "I think you know very well what I mean!" And to her astonishment, he jerked her into his arms and kissed her.

It was a hard, possessive kiss, and as that same giddy burst of excitement that Sara always felt when Yancy kissed her surged up through her, there was a part of Sara that marveled how very different her reaction had been when Hyrum had tried to kiss her. Yancy's mouth was warm and demanding as he kissed her, his teeth nibbling on her lower lip, half coaxing, half ordering her to open her mouth for his hungry exploration. He was very adept at what he did, but Sara doggedly resisted the treacherous desire that threatened to override her senses. Pushing him firmly away from her, she asked tartly, "Is that your answer to everything? A kiss?"

A smile quirked at the corners of his mouth. "Can you think of a better one?"

Resentment welled up inside her at his teasing tone and hotly she began, "I certainly—!"

Yancy's lips on hers cut off the stinging reply, and despite her struggle to escape him, he kissed her deeply and thoroughly, a guttural groan of satisfaction revealing his pleasure. When he lifted his mouth from hers and looked down at her, his eyes filled with emotions she could only guess at, he growled savagely, "You're *mine*! And remember that the next time Hyrum or anybody else attempts to touch you! I don't like my woman entertaining the advances of other men."

Indignation swelled in Sara's breast and her pretty face tinted rosily from temper. "You don't *own* me!

And just where you got the ludicrous idea that you have some prior claim to me—or to my affections—is beyond comprehension!"

Again displaying one of his lightning-swift mood changes, Yancy seemed to relax and, a mocking smile on his mouth, he drawled, "Why, sweetheart, have you forgotten? According to Sam's will and your conniving, we're going to make a baby, maybe two or three, together! I think that explains my 'prior claim,' don't you? I certainly can't stand by and let other men charm you away from me, can I?"

"Oh, stop it!" Sara said exasperatedly. "You have some sort of unhealthy fixation about Casa Paloma and it is time you got over it! Your ancestors may have settled the land generations ago, but it is *only* land, and I don't intend to become a broodmare for your children simply so you can satisfy some driving ambition!" She glared up at him, unaware of how attractive she looked with strands of honey-gold hair which had escaped from the neat braid curling wildly near her cheeks.

An enigmatic gleam in his eyes, Yancy lazily pulled a resisting Sara into his arms. With insulting ease he subdued her struggles and brushed her mouth tantalizingly with his. "Are you so certain, *amiga*, that it is *just* the land that prompts me?" She stared in amazement at him. He kissed her then, his knowing mouth intent upon inflicting a mind-drugging assault, but Sara grimly fought out of his arms, and gazing up into his dark face, she demanded, "What do you mean by that? If it isn't the land, why else would you be so, so . . ." Words failed her and she glared at him.

He flicked a careless finger down her cheek and murmured, "You're an intelligent woman . . . I'm sure if you think about it long enough, you'll come up with an answer."

He began to walk away from her, but she was deter-mined to get a straight reply from him. "Yancy Cantrell, you come back here this very instant!" she ordered him imperiously. "Don't you walk away from me! I'm not through talking to you!"

Yancy glanced back at her, an infuriatingly smug smile on his lips. "Ah, but, sweetheart, *I've* said all I have to say on the matter!"

It was too much, and with a decidedly ferocious lit-tle growl for such a dainty creature, Sara picked up her black silken skirts and raced after him. Catching up with him, she began to pummel his broad, muscular back with her fists. "Don't you *ever*," she exclaimed, almost breathless from her exertions and the anger that flooded her, "walk away from me again!"

Laughing, Yancy turned and caught her flailing fists in his hands. "What a fiery little tigress you can be," he said half teasingly, half admiringly, and there was a soft light in his eyes that suddenly made Sara breathless for entirely different reasons.

His laughter faded and they stared at each other, utter-ly mesmerized. They might have gone on standing there looking into each other's eyes indefinitely, but Tom Shelldrake's voice rang out, shattering the fragile spell that had enveloped them.

"Oh, Yancy! Yancy! I must speak with you!" Tom cried loudly.

Yancy released Sara and looked in Tom's direction. He had not yet seen Tom Shelldrake since he had arrived, and it was only by the greatest effort of will that he did not betray his shock at the changes in the older man.

The years and the war had not been kind to Thomas Shelldrake. He had come home from the battle a broken and shattered man. It wasn't just the terrible wounds that he had sustained, but the sights and sounds that had accompanied the ugly act of war. His nerves were gone, along with the boyish charm he had once possessed. He looked years older than his age of forty-two, his once thick tawny hair lying in thinning, lank wisps across his head. His once bright, laughing brown eyes were dull and lifeless and he seemed to have shrunk, to have become an old man; he bore no resemblance to the jovial, bluff, handsome individual he had been the last time Yancy had seen him. Tom carried his useless left arm in a black silk sling, and Yancy, who had not felt at all kindly toward him previously, was suddenly aware of a burst of compassionate pity. Tom Shelldrake had lost everything—his fortune, his home and his physical well-being—and Yancy was thoroughly ashamed of his earlier observations about the Shelldrakes.

A warm smile crossing his dark features, Yancy walked swiftly toward the older man. When they were close enough, he thrust out his hand and said awkwardly, "Well, Tom, we meet again!"

There was a twinkle in Tom's brown eyes and a hint of his former heartiness was apparent as he clasped Yancy's hand and shook it enthusiastically. "Indeed we do! Indeed we do! And I want to thank you for your generosity! Ann has been telling me about your so-very-kind invitation to us. I won't deny that I have had some grave misgivings about moving to Casa Paloma, but now that I know you're in charge, I can rest easy."

Torn between vexation and resignation, Sara watched the two men, their heads bent together, stroll slowly toward the house. Her mouth twisted ruefully. There was certainly nothing to be gained by trying to continue the argument with Yancy at this point. She would just have to keep a civil tongue between her teeth until she could get him in some private place and make him understand—if she had to take a club to him to do it—that she was *not* going to del Sol, that he was *not* taking over her life and that if he wanted to have the Shelldrakes live with him, that was fine with her! She giggled suddenly. She could almost feel sorry for Yancy—he was probably still reeling from the brash way in which Ann had ruthlessly manipulated events, and now that he'd seen Tom Shelldrake, even if he was angry with Ann's high-handed machinations, Sara doubted that he would withdraw the supposed invitation.

Her sympathy for Yancy, however, was short-lived. Just a few minutes after the two men had disappeared in the direction of the now dilapidated stables, Sara returned to the house to find everything in an uproar. Bartholomew, Tansy and Peggy seemed to be very busy stripping the walls of what few paintings and ornaments remained, and there was a growing pile of selected furniture and household items in the main hallway.

"What are you doing?" she demanded bewilderedly as she watched the three servants darting here and there.

Bartholomew, carrying a gilt-edged mirror from the main salon, replied lightly, "Oh, we are just getting things ready to pack. Yancy has said that we will leave by the end of the week and that we should take only the most essential items with us." He smiled kindly at Sara. "I think I know, of the things that remain, which pieces and objects you would like to take with us."

"I'm afraid that there has been a mistake," Sara said tightly. "*Yancy* may be leaving by the end of the week and certainly he may take *half* of whatever he chooses with him, but the remainder is to stay here—with me!" At their dismayed expressions, she added in a softer tone, "Of course, if you wish to go with him, I understand—but I have no intention of doing so! And *no one* can make me!"

Feeling distinctly out of sorts, Sara retreated to her bedroom. Once there, she found little solace, and because she needed to gain at least some amount of inner tranquility before she had to face Yancy again, she deliberately didn't let herself, even for one second, dwell on the latest disturbing exchange with him. He was arrogant, infuriating, overbearing and far, *far* too sure of himself, and if she *dared* let herself think about him, she'd lose what control of the situation she still retained.

She deliberately skipped the evening meal that night and, ignoring the grumbles of her empty stomach, eventually crawled into bed. She might be hungry, but she wasn't about to confront the combined forces of her household, very well aware that by now Yancy had convinced all of them that they were *indeed* leaving for del Sol before the end of the week. They could all damn well go! she thought grimly as she stared up at the ceiling. *She* wasn't!

To her surprise, she fell asleep almost immediately. How long she had slept, Sara had no idea, but suddenly she was jerked wide awake by the certain knowledge that *someone was in her room*! Her heart leaped to her throat and her eyes strained to pierce the darkness.

A dark shadow drifted toward her bed, and even as she opened her mouth to scream, a hand came down swiftly across her lips. A warm, silky voice murmured in her ear, "Ah, sweetheart, I would have preferred to do this another way, but since you've made it clear that unless I abduct you, you will not go to del Sol, you don't leave me any choice. So abduction it will have to be!"

Yancy! she thought furiously, her fright gone and sheer rage replacing it. She began to struggle wildly, but he only laughed softly as he scooped her up, effectively trussing her up in her own bedcovers. With her head and upper body heavily cloaked by blankets, her cries for help were muffled. She was carelessly tossed over his shoulder, and after giving her a teasing swat on the bottom, he said softly, "Don't worry, *chica*, I have no intention of harming the mother of my children! Now stop fighting me—you'll enjoy your journey to del Sol so much better! And don't worry about the others—they'll follow soon enough! As for now"—he laughed softly again—"it shall be you and me riding away together under the stars. . . ."

PART TWO

ABDUCTION OF
THE HEART

*Lady, cheer up; most of our ills, blowing
     loudly*
*In dreams by night, grow milder when
     'tis day.*

ACRISIUS. FRAGMENT
—SOPHOCLES

9

Sara was so stunned by Yancy's outrageously high-handed actions that even as he tossed her struggling, blanket-wrapped form over the back of a horse like a sack of grain and swiftly tied her to the animal, she didn't honestly believe that he would go through with it. He wouldn't dare, she told herself stoutly. He was only trying to frighten her. But when the horse began to move a few minutes later, the full enormity of her situation dawned on her. *He was abducting her*! He was actually going to spirit her away to del Sol!

A muffled scream of sheer rage burst from her, and like a wild animal caught in a trap, she increased her frantic struggles. He wasn't, she thought furiously, going to get away with this! Sara wasn't by nature a violent person, but it could not be denied that several rather grisly fates for Yancy sped through her mind as she fought against the bonds that secured her to the horse.

Despite her undignified position, several things were clear to her as the moments passed. He had planned this well. She had already figured out from the sounds that there were three horses—the mount Yancy was riding, the beast that carried her and one other. A pack horse? Or was someone else involved in this midnight abduction? If there was a rider on that third horse, he or she was being very quiet, Sara concluded uneasily. As they rode farther away from Magnolia Grove, it was obvious, too, that Yancy wasn't the least concerned about anyone raising the alarm and pursuing them. In growing rage she listened as he whistled softly to himself and urged the horses to a faster pace. *She had to escape!* There wasn't a moment to lose! Every mile took her farther away from safety.

The increased intensity of her unbridled attempts to free herself caused her horse to dance nervously, and Sara smiled grimly. Good! Let Yancy fight with a fractious woman *and* a horse! She couldn't see anything and, trussed up as she was, she could tell little of what was going on around her, but from the horse's actions and the soothing words she heard from Yancy as he tried to calm the uneasy creature she surmised that he wasn't having an easy time of it. After a particularly rambunctious several minutes, brought on by her wild thrashings, the horse was halted and Sara felt a spurt of hope. Maybe Yancy had decided she wasn't worth all this trouble.

Her hope was ill-founded. She was conscious of Yancy bringing his horse alongside hers, and a second later, his hand swatted her smartly on her bottom.

"I know you're angry, sweetheart," he drawled, the amusement in his voice enraging her. "But you're going to have to settle down or I'll be forced to do something that you'll like even less than this!"

A soft growl of sheer fury was his answer and he laughed softly. "I know, I know, you're really annoyed right now, but, *chica*, it's all your fault!" He spoke with such reasonableness that Sara's teeth ground together audibly. "And remember, you didn't give me any choice—you made it very clear that this was the only way you'd go to del Sol. So what was I to do?"

Though muffled, there was no mistaking the furious reply that came from the shrouded figure. Yancy smiled in the moonlight. "Well, you're just going to have to wait a bit before you can get your hands on me. Now settle down and don't give me any more trouble and this whole process will be easier for all of us. And, Sara," he added quietly, with no amusement evident, "don't make me stop again. You won't like what I'll do to you if you keep giving me trouble."

The threat was implicit, and with a bitter sigh, Sara forced herself to relax. For now, at least, Yancy seemed to have the upper hand and she wasn't going to gain anything but grief for herself if she didn't cooperate. For now. It wasn't easy to tamely admit defeat, but she did stop her wild thrashings and tried to find a comfortable position in which to continue the journey.

Unfortunately for her, there was nothing comfortable about the ride that followed. Yancy apparently wanted to cover as much ground as possible before daylight, and despite leading the two other horses, he was able to keep the animals at a fairly swift pace.

At first it wasn't too bad, but by the time they had been traveling for several hours, Sara felt as if she had been beaten up and thrown down a flight of stairs. Every bone in her body ached and she was certain she was going to have bruises that would last for weeks. But she had other, more pressing things to think about and she squirmed around, trying to ease the demands of her body. It was no use, and knowing she wouldn't be able to last much longer, she called out to Yancy, hoping that he could hear her voice clearly enough through the folds of cloth and above the noise of the horses' hooves.

To her relief, the horses were halted a second later and he dismounted and came back to stand beside her mount. With quick, economical movements, he untied her from the saddle and lifted her down. Her legs were unsteady and she swayed against him as he roughly jerked the blankets from around her.

"I told you," he said grimly, "that if you didn't settle down, I'd do something you'd like even less!"

Gulping in great draughts of fresh air, Sara said quickly, "You don't understand! I have to . . ." She flushed and muttered almost inaudibly, "I need to . . . um, I need . . ." Innately shy and horribly embarrassed to confess her predicament, she looked at him beseechingly.

Yancy understood in a moment and his mouth twisted ruefully. "I'm sorry, *chica*. I should have stopped earlier." He gave her a searching glance, then said quietly, "We can do this two ways. You can give me your word of honor that if I allow you some privacy, you won't try to escape . . . or I come with you. Which is it?"

Her body needs urgent, her face hot with mortification, Sara said breathlessly, "I swear! I won't try to run away!" And not waiting to see if he believed her, desperate for relief, she bolted into the bushes.

Yancy waited patiently and when a few minutes later she reappeared, he asked kindly, "Feel better?"

If possible, Sara's face got even hotter. She gave a curt nod and docilely moved toward her horse, standing there silently. When Yancy approached with the ropes and blanket again, she flinched, but it was obvious she wasn't going to put up much of a fight.

There was something so defeated about her as she stood there in the rapidly waning moonlight, her thick hair tumbling wildly about her shoulders, her slim body clearly outlined in her patched muslin nightgown, that Yancy was uncomfortably aware of a tiny ache in the region of his heart. "If you'll promise not to cause any trouble," he said gruffly, "I won't truss you up again."

She threw him a grateful look, and cursing himself for a fool, he lifted her slight weight and settled her gently into the saddle. Glaring sternly up at her, he muttered,

"One sound, one move that I don't like, and it's back the way you were, understand?"

Her eyes very big and green in her face, she nodded, hardly daring to believe that she wasn't going to have to endure the smothering folds of the blanket. Yancy grunted something and went about the business of making certain that her stirrups were the right length.

The fact that she was not garbed for riding became apparent to both of them almost immediately as Yancy's fingers touched her bare feet. He frowned. His warm hands lingered for a second and then, with a sigh, he walked over to the third horse and searched around in the pack on its back.

Returning to the side of her horse, he said dryly, "You might as well dismount and put these on. I don't intend stopping again any time soon, and dressed as you are, you're bound to cause comment if we pass anyone."

"These" were her boots, a floppy-brimmed, woven straw hat, a worn, short calico gown and a pair of boy's knickerbockers. Her mouth tightened as her suspicion that at least *one* member of her household had abetted him in his nefarious actions grew stronger. She jerked the clothing out of his hands and turned her back on him, her nightgown keeping her modestly covered as she struggled into the knickerbockers and pulled on her boots. In order to put on the calico top, she would have to remove her nightgown, and she hesitated for a long moment. She glanced uneasily over her shoulder, and seeing Yancy watching her with open amusement, she muttered something *extremely* unladylike and turned her back on him once more. She took a deep breath and then, in practically one movement, stripped off her nightdress and swiftly shrugged into the short calico gown.

Yancy had a brief, tantalizing glimpse of white, gently rounded shoulders, a stiff little back and a slim waist before the calico hid her charms from his fascinated gaze. For a long moment his eyes lingered on the delightfully shaped derriere revealed by the knickerbockers. She spun to face him and, realizing that he had been boldly staring at her body, said icily, "I hope you enjoyed yourself!"

He grinned and handed her the floppy-brimmed straw hat. "Oh, I did, sweetheart, I did indeed!"

Too infuriated to reply, she jammed the hat on her head and, with lithe grace, mounted her horse. With no clear plan in mind, she kicked the animal into a smart trot. There was a startled yelp from Yancy as he raced for his own horse. It took Sara but a second to realize that this was her chance to escape, that the few precious moments it would take Yancy to remount might be all the time she needed to get away from him. And if her horse was faster than his . . . Filled with excitement, she kicked her horse harder, and as the animal responded by breaking into a dead run, a little bubble of laughter rose up in her chest. She'd show him! But even as elation spread through her, it occurred to her that she really hadn't chosen her moment wisely—she had no idea where she was or in which direction lay safety, and Yancy, on what she suspected was the more powerful horse, was only seconds behind her. She could hear the thunder of his horse's hooves. Any minute now, she had no doubt that he would overtake her. Worse, she had given her word that she'd cause no trouble. After this little stunt, it was very likely—no, probable—that she'd spend the rest of the journey trussed up like a chicken going to market.

Not giving herself time to think, she jerked her horse to a standstill, the animal rearing up wildly on its hind legs and pawing toward the sky at the abrupt reversal. Not a particularly intrepid rider, Sara nonetheless clung gamely to the back of her mount, praying it wouldn't go over backward and kill her in the process. Hardly aware of Yancy, who was pulling his own horse to a far less dramatic stop, Sara fought for several frightening moments to bring the animal under control.

Once her horse had calmed, Yancy, his face grim in the moonlight, brought his own mount alongside and snatched the reins from her slackened grasp. "And what the *hell* was that all about?" he demanded furiously, not about to reveal the sheer terror that had knifed through him when her horse had reared and she had appeared so small and defenseless upon its back.

Her heartbeat returning to normal, and secretly thankful that the dangerous moment was behind her, Sara looked at him and said with disarming earnestness, "I forgot—I gave you my word that I wouldn't try to escape."

Nonplussed, Yancy stared at her for several tense seconds, his fear for her safety gradually ebbing. Finally, when she was convinced that he was going to tie her up again, he scowled blackly at her and said acidly, "Don't *forget* again!"

Fortunately, the pack horse had galloped after the other two animals and Yancy caught it without any trouble. Once again they started off on their journey, Sara's mount obediently falling in alongside Yancy's, the pack horse traveling closely behind.

Sara wasn't any happier with her overall situation, but she was delighted to be sitting upright on the horse and not dangling helplessly over its side, enveloped in countless yards of smothering bedclothes. She was also glad to be more suitably clad, although it felt strange to be wearing clothes without even a chemise or a pair of drawers underneath. Her small bosom and narrow waist needed no corset to define her shapeliness and she often dispensed with wearing one—but no drawers and chemise! It felt decidedly odd, almost decadent, and she was very aware of her breasts pushing and rubbing against the calico and of how the worn knickerbockers clung to her bottom and thighs. It was a queer sensation and made her extremely conscious of her body in a way she hadn't been before.

The moonlight had disappeared, but dawn was not far away and already it was considerably lighter. Sara glanced curiously around her. From the direction of the rising sun, she ascertained that they were riding in a southwesterly direction, and while she knew that they couldn't be more than fifteen miles from Magnolia Grove, nothing looked familiar to her. It was as if they had left civilization behind and stepped off into the untamed wilderness. The landscape was very similar to the uncultivated areas around Magnolia Grove—towering live oaks, spreading magnolia and pecan trees, with multihued green vines and bushes growing rampantly throughout. In the open grassy areas, small spring wildflowers in fantastic shades of blue, pink and yellow bloomed profusely. Under different circumstances, Sara would have enjoyed herself immensely.

As the sun grew higher in the brilliantly blue sky and they continued to ride steadily southwest, she was very glad of the floppy-brimmed hat and her loose, comfortable clothing. The day became very hot and humid, but Yancy showed no sign of stopping, although about midmorning he handed her a thick sandwich of bread and cheese and passed her his canteen. The only time the horses were not moving was when Yancy would allow them to slake their thirst from the small creeks and streams that were scattered throughout the area. To Sara's disappointment, they passed no other riders or wagons, and though she looked surreptitiously around all the time, she had seen no evidence of human habitation. Her mouth twisted. She didn't know why Yancy had wanted her word that she would not try to escape—

there certainly didn't seem to be any place or person to escape to!

It was after noon before Yancy called a halt. Not used to long hours in the saddle, Sara was aching in places she didn't know *could* ache and was fairly melting from the debilitating heat. With heartfelt relief she slid from her horse. Her feet were numb and her legs wobbly after so many hours astride a horse and she felt strange to be finally walking on firm ground again.

Yancy had chosen a pleasant spot to stop. A creek gurgled cheerfully nearby, there was plenty of grass for the horses and there were several patches of welcoming, cooling shade from the clump of live oaks that crowded nearby. The almost hypnotic drone of insects could be heard in the background, and Sara, exhausted by the lack of sleep and the traumatic events, sank down gratefully into the thick spring grass, tossing her hat aside, her tense muscles relaxing fully for the first time since the moment she had awakened to find Yancy in her bedroom.

Oblivious to Yancy as he set up temporary camp, Sara closed her eyes and, a moment later, was sound asleep. It seemed as if she had slept but a minute before she felt Yancy's hand on her shoulder, shaking her gently. As her eyes opened, she realized that several hours had passed, because the sun was considerably lower on the horizon. All her defenses down, she stared up drowsily at him as he lay next to her on the ground, his upper torso propped up by one elbow. Absently she noted the faint black stubble that covered his lean cheeks and chin, the faint creases of fatigue that radiated out from his thickly lashed, gleaming golden-brown eyes. Unaware of the appealing picture she made, Sara lay there innocently blinking up at him like a newly awakened kitten, her beautiful eyes mesmerizing pools of emerald green, her honey-gold hair curling enchantingly around her face.

Yancy thought that he had never seen anything quite so adorable in his life, and before he could stop himself, one hand cupped her cheek, turning her face up to his as his mouth settled gently on hers. He kissed her warmly, his lips moving like a butterfly's caress across hers. He kissed her many times, each time his lips lingering a teasing second longer than the time before, the delicate pressure of his mouth increasing as the minutes passed.

It was an exquisitely sweet torture he inflicted upon them both, his hand on her face softly caressing, his lips moving with slow intoxication against hers. Utterly beguiled by Yancy's lazily sensual kisses, Sara drifted serenely into desire, all her erotic senses singing to life as he wooed and cajoled her with his knowing mouth. There was none of the sudden, violent explosion of passion that usually accompanied their kisses, only a steady, subtle expanding of her awareness of her own body, of the gentle ache in her breasts, of the slight coiling in her belly and of the honeyed warmth that was slowly radiating upward from between her legs to every fiber of her being.

Unknowingly, her arms went around his neck, her slim fingers tangling in his black hair, and for a timeless moment that seemed to satisfy her—the sensation of his crisp dark hair sliding sensuously through her fingers, the sweetness of his mouth moving in drugging eroticism against hers. But as the aching warmth, swifter now, cascaded through her body, she grew vaguely impatient, suddenly wanting him to kiss her fully, to feel his lips harden, to know again the taste of him as his tongue filled her mouth. . . .

She moved restlessly, her fingers clenching and unclenching in the thick darkness of his hair, a soft moan coming from her when he kissed her again, still not giving her what she wanted. This time when he would have lifted his head, her fingers tightened, holding him to her, and shocking herself, she said breathlessly against his mouth, "Kiss me, Yancy! *Really* kiss me!"

Yancy gave a muffled groan and his lips came down hard on hers, all pretense of gentleness gone, his tongue thrusting deeply into the moist, welcoming depths of her mouth. He kissed her passionately, his body gradually lowering itself until he was half lying on top of her.

Sara welcomed his weight, the feel of his chest crushed against her breast exciting, the sensation of his tongue rubbing and gliding against hers sending a current of fire surging upward through her, making her arch and twist from the force of it. This blazing hunger for him had happened so insidiously, so gradually, that she wasn't even aware of the changes in her body, of the wildness in her blood, of the insistent demands of nature coursing through her, and she was too innocent to fully understand how overpowering desire could be to the unwary. Yancy's drugging kisses had thoroughly snared her and she was helplessly swept deeper into passion by the longings of her own impetuous flesh.

Forgotten were all the difficulties between them; there was only now, this moment, this sweet, heady moment when the soft grass was at her back, the cool dappled shade of the oak trees falling across their bodies and Yancy's hard form pressing ardently against hers. The infamous clause in Sam's will, Yancy's horrifying interpretation of it, even his nefarious abduction of her were all forgotten; there was only the heat of his body, the sweet violence of his kisses and the taste of him upon her tongue. . . .

Even his hand at her breast did not break the sensual spell and she shivered as his fingers shaped her and tugged gently at her swollen nipple. When his leg slid between hers, it seemed the most natural thing in the world and she groaned with pleasure as his lips traveled downward, to replace his fingers at her breast, his mouth closing hotly over her nipple.

Coherent thought suspended, Sara was at the mercy of her untutored body, whose every nerve seemed to be driving her toward one thing, and she was powerless to halt what was happening to her. Dimly she was aware of Yancy's heavier breathing, of the increasing urgency of his movements, and in some strange, wonderful way, it added to her excitement, added to the elemental compulsion that was controlling her.

His hands undoing her short gown and flinging it away to reveal her naked upper body aroused no alarm within her, and when he stripped off his own shirt to press his broad, heated chest to her aching breasts, she could only sigh her gratification and push up against him. Sara found the prickle of the thick black hair of his chest intensely arousing and sought to assuage the tinglings in her nipples by rubbing against him in oddly innocent abandonment.

It was nearly Yancy's undoing, and muttering an imprecation under his breath, he suddenly rolled away from her, his hands ripping off his remaining clothing. Before Sara's suddenly riveted gaze, his magnificent body was exposed, from the handsome face right down to the long, aristocratic feet. She could not tear her eyes away, staring in frank delight at all that manly beauty in front of her. Yancy *was* magnificently made, his shoulders broad, his chest deep, his waist narrow and his legs long and powerful. But it wasn't any of those charms that held Sara's rapt attention; it was the sight of his aroused manhood. Yancy was indeed magnificently built ... *everywhere*, but never having seen a fully erect naked man before, Sara had no conception of just how generous nature had been to him, or that he was truly a man among men. She could only stare at him, a strange excitement, a thrill of half fright, half sweet anticipation, flooding through her.

It never occurred to her to stop what was happening between them—it seemed inevitable, a natural outcome of the compelling magnetism that had existed between them from the first moment he had kissed her on the staircase at Magnolia Grove all those years before. Every dream, every half-wistful thought she had ever had of him, had been leading to this moment, and a faint shiver went through her as she realized that in a few moments his hard body would be crushed against hers, that she would become truly his and that her life was never going to be the same again. . . .

And yet she did nothing to prevent it; she could not. Her own body was burning for him, every fiber of her being calling her to him, driving her, rushing her into his arms. When he sank onto the ground beside her once more, she went to him without restraint, her arms clinging to him, her mouth opening eagerly under the passionate onslaught of his. Caught up in the most shockingly primitive demands of her own body, even when he roughly dragged the remainder of her clothing from her, there was no shrinking, no embarrassment— she *wanted* him to see her, wanted him to look at her body, wanted to see his striking amber-gold eyes darken with hungry desire. . . .

Staring in dazed pleasure at the slim, lovely body before him, Yancy felt his throat tighten, and beneath all the savage hunger that raged within him, he was dimly conscious of a strange tenderness. Sara was lovely, lying there in innocent abandon on the bright green grass, her skin nearly as pale as the finest alabaster, her nipples peaked, the color of spring strawberries, and the hair between her slender thighs a downy thatch of golden honey. She was delicately formed, her breasts small but firmly rounded, her waist narrow and her hips curvaceous yet slim and her legs . . . Yancy's gaze lingered for a moment on the shapely length of her legs, imagining himself sinking down between those slender white thighs. . . .

With a groan, he reached for her and kissed her fiercely, his tongue filling her mouth, possessing her, claiming her as he would soon do with his body. But kissing her was not enough; he wanted to taste her everywhere, to learn her scent, her texture, the very essence that made Sara Sara. His lips trailed a line of fire to her breasts, lavishing hot, hungry caresses on each as his hands skimmed her slender body, learning her curves, exploring the softness of her flesh. His movements were increasingly restless, no one area claiming his attention for too long, before he was compelled to seek another, more demanding lure. She aroused and pleased him as no other woman ever had, and against her throat he sang a litany of delight. "Ah, *mi amiga*, you are so *preciosa*, so soft. . . ." His teeth nipped her gently and his hands cupped her swollen breasts as he muttered, "You taste of nectar . . . I could eat you alive, consume you, take you within me, so that you could never escape. . . ." He found her mouth and buried his lips on hers, kissing her with a savage urgency.

Sara welcomed his hungry kiss, reveling in his unabashed desire for her, arching up helplessly against him, her hands caressing his broad shoulders and strong arms. He moved wildly against her, his legs tangling with hers, the heat of his long body burning her, the touch of his hands making her ache and yearn for something as yet unknown. Impatiently his hands slid down her body, resting for a moment on her thighs before he opened her legs and touched the golden-honey curls that grew at the apex of her thighs.

A mixture of fear and pleasure speared through Sara as he lightly rubbed the tender flesh he found there. He kissed her deeply as he played with her, indescribable sensations spiraling outward from his caressing fingers, and she twisted mindlessly beneath his ministrations, the demanding ache within her becoming nearly intolerable. Growling his satisfaction at her reaction, he slid his mouth to her throbbing nipples and with his teeth and tongue he continued to stroke the wildfire that was fueling her wanton behavior.

Sara was burning up, her flesh desperately wanting— no, *needing*—succor from the earthy sensations and emotions that were rioting through her, and her own kisses became more agitated, more demanding, her hands moving over him in frantic excitement. When Yancy delved deeper between her legs, his tormenting finger slowly sinking into the warm, moist flesh, Sara's soft shriek of raw pleasure rent the air and she bucked wildly against his blunt invasion.

"Oh, God! Oh, God!" she cried out, half delirious, half frightened by what was happening to her. "I can't bear it! What are you doing to me?"

"Making love to you, *mi amiga*," Yancy said thickly, kissing the corner of her mouth, never stopping the havoc of his teasing finger. "Making your body ready for mine! Making you feel the same hunger that burns within me. . . ." His lips dropped to her breast and he suckled with passionate vigor. "You are so beautiful," he muttered against her breast. "So warm and desirable, so very . . ." He sighed, as if unable to find the words, and kissed her, his tongue tasting the sweetness of her mouth once more.

Feeling consumed by him, her entire body almost vibrating from the force of the erotic demands that controlled her, she thrashed wantonly beneath his caresses as the most intensely pleasurable feelings seemed to center themselves beneath his lazily thrusting finger. Her hands roamed in increasing frenzy over his broad shoulders and back and daringly she trailed her tingling fingers down the front of him, each time her hand sinking lower and lower. . . .

When she finally touched him, feeling the heat and the size and the texture of him, Yancy groaned deep in his throat. "Enough!" he muttered. "Enough! I cannot bear it any longer either! You're driving me crazy, sweetheart!" He suddenly shifted, his hands firmly holding her thighs apart as he sank slowly between her legs.

Sara's breath caught in her throat and, eyes wide, she stared up at his lean, dark face. This was what she wanted, this was what her body craved and yet she couldn't help the tremor of fearful excitement that shook her as he boldly positioned himself and began to push into the hidden heat between her thighs. Instinctively she stiffened, her hands coming up to shove at his chest, but as if sensing her fears, Yancy slipped a hand between their bodies and gently toyed with her, deliberately stoking the fire, making her forget everything but the rightness of this moment.

Despite the raging desire scalding through him, Yancy took her gently. It was instinctive, something about Sara restraining him, some inner wisdom warning him to exert at least some control over his almost savage need to take her, which ultimately made his possession of her slow and indescribably memorable for both of them.

With a tenderness he hadn't realized he was capable of, he coaxed her body to accept his invasion. Inch by sweet inch, he slid slowly within her, the press of her silken heat against his swollen shaft making him grit his teeth as he fought against the urge to plunge deeply, to sink himself to the hilt in one violent motion. His eyes were closed, his head thrown back as he concentrated on what he was doing, savoring each stirring moment of it, but when he reached the barrier that proclaimed her virginity, his eyes snapped open in stunned disbelief.

The sensation of his flesh joining with hers, of feeling her body widening to accommodate his bulk, made Sara shiver with a strange tenderness for him. Her eyes soft and dreamy, her breasts pushing up against his chest, her arms wound around his neck, she accepted him eagerly, the sudden pain catching her by surprise.

For a long, wordless moment they stared at each other and then something leaped into his amber-gold eyes, something fierce and exultant. He grinned triumphantly and then his mouth came down hard on hers, and inexorably he broke through the barrier and possessed her completely.

Lodged deep within her, Yancy relished his victory, forcing himself to remain still, ignoring the questions that whirled in his head, wanting only to imprint indelibly upon his brain forever this treasured joining. But he could not remain still, the elemental desire to complete the act driving him to move. Mindful of her state, he fought to restrain himself, with a mighty effort pacing himself so that he thrust into her with slow, lazy strokes, unconsciously prolonging the sweetness, intensifying the pleasure for them both.

Yancy had taken her so gently, with such unexpected care, that Sara's pain was gone in a flash. There was only a slight discomfort that faded with every exquisitely tender movement of Yancy's big body on hers. She was willingly dominated by him, reveling in the power of his body, in the way his chest was pressing against her breasts, in the way his hands cupped her buttocks and held her to him as he drove time and again into her welcoming sheath. She was so aware of him, so conscious of everything about him—the taste of his flesh, the musky scent of his body, the terrifying and wonderful things he was doing to her—that when he suddenly stiffened and cried out her name in a strangled, tortured tone, the warm wash of pleasure that eddied through her was a surprise.

Sara's eyes flew open in astonishment, the faint tinglings of her own flesh suddenly absorbing all her attention, and she was hardly conscious of Yancy slipping from between her legs to lie at her side, his arms flung across his eyes. She had thought his possession of her had been the most thrilling event that had ever happened to her, and the feel of him thrusting deep within her had been equally exciting, but the other . . . An oddly satisfied smile curved her mouth. Mmm, the other, she decided dreamily as she stretched like a sun-warmed cat, the other had been, oh, sheer bliss!

Her movement on the grass beside him made Yancy turn to her, and oblivious of his nakedness, he again propped himself up with one elbow and stared down into her face. His dark features expressionless, all signs of his earlier passion gone, he asked harshly, "And now, considering what just happened, would you like to explain to me just what the hell sort of marriage you had with my father?"

10

S ara's sweet feeling of satiation vanished at his words and she flushed. Reality hit her like a lightning bolt and the memory of all the mistrust and animosity that lay between them became disturbingly clear in her mind. With a sick sensation in her stomach, she realized that she had been a fool to forget that Yancy was her enemy, that he mistrusted her and had accused her of the ugliest motives in having married his father. He was also her abductor, and a chill feathered down her spine when it occurred to her that his lovemaking had been a coolly calculated maneuver on his part. He had already sworn that he would be the father of her children. How could she help but suspect that what had been a momentous experience for her had merely been the means to an end for Yancy?

A rush of shame overwhelmed her and she scrambled into a sitting position and grabbed up the short calico gown, which lay nearby. With shaking hands she clutched it to her, hotly aware that it did little to cover her naked body.

Yancy's mouth twisted sardonically. "A little late for modesty, wouldn't you say?"

Sara's flush increased and she muttered something distractedly under her breath as she glanced uneasily around for her knickerbockers.

Yancy wasn't the least bothered by their state of undress and he ripped the short gown from her grasp and growled, "*Por Dios*! Tell me about your marriage! Why were you still a virgin? What sort of dark spell did you cast over my father that kept him from your bed?"

Sara's eyes were fixed beseechingly on the scrap of faded material in Yancy's lean hand and she muttered, "Um, we, um, that's what we decided. Now may I please have my clothes?"

Yancy swore violently. "No! What the hell sort of an explanation is that—you decided? What did you do to my father to get him to agree to such an unnatural state?"

"It was what *he* wanted!" she said tightly, snatching futilely at her short gown.

Yancy easily kept it out of her reach and effortlessly fended off her attempts to grab it. "What *he* wanted!" he exclaimed disbelievingly. "You're lying! My father was a healthy, virile man when you married him—there was nothing to stop the consummation of your marriage."

Unhappily, Sara realized that she was not going to get her clothes back until she had explained to his satisfaction her odd marriage to Sam. Sighing, she said, "Your father and I loved each other, but not in the way you think—it was never like that! From the moment I first met him, Sam always treated me like a daughter—there was never any hint of any other emotion—and I . . ." Sara faltered, her eyes filming with tears when she remembered how warm and kind Sam had been to her and how much she still missed him. She bent her head and said huskily, "Over the years I came to think of him as my father." She smiled wryly. "He certainly worried more about my future than Matthew ever did." She looked up at Yancy, her gaze meeting his scornful stare bravely. "No matter what you think, there was never anything else for him in my heart but a daughter's love for her father."

Yancy snorted. "And I suppose it was because he loved you as a *daughter* that he married you?"

Stung, Sara said sharply, "Yes, it was! He wanted to make certain that I would be protected if something happened to him during the war. He said that he had meant to adopt me, but events moved too swiftly for him to do that, and there wasn't much time before he left to join Lee to do anything *but* marry me!" Sara glanced down at her hands, unable to bear Yancy's contemptuous look. Her voice low, she muttered, "From the beginning it was to be only a marriage of convenience and neither of us ever had any intention of making it anything else. The marriage was arranged solely so that Sam could leave Magnolia Grove knowing that, should he die, he had done everything he could to ensure my future." Her eyes darkened emotionally. "He begged me to marry him! The idea shocked me when he first broached it and I refused, until I realized that only by agreeing could I give him any peace of mind. We had planned to have the marriage annulled after the war, but by then Sam was dying . . ." A lump rose in Sara's throat and she added huskily, "The marriage was simply a way of protecting me and it shows just the sort of fine, generous man your father was—marrying me was a totally unselfish gesture on his part!"

Yancy flashed her a derisive glance. "A touching tale, but I'm afraid that I don't believe you."

Angered, Sara lifted her chin and snapped, "Very well, you don't believe me! What do *you* think happened?"

Yancy's mouth tightened and he leaned nearer to her. "I think," he began in a soft, dangerous drawl, "that it was *you* who suggested the marriage! I think that you were the one who was worried about your future and you made certain, the only way you could, that if something happened to him, if your gullible protector was gone, you'd be taken care of!"

"That's simply not true!" Sara replied in horrified accents. "You hardly know me—how can you believe such an ugly thing?"

Yancy laughed bitterly. "You forget that I have met your kind before. I damn near married someone exactly like you, and while she didn't project the same helpless innocence you do, Margaret knew very well what she was about!"

"I am *not* like Margaret!" Sara said fiercely. "I loved your father! I wanted Sam to be happy and I wanted him to have the peace of mind he needed to be able to leave me alone at Magnolia Grove."

"Oh, and, of course, it never occurred to you that by marrying him you were watching out for yourself!"

Stricken, Sara could only stare guiltily at him. She *had* thought of what being Sam's widow would mean, and she would have been the basest sort of liar imaginable if she hadn't realized that by marrying Sam she was, indeed, watching out for her own future. But her own future had not been the main motivation, she thought painfully. She would *never* have considered marrying Sam if he hadn't pressured her into doing so! She had done nothing wrong! "Yes, I knew that I was securing a future for myself by marrying your father," she admitted. "I'd have been a silly twit not to have realized it. Especially since Sam so very kindly pointed it out to me!"

A look of open dislike on his handsome face, Yancy regarded her blackly. "I'll say this for you. You're a hell of a lot more clever than Margaret ever thought of being!" He laughed mirthlessly. "She'd never have admitted her wrongs, but you—you do it with such beguiling candor that it could easily disarm *most* people!"

"But not you."

His amber-gold eyes swept down her naked body. "Oh, no. Not me, lady. Like I said, Margaret taught me just how deceiving and conniving a woman can be— even a sweet-faced little jade like you!"

Sara's bottom lip quivered slightly and she blinked back the tears his harsh words brought to her eyes. "I see," she said with hard-won calmness, "that since you've already made up your mind about me, there is nothing else for us to say on the subject. But tell me, if I am such a despicable creature, if I am as vile as Margaret, how can you even bear for me to possibly be the mother of your child?" Her clear green eyes met his unflinchingly. "That was the purpose of what we just did together, wasn't it?" Some of her anguish bled through the iron control she was keeping on her emotions and she asked huskily, "Wasn't it all part of your plan? The entire reason you abducted me? To make certain that it was *your* child I conceived? So that Casa Paloma would again belong to someone of Alvarez blood?" Her voice shook slightly. "You cold-bloodedly set out to make love to me—you must have planned all this very well—and you dare to accuse me of being conniving? From where I sit, I can't see that your motives are much different from the ones that you accused me of!"

Yancy grabbed her by the shoulders and shook her slightly. "I never planned a damn thing! Except to take you to del Sol!"

"Oh? You're telling me that what happened was just an accident? That you didn't mean to make me pregnant? That you don't hope that a child will result from what we did today?"

"*Demonio*! It wasn't like that at all! I never meant to—" He broke off and scowled at her. "I only meant for us to stop and rest. You'd been in the saddle since shortly after midnight, and when we came to this place I thought"—his scowl deepened—"I thought that a short rest would be good for you before we traveled any further today."

"Is that so?" she asked sweetly. "You had no intention of seducing me? The idea of making love to me hadn't crossed your mind at all?"

He cursed virulently under his breath and pushed her back onto the spring grass. His dark, handsome face looming above hers, his mouth mere tantalizing inches from hers, he muttered, "You little witch! You have to know that since I kissed you in Sam's office I've thought of *nothing* else but making love to you!"

He kissed her roughly, as if he were angry, but whether with her or himself, Sara couldn't tell; she only knew that letting him kiss her was dangerous and that she dared not allow it to continue. She struggled against him, but he was bigger and very determined and she could not dislodge him, his warm, long, muscled length pressing her deeper into the grass. His lips were demanding as they moved over hers, his tongue bluntly forcing itself into her mouth.

Dizzily Sara fought what was happening, frantic to stop him before things went too far. Finally she managed to get an elbow between their locked bodies and twisted her mouth away from his.

"Stop it!" she choked out. "Don't make things any worse than they already are!"

They were both breathing hard and for a long moment they stared at each other, their faces still close together.

The dark desire faded from Yancy's eyes and, a bitter cast to his mouth, he muttered, "I didn't intend this either . . . I . . ." A half-angry, half-bewildered expression crossed his face. "I get near you and I stop thinking about anything but how sweet your mouth would taste, or how much I want to bury myself within you . . . how slick and hot you would feel, how tight, how much pleasure you would give me." He paused, his eyes boring into hers, and he said thickly, "You must believe, Sara, I never meant for this to happen." Honesty made him add, "At least not now. Not here and not like this. I really only meant to give you a respite from our journey. You *have* to believe that when I woke you, it was only to tell you that we had to be leaving. I never meant to kiss you. . . ." He swallowed, his eyes dropping to her soft mouth. "It just happened . . . I didn't plan it. You were just so sweet and irresistible—I meant to kiss you just once, but . . ." Almost compulsively, he brushed his mouth near the corner of hers. "But once I kissed you, I could not stop myself . . . I wanted you." He slowly kissed her again, his lips dragging erotically against hers. Huskily he said, "I want you again . . . now. . . ."

His kiss was black magic, but knowing that if she didn't escape him now, before the demands of her own body befuddled her, there would be *no* escape, Sara tore herself from his embrace and scrambled hastily to her feet. Avoiding looking in his direction and the carnal temptation he offered, she shakily gathered the rest of her scattered clothing and ran blindly to the small creek that edged the area where they had stopped. Dropping her clothes on the dry ground, she stepped right into the rushing water, glad that the creek was deeper than it looked. The sun-warmed water rose almost to her hips. She had a savagely instinctive need to wash the signs and scent of their coupling from her body, as if by destroying any outward evidence she could also obliterate the fact that it had ever happened. Again and again she dunked herself under the water, her hands scrubbing her flesh, frantic to completely erase the tiniest remnant of their passion.

Sara wasn't even aware that she was crying, the tears streaming down her face, until Yancy, having joined her in the creek, pulled her into his arms and said softly, "*Preciosa*! Don't cry! I never meant—" He cursed under his breath and muttered, "I'm sorry. I swear I won't touch you." His mouth twisted bitterly, for he was too aware of his shortcomings where she was concerned. "I mean, I swear I'll try not to touch you again—you're just too damned appealing for your own good!"

She looked up at him. "Then let me go," she said huskily. "Take me back to Magnolia Grove."

Yancy's arms tightened around her and his half-remorseful, half-indulgent expression vanished instantly. His mouth set in hard lines, he said, "No. Don't ask that of me!"

Angrily Sara pushed herself out of his arms and, heedless of her nakedness, waded from the creek. Swiftly donning her clothes, she paid no attention to Yancy as he slowly left the water and garbed himself.

Yancy watched her closely, disturbed and uneasy at the stony set of her lovely face. *Por Dios*! What the hell was he going to do with her? It wasn't meant to be this way! The look on her face tore at his gut, filling him with an angry, guilty despair. He *hadn't* meant to make love to her . . . not this soon anyway, and it had had *nothing* to do with giving her a child or Sam's will!

Walking over to where she stood near the horses, he cleared his throat and muttered, "I made a fire and there's some coffee and sandwiches. I think it might be a good idea if you ate and had some coffee before we leave."

Sara flashed him an angry glance. "Don't be nice to me!"

Yancy held on to his temper with an effort. "Not nice," he finally said. "Sensible! There are still several hours of daylight left and I intend for us to ride until dark. Eat something now or not—but be warned, *chica*: you'll be damned hungry before we stop and make camp."

Sara would have liked to throw his offer of food in his face, but her stomach rumbled just then and she spun on her heels and stalked over to where a small fire burned. In an unfriendly silence, they drank the boiled coffee and ate the thick sandwiches that Yancy had brought with him.

It was only when they were remounted and preparing to ride on that Yancy spoke. His horse standing next to hers, the reins of her mount and the pack horse's lead rope firmly held in one of his hands, he looked at her averted profile and said softly, "Sara, I can't undo what's been done—I don't even know that I want to—but you must believe that I didn't plan what happened."

"I asked you to believe me about Sam, but you didn't. Well, now it's my turn to return the favor." She flashed him a look full of fire and, her eyes dark and stormy, said fiercely, *"I don't believe you!"* Averting her face once more, she stared blindly in the opposite direction from him.

Yancy studied the delicate, stony-faced profile presented to him for a long time, stunned by the feeling of pain that knotted in his chest. His mouth tightened. *Cristo!* He was *not* going to be taken in again by a pretty face! No matter what strange and powerful feelings she aroused in the region of his heart—he'd suffered through that once and wasn't about to do it again—no matter how tempting the bait! Margaret had wreaked enough havoc and anguish in his life to last him until the end of his days, and no matter how beguiling Sara appeared, no matter how sweetly vulnerable she looked, no matter how desirable he found her, he was *not* going to fall into that trap again! Not ever!

His voice clipped, he said, "Have it your way, then!"

The silence that now accompanied them on their journey was not pleasant, and though they had not spoken often previously, there was not one word exchanged between them during the next several hours. The stop had delayed them far longer than Yancy had planned, and since he had a specific destination in mind for their night's camp, he pushed them hard, even continuing to ride long after the sun had set.

Not a seasoned horsewoman, although she had ridden off and on all her life, Sara ached in every bone and muscle of her body as the miles passed. As the light faded and the darkness descended, she was thoroughly miserable, hungry, weary and achy, but she bore it all without an outward sign of distress. She swore she'd *die* before she'd ask Yancy to stop, but she couldn't help the grateful little groan that came from her when Yancy finally halted the horses and said, "We'll camp here for the night."

It was too dark for Sara to distinguish much about her surroundings, but she gathered from the faint gurgle of running water and the scattered dark shapes of trees that it was a spot very similar to the place they had stopped at earlier. She dismounted clumsily, shoving away Yancy's hand when he offered to help her. Teeth gritted together, she muttered, "Don't touch me!"

Yancy sighed exasperatedly and turned away, busying himself with securing the horses and unsaddling them. Sara stood there glaring at him uncertainly until he said coolly over his shoulder, "If you're not going to help, go find somewhere to sit down and stay out of my way."

Normally the most considerate of creatures, Sara tossed her tangled hair and said sharply, "Since I'm here under duress, I don't think you can reasonably expect me to help you in any way!"

He slanted her an unreadable glance in the darkness. "Yeah, sweetheart," he said acidly, "I'm sure that I can't expect you to do *any*thing reasonably!"

"I'm glad we understand each other!" she retorted.

The open hostility between them did not lessen, and after bolting down another meal of sandwiches and coffee, Sara was glad to seek relief in sleep. Earlier Yancy had placed her saddle a little distance from the small fire he had started and had thrown down a couple of blankets. "Madam's bed," he had said dryly.

At first glance, it didn't seem very inviting, but after what she had gone through since the last time she had been in a bed, Sara found it more comfortable than she would have suspected. Her head resting on the saddle, her belly full, and wrapped in her blankets, Sara was asleep almost the instant she lay down.

The same couldn't be said for Yancy. He sat at the side of the lazy little fire, his brooding gaze locked onto Sara's sleeping form. She was, in more ways than he cared to think about, a dilemma for him. He had planned her abduction to del Sol with an almost lighthearted zeal, certain in his own mind that it was what he needed to do in order to protect Sara from her own foolishness. Her idea of living at Casa Paloma was ludicrous—the damned place was in danger of falling down, and in trying to repair it, she'd end up squandering every penny she'd inherited from Sam. His mouth thinned. Not that he really cared. It just wasn't practical, he told himself grimly. And there was the matter of Sam's will.

Por Dios! What in hell had Sam been thinking of when he had tied up the disposal of Casa Paloma in such a way? Even if Yancy believed that Sara had been instrumental in convincing Sam to put such a requirement in his will, he had trouble persuading himself that Sam had been so totally besotted to go along with her scheming. Hadn't his father learned anything from Margaret? Besides, Sam had known how *he* felt about Casa Paloma! Yancy smiled bitterly. Hell! He'd threatened to kill Margaret to keep *her* from getting her grasping claws on the place—what did his father think he'd do to Sara? Sam would have had to know that he'd do everything in his power to make certain that Casa Paloma returned to the Alvarez lands.

In the act of taking a last sip of coffee from his tin cup, Yancy froze. Of course! That conniving old bastard! Even from the grave he was trying to manipulate him! His mouth twisted. And this time Sam had baited the trap with an almost irresistible lure—Sara!

Frowning, Yancy tossed aside his empty cup. Had Sam known how attractive he found Sara? Had his father put in that damnable clause simply to ensure that he was well and truly snared?

Yancy shook his head bewilderedly. Despite their differences, and there had been many, he would never have believed his father capable of such devious maneuverings. Sam had been a kind, generous man, which gave credence to Sara's version of the situation, but his father had also been weak-willed and easily swayed, and Yancy found it impossible to believe that Sam had methodically thought out a plan that would unite his widow and his son. And yet the unsettling idea nagged at him that Sara might be telling the truth. . . . Yancy was suddenly suffused with a powerful wash of hope, but then it faded almost immediately, Margaret's memory and her betrayal inexorably rising through him. No! He was not being tricked again! Never again would he lose his head over a pretty face and a beguiling smile! Never!

There were, he finally decided wearily, no easy answers and none that fully satisfied him—not even blaming everything on Sara! And, the Lord knew, he would have liked to do just that! Grumbling and swearing under his breath, he eventually settled himself next to her on the ground. Time had a way of revealing all truths and he sure as the devil wasn't going to resolve anything tonight. Tomorrow and in the days that followed he would plumb the riddle of Sara Cantrell.

Instinctively, his body curved itself spoon-fashion along Sara's. Yancy told himself his position was necessary because he needed to be close to her in case she tried to escape. He was an incredibly light sleeper and he was confident that she couldn't make the slightest move without waking him. As for her escaping—his horses were trained to obey only his commands, a necessary precaution when one lived as he had amidst Indians who were famous horse thieves. As a further precaution, he'd hidden her boots! Even if she did manage to slip away from him as he slept, without a horse and barefoot, she wasn't going to get far. Smiling at his own cleverness, he fell asleep.

11

The next morning, Yancy wasn't smiling, nor was he feeling particularly clever. He had slept well and nothing untoward had occurred—Sara was still sleeping deeply at his side when he woke at first light—but despite a restful night, Yancy was irritatingly aware that none of his problems had been resolved. Sara was *still* the dilemma she had been before he'd gone to sleep, and the chilly shoulder she gave him as their long trek continued did not abate one jot!

The journey to del Sol was not something that Sara ever looked back on with any pleasure. They spoke only when necessary, both of them keeping the communication between them to a bare minimum. The journey was not particularly dangerous or arduous, although Yancy did keep them in the saddle for long hours, but Sara welcomed it—at least the passing scenery afforded some view other than the abominable sight of her arrogant, overbearing, *wretched* abductor! At first Sara remained totally aloof when Yancy would set about making camp for them, but eventually her conscience pricked her, though why it should she couldn't guess, and she began to take a more active role in the day-to-day chores. By the time they had been on the trail for ten days, they had worked out a system between them and could make a comfortable camp in a matter of minutes.

Despite the animosity that fairly shimmered in the air between them, it was not a time that was completely *un*pleasant. The countryside they rode through had an almost tropical lushness to it that delighted the eye and beguiled the senses, and after the first several days, as she became more used to her horse and saddle, Sara found that she thoroughly enjoyed riding. She was free of the cares and demands that had rested for too long on her young, slender shoulders at Magnolia Grove, and even with all the difficulties that lay before her, Sara's spirits rose with every mile that passed. She was strangely eager to see del Sol and the chaparral and brush country that surrounded it.

After the long hours in the saddle, she looked forward to camp each evening, and since there was little to distract her, she spent most of the time musing at the queerness of fate before retiring to her rough bed upon the ground. Often, after a hasty meal of corn bread, which was baked in the hot ashes of the campfire, and a savory stew of whatever game Yancy had killed, Sara was reminded of similar nights with her father. Happy memories would flood her and she would smile to herself, enjoying the tranquility of the moment. Sometimes, though, sipping her hot coffee, she would stare at the leaping red-and-gold flames, wondering about the life she might have had if Matthew had not gambled away Mockingbird Hill—or if he had not been so foolish as to get himself killed. She would give herself a shake, not willing to dwell on the not-so-pleasant past.

As they continued to ride, the terrain and vegetation changed gradually, the land becoming drier and less overpoweringly tropical, the tall, stately trees, rampant vines and profusely blooming wildflowers slowly disappearing. The soil was no longer the fertile bottomland so prized by the planters and the country became more open, the horizon extending endlessly before them. The days were hotter, too, less humid the farther inland they rode, but Sara grew used to the blistering heat of the hot yellow sun.

By mid-May they had reached the vast rolling prairies, riding through grasses that were waist-high and past patches of thorny acacia, tall prickly pear and mesquite. Near the creeks and streams, the growth was luxurious, cottonwoods and black willows crowding next to one another, and Sara was astonished by the incredible variety of wildlife they saw. Vast herds of mustangs and long-horned cattle roamed everywhere, yet the country was also full of rabbits, turkeys, quail, deer and antelope. At night they were serenaded by the mournful howls of the coyotes and big lobo wolves, the frightening scream of the occasional panther making itself heard now and then.

Sara had kept the conversation to a minimum between them, but one night after they had eaten, curiosity getting the better of her, she asked suddenly, "How much farther is it to the rancho?"

Yancy smiled. "You've been on it the past two days." Ignoring her openmouthed amazement, he went on smoothly. "I reckon we'll sleep in real beds tomorrow night."

Despite all the reasons why she shouldn't be, Sara was eager and intensely curious to finally see del Sol. It was late afternoon the next day when they topped a small rise and she caught sight of a black dot in the distance, and her heart leaped. Glancing across at Yancy, she asked excitedly, "Is that it? Is that del Sol?"

Yancy nodded slowly. "*Sí*, that is my home." He paused, his amber-gold eyes resting for a long time on her lovely features, and Sara was aware of an odd air of cautiousness about him—almost, she thought in surprise, as if he were *shy* . . . or uneasy about her reaction to del Sol. Just when the silence was becoming uncomfortable, he turned his gaze forward and said quietly, "I hope you will be happy here."

He kicked his horse into movement, and as Sara's followed obediently behind, they began to ride toward the place that was at the moment only a mere dot on the horizon. Sara was introspective as they rode toward del Sol, her thoughts on Yancy's odd behavior. It took her a few minutes to guess the reason behind his inexplicably wary air—*Margaret*!

Sara wasn't too surprised at Yancy's protective reserve. From everything that she had ever heard about Margaret's lone trip to del Sol, it was glaringly obvious that Margaret had plainly *loathed* the place! In fact, Margaret's open detestation of the very idea of living at del Sol was what had, supposedly, driven her into Sam's arms. It was only natural that Yancy would be a bit uneasy about Sara's reaction.

A gentle smile curved her mouth. It shouldn't have, but somehow that almost shy air about him melted some of her resentment against him and his arrogant behavior.

As they approached del Sol, Sara realized that the dot was actually a cluster of buildings, and with every mile they rode, it became apparent that Yancy's home was not just a house but an entire village. The site was breathtaking; the rolling prairies of rich grass, broken only by the trees and bushes which lined the streams and creeks, seemed to go on as far as the eye could see. Del Sol had been built on a slight rise, near one of the sparkling blue-green streams, and as they rode closer, Sara marveled at the abundance of towering trees and abundant grass that grew in the area. Fanning outward from the hacienda—and there was no mistaking its stockade-like walls or its imposing size and height—were several far less grand structures, small *jacales* and barns, a gleaming white church and other squat adobe buildings. There were corrals and patches of cultivated ground, orange trees and grapes laid out in tidy areas, and in other places the bright green of newly planted corn was unmistakable. As they rode between the buildings, chickens, pigs and goats, squawking, oinking and bleating, scattered in front of their horses.

Sara's senses were vividly assaulted as she tried to absorb everything—the blinding white of the buildings, the scent of orange blossom in the air, the excited sounds of children and the herds of cattle and horses that grazed in the distance, their movements carefully monitored by swarthy-skinned riders on tough little mustang ponies. There was a narrow dusty trail which meandered through the area, leading to the hacienda with its thick, protective walls glistening as bright as new-fallen snow, and some of Sara's exhilaration with her surroundings faded. Del Sol was, after all, to be her prison.

They had barely reached the first buildings before they were suddenly greeted exuberantly by a mob of dusky-skinned, half-naked, bashfully smiling children and dark-eyed, laughing women wearing shawls in brilliant colors of blue, scarlet and yellow and sombrero-clad men in loose, baggy white pants. The warm afternoon air was filled with cries of delight.

"Ah, Senor Yancy, you have returned to us!"

"It is El Patrón! Hurry, hurry, El Patrón is here!"

"Senor! Senor Yancy, long have we waited for you!"

"Oh, senor! It is *good* to have you back with us again!"

Their progress was slow as Yancy stopped to talk with people. Small children were continually being eagerly introduced and held up and thrust forward for his inspection, and Sara was startled at the depth of respect and affection that was lavished on him. It was obvious that he was greatly loved and that these people looked upon him as very nearly a god. Sara snorted.

No wonder he was such an overbearing, imperious devil!

Eventually the small crowd fell behind them and Sara and Yancy rode through the huge, beaten-iron gates that guarded the entrance to the hacienda grounds. Sara had been halfway prepared for what she would find inside, but even so, she sat there staring spellbound at the inviting loveliness that lay before her.

Another world, a world of graciousness and wealth, a world that would have been greatly familiar to an old-world Spanish grandee, had been created behind those massive eight-foot-high walls. The hacienda site encompassed nearly five acres, and where there were no buildings, from what Sara could see, it was composed of stretches of green lawns dotted with neat rows of orange and olive trees, and scattered in charming disarray were other shrubs and trees more native to the area. She spied a stream flowing gently through a far corner, but immediately in front of her was a flagstone courtyard, a magnificent three-tiered fountain bubbling with sweet, clear water in its center. Beyond the courtyard lay the stately hacienda. The two-storied, pale ocher building looked larger than it actually was. Wide, covered, blessedly cool walkways with gracefully arched openings and balconies with delicate iron grillwork surrounded the main structure. Purple bougainvillea draped itself attractively near one corner; a heavily scented pale pink rose climbed at the other and a jasmine-festooned portico jutted out into the courtyard. Sara was utterly enchanted.

Here again, as it had been through the village, they were suddenly inundated by a crowd of excited, dark-eyed, dark-skinned Mexicans, their pleasure at Yancy's return obvious. It was several moments before Yancy could even dismount from his horse and a few moments after that before he turned to Sara. Aware of several discreetly speculative glances sent her way, Sara wondered just what Yancy would tell them about her; she understood a smattering of Spanish, as did most people who had lived in Texas for any time, but her command of the language was not great. When Yancy's hands tightened around her waist and he swung her gently from the saddle, she had no trouble picking out the word *novia*, however, from the swift stream of Spanish he spoke to the gathered crowd.

There were unmistakable cries of gladness and voluble congratulations, and keeping a smile on her face, Sara hissed out of the corner of her mouth, "I am *not* your *novia*! How could you tell them that I am your fiancée!"

Yancy drew her nearer to his side, and keeping one arm ruthlessly anchored around her waist and an easy smile on his mouth, he murmured, "But you are, sweetheart. Did you think that I would allow my children to be born without my name?"

Her smile faltered just a tiny bit, but her eyes sparked dangerous green fire, and she muttered, "I'm not pregnant—and I'm not about to be married for my broodmare capabilities!"

Yancy's arm tightened almost painfully around her waist, and to the delight of the onlookers, he pulled her to him and kissed her soundly. Against her stinging lips he whispered, "Has it ever dawned on you, my prickly little dove, that I may not give a *damn* about your 'broodmare capabilities'?"

When Sara stared up at his dark face in astonishment, he laughed and kissed her again—much to the vociferous pleasure of the onlookers. Not giving Sara a chance to recover, Yancy began to introduce her to those gathered around them, explaining to her that these were the house servants and that many of them were descendants of the family retainers who had followed the first Alvarez from Spain into Mexico and then into Texas. Sara smiled and nodded, nodded and smiled and wondered if she would ever remember any of their names. Not that it mattered, she told herself stoutly; she wasn't going to be staying here long! She kept reminding herself grimly of that fact when, eventually, the group dispersed and a smiling, black-eyed beauty near her own age led her through the house and along a cool, shaded walkway at the rear to a spacious room in one of the wings of the sprawling building.

As they walked, Sara had a glimpse of large, airy rooms, the cool tile floors broken here and there by richly hued rugs, the furnishings an elegant mix of the simple Mexican style and the darker, heavily carved fashion of the Spanish. She was enchanted to discover that at the rear of the house there was another courtyard, in the center of which was an almost exact duplicate of the three-tiered fountain in front. The hacienda was shaped like U, the three sides of the house enclosing the smaller courtyard, the covered, arched-opening walkways endowing it with a cozy, private feeling. Again there were bougainvillea vines and roses strewn along the iron-worked balconies of the upper floor, white jasmine twining here and there, and the heady scent of jasmine and damask roses mingled with the faint hint of orange blossom in the warm air.

Under different circumstances, Sara would have thoroughly enjoyed herself, and as it was, she had to remind herself constantly that she was not here by her own choice—this was no *visit*! The sight of the wide mosquito-netted bed had every bone in her body yearning to test its softness, and when the woman at her side said softly, "I speak some English—that is why Senor Yancy asked me to show you to your room and told me that I am to be your maid. He said that you were very tired from your journey and he thought that the senorita would enjoy a bath. Should I have one prepared for you?" Sara thought she would swoon with pleasure.

Her delight obvious, Sara replied warmly, "Oh, I would like it above all things!" Smiling with disarming charm, she looked at the woman before her and admitted honestly, "I am afraid that I do not remember your name."

The woman chuckled and said, "I am not surprised! My name is Maria Chavez. I am married to Senor Yancy's head vaquero and my *madre* is the housekeeper, Dolores Fernandez, and my *padre* is Juan, El Patrón's bookkeeper. You met them just a few minutes ago, except for Esteban, my husband."

Sara shook her head. "I'm sorry, but I don't remember them at all!"

Maria smiled. "Do not worry, senorita, you will have all your life to learn our names and know our families. Now, if you will excuse me, I shall see about your bath."

It was only after Maria had left that it occurred to Sara that she had not corrected Maria's "senorita," and she wondered if Yancy had mentioned the fact that she was his father's widow. Somehow she rather doubted it!

The bath was wonderful, everything she had dreamed it would be, and after all the weeks of hasty morning scrubs in cool streams and creeks, it was bliss to relax in the warm, jasmine-scented water and to lather her entire body with a delicately perfumed soap and to wash her hair until it was so clean it squeaked.

Maria had brought her a pitcher of sangria, and sipping the wine-and-fruit-juice punch, wearing nothing but a large white towel, completely relaxed from her bath, Sara allowed herself the luxury of trying out the bed. It was as soft as she had imagined, and she carefully set down her glass of sangria on a pine table near the huge bed and let her slender body slowly melt into the welcoming softness of the feather-filled mattress. For a moment all her troubles vanished and before she was aware of it, she drifted off into a deep sleep.

Dusk was falling when Yancy entered her room and found her still asleep. In the intervening time, he, too, had bathed and changed his travel-stained clothing, but there had been no rest for him—the rancho had been in the capable hands of his staff all during the long years of the war, but there was a multitude of news and information that he needed to absorb. Only once, immediately after Lee had surrendered to Grant at Appomattox, had he been able to return to the rancho before now. That trip after the war had been lightning-swift—more to apprise his people that he was alive and well and that he would resign his commission and return to them permanently just as soon as it was possible. Listening to the reports of his men had taken him longer than he had planned, and he had learned that for all his eagerness to return, the affairs of the rancho could have gone on at the same placid pace indefinitely without his hand at the helm. But all that was going to change now.

El Patrón had finally returned, and he had plans for the future.

Of which, he thought pensively as he stared down at Sara, not a few involved this mesmerizing little creature lying there so defenselessly in front of him. His expression was both jubilant and troubled as he continued to gaze at her slender form, his eyes lingering on the shapely legs revealed by the towel. What the devil was he going to do with her? A smile lifted one corner of his mouth. Oh, he knew what he wanted to do with her—getting her to agree with his plans was the problem!

It had been no ruse when he had introduced her to his people as his *novia*—long before they had reached del Sol, he had decided that he was going to marry Sara, no matter how much he mistrusted her or how much her avaricious tendencies disappointed and infuriated him. Even before he had set eyes on Sara again, he had decided that his own marriage was long overdue and that before the year was ended, he would have himself a bride. He had three logical, eminently practical reasons for this decision: he would be thirty-five years old next February, he owned a vast estate and was incredibly wealthy . . . and he had no heir. It was time he gave some serious thought to the next generation, and unfortunately—at least he'd always considered it unfortunate in the past—legitimate heirs could not be begotten unless one had a wife.

Which brought him to Sara. With something perilously close to tenderness, he gazed at her, noting the sweet curve of her cheek, the soft temptation of her mouth and the sensual lure of her half-naked body. But even more than these obvious charms, something about her had always called to him, he couldn't deny it—no matter if she had schemed to get her grasping little hands on his fortune! It was true, Sam's will did force his hand, but he doubted that even to regain Casa Paloma would he have tied himself to a woman he hated or to one who didn't arouse him.

He smiled faintly. There was no doubt that Sara aroused him. Even now he could feel his body hardening, desire running through him, and the urge to lie down on that bed beside her and kiss her awake was nearly overpowering, but he held back. He had been oddly relieved that she was not pregnant, that no child would result from that unbearably sweet coupling beneath the live oaks, and for reasons that he dared not explore too closely, he didn't want her to believe that it had been only to meet the requirements of Sam's will that he had abducted her and made love to her. For those same unexplored reasons, it was also important that Sara understand that his willingness to marry her had nothing to do with that damned will.

And yet, with blunt candor he coolly admitted to himself that the conditions of his father's will made her the most logical candidate for his hand, and if he viewed the situation unemotionally, it shouldn't matter to him at all *what* Sara thought of his reasons for marrying her. A hard expression suddenly crossed his face. Considering how she had schemed to put him in precisely this position, she should be ecstatically pleased that her plan had actually worked!

It was that hard expression on his dark face that Sara saw when she first woke, and the sight of it galvanized her. She sprang upright, frantically clutching her slipping towel. "What are *you* doing here?" she demanded breathlessly, unaware of how seductive she looked with her golden-honey hair falling in tumbled waves around her bare shoulders and her long legs showing from beneath the towel.

"Now, is that any way to greet your *novio*?" Yancy drawled, a glint of devilment dancing in his eyes, his thumbs hooked into the wide black belt he wore around his lean waist.

"You're not my *novio*!" Sara spat furiously, her cheeks flushed with temper. "You may have abducted me from Magnolia Grove and presently you might have me at your mercy, but under no circumstances am I ever going to consent to marry you!" Rashly, she added, "And you can't make me!"

She knew it was a mistake the moment the words left her mouth. His lazy air vanished and, his mouth grim, he reached for her, jerking her into his arms.

He kissed her bruisingly. "You silly little fool—I can make you do anything I want," he growled against her mouth. "You forget that you are in my domain now.

There is a priest in the village, a priest who owes his living to me, and all around you are my people. Do you really think that I could not have my priest marry us—that I need *your* cooperation to accomplish our marriage?" He laughed, some of his anger vanishing. The brutal hold on her arms lessening, he said easily, "Sweetheart, you can't stop me from doing whatever I damn well please! And you would do well to remember that fact! Try my temper too far and you might come to rue the day you met me."

His words frightened her, but she had no intention of letting him know that, and lifting her chin pugnaciously, she said fiercely, "I *already* rue the day I met you, so it would seem that I have nothing to fear!"

Yancy stared at her for a long moment, an odd smile slanting across his face. He pulled her back against him and brushed his mouth against hers. "Then I have no reason not to do as I please, do I?"

Before Sara had time to guess his intent, he was pushing her down into the welcoming softness of the feather bed. They fell together, Yancy's big body half covering hers, his mouth closing unerringly over hers.

Infuriated by his actions, Sara fought him, but the towel proved no barrier to Yancy's seeking hands. Effortlessly he flung it aside, and as his lips slid like sweet fire down her throat to her breasts, she groaned half in pleasure, half in rage at what he was doing to her. Determined not to give in to him, she stubbornly tried to ignore the sweet sensations beginning to course through her body, but for just a moment, when his hand traveled down her belly and she knew what he was seeking, she almost forgot why she was fighting him. . . .

His seeking fingers found the slick, moist warmth between her thighs and Sara's whole body fairly hummed from the sudden stab of desire that shuddered through her.

It would be so easy, she thought hazily, so easy to lose herself in his arms, so easy to let him seduce her into compliance, so easy . . .

She was still trembling on the brink of capitulation when Yancy rose from the bed and hastily stripped away his clothing. It was a tactical error on his part, because while he was swift in his actions, it gave Sara just long enough to realize how dangerously close she was to letting him manipulate her once more.

She had hesitated almost too long, but even as Yancy's naked body came down on the bed beside her, she rolled away from him, intent upon putting a safe distance between them. Yancy would have none of it, though, and in spite of Sara's fists beating on his chest, he pulled her closer to him. Her hands caught between their thrashing bodies, she suffered his kiss, and while there was fire in her gaze when he lifted his head, it was the fire of fury, not passion.

"Let me go!" she hissed at him, her face flushed and her eyes bright with anger. What he might have replied was lost when the door to their room opened unexpectedly.

Startled, Sara turned to look in that direction and she was suffused with embarrassment, as was poor Maria, who stood frozen in the doorway, carrying a tray of fresh sangria and warm, fragrant sweet cakes. Maria instantly averted her horrified gaze and, not looking in their direction, hastily placed the tray on a nearby table and beat a frantic retreat from the room.

Sara's cheeks were every bit as red as Maria's had been, but Yancy . . . Yancy sprawled out beside Sara on the bed and let out a whoop of laughter. Scrambling upright and clutching the towel protectively in front of her, Sara glared at him.

"I don't find this at all amusing!" she said tightly.

Yancy only smiled at her. "Don't you, sweetheart? Well, quite frankly, from my point of view it couldn't have turned out better!" His eyes dancing with wicked satisfaction, he drawled, "Now try telling everyone that you are not my *novia*!"

⚭ 12

For a long time after Yancy had left her, an infuriatingly smug smile on his hard mouth, Sara remained on the rumpled bed, staring blindly at the swaths of mosquito netting overhead. Her thoughts were not kind.

Aware that she was accomplishing nothing by just lying there, Sara eventually roused herself. Appropriate apparel seemed to be her most immediate need and she viewed the heap of travel-stained clothes on the floor near the brass tub with distaste. Although she hadn't seen any of the contents, she knew that in the saddlebags on the pack horse there were other things to wear—on one of their friendlier days, Yancy had told her that he'd had Tansy pick out several items for her to wear until the remainder of her clothes arrived at del Sol. At the moment, however, the decidedly shabby calico gown and well-worn knickerbockers seemed to be her only choice. Clasping the towel more tightly around her naked body, she reluctantly approached the pile on the floor.

Fortunately, before she was forced to don the soiled clothing, there was a loud rap on the door, and at Sara's command, the heavy mahogany-and-iron door was pushed open. Maria stood in the opening, holding the heavy leather saddlebags in her arms. Not meeting Sara's eyes, with no sign of her former warm friendliness, Maria marched across the room and laid the saddlebags on the bed. Stiffly she muttered, "Senor Yancy said that you would need these things. Would you like me to unpack them for you and hang the garments in the wardrobe?"

Sara's cheeks flushed, hot shame flooding through her at the memory of Maria's stunned face when she had seen her in Yancy's arms. It was obvious, too, that Maria was still very embarrassed by the intimate scene she had interrupted earlier and that she heartily disapproved of such a shocking breach of morality. It was depressingly obvious that Sara's reputation had been gravely damaged and that in Maria's eyes she was a fallen, disgraced woman.

Sara sighed, resentment against Yancy building in her breast. Quietly she said, "Thank you for bringing me the clothes, but no, I don't need you to unpack for me—I can do it myself." She sent Maria a tentative smile and added lightly, "As you can see, there really aren't that many things."

Maria ignored her friendly overture and merely nodded and said coolly, "Then if you don't need me, I shall be on my way." Her body rigid with disapproval, she turned around and began to walk away. At the door, her back still to Sara, she said reluctantly, "There is a bell rope by the bed. If you want me, all you have to do is pull it—it rings a bell in the kitchen."

What Sara would have liked to do with the heavy velvet rope was to put it around Yancy's neck and strangle him, but she only said meekly, "Thank you, Maria. You've been very helpful."

Her depression growing, Sara unenthusiastically turned her gaze on the dusty saddlebags. Crossing to the bed, she began to unpack, pleased to see the amount and variety of clothing that Tansy had managed to stuff into the saddlebags. She shook out two gowns and a calico wrapper, and laid aside three pairs of fine muslin drawers and two delicately embroidered chemises, along with a whale-bone corset. There were several other items that Tansy had thoughtfully packed, and after dressing herself in underclothes and a dark green, heavy skirt, which she topped with a favorite puffed muslin chemisette, Sara busied herself with hanging up the remaining garments in the cavernous wardrobe, which took up nearly one entire wall of her bedroom. She was furious at Tansy's betrayal, but she had to admit that Tansy had included just about everything she would need—even a chintz wrapper and a much-preferred soft muslin nightgown.

Feeling adequately armored by her undergarments, drawers, petticoat and chemise, and once her hair was neatly arranged in its usual tidy cornet of honey-colored braids, Sara straightened her shoulders and ventured forth from her room. She was aware that if word of her indiscretion with Yancy had spread to the other servants, Maria's attitude toward her was likely to be repeated by everyone else. Sara was not as serene as she looked as she strolled down the wide covered walkway toward the main part of the hacienda. Inwardly she was shaking and nearly sick at the thought of being the object of everyone's condemnation. Much to her great relief, it appeared that Maria had held her tongue, for the two servants she passed on her way smiled warmly at her and greeted her shyly.

Darkness had fallen, but the walkways were lit by the soft glow of lanterns hung on either side of graceful arches, the patio bathed in a faint golden light. If Sara had thought the patio beautiful and appealing earlier, seeing it now by lantern light utterly beguiled her. The sound of the tinkling fountain drew her, and she was delighted to note the bright flashes of goldfish swimming lazily in its depths.

Everything about del Sol that Sara had seen so far enchanted her, from its dark-eyed, soft-spoken people to this lovely, inviting flagstone patio, and she wondered with a frown how Margaret could have taken such a vehement dislike to the place. Granted she had not explored the entire hacienda, but obviously it was an unexpected oasis of luxurious comfort and opulent elegance in the vast, trackless wilds of Texas. And even if, during her one and only visit, the place had been crumbling and neglected as others had indicated, couldn't Margaret have seen its obvious potential? Had she been blind? Or had she used the condition of del Sol at that time as an excuse to throw herself into Sam's arms? It was a disturbing idea and deliberately Sara turned her thoughts to other things; she had enough to worry about without speculating uselessly on the motives of a woman long-dead . . . a murdered woman.

Standing there in the tranquil, softly glowing golden patio, for a second Sara was conscious of a frisson of uneasiness down her spine. Had Yancy killed Margaret? Was she now in the hands of a murderer? Again instinct told her that she was foolish to think such thoughts, but she was conscious that until Margaret's murder was solved neither she nor anyone who had been touched by Margaret's malignant personality would ever be completely free from unexpected moments of ugly suspicion and fear.

Muttering exasperatingly to herself, with an effort Sara firmly wrenched her mind away from further unproductive musings, and after one last look at the bright red-and-gold flashes of the darting fish, she continued on her way to the front section of the hacienda. Entering the commodious main *sala*, Sara hesitated, uncertain of her destination. The sound of male voices came to her and as she turned in their direction, she spied Yancy walking toward her, tall and breathtaking in a white, full-sleeved shirt open at the throat and a pair of well-fitting black breeches and boots. At his side, almost trotting to keep up with his long stride, was a much shorter, roundly shaped older gentleman who wore the frock and accoutrements of a priest.

Sara's heart sank. A *priest*! A ghastly sensation passed through her. What if Yancy had told the priest of their earlier intimacy? The thought of facing the moral outrage she was certain she would see in the little priest's eyes almost made her run from the room. Telling herself that *she* had done nothing wrong, that Yancy's soul was no doubt blacker than Satan's himself, she forced herself to remain where she was, a polite smile fixed on her mouth.

A mocking gleam in the depths of his amber-gold eyes, Yancy sauntered near her and murmured, "Ah, there you are, my dear! Let me introduce you to Padre Quintero. I have invited him to share our *antojitos* with us this first night in your new home, and he is most eager to meet the woman I intend to marry."

Wishing fiercely that she had the courage to shout out the truth, Sara felt her smile become even more fixed, but she did not refute Yancy's words. Mentally cursing herself for being such a coward, she politely nodded to the little priest, relieved yet puzzled that Padre Quintero displayed no condemnation toward her.

Once the initial introductions were completed and they had seated themselves in comfortable chairs of rich oxblood-red Spanish leather, Padre Quintero leaned forward with a twinkle in his brown eyes and lightly patted Sara's hand where it lay on the arm of her chair. "Yancy has already explained your situation to me," he murmured gently, "and while I abhor the fact that he deemed it necessary to marry you first in a civil ceremony in San Felipe, I cannot express how elated I am that he wants to do the proper thing and marry you again, here at del Sol among his people, in a Catholic service."

How she kept from gaping like a village idiot at the smiling little priest, Sara never knew. Recovering herself slightly from what she had just heard, Sara shot a fulminating glance at Yancy. What an unscrupulous *devil* he was! Telling the priest that they were already married! She had to admit, however, that he had certainly concocted a clever lie to salvage her reputation with his people, and she supposed she should be grateful for his quick action. Regrettably, she wasn't—not in the least! Forcing a bright smile on her face, she tore her furious gaze away from the mocking amusement in Yancy's eyes and looked at Padre Quintero. "Oh, you can always trust my *husband*"—and she nearly choked on the word as she said it—"to do whatever *he* considers appropriate!"

Yancy sent her a seraphic smile, and for one moment Sara was so consumed with rage that she actually saw scarlet spots dance in front of her eyes. There were several similar incidents like that during the time that followed, but somehow she got through the remainder of the evening, her temper not at all helped by Yancy's infuriatingly solicitous behavior or the provocative glances he sent her way when he had said something particularly provoking.

It was with great relief that she finally bade the chatty little priest good night and fled to the sanctuary of her room. But even there solace was denied her. An embarrassingly penitent Maria was waiting for her, and Sara had hardly stepped through the doorway before Maria exclaimed, "Oh, senora, can you forgive me! I did not know that you and Senor Yancy were already married!" Her dark eyes full of misery and begging for forgiveness, she said breathlessly, "It was very wrong of me to act as I did in any case, but once Senor Yancy came to me and so kindly explained about your marriage in San Felipe, I understood completely." Maria hung her head. "I should not have burst in on you that way, and truly, it was very wrong of me to treat you so coldly. I am so ashamed! Will you forgive me?"

Feeling absolutely wretched about Maria's unnecessary abashment and furious with Yancy for creating this situation, Sara said quickly, "Oh, please, do not even mention it! You did nothing wrong. Let us *forget* it!"

Her face wreathed in smiles, Maria breathed, "Oh, senora! You are so kind! No wonder Senor Yancy loves you so!" Shyly, she added, "I knew that there had to be some explanation. Senor Yancy is such a *good* man— he would do nothing that was improper!"

Her teeth fairly grinding together, Sara managed to say "Oh, yes! Senor Yancy is indeed a paragon! Now, if you will excuse me, I would like to retire for the night."

Her eyes lowered, a smile twitching at the corners of her mouth, Maria said archly, "Ah, I understand—the senor is impatient to join his bride. I shall leave you immediately and not disturb you again until the morning." She smiled slyly. "*Late* in the morning."

Only when the door had closed behind Maria's voluptuous figure was Sara able to give full vent to her frustration. Muttering and swearing disgracefully, she threw herself down on the bed and beat her fists into the feather-filled mattress. By envisioning all of the horrible fates she would like to inflict upon her tormentor, she was able to release the worst of the bottled rage within herself. Eventually she felt a little better—besides, there was no fate *too* horrible for him!

The next several days passed in an angry red haze for Sara, her jumbled emotions veering wildly from mournful defeat one moment to blazing defiance the next. By the time she had been at del Sol for the better part of a week, only one thing was clear in her mind: *she had to escape*!

Everything that Yancy had stated was true. Padre Quintero would eagerly do just as Yancy asked, and it had become painfully clear to Sara that all the inhabitants of del Sol were willing to lay down their very lives for El Patrón! No one would lift a finger to prevent him from doing exactly as he pleased, and she knew that they would think her mad if she spoke against him. Certainly they would not believe that their beloved Senor Yancy had lied to them! Not everyone understood about the civil ceremony in San Felipe, but all were overjoyed at the prospect of seeing El Patrón marry her again in the village church, and preparations for the wedding were in full swing.

To Sara's growing horror, despite her furious, private denunciations of his actions and her oft-stated determination to *die* before she would marry him, events seemed to be moving along very smoothly in precisely the direction that Yancy wanted. Effortlessly waving away her increasingly frantic and violent vows never to marry him, Yancy had coolly set the date for their marriage for Wednesday, the fifth of June—a day that was coming terrifyingly near.

Each morning she woke to the frightening knowledge that the date of her marriage was twenty-four hours closer and that there was no way of stopping it from taking place. Except, she thought grimly, if there was no bride for the groom to marry . . .

Having decided upon her course of action and knowing that time was her enemy, Sara began to plan her escape, and she was thankful that she had free rein of the hacienda compound itself. There was not a moment to lose, and within two days of her decision to escape, she had already gathered and hidden a sizable cache of goods that she would need on her dangerous journey. Secreting food and water, even a knife and an old-fashioned pistol and extra ammunition, had not been difficult. Suitable clothing was near at hand—her boy's knickerbockers, boots and the few short gowns she had worn for the trip to del Sol would certainly be sufficient for her return to Magnolia Grove.

Sara had learned a great deal on the journey to del Sol and she had every intention of putting those skills she had perfected on the trail to good use. She knew it was a hazardous, even foolhardy undertaking that she was planning, but being forced to marry Yancy Cantrell seemed to her to be the greater of two evils. She would rather risk her life in the vast wilderness of Texas than meekly become his bride.

As she lay alone in her comfortable featherbed, her stomach full of the hot, spicy meal that had been expertly prepared by Dolores, the nearly finished, lovingly sewn wedding gown of fine white satin and pearls hanging on the mahogany wardrobe, memories of Yancy's smile and his devastating lovemaking drifting through her mind, she sometimes wondered if she wasn't moon-crazed. She was determined to run away from a situation most women would have joyously accepted—a handsome, wealthy man, who made her flesh sing with pleasure and her heart pound with excitement, was intent upon marrying her. What, she had asked herself miserably, was so *dread*ful about that?

Sara couldn't explain it, not even to herself. She knew it had much to do with the will Sam had left and with Yancy's unwillingness to believe her explanations about her marriage to his father, as well as his frank inability to allow her any say in what was *her* future, too! That and the fact that he had never once mentioned the word "love." . . .

A little tear ran down her cheek. He didn't love her, that was obvious. He wanted her; he desired her body and he had taken great delight in making love to her during those never-to-be-sufficiently-regretted times that she had lain in his arms, but he had never indicated that there was a deeper emotion behind any of his actions. He had—damn him!—put forth several logical, practical, eminently *suitable* reasons for their union, but had never a word of love.

To Sara's dismayed relief, a state which clearly reflected her chaotic emotions, he had made no attempt to make love to her again since they had been at del Sol. He had, in fact, attempted no improper intimacies with her at all, and he was always infuriatingly polite to her and treated her with a mocking respect that made her long to soundly box his ears. When he kissed her, and she couldn't help but notice that he seemed to seize every opportunity to do so, they were teasingly chaste, gentle kisses, which she found disturbingly dissatisfying. Having known his full possession, she was unhappily aware that her body was now beset with powerful, elemental needs that it had never experienced before. There had been several nights recently when sleep had eluded her and she had tossed and turned, yearning, *aching* to have him touch her. From the hint of laughter she sometimes glimpsed in his eyes, she had the unpleasant sensation that he was very conscious of just how very unsatisfying she found his mockingly austere salutations. . . .

It was clear—she had to escape! And she had chosen tonight to do it. She had schemed and planned to the best of her ability and everything was in place.

The hour was well after midnight, and scrambling into her clothes—the knickerbockers and the same short calico gown she had worn on the journey to del Sol, only now freshly laundered and clean—she stole from her room and crept to where she had hidden her cache of supplies. Hefting the saddlebags, which to her good fortune had been inadvertently left in her room, onto her slender shoulders, she stealthily made her way toward the far wall of the stockade. It was here that she had been shown the small stable, where a few horses were always kept in case of trouble. To her delight, she had discovered that the mare she had ridden to del Sol, Locuela, so named for her friskiness as a filly, was one of the horses in the stable. It was actually the knowledge that Locuela was so near that had first put the thought of attempting an escape in Sara's head.

Slipping inside the stable, Sara crooned to the mare and swiftly saddled and secured the saddlebags to her. Then, her heart thundering in her breast and Locuela's reins in her hands, Sara stepped out of the stable. She had already noted the small, iron-barred gate not far away in the stockade wall, and silently leading her horse, she hurried toward it.

Carefully, holding her breath as she did it, she slowly pushed open the gate. There was one small squeak that brought her heart into her mouth, but the next moment the gate was completely open. Once they were on the other side of the stockade wall, Sara instantly mounted Locuela and urged her away.

She kept the horse well away from the village, circling widely around the clustered buildings. Her nerves were exquisitely stretched, her eyes darting this way and that, trying to pierce the darkness, her ears straining to hear the slightest sound of discovery. Once, when a dog barked, she started so violently that Locuela snorted loudly at the sharp tug on her reins.

Finally they were far enough away from the slumbering village to escape detection, but because of her unfamiliarity with the area and the smothering blackness of the night, Sara still kept Locuela at a slow, steady pace. She glanced now and then at the stars overhead, praying that she was heading in the right direction.

As the hours passed and del Sol fell farther and farther away, the sky gradually lightened and Sara was filled with a sensation of fierce elation. Letting out a whoop of sheer exuberance, she kicked Locuela into a distance-eating canter. She had done it! She had freed herself from Yancy and she was now on her way home!

She made good time all during that day. The heat seemed less intense than it had been the day before and Locuela was fresh and eager to go, so Sara saw no reason to lessen their pace. Her escape would be discovered all too soon, but she was relying on the fact that unless she rang, Maria never came to her room until late in the morning. No one, probably not even Yancy, would be alarmed if she was not in her room even then; everyone would assume that she was somewhere around the hacienda grounds, and it would be several more hours—possibly, if she was very lucky, close to early evening—before it was obvious that she had fled. Locuela's absence was bound to be noticed, but Sara was hoping that it would be a case of the stable boy thinking that one of the vaqueros had needed the mare and had taken her. Her greatest fear was that Yancy would be told the moment the mare's disappearance was discovered. It would take him only a second to realize what had happened.

Suddenly terrified of being Yancy's prisoner again, Sara kicked Locuela into a dead run, and for over a mile they flew across the ground at a breakneck speed. Finally, though, common sense reasserted itself and she pulled the mare back into a more normal pace. Running her mount into the ground wasn't going to gain her anything!

Sara made camp that night near a thicket of chaparral, a narrow, sluggish stream of water flowing nearby. She was feeling very pleased with herself and there was a smile of satisfaction on her lips when she drifted off to sleep, the small fire she had built casting flickering shadows over her slender form.

It was Locuela's loud, agitated snorting that jerked her awake, and for a moment she was disoriented. Locuela was dancing nervously around a branch of acacia brush where Sara had tethered her, and Sara heard the mournful and terrifyingly near howl of a lobo drifting through the night air. As the mare continued to move restlessly and snort, the lone howl was joined by several more, and a shiver of unease went down Sara's spine. The fire had died to just a few glowing coals, and hastily she grabbed a couple of pieces of deadwood she had gathered earlier and tossed them on the coals. It took a moment or two, but soon there was the merry cackle of burning wood and as the flames leaped higher, she was able to see the occasional red gleam of eyes and the sinister dark shapes gliding just beyond the light of the fire. *Lobos!*

Yancy had warned her about them on their journey to del Sol. The lobos were big, fierce wolves, and with all the abundant game in the area, they had flourished, their numbers growing every year. They were brave, tenacious, bold hunters, able by the sheer numbers of their pack to pull down a full-grown horse or a long-horned bull. They showed no fear of humans, but normally they weren't a problem, and it was highly unlikely that they would attack her. Sara swallowed painfully. If *she* wasn't their target . . . They must have gotten Locuela's scent and come to investigate.

It was one of the most unnerving moments of Sara's life. She was alone in an enormous wilderness, with only an old Spanish pistol for protection, surrounded by a pack of large, feral predators that seemed to have decided upon her horse for dinner—and without Locuela, she was doomed!

One of the wolves, a big, powerful black, suddenly loomed up out of the darkness. With a scream of ter-

ror, Locuela reared and broke loose from where she had
been tied and galloped frantically off into the night. The
wolves followed her.

There was nothing Sara could do. The horse was
gone, the sound of her hoofbeats already disappearing,
the lobos in swift, inexorable pursuit. Frightened and
appalled, Sara piled more wood on the fire and huddled
near it, pulling all her gear near her as if those inani-
mate objects could protect her. She tried not to think of
Locuela's fate, or of what her own might be . . .

It was an endless night. She dozed uneasily by her fire,
one hand tightly clutching the pistol she had taken from
the saddlebags, the other the heavy leather saddlebags.
She was now truly on her own.

When dawn was only a mere hint of rosy-hued orange
on the horizon, she woke from her apprehensive and
decidedly *un*restful slumber. Glancing around at the
empty, endless horizon of grass and brush, Sara shivered and her spirits sank even lower. Daylight had not
improved her situation.

Finishing her last cup of coffee, she repacked her
cooking utensils and filled her canteen from the stream.
It never occurred to her to give up. She didn't have a
horse, but she had two good, strong legs and at least
some provisions. The saddle, of course, would have to
be left behind, and after hoisting the saddlebags onto
one shoulder, she draped the saddle blanket on her other shoulder and, without a backward glance, began to
trudge in the direction in which she hoped Magnolia
Grove lay.

She walked steadily, stopping only now and then to
rest in the scant patches of shade infrequently offered
by the chaparral and the few mottes of stunted trees that
broke the monotony of the horse-belly-high grass. There
was a dogged determination about Sara as she traveled.
At first, she didn't let herself even *consider* failure. She

kept her thoughts trained on how surprised everyone was going to be when she eventually showed up at Magnolia Grove.

Keeping the notion of success in the forefront of her mind helped, but it could not compensate for the swiftly dwindling supplies, or for the fact that she had found no water since she had left the little stream where the wolves had frightened away Locuela. During the day the sun burned down relentlessly on her slender form. But the nights were the worst. At night the howls of the wolves kept her awake, robbing her of the deep sleep she needed so desperately. And it seemed that they were following her, that every night the howls came closer. . . .

She was so tired. So thirsty. And crazy, she thought gloomily. Had she really believed that she could find her way back to Magnolia Grove? And would it have been so awful to have been married to an exciting man like Yancy Cantrell? Wouldn't being his wife have been a far better fate than dying out here all alone, where not even her bones would be found?

Suffering from lack of water, exhausted from lack of sleep and the long, fatiguing days spent walking and walking and walking, Sara gradually began to leave a sad little trail of discarded items behind her as she tried to lighten her load. By the fifth day her concentration had grown fuzzy, and when she dropped the saddlebags she wasn't even aware of it—or of the direction she was traveling in, although she sensed that something was wrong. Just before dusk, when she passed a distinctively half-hollowed, stunted oak that she recognized from having seen the previous morning, she knew that her most terrifying fears were real—she had been traveling in circles! Unable to help herself, she sank down miserably on the ground, her back against the tree, her knees against her chest, and allowed the tears she had kept at bay full rein.

She cried bitter, bitter tears, but eventually she roused herself. She had to go on. If she stopped here, she would die by this blasted oak tree, but if she moved on, there was the fervent hope that soon she would find water. Grimly Sara struggled to her feet. She still had her knife, the canteen and the pistol, and she was *going* to find water! Her shoulders belligerently squared, she gamely set off, determined that she would not be defeated.

She was passing through an area of thick chaparral, and as darkness began to fall, she commenced looking around for a place to camp for the night. The sudden howl of a wolf not far from where she was gathering wood startled her.

She dropped her armload of branches and twigs, her heart pounding in her chest, and looked nervously around. She could see nothing, but the sound came again, closer this time. As she stood there frozen, she heard an answering cry. She swallowed. Oh, God! Oh, God! Surely not!

But as the minutes passed and the blood-chilling howls of the wolves seemed to come from all around her, it appeared that her plea had gone unanswered. The big lobos had found their prey for tonight—*her!*

∽ 13

Too scared to move, Sara stood there frozen, the sounds of the nearing wolves echoing in her ears. She told herself that she was imagining things—that it was some other prey that had caught their deadly attention. The hair-raising, mournful sounds died away and a wave of relief swept over her.

Laughing nervously to herself, she bent over to pick up the fallen firewood. A series of soft, excited yelps broke the air just behind her and caused her to straighten with a jerk. The sounds were noticeably closer and she knew then that she had been fooling only herself. The wolves were after her.

Frantically she looked around for a place of safety, but there was none—only the looming, shadowy forms of the prickly chaparral scattered here and there. None was high enough or thick enough to offer any protection from a wolf attack, and her heart squeezed with terror. She had the pistol, but once all the bullets were gone, what was she going to do? Use the knife?

A sudden loud howl nearer than all the others made her whirl around and stare through the gathering darkness in that direction. They were closing in, but it was the sight of a long, lean, sinuous form gliding silently through the brush that finally broke the paralysis that seemed to have frozen her limbs.

She had to move. *Now*! Jaw clenched determinedly, she set off with an outwardly confident stride—there was not going to be any sign of weakness or faltering about her!

Her mind working at a furious speed, she cast about for the best place to make a stand. Like a ray of hope, the memory of that half-hollowed oak flashed into her mind. If she could reach it . . . Spotting two more sinister shapes slinking through the ever-increasing darkness, Sara swallowed painfully. She had to reach that oak! Once she had climbed inside that hollow, it would provide her with the only protection she was going to find for miles.

How far back had she passed it? Her pace increased, and to her great alarm, she heard the brush behind her rustling loudly—as if several large bodies had pushed through it. The wolves were not making any attempt to hide their presence and Sara could clearly hear the sound of their panting, the occasional excited barks and yelps that told her only too well just how very closely they were following her.

Trying not to think about the wolves, she anxiously scanned the area in front of her. Where was that damned tree? One of the bigger wolves slunk nearer and she clutched her pistol even more tightly and pulled back the hammer, the click exploding loudly through the night air. A muffled yelp to her left had her eyes darting there nervously, and nearly choking with sheer terror, Sara spied three or four steadily padding wolves, keeping pace with her.

Her stomach lurched as she realized that with the pack already on three sides of her, it was now herding her to where its leader would strike. She swallowed painfully, the urge to run blindly almost overpowering.

The huge, powerful wolf appeared without warning in front of her, a yellow-eyed black that sprang out of nowhere, its gleaming fangs the only thing Sara saw before she instinctively raised the pistol and fired. Her aim—thank God!—was true, and the wolf yelped agonizingly as it fell at her feet. The sight of the twitching corpse and the sudden cacophony of howls that broke the night air shattered the last of Sara's composure, and throwing caution to the winds, she began to run as fast as her exhausted legs would carry her.

How long she ran she never knew, the ghastly fate that awaited her if she were to falter or stumble lending her a speed and stamina she had never known she possessed. Darkness surrounded her, only the feeble light of the partially full moon guiding her way as she sped through the night.

Suddenly a wolf exploded out of the brush to strike at her legs, but again the pistol spat and the big animal spun around, biting at where the bullet had entered its body.

Briefly, the wolves seemed to fall back, and Sara was filled with the painfully fervent hope that the damage she had inflicted with the pistol had given them a distaste for her. The respite was momentary, however, for all too soon the sounds of renewed pursuit rang in her ears.

Her legs felt like lead, her breathing so labored that she feared she was going to fall down, never to rise again; and it was then, its twisted shape unique and utterly lovely to Sara, that the half-hollowed oak, outlined by the frail silver light of the moon, loomed up before her. Nearly hysterical with fear and relief, she ran with increased vigor, not even aware that she was laughing and crying at the same time.

That short, blessed lapse in the chase by the wolves gave Sara barely enough time to scramble up the stunted oak and into the narrow hollow opening that was over five feet above the ground. With a pious prayer that the hollow was not home to something deadly or vicious, she dropped her shaking limbs into its welcoming sheath just as the braver members of the pack hurled themselves against the tree, leaping up and snapping at the empty air as Sara disappeared within the shelter of the oak.

The hollow was snug, Sara's shoulders and back pressed against the sides of the tree, and there was barely enough room for her to bring her arms up in front of her as she shot wildly at the persistent wolves that clawed and sprang up at the entrance of her fortress. Safe for the moment, she began to quake with reaction, her limbs trembling violently, her hands shaking so badly she could hardly grip the pistol.

The wolves were all around the tree, and from her vantage, she could hear the frightening noises of their whines and snarls, the sound of their clawing feet as they attempted to dig her out of her hiding place. They did not attack continuously. There were long periods of time when Sara thought that perhaps they had given up and gone away, only to have the pack suddenly begin the attack anew.

It was a very long night. Between attacks, when exhaustion claimed her, she dozed lightly, uneasily, waking the instant the wolves would launch another attack.

When the first rosy light of dawn began to creep across the purple-hued horizon, Sara awakened foggily from her latest strained nap. She was vaguely aware that it had been quite some time since the last assault by the wolves and she listened intently. There were no longer any sounds of the wolves, and after waiting several moments more, she moved stealthily and risked taking a peek outside her snug little hollow.

At the base of her tree lay the bodies of three wolves she must have killed during the night, but beyond that, in the ever-spreading light of day, there was not another wolf in sight. Hardly daring to believe that her ordeal was over, she continued to glance cautiously around, her ears straining to hear the slightest hint of danger. There were no sounds in the warming air but the sweet song of birds and the faint drone of insects.

Too afraid to do otherwise, she waited a while longer, and it was only when the sun was fully risen that she warily began to crawl out of her hiding place.

She had survived the night, but night would come again, and with it the wolves. . . .

This stunted, blessed hollowed oak was the only safe place for her once darkness fell—she dared not go very far from it or the fate she had escaped last night would truly be hers. Yet if she did not leave its safety, if she did not seek out food and water, she might as well just sit here and let the wolves find her again—she would die anyway!

Bleakly Sara glanced around her, an endless expanse of grass and chaparral meeting her eyes wherever she looked. Oh, God! How could she have been so foolish! So stupid!

Furious with herself, she stood up. She couldn't just stay here and do nothing! She glanced over to where the three dead wolves lay on the ground. She dared not leave them there because of the stink they would produce and the scavengers they would attract. Swallowing her rising gorge, she spent the next several minutes dragging the heavy bodies as far away from the vicinity of the oak tree as possible.

The dead wolves disposed of, Sara took another, longer look around her. She didn't rate her chances of finding either water or food very high, but she had to try. She wasn't, she vowed fiercely, going to die without a struggle.

No matter what she found—unless, of course, it was another place as safe as the hollowed oak—she intended to return well before dusk, and she didn't like to think about what she was going to do if she found no water or food.

Sara found nothing that morning. More terrifyingly, she discovered that her body had reached its limits and that she was not going to be able to travel as far away from the safety of the hollowed oak as she had first thought. After a scant two hours, breathing hard, she half walked, half stumbled back to the oak. Collapsing in a shambles at the base of the tree, just as the sun reached its zenith in the brilliant blue sky, Sara finally gave up. She was going to die. Scrambling up painfully into a sitting position, her back resting against the tree trunk, her knees bent, her arms lying on top of them, she searched the horizon. How flat and unchanging the landscape seemed, and yet she knew that wasn't true. There were all sorts of little draws and rises here and there to break the monotony of the land, but they weren't obvious; they just blended into the sea of grass and chaparral.

She fixed her sleepy gaze in the direction in which she thought that del Sol might lie and wondered what Yancy was doing at this moment. She smiled faintly. Probably cursing her very name. And the fact that he had lost all chance of ever regaining Casa Paloma. Paloma would now go to Bartholomew and Tansy, and Sara sincerely hoped that they would live a long and happy life there— just as she had planned to do.

She sighed. It didn't matter. Nothing mattered. Her eyelids started to flutter shut and then she frowned. What was that? On that slight rise? A silhouette? Was it *the* dream again? Would she see the Dark Rider of her dreams one last time?

She straightened, her sleepiness vanishing. It *was* a silhouette! The unmistakable shape of a horse and rider . . . A tall, dark rider, his wide-brimmed black hat shading his features as he carefully scanned the horizon. Dimly she noted the smaller chestnut pack horse he led behind him and that there was something familiar about the animal—*Locuela*?

Sara didn't need to see his face to identify the dark rider. There was such arrogance and purposefulness about him as he sat in the saddle, easily controlling the restive big buckskin horse; such suppressed power in that long, lean form that she knew it could be only one person—Yancy Cantrell!

She smiled mirthlessly. Of course he would come after her. She was too important to him. Or rather, her *children* were important to him—vital, in fact. Without them, he lost all claim to Casa Paloma. . . .

Sara made no attempt to attract his attention. With a fatalistic calm she simply waited, too weary and defeated to move. Yancy had tracked her this far, and he would find her soon enough without any help from her.

But overriding all other emotions was a fervent thankfulness that he *had* found her—for whatever reasons. And because he had come after her, she was going to live, *not die here*! A profound sense of gratitude swept over her. Yancy had saved her life! No matter what the future brought, she would never forget that fact. *Yancy had saved her life*!

He rode steadily in her direction, stopping now and then to study the signs on the ground. He had come within two hundred feet of her resting place at the base of the oak before he glanced up, almost instinctively, and spotted her slender, shade-dappled form.

The buckskin suddenly erupted into movement, thundering swiftly toward her, the small chestnut galloping wildly to keep up. Not six feet away from where she lay, at the sharp jerk of the reins, the buckskin plunged to a savagely abrupt stop, rearing and pawing the air at such rough treatment. Before the horse's hooves touched the ground, Yancy had already swung out of the saddle and was at Sara's side.

His hat hid his expression, but Sara was groggily aware of the way his hands trembled when he reached out to touch her, the sudden catch of his breath when his gaze met hers. His amber-gold eyes blazed with some strong, undefined emotion and then she was in his arms, his mouth moving urgently against the sweat-dampened hair at her temple.

Yancy held her for a long time, hardly daring to believe that he had found her and that she was still alive. He had faced war, Indian attacks, cannon fire and death, but *nothing* had ever terrified him as much as Sara's disappearance! It was only when Sara croaked, "Thirsty," that he was able to tear himself away from her and go to his horse for the canteen.

As tenderly as a mother tending a child, he guided the cup to her lips and allowed her to sip a little water. Despite her plea for more, he shook his head. "No, sweetheart," he said gruffly, his throat tight with emotion. "Too much would be just as bad for you as too little. In a few minutes you can have some more." He poured another cupful, and dipping his scarlet bandanna into the water, he carefully washed her face, letting the cool water drip down her neck to settle between her breasts.

Sara sighed gratefully. It was heaven. Her eyes closed, she asked wearily, "How did you find me?"

Yancy's features hardened. Looking at her wan features, he decided savagely that it was just as well that she was half dead—otherwise he might be tempted to thrash her senseless! Staring at the signs of her ordeal which marked her fair skin, his expression softened and he said huskily, "You didn't make my task any easier by heading off in the wrong direction!"

Sara's eyes flew open. "The wrong direction?" she croaked. "Wasn't I traveling toward Magnolia Grove?"

Yancy shook his head and smiled grimly. "If you'd kept on in the direction you were going, you'd have ended up in Mexico eventually! And because it never occurred to me that you'd go anywhere but to Magnolia Grove, I didn't even bother to look for any tracks—I simply mounted my fastest horse and took off after you. It was two days later before I realized that I had miscalculated and returned to del Sol—not, I might add, in the kindest frame of mind! I immediately organized a search in *all* directions fanning out from the hacienda, and that afternoon we managed to find your trail. Locuela came trotting merrily up to us the next morning . . . it was rather a nasty moment." Yancy's mouth tightened, a bleak expression entering his eyes. "It was obvious that she had somehow escaped from you—she'd broken one of her reins—and it was equally obvious that she had been run and run hard."

"Wolves," Sara muttered. "She got frightened and broke away. I thought they had killed her."

"Not Locuela—she's a tough old mare," Yancy said lightly. "And smart. Even in a blizzard she could find her way to del Sol and she can always find water, which is one of the reasons I usually have her with me"—his voice deepened—"and why I didn't really worry about you until we found her roaming free."

A small silence fell, Sara's eyelids fluttering shut. Yancy stayed where he was, hunkered down beside her, his gaze fixed intently on her exhausted features. After a bit, Sara asked, "Do you think I could have some more water now?"

Yancy poured another cupful of water from his leather canteen, and handing Sara the tin cup, he said gently, "Drink it slowly, *chica*—there's more where that came from, so there's no reason to gulp it down."

Sara smiled tiredly, and fighting against the instinct to do just that—gulp it—she forced herself to take dainty sips. The water felt so good sliding down her parched throat. The coolness. The wetness. Like nectar. With her eyes shut, she just lay there, the taste of the sweet, sweet water lingering on her tongue.

There was little conversation between them. All through the long, hot afternoon, Yancy periodically gave her small amounts of water, frequently bathing her face and neck and arms to help provide more moisture to her depleted body. The loud, persistent rumbling of her stomach had made him smile and hand her a piece of jerked beef. The beef was hard and tough, the texture of boot leather, but Sara was certain that she had never tasted anything so delectable in her life before, except, of course, for the water. . . .

The worst of the heat of the day had vanished when Yancy said abruptly, "I spotted a small water hole with a stand of cottonwoods a few miles back. It'll be a good place to camp tonight."

It *was* a good place for a camp, with plenty of clear, cool water, the leafy cottonwoods providing a modicum of shelter, as well as deadwood for a fire. Yancy had carried her to the campsite on his horse, her slender body protectively cradled in his arms; Locuela, loaded with supplies, trailed behind them. It had been a short ride to the new location, and lying now on a blanket on the ground with Yancy's saddle as a pillow for her head, Sara watched listlessly as he went about setting up camp.

She was so tired, and though she was no longer nearly crazy with thirst, she *was* hungry. Plaintively, she finally asked, "Could I have another piece of jerky?"

Busy with starting a fire, Yancy glanced over his shoulder at her. He grinned for the first time, his teeth flashing whitely in his dark, beard-stubbled face. "You must be feeling a little better if all you can think about is your stomach."

Sara made a face, wrinkling up her nose delightfully at him. "It's not *all* I can think about. A hot bath would be heavenly and a real bed utterly divine, but right now food seems more important!"

Yancy's grin faded and a shadow crossed his face. His words clipped, he said, "But you ran away from all those things, didn't you?"

She had been so thankful to see him, so *glad* that she wasn't going to die beneath that hollowed oak, and he had been so kind, so gentle with her all afternoon that she had momentarily forgotten all that lay between them. Her eyes dropped and she bit her lip. "Yes, I did."

Yancy's mouth hardened, and biting back the angry, corrosive words that flowed up into his throat, he looked away. Taking a deep, calming breath, he said coolly, "We'll talk about that later. Right now, before it gets any later, I'm going to shoot us some fresh meat."

Grateful that he had changed the subject, she watched uneasily as he mounted his horse and pulled his rifle from the scabbard. Suddenly swamped by an unspeakable fear at being deserted, Sara had all she could do to prevent herself from calling him back when he rode away. She knew he was coming back; Locuela was securely tied to a stout cottonwood, a tidy pile of supplies not far away; there was fire and water nearby, yet Sara was terrified to be left alone. Last night's events were too fresh, too vivid in her memory, and helplessly, tears burst from her eyes when he vanished from view.

There was nothing to be scared about, she told herself fiercely. She was safe. Yancy wouldn't desert her. He would come back. She had *nothing* to fear.

It was easy to tell herself she had nothing to fear, but she started and jumped at every strange sound for the next several minutes. Yancy had been gone about half an hour when she heard the sounds of a shot drifting on the air. To her intense relief, a short time later he rode into camp, a small deer tied across the cantle of his saddle.

Sara ate well that night, even though Yancy cautioned her not to overeat. For once she followed his advice without any argument, but it was with a full stomach that she finally fell asleep near the fire. The sounds of the wolves howling in the distance woke her during the night, but the sight of the fire burning brightly and the feel of Yancy's big body wrapped securely around hers spoon-fashion calmed the instinctive terror she felt when she heard the chilling cries of wolves. Snuggling closer to Yancy's warm body, she fell asleep again almost immediately.

It took them only two days to reach del Sol, and Sara was appalled to discover that she had spent much of her time wandering in circles. There was not much conversation between them as they traveled back to the hacienda. At Yancy's blunt command, Sara rode on his horse with him, again cradled by his strong arms, her cheek resting on his chest, the powerful beat of his heart a soothing melody to her ears.

There was such open joy at her safe return to del Sol, the Mexicans crowding close to the big buckskin to reverently touch her hand or foot, that Sara was unbearably moved and filled with guilt. She hadn't done anything wrong, and yet . . .

At the hacienda itself, after carrying her to her bedroom, Yancy left her in the hands of the women and she was crooned over and coddled by Maria and Dolores and the other house servants. A delicate chicken broth was instantly pressed upon her, and against her feeble protests, Maria tenderly bathed her and gently rubbed a soothing lotion into her parched skin. With soft scoldings and gentle threats, Maria placed Sara in bed and finally left her alone.

Sara slept soundlessly that night, not even aware when Yancy entered the room and, lighting a candle, stood looking down at her. He stared at her for a long time, noting the silky strands of honey-gold hair spread out across the white pillow, the long lashes lying like tawny fans against her cheeks and the sweet curve of her tempting mouth. The expression on his face was darkly brooding. A deep sigh came from him and with exquisite tenderness he dropped a kiss on her forehead and silently departed.

Possessed of a strong, healthy body, Sara didn't take long to recover, and within a week there were no signs of the horrible ordeal that she had undergone. She was treated with such kindness by everyone, including, to her amazement, even Yancy, but she kept waiting tensely for the moment of retribution to fall upon her. Not one word of reproach or angry denunciation had been leveled at her, and Sara's guilt had grown to enormous proportions. Everyone just seemed so *happy* that she had been returned safely—Yancy had even concocted a simple tale to explain what had happened. And not one person, not even chubby Padre Quintero, had given the slightest indication of disbelief that, at *Yancy's* suggestion, she had gone exploring on her own and become lost. . . .

Daily Sara basked in the warmth and the concern of the people of del Sol, and nightly, twisting restlessly in her big, lonely bed, she felt gratitude to Yancy for saving her life, as well as for sparing her an embarrassing explanation for her foolhardy actions. The potent, dangerous combination of gratitude and guilt which she felt led Sara to decide that she *would* marry Yancy after all. She *owed* it to him. Like a flash of lightning across a purple summer sky, it occurred to her that there was also another, more compelling reason to marry the Dark Rider of her dreams—*she loved him*! Had been in love with him for weeks! It didn't matter that he didn't love her—in that first moment of discovery, she was positive she had enough love for both of them. She would be a *good* wife to him and someday, just perhaps, he might come to love her. . . . A tremulous smile curved her mouth as she admitted giddily that the future had suddenly acquired a remarkably rosy hue. *She loved Yancy Cantrell*! And she had every intention of marrying him!

It hadn't escaped her notice that the date originally planned for their wedding had come and gone and that Yancy had made no mention of a new date. It also hadn't escaped her attention that he acted very circumspect around her and watched her with an aloof, brooding intensity that made her just a little uneasy. Oh, but he was so very kind to her these days. And oh, so dear! So *very* beloved! How could she have been so stupid as to run away from the very thing that her heart demanded?

It had occurred unhappily to Sara that perhaps the reason there had been no further mention of marriage between them was because Yancy was fearful of pre-cipitating another rash, *moronic* escape by her. He *never* had to worry about that again! she vowed fiercely. And tomorrow morning, she thought with a flutter of nervous anticipation, she would seek him out and tell him that she would marry him and give him a child for Casa Paloma.

PART THREE

DECEPTIONS OF
THE HEART

*It oft falls out,
to have what we would have, we speak
not what we mean.*

MEASURE FOR MEASURE
—WILLIAM SHAKESPEARE

∽ 14

It was easy to make the decision to offer to marry Yancy in the protective cloak of darkness, but it wasn't so easy to actually carry it out in the revealing light of day, and Sara procrastinated as long as she could. After spending half the morning selecting and discarding items from her meager wardrobe, she finally settled on the rose-bordered calico gown that Tansy had packed for her. She fussed an inordinately long time with her hair. Eventually, she left it in her normal tidy cornet of braids. Taking a long, last look at herself in the cheval glass, she breathed in deeply and marched resolutely toward the door.

It was with a feeling of anticlimax that she learned from Maria that Senor Yancy would not return to the hacienda until late this evening. He had gone with Maria's husband, Esteban, to oversee the castrating of several wild bulls that had been captured on Tuesday.

Sara wandered restlessly around the hacienda and its grounds all day, eager for Yancy's return, yet dreading it, too. As the hours passed, she began to question the wisdom of her decision, but then chided herself for her doubts. *Of course* she was doing the right thing, the only moral thing she could do after Yancy had been so good and kind to her.

Dusk had fallen by the time Yancy returned that evening. Seated on the rim of the goldfish pond, Sara started anxiously when she heard the sounds of the commotion that heralded his arrival home. Her mouth went dry, and nervously wiping her hands on her gown, she slowly stood up.

He looked tired and dusty, his breeches and boots covered with a fine layer of Texas dirt, his white shirt sweat-stained and soiled, and Sara's foolish heart leaped with joy at the sight of him. Carrying a plain black sombrero in one hand, he walked over to her, stopped in front of her and said quietly, "Maria said you wanted to see me."

This wasn't quite how Sara had planned it, but before she could lose her courage, she blurted out, "Do you still want to marry me?"

Something flashed in his eyes and he replied softly, "More than anything in the world."

Sara gulped. Well, naturally he'd say that—he wanted Casa Paloma; she just wished that she wouldn't feel such a silly rush of pleasure when he said things like that! Not looking at him, she stammered breathlessly, "I k-k-know that the only reason you want to marry me is so that we can m-m-make . . . h-h-have a child." Forcing herself to gaze into his beloved face, she confessed disarmingly, "I have acted very silly! It doesn't matter that ours won't be a love-match—a lot of marriages aren't! I am so very grateful that you saved my life and . . . and even though we don't love each other doesn't mean that I can't be a good and dutiful wife to you. I *will* be a conscientious and obedient wife—I swear it!"

"I see," Yancy drawled slowly, an unreadable expression on his dark face. "Let me make certain that I understand you," he said dryly, his eyes never leaving hers. "You are grateful to me, and because you are grateful to me, you are agreeing to marry me and have my child?"

Sara nodded, her lovely emerald-green eyes clear and guileless as she stared up at him, glad that he understood the situation. This was what they needed—plain speaking! There would be no misunderstandings between them.

"And you think that's what I want?" he asked silkily, a dangerous note underlying his words. "An obedient, *dutiful* wife?"

He made the words sound ugly and distasteful and Sara frowned slightly, a shiver of unease sliding down her spine. The expression on his face wasn't very encouraging either, and she had the curious impression that he was holding back his formidable temper with a great effort.

"Don't you *want* to marry me?" she asked in a troubled voice.

Yancy swore softly under his breath and, dropping the sombrero to the flagstones, dragged her roughly into his arms. He kissed her fiercely, his mouth bruising hers, his fingers digging painfully into the soft flesh of her upper arms.

Sara struggled in his embrace, confused and frightened by his reaction. Her fists beat frantically against his broad chest and she desperately tried to twist her head away from the savage assault of his lips against hers.

As suddenly as the kiss had begun, it was over, and thrusting her from him, he stared enigmatically at her flushed features. "You were not," he said coolly, "being very dutiful!"

Sara swallowed, reminding herself that he had saved her life and that she had just sworn that she would be a good and obedient wife to him. "I'm sorry," she muttered. "I didn't mean to . . . to . . . You surprised me—next time I'll do better."

Yancy growled something vicious under his breath, and picking up his sombrero, he said tightly, "I'm afraid that as my wife, you'll have to do a great deal better!" He fixed her with a hostile stare and inquired acidly, "Are you certain that your *gratitude* will allow you to put up with my demands?"

Confused and dismayed by his reaction, not understanding why he seemed so angry and brutal, but trying gamely to stay on the course that she had decided upon, Sara docilely nodded her head. A blush staining her cheeks, she said low, "I understand what you require of me and I p-p-promise that I won't be such a ninny the next time you kiss me or anything."

Her words were meant to placate him, but they seemed to enrage him even further and his eyes gleamed like golden fire. "Oh, Jesus! Spare me *that*!" Pinning her to the spot with his furious gaze, he lifted her chin with one hand and said grimly, "But since you seem determined to sacrifice yourself, I'll talk to Padre Quintero about arranging our marriage. In the meantime, Sara, think about this—I can *buy* complaisance and meekness, I don't need to marry it!"

Spinning on his heels, he disappeared, leaving Sara to stare after him in bewilderment. She'd done what he wanted—agreed to marry him. Why was he so angry about it? He was getting everything he wanted; she'd even made it clear that she understood the need for a child to inherit Casa Paloma. So why was he so *very* angry?

It was a question Sara was to ask herself repeatedly over the next few weeks. The date for their wedding had been set for the twenty-sixth of June, and as the day drew nearer, Yancy's temper seemed to become even more volatile. Idly Sara had inquired if he thought that Bartholomew and the others from Magnolia Grove would arrive in time for their nuptials and had had her head nearly snapped off for her pains. Roaring and snarling around the hacienda, he was like an enraged tiger, his manner to Sara particularly insulting and infuriating. More than once, the urge to slap his arrogant face made her fingers tingle, and with increasing difficulty she held her tongue and the sharp retorts she would have liked to hurl back at him. Her sincere feelings of gratitude were wearing exceedingly thin, especially in the face of his provoking attitude toward her. It was almost as if he were *trying* to make her fly into a rage.

Yancy was so unusually black-tempered that even the household servants began to look at him askance. From the little she gleaned from Maria, it wasn't just the servants in the hacienda who bore the brunt of his wrath. Esteban had said that he was like a maddened bear, the way he snapped and growled at everyone and charged violently around the rancho.

Fortunately, Sara saw little of him; he rose before dawn and was gone from the hacienda at first light, and on many nights darkness had fallen long before he returned, the signs of exhaustion obvious in his dark, lean face. The prospect of their coming marriage apparently was *not* giving him any joy!

Sara had begun to dread those nights when he did return early. Garbed in a pair of black *calzoneras*, which clearly revealed the muscled length of his legs, the silver filigree buttons left undone from knee to ankle, and in a long-sleeved, billowy scarlet shirt, his booted feet stretched negligently out in front of him, he would lounge majestically in one of the leather chairs in the main *sala* and, drinking an astonishing amount of brandy, would stare broodingly at Sara. He looked so handsome as he sprawled there, his tousled black hair gleaming, the finely molded, slightly cruel-looking mouth and arrogant cheekbones betraying his Spanish heritage. He seldom spoke to Sara during those nerve-racking evenings, and then only to utter the most provoking and aggravating comments imaginable, and she wondered with increasing apprehension if this was how they would spend the remainder of their days together. What had happened, she wondered miserably, to the laughing man who had kissed her senseless and made her pulses race with just a look from underneath his long lashes?

It was decidedly unnerving to be the sole object of that unblinking, golden-brown gaze, and Sara was thankful that Maria had found some sewing for her to do when Yancy was at the hacienda in the evening. Concentrating on her neat stitches, she could ignore his disquieting presence for the most part, and when he did say something particularly infuriating, she could vent some of her temper by repeatedly stabbing the needle through the fabric and pretending it was any number of vulnerable parts of his anatomy. It wasn't quite as satisfying as slapping his mocking face, but it did provide some relief from the anger that surged up inside her, and the thought of a lifetime of hiding her feelings, both the love she felt for him and the rage he seemed to deliberately arouse these days, was definitely daunting.

On a hot June night, three days before their wedding, they were sitting on the lantern-lit patio at the rear of the house, seeking what coolness could be found. Sara was seated on the rim of the fountain, pensively watching the antics of the gracefully swimming goldfish, occasionally amusing herself by dipping her fingers in the water to tease any that came near where she sat. Yancy lounged half hidden in the shadows.

Unknowingly, Sara made a delightful picture. She had left her hair loose, and having caught the honey-gold strands with a watermelon-pink silk ribbon, she had fashioned a frivolous knot of curls that fell from the top of her head. Her gown was in a shade of silk which matched the ribbon, with a dropped bodice that left her slender shoulders and a modest amount of her firm young breasts bare. The garment, her second-best ball gown from better days at Magnolia Grove, was very becoming to her delicate shape, clearly defining her slim waist before falling in a series of delightful ruffles to her feet.

Yancy, sipping brandy, watched her through hooded lids. He was garbed this evening in a pair of black, tight-fitting *calzoneras* trimmed along the outer edge with gold-tinsel lace; a scarlet sash was tied around his lean waist, and his fine white cambric shirt was opened halfway, the curly hair which covered his muscular chest appearing even blacker against the pristine white of his shirt.

Sara had tried all evening to keep her gaze averted from that broad expanse of hair-roughened chest, but she couldn't help remembering what it had felt like beneath her fingers, remembering with a little shiver of excitement the warmth and power of its muscled width. Their wedding was in three days and despite deep feelings of misgiving, her rebellious body was already anticipating Yancy's intoxicating lovemaking.

She sneaked a shy glance in his direction, her eyes unconsciously lingering on the length of his long legs, intensely aware of the latent power and blatant sensuality of his tall, hard body as he lounged there in the shadows. In just a few days, she thought breathlessly, he would come to her in all his naked splendor, that glorious body of his possessing hers and transporting her once again to those all-too-new erotic heights. To her shocked mortification, her nipples suddenly swelled and hardened, protruding noticeably against the watermelon silk of her bodice.

She jumped up nervously, her one idea to escape from his unsettling presence. Looking everywhere but at him, she said, "It's late. I'll say good night to you now."

His face hidden by the shadows, he drawled, "Running away, sweetheart?"

Startled, Sara glanced at him. "What do you mean? I'm not running away!"

"Aren't you?" he asked caustically. "Seems to me that since your *gratitude* compelled you to so graciously offer to marry me, you run and hide the moment I get within six feet of you."

As she stared at him in openmouthed astonishment, he stood up and drained his brandy glass. With a violent movement that made her gasp, he smashed the crystal snifter against one of the stone archways, the sound of shattered glass echoing through the tranquility of the night air. Indifferent to the destruction he had just wrought, he stepped nearer to Sara. Catching her chin between his fingers, he tipped her head up, stared intently into the mysterious green pools of her eyes and asked, "And just what are you going to do Wednesday night after we have said our vows before Padre Quintero? Run away then, too?"

Bewildered and uneasy, Sara stared back at him. "I promised that I would be a good wife to you. . . ." She blushed delightfully. "In *all* ways."

"Will you?" he asked silkily, his fingers tightening on her chin. "I've wondered lately if this was how you trapped Sam into an unconsummated marriage. Such shy, demure ways I've seen recently. Such sweet forbearance! Such gentle, nunlike meekness! And yet I've tasted your passion. I know the fire that is within you, a sweet fire that, having once known, a man would be willing to burn in forever. Is that how it was with my father? Did you promise him heaven before the wedding, only to consign him to hell after the ring was on your pretty little finger?"

All of the resentment she had been hoarding up these past weeks suddenly erupted throughout Sara and she jerked her chin free of his hold. Bosom heaving with temper, she glared at him and, surprising both of them, gave him a ringing slap across his taunting mouth. "Shut up!" she hissed furiously. "You've just exhausted my supply of tolerance for your boorish comments and I will *not* stand here and *meekly* listen to you insult me—or your father!"

He grinned tightly, his eyes gleaming brightly in his dark face. "Ah, the little cat is finally showing her claws! I've wondered where she'd gone to lately. I was afraid that your *gratitude* might have destroyed her."

"Will you stop harping on my *gratitude*!" Sara snapped, her cheeks flushed and her hands on her hips. "I'm *sick* of it, do you hear me? If you mention it one more time, I swear I'll do you a violence!"

To Sara's dumbfounded amazement, he smiled hugely and before she could guess his intent, he casually reached out and jerked her against him. His hands on her upper arms holding her prisoner, his lips came down hard on hers and he kissed her deeply, urgently, his tongue boldly and thoroughly plundering her mouth. Raising his lips from hers dizzyingly endless moments later, he murmured, "Welcome back, little spitfire—I've missed you!"

If anything, Sara's temper soared even higher. "You've a blasted funny way of showing it!" she shot back, not one whit appeased by his words. Struggling out of his embrace, hands on her hips, she glared at him. "You've been as pleasant as a nose-stung bear these past weeks and I'm not going to put up with it anymore!" She took a deep breath and added grimly, "I've told you the truth about my marriage to Sam, and if you choose not to believe me, that's *your* problem—but you've insulted me and your father for the last time, do you hear me?" Acidly she finished, "I must say, the fact that you are determined to marry me, believing me the foulest sort of creature alive, makes me wonder about *you!*"

Yancy grimaced, Sara's shafts going home with a vengeance. He *had* been a bastard lately. Ruefully, he said, "I *have* been unbearable lately and my only excuse is that your offer to marry me out of gratitude struck me on the raw." He flashed her a dark look. "No man likes the idea of being married because of *gratitude!*"

He made the word sound incredibly nasty and Sara gaped at him, some of her anger fading. Not willing to let the implications of his words sidetrack her from the far more important issue of her marriage to Sam, she asked tightly, "And my marriage to your father? What about it?"

Yancy sighed and his mouth twisted. "You don't give any quarter, do you, lady?" And at Sara's vehement shake of her head, he added bluntly, "Your marriage to Sam was a handy weapon . . . but I think it's served its usefulness."

Sara's eyes narrowed. "What does *that* mean?"

He grinned, a mocking light dancing in his eyes. "Why, only that I've known for weeks that you must have been telling the truth."

Not giving her a chance to comment—even if she could have thought of *any*thing to say to his outrageous statement—he spun her around and, swatting her playfully on her bottom, he said teasingly, "There will be no more confessions tonight! Run along to bed, *chica!* I hope you sleep well—you're certainly going to need plenty of rest for our wedding night!"

Indignantly Sara jerked around with the clear intention of continuing the battle, although she was no longer clear what it was that she was fighting for, but Yancy was walking away from her . . . *whistling!*

To her astonishment, Sara *did* sleep well that night, and if her dreams were full of indecently explicit acts with a certain infuriating, bewildering, oh, and *complete-ly* fascinating black-haired devil with mocking amber-gold eyes, she preferred not to dwell on that fact. She woke with a ravenous appetite and with a decided sparkle in her green eyes. Fighting with Yancy was *very* stimulating!

Another long day stretched before her, but for the first time since she had returned to the hacienda, Sara was actually looking forward to the evening and another skirmish with her impossible husband-to-be! There was a new spring to her step and she couldn't seem to stop smiling, although she had no idea why it should be so. When Maria brought her a fresh pitcher of lemonade and some freshly fried *sopas* filled with *picadillo dulce*, a sweet, spicy combination of raisins and pork, Sara was actually humming happily to herself. Maria said nothing until after she had placed the tray on a black iron table; then, hands on her hips, a twinkle in her dark eyes, she murmured, "I would very much like to have been a tiny bird last night."

Sara glanced up at her and Maria grinned. "Senor Yancy, who has been a snarling tiger for weeks, left this morning smiling and whistling, and now I find you sitting here all alone with a silly little smile on *your* face! It does not take the village wise man to guess what has happened!"

Sara blushed hotly right up to the roots of her hair and, pouring herself a glass of lemonade, said with a valiant attempt at airiness, "Why, I have no idea what you're talking about—*nothing* happened!"

Maria snorted and had just started to go back into the house when they both heard a noisy hullabaloo which came from the direction of the village. They exchanged a startled glance and then, as one, the two women hurried to the front of the hacienda. Sara had no thought of danger as she picked up her skirts and petticoats and sped down the broad steps of the portico and ran past the huge three-tiered fountain in front to the iron gates that were standing open this hot June day. The sounds they heard were not those of fear, but of excitement.

Dolores and Juan had joined Maria and Sara, and together the four of them spilled through the gateway. With hands shading their eyes from the blinding sunlight, they stared at the procession winding its way snakelike along the village street.

There were a half-dozen riders on horseback accompanying three wagons of varying sizes, each wagon obviously heavily laden. Sara recognized Yancy on his favorite mount, the big buckskin, and some of the other riders as del Sol vaqueros, but it took her a second or two before she realized that the tall, dark man on the bay gelding was Bartholomew! Having recognized Bartholomew, she understood instantly what she was seeing—the household from Magnolia Grove had arrived!

It was indeed the household from Magnolia Grove. Not only Bartholomew, Tansy and the other three servants, but Ann and Thomas Shelldrake as well as a sullen-faced Hyrum Burnell. But Sara barely noticed anyone but Bartholomew and Tansy. Bartholomew had hardly dismounted from his horse before she excitedly flung herself into his arms, suddenly realizing how *very* much she had missed him!

Bartholomew smiled down at her and asked teasingly, "Does this mean that you have forgiven us our part in your abduction?"

Happiness bubbling up inside her, Sara scowled with mock fierceness. "I shall never forgive you!" she exclaimed sternly. "It was a mean, underhanded trick to pull on me!" Then, unable to maintain her facade, she burst out laughing. "Oh, Bartholomew! I have missed you so!"

"Is that my man you are pestering, young lady?" demanded Tansy from her seat in one of the wagons. Dark eyes dancing with amusement, she went on. "I just don't know what the world is coming to these days—turn my back for an instant and what do I find? Some cheeky young thing is hugging and kissing my husband!"

Yancy had dismounted from his horse, and after helping Tansy down from the wagon, he sent Sara a mocking glance before saying to Tansy, "You won't have to worry about that cheeky young thing much longer. We're getting married in two days and you can be assured that, as my wife, she won't be running up and throwing herself at strange men!"

The wagons were in a semicircle in front of the gateway to the hacienda, the outriders and their horses crowding close. Out of the corner of her eye Sara saw Hyrum's mouth tighten, but he gave no other sign of his reaction to the announcement. Such was not the case with Ann Shelldrake.

"*Married*!" Ann exclaimed furiously, her blue eyes snapping with displeasure. She was seated regally in the second wagon, the old black man, Noah, who was driving the wagon, at her side. Her gaze locked on Yancy's dark face. "You're not actually going to marry her, are you?"

Yancy carelessly pulled Sara to his side and draped his arm possessively around her slender waist. He cocked an inquiring eyebrow at Ann and said bluntly, "That is certainly my plan, and I fail to see what business it is of yours!"

Ann flushed angrily, but recalling that she was Yancy's guest—his not-exactly-welcome guest—she controlled herself. Forcing a conciliatory smile onto her lips, she said, "Forgive me! I was just taken aback, knowing as I do your views on marriage." A sly expression in her eyes, she murmured, "How bizarre! I don't know that

I've ever *heard* before this of anyone marrying his own stepmother!"

Yancy's eyes were hard as they rested on Ann's lovely features. "I'm sure," he said grimly, "that there are any number of things that you have never heard of in your narrow little world!"

"Oh, dear!" Ann said, prettily contrite. "I've angered you! I'm so sorry—I never meant to!" She smiled coquettishly at him. "My dreadful tongue—you know how it runs away from me! Come, now, let us put it behind us and help me down from this horrid wagon! I vow I am sick to death of it after all these weeks in the wretched thing!"

Yancy looked at her for a full moment and then said deliberately over his shoulder, "Hyrum, since you invited yourself along, make yourself useful and help Mrs. Shelldrake down from the wagon."

Ignoring Ann's indignant gasp, Yancy drew Sara along with him and, approaching the last wagon, stopped and smiled up at Tom Shelldrake and Peggy. Addressing his words to Tom, he said warmly, "Hello, sir. I hope that the journey was not too hard on you."

Tom Shelldrake looked worn and tired and it was obvious that his bad arm was aching, the way he kept rubbing it with his other hand. He smiled wanly and murmured, "Not too hard, son, but I can't deny that I'm glad I'll be able to sleep in a real bed tonight and not on the ground!"

Yancy grinned at him. "It will be my pleasure, sir, to see that you sleep tonight in the softest feather bed in the hacienda! May I help you down?"

It was apparent as he scrambled down awkwardly that Tom was grateful for his help, and Sara stared at Yancy curiously. He was such a confusing mixture. Hard. Kind. Arrogant. Demanding and yet capable of being so very tender and thoughtful. So would he have been with his father, and she was aware of a tight little knot in her chest when she thought of the time that Sam and Yancy had missed together. Time that could never be recaptured or undone . . .

It was a busy afternoon and Sara was pleasantly tired by the time the last object from Magnolia Grove had been unloaded from the wagons and placed momentarily in the storehouse near the hacienda stables. Ann and Tom had disappeared into the grand suite of rooms that Yancy had told Maria to give them, and from the numerous trips made by the various servants throughout the afternoon to those rooms, Sara guessed that Ann was reveling in the delight of having people at her command once more.

Bartholomew, Tansy and Peggy were happily settling into a small adobe house which Sara had previously noticed sat off to one side of the hacienda. A little frown between her brows, she watched as Tansy bustled merrily around, familiarly stowing their few belongings here and there. Tansy seemed to know exactly where everything should go and Sara finally asked, "Have you been here before?"

Tansy glanced at her in surprise. "Of course! This has always been Bartholomew's quarters whenever Master Sam was at del Sol. You forget that Bartholomew saw Master Yancy born and that Master Sam often left him here with Master Yancy and his mother when he had to be at Magnolia Grove. Del Sol is almost as familiar to us as Magnolia Grove—we have always considered the rancho our *real* home."

Despite the arrival of the inhabitants of Magnolia Grove, that evening was very quiet—the Shelldrakes remaining in their suite and all the others busy settling into their new quarters. Sara knew that Noah and his woman, Mercy, had been given a tiny house in the village to stay in and she wondered where Yancy had put Hyrum. Hyrum was a good man. She was positive that, given the chance, he would work hard for del Sol. Hopefully, Yancy would put aside his unfair animosity and realize that Hyrum could be an asset to the rancho. Mostly, she just hoped that Yancy would treat the former overseer of Magnolia Grove with the same polite courtesy he extended to all the people who served him.

Sara didn't see Yancy or any of the others that evening, but she was aware that their arrival had changed the even tenor of the hacienda and that her wedding was less than two days away. . . . She woke the next morning with an odd heaviness of spirit and realized guiltily that while she was delighted that Bartholomew and the other servants from Magnolia Grove had arrived, the presence of the rest of them—the Shelldrakes and Hyrum—was not as pleasing to her. The three of them were indelibly linked in her mind to that unhappy time following Margaret's murder, as well as to the dreadful days following Sam's death. It was a curious distinction. Bartholomew and the others had all been present during those times, yet it was only those three, Ann, Tom and Hyrum, who aroused in Sara a sense of uneasy gloom.

With an effort she pushed aside her thoughts and sprang from her bed. No one seeing her a half hour later would ever guess that she had been the least bit melancholy when she had awakened that morning, because she was smiling warmly and a sweetly serene air seemed to surround her.

Having eaten a light repast in her room, she was eager to locate her personal belongings from Magnolia Grove. The scanty wardrobe packed by Tansy had definitely begun to pall and she was looking forward to wearing something other than the watermelon silk that evening. When Maria appeared in answer to her pull of the velvet rope, Sara said brightly, "In the confusion yesterday, someone neglected to bring my trunks and things to my room. Do you know where they put them after they were unloaded from the wagons?"

Maria looked surprised. "*Sí*! Senor Yancy ordered them taken to his rooms." Smiling archly, she added, "After tomorrow night, his rooms will be yours—where else would your belongings be?"

Some of Sara's serenity slipped and she cursed the blush that suddenly stained her cheeks. Not meeting Maria's laughing eyes, she said with false nonchalance, "Oh, naturally, that's where they would have taken them! How silly of me to have thought otherwise!" She started to breeze out of the room, only to stop abruptly at the door. Making a face, she glanced at Maria. "Could you please show me the way to Yancy's rooms?" she asked meekly.

Maria laughed and said warmly, "Come along, *chica*. They are just down the walkway."

Yancy's quarters consisted of two grandly furnished, enormous rooms connected by a charming sitting area and two large dressing rooms. Sara felt slightly intimidated by the size and richness of the quarters, but spying three leather-bound trunks resting in the middle of the smaller of the two bedrooms, she forgot everything but the happy prospect of reacquainting herself with her belongings. She and Maria spent a pleasant morning unpacking and hanging her clothes in the huge mahogany wardrobes that lined two walls of one of the spacious dressing rooms. A few personal objects, her silver-backed brushes and combs that Sam had given her on her eighteenth birthday and two exquisitely shaped crystal flagons, now rested on the gleaming top of a satinwood dressing table. She had little jewelry—most of the expensive jewels that Sam had given her had been sold to finance the war—but she did have a few small trinkets which she placed carefully in one of the smaller drawers of the dressing table.

Maria watched her with a frown. "Have you no jewelry box?" she finally asked.

Sara smiled at her. "No, but it doesn't matter. I don't have that much jewelry anyway."

Maria was not happy. She liked everything in its place, and it was unseemly that the soon-to-be-mistress of the hacienda had to put her jewelry loosely into a drawer like some ill-bred *tabernera*! A thought occurred to her. Beaming, she said happily, "Oh, wait! I know! There is a carved box in Senor Yancy's wardrobe that will hold everything just fine!"

Spinning on her heels, she raced into Yancy's room, to return a few minutes later carrying a richly carved box of some dark wood. Approaching the big, high, old-fashioned bed which dominated Sara's new room, Maria shook the box lightly, and hearing something rattling inside, she said, "I don't know what he has in here, but I'm sure he won't mind if we put it someplace else and you use the box temporarily."

With Sara at her side, Maria opened the box and flipped its contents onto the brilliant sapphire quilt which covered the bed. There was only one thing in the box Maria had taken from Yancy's wardrobe, and Sara gasped as she stared at the ornate silver dagger that lay glittering in the sunlight that poured onto the bed. She recognized it instantly. The last time she had seen that dagger, it had been buried in the breast of Margaret Cantrell.

∽ 15

As Sara stared in horror at the silver dagger lying so innocently on the sapphire quilt, there was a sound behind her, and she whirled around to see Yancy standing in the doorway of the sitting room. Unaware of the tension coiling through Sara, Maria glanced at him and said smilingly, "Oh, senor, it is good that you are here. I have just told your *novia* that you won't mind if she uses this box to hold her jewelry. You yourself can now reassure her."

His dark face revealing nothing, Yancy said, "*Gracias*, Maria, I shall do just that. In the meantime, would you mind leaving us alone, because there are some things I'd like to discuss with my *novia*."

Oblivious of the undercurrents between the other two, Maria smiled knowingly and hurried from the room. Silence greeted her departure, and for an endless time Yancy and Sara stared at each other across the expanse that separated them. Sara's emerald eyes were full of accusations; Yancy's amber-gold gaze was opaque and watchful.

Sara didn't like the thoughts that were churning through her brain. She had convinced herself that Yancy had not murdered Margaret—even now her heart shrieked out that things were never what they seemed, that there was an explanation, that the man she had agreed to marry, a man she loved deeply, could *not* have committed cold-blooded murder. And yet ... All the evidence had always pointed to Yancy, and despite the agony in her heart, the cool logic of her brain told her that a murderer could wear many faces, and that sometimes blackhearted villainy hid behind a charmingly handsome visage. Sometimes the most loathsome evil could take the form of a tall, broad-shouldered man with a mocking smile and a beguiling manner....

Her accusing green gaze on his, Sara asked stiffly, "Is that the same dagger?"

Yancy smiled thinly, and walking with that careless, predatory grace of his across the room toward her, his eyes never leaving hers, he inquired silkily, "Do you really want to know? Haven't you already made up your mind that not only is that the dagger that killed Margaret, but it was my hand that drove it into her breast?"

Sara met his gaze squarely, wondering miserably how events could have changed so swiftly between them. She had been happy five minutes ago, actually looking forward to their marriage in less than two days, certain that whatever obstacles lay ahead could eventually be settled. And now ... Sara swallowed with difficulty. And now they were staring at each other like bitter antagonists.

When she remained silent, her expressive features mirroring all the chaos roiling inside her, Yancy's grip on his temper broke, and he reached out and dragged her up next to him. "Damn you!" he cursed softly. "Which is it? Either I killed Margaret or I didn't! What am I, Sara? The man you intend to marry, or a murderer?" At her look of agonized indecision, he swore under his breath and disgustedly threw her from him.

Sara fell against the bed and the shock of his violent action loosened her tongue. Tears stinging her eyes, she cried passionately, "You're unfair! All the evidence always pointed to you! You've never *denied* killing her!

Not once! And now I find in your possession the weapon I know killed her—a weapon you and Sam told me wasn't there—and you want me to just blindly trust you? Why should I?"

Hands on his lean hips, he regarded her bleakly. "Why should you indeed?"

He turned on his heel and began to stride from the room. At the doorway, he stopped and looked back over his shoulder at her as she half lay, half stood by the bed, the tears drying on her face. She looked so young and defenseless, so tempting and desirable. Something clenched painfully in his heart and he said levelly, "This doesn't change anything. We'll *still* be married on Wednesday—if I have to tie you up and carry you spitting and clawing before Padre Quintero."

Sara sank down onto the sapphire quilt, cocooned in the deafening silence of the room after Yancy had left. For a long time she stared intently at the silver dagger on the bed, almost *willing* it to somehow reveal the secrets held in its lethal beauty.

Could she have been wrong? Could her heart be wrong? Had Yancy killed Margaret?

She thought about it for hours, just sitting there staring dully at the dagger but not really seeing it anymore, her mind on those events that had taken place so many years ago. Almost as if it had happened yesterday, she could recall everything she had seen and heard that first night at Magnolia Grove. The house had been filled with any number of people who had good reason to wish Margaret dead—the Shelldrakes, Hyrum, even Bartholomew! Someone could argue that Sam had as good a reason as anyone for killing Margaret. Yancy, she concluded slowly, was not the *only* person who would have liked to kill Margaret—just the most obvious!

Sara sighed dejectedly. All of this useless speculation, she admitted glumly, trying to guess who had been

Margaret's killer, was wasting time. She was avoiding the only question that mattered, the agonizing question that she had to answer once and for all: did she believe that Yancy had killed Margaret?

Sara couldn't honestly answer that question. She loved him. She did not *want* to believe that he could be a cold-blooded murderer. But he could be, she confessed miserably. He *could* have murdered Margaret. He was obsessed by Casa Paloma—hadn't he boldly kidnapped her, and wasn't he determined to marry her and get a child to inherit Casa Paloma? Didn't those actions indicate that he was a man capable of letting *nothing*, not even murder, stand in the way of what he wanted?

Sara's mouth twisted. There were only two things that she knew for certain: she *loved* Yancy Cantrell and she had *never* been fearful of him, had never felt that her life was in danger from *him*! Whether he had killed Margaret or not had nothing to do with *them*, she thought fiercely.

Bleakly aware that she was being weak and unfair to both of them by simply burying her head and hoping that the problem would go away, but incapable of doing anything else, she rose from the bed and reluctantly picked up the dagger. Walking into Yancy's room, she laid it on the top of a massive, heavily carved bureau and quickly left his quarters.

The shady, covered walkways were deserted—it was siesta time—and, glad that no one was about, especially Yancy, Sara rushed into her own room, slamming the door shut behind her. Eyes closed in relief that she had reached the solace of her own room, she rested back against the door's wooden bulk. Safe.

"*Sara*! Where did you come from? You startled me, child!" exclaimed Ann loudly, not ten feet away from her.

Suppressing a heartfelt groan, praying fervently that

she had been mistaken, Sara opened her eyes. Her ears had not deceived her—Ann Shelldrake was in her room!

Garbed in a gown of pale blue silk, her blond ringlets tied neatly at her neck with a white bow, Ann was standing at the end of Sara's bed. She looked, Sara thought idly, almost guilty. As if she had been caught doing something she shouldn't be doing.

Sara frowned slightly. "What are you doing in my room?" she asked quietly. "Were you looking for me?"

Drifting regally toward her, Ann quickly recovered her composure and said lightly, "Why, yes, I was, my dear." She smiled at Sara. "I had hoped to find you alone—we *must* talk about this ridiculous notion of your marrying Yancy on Wednesday. It simply cannot happen! I forbid it!"

"You forbid it?" Sara repeated dumbly. "How can you? And why?"

Ann laughed harshly. "Well, I can't *actually* forbid it, but, my dearest child, think! You cannot want to marry him! He is a murderer!"

"Is he?" Sara asked tightly. "No one has ever proved that."

Ann's face hardened. "Don't tell me he has so besotted you that you believe him *innocent*?"

Ann's question cut to the bone, but Sara could not bring herself to share the uncertainties in her own mind with the other woman. Her voice cool, she said, "I don't think that this is any of your business."

"Listen to me, you little fool!" Ann snapped. "Marry Yancy Cantrell and you will regret it for the rest of your days."

"That may be," Sara agreed equitably, "but isn't that my decision to make?"

"Oh! I don't know why I bother! There is just no talking to you!" Ann said impatiently. "You're determined to ruin your life!"

Sara smiled bleakly, and stepping away from the door, she said quietly, "That may be. We'll just have to wait and see, won't we? Now, if you don't mind, I'd like to be alone, and I'd appreciate it if you didn't come into my room uninvited again."

"*Well!*" Ann said indignantly. "Haven't we turned into a haughty madam! And the ring is not even on your finger yet!"

"Ann, let it be. I'm marrying Yancy on Wednesday and there is nothing you or anyone else can say or do that will change my mind. Now, please, leave me alone."

"We'll just see whether you marry Yancy on Wednesday! You just wait!"

Ann swept furiously from the room, the door banging shut behind her flying silken skirts.

Rubbing a hand wearily across her forehead, Sara wandered over to a high-backed chair and sat down in it, wondering how she had endured Ann's tempers and tantrums all these years.

It was odd, but the exchange with Ann had clarified certain things in her mind. She *was* going to marry Yancy on Wednesday, and her decision had nothing to do with his threats to go ahead with the wedding regardless of whether or not she consented. She loved him and she wanted to marry him and she realized that she had indeed spoken the truth to Ann—there was *nothing* that anyone could say or do that would shake her from that firm resolve!

The day before the wedding was like the lull before the storm. Sara had nothing to do with the actual arrangements; Yancy, Maria and the others were taking care of all the little details. Sara was aware of the excited bustle that seemed to permeate the very hacienda, but it didn't touch her. Bartholomew and the other servants from Magnolia Grove had obviously been pressed into last-minute service for the great day. Her lovely wedding dress hung in all its finished glory in the front of the wardrobe, and Maria and Tansy had been quarreling amiably over which one of them should have the pleasure of dressing her and arranging her hair the morning of the actual ceremony.

Sara hadn't seen Yancy since their confrontation over the dagger—he seemed to be avoiding her and she didn't know whether she was glad or disturbed by his actions. The few times she'd seen Ann, the older woman had simply given her a cool greeting and then managed to pretend that Sara wasn't even in the same room with her.

Time seemed suspended to Sara the day before she would marry Yancy, the minutes and hours moving in slow, inexorable motion. By late afternoon, when the worst of the heat had dissipated, she was thoroughly bored and sick of her own company and decided that a walk to the stable to see Locuela would be a pleasant diversion. Donning a wide-brimmed, woven straw hat, she begged some dried apples from Dolores in the kitchen and strolled off.

Since their misadventure together, Sara had grown very fond of the little chestnut mare and had been inordinately pleased when Yancy had told her some days ago that she could consider Locuela her own personal mount. She had made several of these excursions to give Locuela some special treat, and the mare had quickly learned that Sara's presence indicated a tasty morsel was in the offing. Locuela, having caught her scent, was whickering to her even before she entered the shadowy coolness of the stable. Grinning, Sara walked over to the mare's stall and presented the dried apples. She spent several enjoyable minutes with Locuela, scratching her neck and crooning silly nonsense to the mare as the treats were daintily consumed.

Eventually, giving Locuela one last pat on the shoulder, she turned away, intending to return to the hacienda. She had taken only two steps toward the wide double doors of the stable when Hyrum suddenly appeared before her. They had not spoken privately since his arrival; as a matter of fact, Sara had not seen him since that day. Yancy had only indicated rather sourly that, in view of Hyrum's service to his father, he would give him a chance to prove his worth at del Sol.

Smiling pleasantly at him, Sara said warmly, "Hyrum! How good to see you! I hope that you are settling in well and that you're finding the rancho to your liking."

Hyrum ignored her friendly greeting. "Are you really going to marry *him* tomorrow?"

Sara stiffened. "Why, yes, I am," she replied in a much cooler tone of voice.

"How can you, after what he did?" Hyrum demanded hotly. "How can you bring yourself to marry a black-hearted murderer?"

Sara sighed. She really was getting tired of everyone trying to convince her not to marry Yancy, and she was getting even more tired of hearing him called a murderer! Fixing Hyrum with a stern glance, she asked softly, "Are you so certain that he killed Margaret? You had as much of a motive as he did."

An uneasy expression crossed his face. "What do you mean by that?"

"Only that I overheard a conversation between you and Margaret and I know that she threatened to get Sam to fire you and hire a new overseer. She was going to tell Sam that you were pestering her with unwanted attentions."

Hyrum looked thunderstruck. "You know about that?"

Sara nodded. "And it gave you a very good motive."

"But I didn't kill her!" he said passionately. "I despised her, but I wouldn't have harmed her! Besides," he added sullenly, "it was Yancy who swore he'd kill her before he'd let her have Casa Paloma."

"That's true," Sara said agreeably, "but do you have any proof that he actually did it?"

"Everyone knows he did it! *Everyone!*" Seeing that Sara was not overly impressed by his argument, he added spitefully, "And everyone knows that he's marrying you for only one thing—to get his greedy hands on Casa Paloma!" When Sara made no reply, but only stood there regarding him sadly, Hyrum suddenly grabbed her and pulled her into his arms. "Sara, come to your senses before it's too late! Don't throw your life away!" he cried. "Marry him tomorrow and you'll regret it for the rest of your life!"

Gently disengaging herself from his embrace, she stepped away and said with quiet dignity, "I appreciate your concern. And because I know you have only my best interests at heart, I will pretend that you did not just vilify the man I am going to marry—a man, I might add, who has given you shelter and who is willing to let you prove yourself. Why don't you give him the same chance?"

Hyrum stared at her as if she had gone mad. "What has he done to you? Why are you acting this way? What happened to your plans for Casa Paloma?"

Sara had no answers for him and she turned away, realizing unhappily that she could not, *would* not, explain herself to him. Hyrum's hand on her arm jerked her back in his direction. His even features flushed an unbecoming shade of red, his pale blue eyes narrowed and hard, he said contemptuously, "And I thought you were different! You're just like Margaret—as long as there is a fortune involved, you'd sell yourself to the devil himself!"

"I think," Sara gritted out tightly, "that you've said just about enough! You, more than anyone else, have no right to judge me—or Yancy! Now, let me go before you make me say something we will both regret."

With a disgusted gesture, Hyrum released her arm. "Think about this, Sara," he said harshly. "You can order me to stop telling you things you don't want to hear, you can even run away from me—but if you marry Yancy Cantrell, after tomorrow you'll *never* be able to run away from *him*!"

Thoroughly ruffled by the unpleasant exchange with Hyrum, Sara fairly bolted from the stables. She had made up her mind to marry Yancy, but she couldn't deny that being met by such violent opposition to that decision was not a trifle unnerving, especially in view of her own uncertainties. She was determined not to let herself start questioning the wisdom of what she was doing, but, by heavens, it certainly wasn't easy!

She was still slightly flustered and a little out of breath by the time she reached the patio, and she was hoping to find a cool, shadowy corner in which to sit, *alone*, and recover some of her composure before she had to face anyone else.

Tom Shelldrake, his bad arm resting in its usual sling, was sitting near the fountain, idly watching the bright-colored flashes of the goldfish when Sara entered the patio, and she almost groaned out loud. There were several reasons for her *not* to like Tom, but she did. He was so patently grateful for the help that Sam had given him after the war, and while he could sometimes be as arrogant and overbearing as Ann, he was, like Sam, a basically good man—despite his deplorable affair with Sam's wife. In the beginning Sara had wondered how Tom had allowed himself to enter into an adulterous liaison with his best friend's wife, and she had long ago decided that he had probably been more a victim of Margaret's manipulations than a philandering male. He and Sam both had been flawed in some respects, especially where Margaret was concerned, but Sara had never forgotten Tom's kind manner to her that first night at Magnolia Grove, and he had been exceedingly comforting to her in the terrible days following Sam's death. Putting a gracious smile on her lips, she walked up to him.

"They're very pretty, aren't they?" she said by way of greeting.

Tom glanced up and smiled. "Indeed they are, but not nearly as lovely as you, my dear!"

Sara laughed and sat down beside him. "You're very gallant, kind sir!"

"Ah, Sara, it is good to hear you laugh—you haven't had much laughter in your life, have you?"

Sara smiled gently, noting Tom's worn features. "Oh, don't worry about me! I've had my fair share!"

Maria appeared just then, bearing a large silver tray with a pitcher of sangria, some glasses and a pottery bowl of crisp-fried *buñuelos* sprinkled with cane syrup. Seeing Sara, she exclaimed, "Oh, I did not know that you were joining the senor! Would you like me to bring you a bowl of *buñuelos*, too?"

Sara shook her head. "No, no, that won't be necessary, but since there are already extra glasses, I shall enjoy some sangria."

After Maria had poured them each a glass of sangria and had departed, Tom and Sara sat there in companionable silence, sipping their sangria and watching the fish swim. It was a very tranquil setting, and sitting beside Tom on the broad rim of the fountain, Sara felt some of the tension caused by her bitter exchange with Hyrum slowly dissipate.

The heat of the day was waning, but the drowsy buzz of the multitude of insects could still be heard, and Sara decided that this was one of her favorite times of the day. Soon the purple, cooling shadows of dusk would fall, followed by the star-studded black cloak of night, but this brief interval between daylight and dusk always seemed so restful to Sara. She took another sip of sangria and let out a sigh of contentment.

Tom glanced at her. "A sigh? A happy one or sad?"

Sara smiled. "Neither—merely contented."

"Are you, my dear?" Tom asked with quiet intensity, his weary brown eyes fixed intently on her face. "You have no reservations about the step you are taking tomorrow?"

Sara grimaced. "Certainly I have reservations—didn't you before you married Ann? Doesn't everyone on the eve of such a momentous undertaking question themselves about the rightness of it? Wonder if they are making a mistake?"

"In your case, I would think that you would wonder a great deal more than others!"

Sara met his troubled gaze squarely. "Because of the murder? Is that what you're referring to? Margaret's murder?"

It was Tom's turn to grimace. "I know that it is none of my business," he said slowly, "and I do not mean to intrude, but surely, my dear, you must have some deep reservations about the wisdom of marrying a man accused of murder."

Sara stared off into the distance, wishing that he had not broached the painful subject of Margaret's death; she was becoming downright irritated at the way everyone just *assumed* that Yancy was guilty. But there was such gentle sincerity in Tom's voice, such concern, that Sara's defenses were instantly breached, and in a low voice she admitted, "There are times that I wonder if I am a fool, and others . . ." Her voice trailed off and she took a quick sip of her sangria. Fixing her clear emerald gaze on him, she asked abruptly, "Do you think he killed Margaret?"

Shelldrake looked uncomfortable. "Sara, I . . ." He sighed heavily and then said honestly, "Yes, I'm afraid that I do—his violent temper was, is, known by everyone, that and the fact that he absolutely *despised* Margaret. He had a compelling reason for murdering her, and it was common knowledge that he had threatened to kill her numerous times. There was no one else it could have been but Yancy!"

Sara's gaze never wavered and she said softly, "But that's not true. Margaret was, with the exception of Sam, universally hated. There are any number of people who could have had as good a reason as Yancy's to kill her." Gently, she added, "Even you."

"What the devil do you mean by that?" Tom demanded sharply, a faint flush of anger staining his cheeks.

Sara's mouth twisted wryly. She would have given a great deal not to be dragging up all the old, painful wounds—particularly, she did not want to hurt or offend a man she liked very much—but she had no choice. Taking a deep breath, she said bluntly, "Only that I overheard a conversation between Margaret and Ann the night before Margaret was killed, and I know about the affair you had with Margaret . . . and the fact that the child she carried might have been *your* baby! According to your wife, you were worried that knowledge of the affair might come out and that it would ruin your chances for the judgeship. Some might say that both you and Ann had a good reason to want Margaret dead. I'm not accusing you or Ann of murdering Margaret, but don't you see," Sara said passionately, "if suspicion could fall, even for a moment, on someone like you, then you must admit that there were all sorts of people besides Yancy who hated Margaret enough to have killed her. Even Bartholomew had a motive; Hyrum had a reason, and it can also be argued that Sam, if he'd found out about her affair with you, could have wanted her dead.

Oh, don't you see what I'm trying to say? *Any*one could have murdered her—not *just* Yancy!"

"Oh, but I do see!" Tom said stiffly, a frigid expression on his usually amiable features. Rising to his feet, he looked pityingly at her. "What I see is a self-centered, ungrateful, *thoughtless* young woman, so determined to marry the Cantrell fortune that she is willing to cast stones at anyone in order to convince herself that her fiancé is innocent!"

"It's not that at all!" Sara denied fiercely. "I only wanted to point out that there are *others* who might conceivably have killed Margaret!"

"Well, you've certainly pointed it out, I must say!" Rounding on his heels, Tom stalked off, outrage in every line of his body.

Dismayed, Sara watched him go, wondering how she could have let her wretched tongue alienate a man who had been a comforting friend to her these past years. Maybe he was right, she thought forlornly; maybe she *was* casting around for someone else to take the blame for Margaret's murder. Feeling particularly depressed and uncertain, Sara left her perch by the fountain to take a stroll around the grounds of the hacienda. Dusk was falling and there was little to see in the failing light, but the gloomy shadows of gathering night suited her bleak mood just fine! She wandered aimlessly for quite some time and then, realizing that the hour was growing late, began to make her way back toward the hacienda.

The scent of tobacco suddenly drifted on the night air, and glancing around, Sara spied the glowing tip of a cheroot. She could barely make out the long outline of a man's figure as he lounged against the outside wall of the hacienda, but from the way her pulse jumped and her heart began to race, she knew who watched her in the darkness. Stilling her crazy senses, she walked over to him. "Spying on me?" she asked dryly. "Afraid I'll try to run away again?"

Yancy took a drag of the cheroot, then flicked it carelessly onto the ground. He was lounging negligently, one knee bent, one booted foot resting against the adobe wall, and when Sara came nearer, he lazily pulled her into his arms. Searching her lovely features in the faint light of the rising moon, he asked, "Would you? Run away?"

His mouth was inches from hers, his breath warm and smoky, and Sara was suddenly almost giddy with desire. Making no attempt to escape from him, she met his seeking gaze and smiled ruefully. "No, I won't run away. Once was quite enough, thank you very much!"

His lips quirked slightly, but he said dryly, "*Querida*, that wasn't exactly the answer I wanted . . . and you know it!" He brushed his lips tantalizingly across hers. "Since you won't take the hint, I'll have to put it more bluntly. Are you going to marry me tomorrow?"

Sara slowly nodded her head, her eyes never leaving his. "I don't have much of a choice, do I?"

"No," he breathed thickly; "no, you don't!" He kissed her then, a kiss of such sweetness, of such suppressed passion, that the world spun dreamily out of control for Sara and she trembled in his embrace. When he lifted his head a lifetime later, she could only stare dazedly up at his dark face, her lips raptly parted, her eyes softly glowing. He smiled. "Run along to bed, sweetheart. You won't get much sleep tomorrow night—that I can promise you!"

Sara wandered slowly back inside the hacienda. In her room, she noted the lamp by her bedside which one of the servants must have left for her, and slowly she began to undress, her starry-eyed mood still upon her. Wearing her nightgown of soft, worn muslin, she undid her hair and idly began to brush the long honey-gold locks.

Tomorrow was her wedding day. This time tomorrow night she would be Yancy's wife. . . .

A dreamy smile on her lips, she finally put down the brush and walked over to her bed. She was on the point of blowing out the lamp and climbing into bed when something made her take a second glance at the smooth expanse of the covers. A little frown wrinkled her forehead. That was the problem—the covers *weren't* smooth. Right in the middle, where she would lie, there was a slight hump, its rounded shape seeming to undulate now and then with a mesmerizing movement.

Sara's blissful mood vanished and her mouth was suddenly dry. With a shaking hand, she grasped one end of the covers and flung them aside.

She leaped back instinctively at the sight of what lay curled up on her bed: ring upon ring of lethal coils, its flat, triangular head pointed in her direction. A *rattlesnake*!

In horror, Sara gasped and staggered back even farther out of striking range of the snake, and only then did she hear the warning buzz of its madly vibrating tail. The snake, a large one, was tightly coiled and ready to strike, and for one mind-numbing moment Sara could only stare at it, hardly daring to breathe as reality hit her. *Someone had deliberately put a rattlesnake in her bed*!

∞ 16

Frozen in atavistic horror, Sara just stood there staring at the snake, her thoughts jostling wildly through her brain. Was she out of range of the venom-filled fangs? In trepidation, she eyed the four feet or less that separated them. Yancy had once told her that a rattlesnake could strike up to two-thirds of its body length, but how long did they grow? she wondered almost hysterically. Five feet? Six feet? Longer? More importantly, how long was *this* rattler?

Beyond its constantly flicking forked tongue, the snake was not moving. It was tightly coiled, its head tucked down close to its body, its black eyes never leaving Sara.

Carefully, Sara took a step backward. When the snake remained undisturbed, she took another one. Feeling a little safer, she glanced around nervously for some sort of weapon. There was none. She considered backing up to the door and going after help, but the notion that the snake could slither off her bed and hide itself somewhere in her room while she was gone was utterly unnerving. No. She wasn't taking her eyes off the damn snake until it was dead!

Some of her terror was fading, but she was aware that she was still shaking slightly and that her heart was beating very fast. She was more scared than she cared to admit. Again she glanced around her room for a weapon. Her eyes fell upon the heavy dark crucifix on the wall. She glanced back at the snake. Then at the crucifix.

Could she use the crucifix like an ax? Was it long enough? She eyed the snake again. She swallowed. Cautiously, she edged near the wall and reached up and grasped the crucifix. It was a long and narrow wooden crucifix, the cross arms nearly two feet wide, the base perhaps three, the figure of Christ beautifully and delicately carved.

Her hand fastened around the end of the crucifix and she lifted it gently from the wall, reassured by the balance and weight of it in her grip. The crucifix firmly grasped in one hand, her eyes on the snake, she took a careful step nearer to the bed. The snake moved slightly, its head rising upward just a fraction, almost as if it sensed danger. Sara glanced at the crucifix held in her hand like a club and a bubble of hysterical laughter rose in her chest. Most people merely prayed to Christ for some mysterious, miraculous intervention in their lives, but tonight Christ was to play a decidedly *active*, practical part in her life!

She took another deep breath, tightened her grip on the crucifix and, moving swiftly, stepped within range and struck at the snake at the same time. The snake lunged at the crucifix, and not even aware that she did it, Sara gave a soft little scream of pure fright. She retreated slightly; then, grimacing and gritting her teeth, she closed the distance between them and struck again at the snake. This time her blow connected.

It seemed like hours, but it could have been only moments later that the snake was dead. Trembling with reaction, Sara dropped the bloodied crucifix and staggered backward from the bed. A hand to her mouth, her eyes wide and dilated with remembered terror, she stumbled farther away from the carnage on her bed.

The door suddenly opened behind her and, a merry smile on her face, Maria came in carrying a small tray with a pot of creamy, sweet hot chocolate and a delicate china cup and saucer. "Ah, *bueno*! You have not gone to bed yet. I thought you might enjoy a cup of chocolate before you retired."

Maria caught sight of the expression on Sara's face and her smile faded. Then she saw the snake on the bed—or rather, what remained of the snake. The tray crashed to the floor and she let out a shriek that was no doubt heard in Mexico. "*Ay*! *Ay*! *Cáspita*! What has happened here? Are you hurt? The snake did not bite you, did it?"

Maria had barely stopped speaking before Yancy appeared in the doorway, his pistol in one hand, the expression on his face dangerously fierce. He took in the scene in one comprehensive glance and then he was across the room, his arms closing tightly around Sara's trembling body. His mouth pressing gently against her temple, he asked urgently, "Did it strike you?"

Against his warm chest, Sara shook her head vehemently, her body shuddering afresh with reaction, the feel of Yancy's strong arms around her the most blessed sensation in the world. Now that it was over, now that she was safe, she suddenly burst into tears, great, gulping sobs racking her.

Wordlessly, Yancy scooped her up in his arms and strode from the room. As he passed Maria, he said curtly, "Get rid of it and send Esteban to me immediately." He looked down at the shattered pot and the spilled chocolate. "You might also prepare another tray for her. Bring it to my rooms, along with the rest of her clothes—she's *never* sleeping in here again!"

With Sara protectively cradled in his arms, Yancy swiftly reached his rooms. Kicking open the door, he crossed the lamplit room and with exquisite tenderness deposited Sara in the middle of his big bed. When he went to rise, Sara's arms tightened around his neck and she whispered, "Don't leave me—not yet."

Yancy smiled slightly, and laying aside his pistol, which was still in his hand, he sank down slowly beside her, aligning his big body next to hers. He kissed her ear and murmured, "You *do* know that Esteban and Maria are going to be here in a few minutes? I wouldn't want to start something I couldn't finish. . . ."

Some of her primitive fear ebbing away, she glared up at him. "*That* wasn't why I wanted you to stay!"

He smiled even more, a mocking gleam in his amber-gold eyes. "I didn't think so . . . but you're not thinking about what happened anymore, are you?"

Sara looked at him in surprise. She wasn't. And she wasn't going to either, she thought with a shudder. Yancy kissed her then, fully on her lips, his tongue sliding hungrily into her mouth. With a wantonness that shocked her, she returned his kiss and he growled low in his throat, his arms crushing her to him, his tongue delving even deeper.

With an effort, he finally lifted his lips from her throbbing mouth and, staring down into her face, said thickly, "Tomorrow night, respond as sweetly and I shall know that there is indeed a heaven on earth!"

He got up from the bed, picked up the gun and carefully slipped it into the holster that was draped over the back of a chair. He had just turned to look back at Sara when there was a sharp rap on the door. At his command, the door opened to reveal Esteban Chavez, an anxious expression on his darkly handsome features, his sombrero held in his hand.

"Senor! Maria has told me what happened. How could this terrible thing have occurred?"

Yancy shrugged, and with a warning in his gaze, he cut his eyes in Sara's direction, and murmured, "We'll talk about it outside, just as soon as Maria arrives—I don't want to leave her alone."

Maria arrived a few minutes later, a freshly prepared tray in her hands and some pieces of clothing draped over her arm—in anticipation of the wedding, everything except for a few items had already been moved into Sara's new rooms. Clucking like a hen with one chick, Maria barely acknowledged the men, but hurried over to the bed.

Seeing that Sara was in safe hands, Yancy motioned to Esteban and the two men walked to the door. Just before he left the room, Yancy said to Maria, "Don't leave her! We'll be back in a few minutes." Closing the door firmly behind him, he looked carefully around the deserted courtyard and empty walkways. Satisfied that no one was about, he offered Esteban a smoke and both men lit the long black cheroots. They smoked in silence for several minutes; then Esteban said quietly, "It is a strange thing, senor, that snake in your lady's room."

His eyes hooded, Yancy nodded. "Damn strange! *Por Dios*! There hasn't been a rattlesnake spotted inside the compound since I was a boy. Before then, once in a while one would be found warming itself on the courtyard stones, but *never* in the hacienda itself, much less coiled in somebody's bed!"

Esteban regarded Yancy's shuttered features in the darkness. "Do you think," he asked carefully, "that someone meant to harm your *novia*? That it was done deliberately?"

Yancy looked full at him, and at the savage fury glittering in the depths of those golden eyes, Esteban glanced quickly away.

"Yes, I think it was done deliberately," Yancy growled, a note in his voice making Esteban *very* glad that he was not the person who had done this evil thing. "And I would hazard a guess that we don't have far to look for the culprit!"

Esteban glanced at him. "You think it is one of the gringos?"

Yancy tossed aside his half-smoked cheroot with a violent motion. "Who else?" he snapped. "Sara has been here for weeks and nothing like this has happened. *They* have not been here more than three days and already my *novia* has found a rattlesnake in her bed! Wouldn't that make you just a little suspicious?"

Esteban nodded. "*Sí*! But which one? And how do you mean to discover the evil one? They are not likely to tell you the truth if you were to ask them."

"I know. But I want you to question the servants. Find out if anyone saw one of the gringos near Sara's room this evening. Find out, if you can, who caught the snake—Hyrum is the most likely prospect for that, since he has had complete access to the rancho." Yancy frowned. "The Shelldrakes have *appeared* to stay strictly inside the hacienda, and I can't imagine Senora Shelldrake wrestling with a rattlesnake herself, although I *can* see her plotting such a thing! Senor Shelldrake has a crippled arm, which would make capturing a live rattlesnake rather chancy, but I'm not eliminating any of them for the time being." He looked grimly at his head vaquero. "One last thing—pick a couple of our most trustworthy men and assign them to watch my *novia*. Tell them to do it without making themselves noticed. Quietly, *mi amigo*."

Esteban nodded and the men talked in low voices for a few minutes longer. Then, tossing aside his cheroot, Esteban left Yancy, disappearing into the darkness of the night.

Again Yancy's eyes did a slow, thorough appraisal of the area, but seeing nothing to arouse his suspicions, he turned and entered his rooms. Maria was sitting in a chair beside the bed, where Sara was comfortably ensconced, a pile of pillows at her back as she sipped the hot, sweet chocolate.

There was still remembered terror lurking in the depths of her lovely eyes, but wearing a clean, fresh nightgown, her face looking as if it had been thoroughly scrubbed and her hair caught up in a wide band of green silk ribbon, she bore few traces of her recent ordeal. She looked, in fact, Yancy thought with a sudden quickening of his breath, just as he had so often imagined. A faint, sensuous smile curved his bottom lip. Well, perhaps not *exactly* as he had pictured her; in his reveries she was usually naked, and her maid was not sitting at her side, chatting blithely away about all the delicacies that had been baked and cooked for the wedding feast tomorrow!

It was obvious that Maria was doing her best to keep Sara distracted from what had happened, and the tiny smile that lurked at the corners of Sara's mouth and her relaxed air revealed that Maria was doing a very good job of it, too! Yancy noted grimly, however, that Sara lay *atop* the covers, a gaily woven blanket merely thrown across her lower limbs. He suspected that it would be a long time before she could ever crawl into bed without remembering the rattlesnake, and his eyes hardened. Someone was going to suffer a rather nasty fate because of tonight's doings!

None of his thoughts showed on his face, though, as he strolled up to the two women. At his approach, Maria sprang to her feet and murmured, "Unless there is something more you wish of me, I shall be gone—*mi madre* and I plan to bake more *fruta de horno* before we retire for the night." Despite all the questions he glimpsed in her eyes, Yancy was grateful that Maria had deliberately made no mention of the snake, nor of what he and Esteban had talked about outside.

There was an awkward little silence after Maria had departed, but, carefully putting down her cup and drawing her knees up protectively to her chest, Sara tried for a light note. "Does that happen often at del Sol? Rattlesnakes crawling into beds?"

Yancy scowled. He would have preferred not to talk about what had happened—at least not right now. Sara looked fairly serene and he wanted her to stay that way! Mostly, he just wanted her safe and happy and to forget about the damned snake! And as for the culprits . . . An ugly smile touched his chiseled lips. Someone was going to find out just how cruel and heartless a man with the blood of the conquistadors in his veins could be!

But, aware that for her own safety Sara needed some plain speaking about what had happened, Yancy took the chair that Maria had vacated and stretched his long legs out in front of him. "No, it doesn't!" he said baldly. "And it *shouldn't* have happened at all!"

Sara shuddered slightly. In a small voice, she said, "Someone tried to kill me, didn't they? If I hadn't seen it before I got into bed . . ." She swallowed. "It would have struck me, perhaps even several times, before I realized what was happening. I could have *died*!"

Yancy cursed violently under his breath and in one swift movement left his seat and went to lie on the bed beside Sara. As natural as breathing, she came into his arms. After settling her comfortably beside his long length, he said bluntly, "I don't think there is any question about that! The question is who and why."

Her cheek resting against his warm chest, her fingers nervously playing with the buttons on his shirt, Sara muttered, "I'm glad you didn't try to tell me that I was imagining things."

Above her head, Yancy said dryly, "That would have been rather difficult, don't you think, when I was faced with such convincing evidence? Unless, of course, you wanted more attention and placed the snake there yourself?"

Her head jerked up at his words, her lips half parted in outrage as she glared at him. It was the last thing on his mind, but as he stared at those sweetly shaped lips, Yancy forgot everything but how much he wanted to kiss her again, to press his lips against hers and feel her yielding mouth beneath his, to assure himself that she really was warm and *safe* in his arms. With a muttered imprecation, he tightened his arms, and his mouth descended to fasten urgently on hers. She melted into his embrace, her arms going around his neck, her mouth opening eagerly for the impatient exploration of his tongue.

Sara's brush with danger had left them both shaken, and now, as they lay in each other's arms, a primitive urge to affirm, to celebrate the intoxicating knowledge that they were *alive*, suddenly swept over them. They kissed with a frantic urgency, their hands desperately tearing at hindering clothing until they were naked together, their limbs entwined. This was no gentle seduction, no sweet lovemaking. Yancy's hands were hard, almost rough as they explored her body, his kisses fierce and demanding, and Sara shivered in excitement at the barely suppressed violence of his caresses. Her fingers tightened pleasurably in his hair when his teeth tugged ungently at her aching nipples and she moaned softly when his hands boldly opened her legs.

There were few preliminaries, both of them already half mad with the reckless need to join their bodies. His fingers explored her swiftly, and finding her moist and welcoming, Yancy growled low in his throat. Catching her hips, he lifted her to him and in one swift motion buried himself within her tight slickness.

He rode her hard, his mouth crushed against hers, his hands on her hips, ruthlessly holding her where he wanted as he drove himself deep inside her time and time again. The need to spill his seed, the instinctive prompting to pour into her the very essence of himself, was overpowering, and as the sweet pleasure began to rise inexorably within him, his pounding against her became almost frantic.

Sara found this wild, almost savage lovemaking shockingly erotic, Yancy's utter domination of her body so strongly arousing that her fingers dug into his broad back with increasing delight every time their bodies met. The feel of him, of his big body moving on hers, filling her, possessing her, made her tremble beneath him; the sensations, the spiraling desire, combining inside her until she was aware of nothing but the fierce hunger within herself to reach that peak of pleasure she knew would soon be hers.

Their bodies met and parted with increasing urgency and Sara stiffened as the first spasms exploded through her; Yancy's hands tightened on her hips and a primitive, jubilant cry burst from deep in his throat as he furiously pumped his seed into her.

They lay together a long time, Yancy unable to bring himself to move away from her as Sara's fingers absently toyed with the curly hair at the nape of his neck. They kissed lazily, the frantic, almost savage urgency of their lovemaking having vanished. It was sometime later when Yancy finally slid off her body, but he did not leave her; his arms pulled her tightly to him and eventually they slept, the rattlesnake and the danger to Sara the last things on their minds.

When Sara woke, she was alone in Yancy's bed, and a little flush stained her cheeks when she remembered the previous night's violent mating. Then she smiled, a woman's secret smile that has driven men to distraction for centuries.

Stretching luxuriously, aware of sweet aches in her body that had not been there before Yancy's lovemaking, she lay there staring dreamily at the ceiling. Today was her wedding day. Before another night fell, she would marry the man she loved.

Humming lightly to herself, she pulled the bell rope that would summon Maria. Breakfast, or *desayuno*, as Maria referred to it, first, and then a long, relaxing bath.

A half hour later, having eaten her light repast, Sara sank blissfully into a tub of rose-scented hot water. Maria had placed a screen around the tub, and from the other side, Sara could hear her chattering away as she laid out the garments Sara would need for the day. Neither one of them had made mention of last night's nearly tragic event, and even when the memory of the snake tried to intrude into Sara's consciousness, she pushed it viciously aside. This was her wedding day! She was *not* going to let anything spoil it!

Unfortunately, it was at that moment that the door to the suite of rooms suddenly flew open and Ann rushed in. "Where is she?" Ann cried in great agitation. "Is she all right? I just heard the awful news!"

Sara sighed. She didn't really want to face Ann right now, but, rising from the tub and wrapping a towel around her body, she said easily enough, "I'm right here, Ann. And as you can see, I am unharmed. I was frightened last night and it was a horrible experience, but I am just fine."

"Oh, you poor darling!" Ann exclaimed warmly, a sympathetic expression on her face as she came over to Sara. "What a terrible thing to have happen! Why, if you hadn't seen the snake, who knows what the outcome would have been!"

Hoping that Ann would have enough sense to let the subject drop, Sara seated herself on a velvet-covered stool before the satinwood dressing table and murmured, "It's over! And I would prefer not to think about it anymore." Her eyes met Ann's in the mirror which hung over the dressing table. "Today is my wedding day. I don't want to ruin it with ugly memories."

Ann's expression changed to one of horrified disbelief. "Oh, but, Sara, you can't possibly mean to go through with it! Not after what happened!"

"That's exactly what I mean! It was an unfortunate experience, one I don't want to repeat, but it changed nothing!"

Ann looked impatiently over at Maria, who was still lovingly laying out Sara's wedding garments on the bed. "Leave us!" Ann said in her most imperious manner. "I wish to talk to your mistress in private."

Maria glanced at Sara, and at Sara's faint nod, she withdrew from the room. Crossing to stand behind Sara, Ann rested her hands on the younger woman's shoulders and said, "I know that I have often been a trial to you— I *know* I'm arrogant and demanding—but you have to believe me when I say now that I have your best interests at heart. I'm very fond of you and I don't want you to be hurt. You *cannot* marry that man! Not after what happened last night!"

"What in the world are you talking about? Why should last night change anything?"

Ann seemed to hesitate. Then she took a deep breath and, her eyes locking on Sara's in the mirror, said softly, "Sara, Sara! Don't you realize what happened? Don't you understand the danger you are in? Hasn't it occurred to you that you could have *died* last night? And if you had died, Yancy would not be forced to marry you today to gain control of Casa Paloma!"

Impatiently Sara dragged a brush through her honey-gold curls and tried not to let Ann's ugly words destroy the happy glow that surrounded her. Aware of the other woman's fixed gaze, Sara looked away, wondering bleakly why Ann seemed to thrive on discord and why she *always* twisted things and interpreted events in the

most distasteful light possible. The best way to deal
with Ann, Sara had learned painfully, was to simply
ignore her, but it was hard to do that, particularly when
Ann's "Yancy would not be forced to marry you" rang
so unpleasantly in her ears. Out loud she said exasperatedly, "Have you forgotten that if I die without issue,
it is Bartholomew and Tansy who inherit the land, *not*
Yancy?"

"No, I haven't forgotten," Ann replied gently. "But
don't you see that also gives Bartholomew and Tansy a
very good reason for wishing you to die?"

Sara frowned. She hadn't considered that aspect, but
if she had, she would have dismissed it for the foolish notion it was—Bartholomew and Tansy wouldn't
harm her! And from nowhere came a flashing moment
of doubt. Or would they? If she died without a child,
they *did* inherit Casa Paloma. She shook her head vehemently in denial, firmly dispelling the unworthy thought.
After the scene yesterday, she should have known that
Ann would try to poison her mind with more of her malicious barbs. Ann had a wonderful way of planting little
seeds of doubt and then carefully nurturing them along
until the results she wanted came to fruition. Well, Sara
wasn't going to let her get away with it this time! Bluntly she asked, "Ann, which is it? First you implied that
Yancy wanted me dead; now you're casting suspicion on
Bartholomew and Tansy." Dryly she added, "Or perhaps
you think all three of them are in collusion together. Is
that it?"

Ann's hand tightened on her shoulders. "Why is that
so impossible to believe?" she demanded with such passionate sincerity that Sara was startled. "Bartholomew
is Yancy's uncle, or have *you* forgotten that fact? And
Yancy's real objection to Casa Paloma is that it sits
well inside the borders of del Sol. If you were dead,
without issue, what would stop him from paying off

Bartholomew and Tansy? If you were dead, Yancy could *still* have Paloma, but he wouldn't be shackled to a wife he never wanted! Bartholomew and Tansy would have a fortune and *they* wouldn't be bound to a run-down, worthless bit of dirt in the wilds of this godforsaken country! Do you really think that after having been a slave most of his life, despite his Cantrell blood—or perhaps *because* of it—Bartholomew wouldn't leap at the chance to gain a fortune? Or that Tansy hasn't been resentful of her position? No one denies that there is a strong bond between Yancy and Bartholomew. They *could* have planned it!" Ann's eyes filled with tears. "Oh, Sara, don't you see that I'm only trying to help you? For once stop thinking of me as your enemy and realize that I am trying to help you!"

"Yancy wouldn't . . ." Sara got out from between stiff lips, her thoughts whirling. It was Ann's manner rather than what she was saying that had shaken Sara and made her listen to what the other woman was saying. Coupled with Ann's apparent concern and candor, her words made a terrible sort of sense, but Sara fought against the idea of even considering that there might be a hint of truth in what Ann had said. Clinging to the one thing she believed with all her heart, she muttered, "Yancy wouldn't harm me!"

Ann gently turned Sara around to face her, and kneeling on the floor before her, she clasped Sara's limp hands in hers. "Listen to me!" she began fiercely. "You are so young and innocent. You don't know the blackness that is within some people. Right now, all you see is Yancy's handsome face and his charming manner. But he is the vilest blackguard imaginable. You must believe me!"

"Why are you doing this?" Sara asked dully, all her earlier pleasure in the day utterly destroyed. She didn't want to think about what Ann was saying; she didn't want to give credence, even for a moment, to the terrible possibilities Ann was putting before her. She didn't trust Ann; she *did* trust Bartholomew and Tansy, and yet . . . Her green eyes full of misery, she demanded desperately, "What do you possibly hope to gain by these lies?"

"Nothing! I simply want you to think about what you are doing! Stop the wedding. Don't tie yourself to a man who may have already murdered one woman."

Painfully Sara said, "If there is even the faintest hint that what you say is true, wouldn't my marrying him ensure my safety? If I become his wife, wouldn't he be assured that his child would inherit Paloma? He wouldn't need to kill me to accomplish that!"

Ann smiled pityingly. "And what about afterward? What about after your child is born? Yancy wouldn't *need* you anymore! You would have served your purpose. And Bartholomew and Tansy? Do you think they are just going to calmly stand by and allow you to give birth to a child who will effectively ruin their chance to inherit Casa Paloma? Sara, think! They don't have any money—they could do nothing with the rancho except sell it. The land is worthless to them . . . but they could sell those useless acres to Yancy for a small fortune!"

Sick at heart, angry with herself for listening to Ann's ugly words and yet unable to completely banish everything that the woman had said from her mind, Sara gently removed her hands from Ann's and said wearily, "Let it be, Ann. I will not believe that any of them is capable of such convoluted, wicked ideas! And I *am* marrying Yancy today."

Ann stood up. "I see," she said slowly, idly twitching the full skirts of her rose-striped calico gown into place. A defeated expression in her blue eyes, she asked quietly, "Is there nothing I can do to convince you that you are making a mistake?"

Sara smiled weakly. "No, I'm afraid not. You see, I love him. . . ."

"And has he admitted that he loves you? Does he?" Ann asked insistently. "Does he love you?"

The stricken look on Sara's expressive little face was answer enough and Ann smiled bleakly. "You see. You know that he doesn't love you and yet he is insisting upon this wedding. It is only by the greatest good fortune that we arrived before the ceremony. Doesn't that strike you as odd? That he is in such a hurry to have that ring on your finger that he couldn't even wait until we arrived?" There was a rueful cast to Ann's mouth as she said, "I am the first to admit that I am not very matronly, but, Sara, to the best of my ability, which I'll also admit is not very great, I *have* tried to act in at least a sisterly capacity to you these past few years. We have been through some shattering times, you and I. . . ." Ann sighed. "I just don't want you making a mistake you'll regret for the rest of your life."

Deeply touched by Ann's sincere manner and words, Sara smiled faintly. "I appreciate your concern, I really do, but I think your worries are misplaced. Yancy may not love me, but he is kind to me. He has been very good to me."

Ann nodded, a thoughtful expression in the depths of her eyes. "I'm sure he has, child. After all, why wouldn't he be? You're going to give him exactly what he wants—Casa Paloma! But I wonder if you would go along with his plans so meekly if you knew that there was another woman involved . . . that the reason he does not love you is because his heart is already given to another."

Sara's mouth went dry and a knife blade seemed to slice right through her heart. "What are you talking about? There is no other woman!"

Ann shook her head sadly. "Oh, but there is. Didn't you even once wonder why Yancy agreed so readily for me to come to del Sol?"

Dazedly Sara shook her head, denying the awful enormity of what Ann was suggesting—that she was Yancy's mistress and that he had brought her here for his own pleasure. It was lies, lies, *lies*! It had to be more of Ann's malicious contorting of the facts. It *had* to be! Ann and Yancy were *not* lovers! They had *never* been lovers. Yancy couldn't have brought his mistress to the very home he intended to share with his bride. He *couldn't* have!

"It's not true!" Sara cried in a shaken voice. "You're lying. I know you are!"

"Oh, but I'm not," Ann replied gravely. "Shall I prove it to you?"

For several minutes after Ann had left the room, Sara had rubbed her arms, as if she could wipe away the stain of having agreed with Ann's plan to prove that Yancy was indeed her lover. She felt disloyal and unclean and the ache in her heart was nearly intolerable. Bleakly she stared at her pale reflection in the mirror.

She didn't want to believe one word of what Ann had said—not about Yancy, not about Bartholomew and Tansy; she certainly didn't want to start speculating that they *might* have plotted against her. In her heart of hearts she was positive that Ann was lying, manipulating facts to suit herself.

Usually she could spot what Ann was after, but this time Sara could think of no satisfying reason for Ann to make up such outright lies. Whether or not she married Yancy was not going to change Ann's circumstances— Ann would *still* be dependent upon Yancy's goodwill. And while it might be argued that Ann would prefer to be indebted to Sara rather than to Yancy for her continued support, Sara didn't really think that was a good enough reason to explain away everything that Ann had said. And Ann had nothing to gain if Sara were to die without issue and Bartholomew and Tansy were to inherit or sell Casa Paloma to Yancy.

Sara stood up and unhappily began to dress in an older gown of yellow calico. Tears welled up into her eyes when she looked at her wedding gown—pale pink muslin lavishly sewn with pearls and lace—lying on the bed where Maria had so reverently spread it. How happy she had been just a short time ago! Before Ann had come into her room. . . .

A small ormolu clock on the mantel above the fireplace in Yancy's room suddenly rang out the hour, and Sara's face tightened. It was time. The hour she and Ann had decided upon. Her heart full of dread, her spirits desolate and uneasy, Sara reluctantly left the bedroom and began to walk with heavy steps toward Ann's room.

If Ann had told the truth, and Sara was praying desperately that Ann had lied, she knew what she would probably find when she pushed open the door to Ann's room. Even so, even prepared for it, Sara was still shocked when she opened the door and caught sight of Yancy locked in a torrid embrace with Ann. Their bodies were crushed together, Yancy's hands at Ann's waist, her hands tangled in his dark hair, their mouths passionately molded together. Reeling in pain, Sara gave a small, wounded cry.

Hearing that soft, broken sound, as if feeling the sting of a scorpion, Yancy jerked his head away from Ann, and with a violent movement, he thrust her away from him and swung around to meet the hurt accusation glittering in Sara's green eyes. Across the room they stared at each other, Yancy's dark face revealing nothing, Sara's lovely features revealing all too clearly just what she thought.

"Oh, dear!" Ann exclaimed prettily. "I didn't expect you. . . . I'm so sorry you had to discover us this way, my child, but there is really a very simple explanation for what you just saw. Really, Sara, it is very innocent and not at all what it looks like. Yancy had just agreed to give Tom and me a small place in the village all our own, and I was just thanking him."

Neither Yancy nor Sara paid her any heed, each one's attention fixed wholly on the other. Sara stared at him for a timeless moment longer and then, with a tiny, anguished moan, spun around, yellow skirts flying, and ran out of the room. Yancy remained standing where he was for a long minute and then he slowly pivoted on his heels to look at Ann.

His face grim, he said softly, "You planned that very well, Ann. I must congratulate you."

Ann looked puzzled. "I'm afraid I don't know what you're talking about. Whatever do you mean? I *explained* to Sara what happened, didn't I? I don't see how you can blame *me* if she misinterpreted what she saw! I *was* only thanking you for your generosity!"

Yancy smiled unpleasantly. "Believe me, at this moment I have no feelings of generosity for you—as a matter of fact, I'm divided between throttling you and ordering you to pack your bags and get the hell off my land and out of my life!"

A flicker of unease crossed Ann's face and she said hastily, "It is unfortunate that Sara misinterpreted what she saw, but it wasn't my fault! And to make these threats to me is very unkind! Where would poor Tom and I go if you threw us out? If you abandoned us, we would have no place to go. The journey here was very tiring for Tom—he is not very strong, and for you to heartlessly condemn us to hopelessness would be cruel beyond belief."

"Odd, but I don't remember mentioning Tom's name in connection with throwing *you* off the rancho!" Yancy said coldly.

Ann's eyes dropped demurely and she murmured, "But do you really think that Tom would allow you to deny his wife a place to live and *not* share my fate?"

She had him there and Yancy knew it. "I always thought that you were the 'nice' one," he said grimly, "that it was only Margaret who was a malicious bitch. I see that I was wrong."

"Oh, Yancy! You can't honestly think that I set this up deliberately. Tell me that's not what you're thinking."

"I'm thinking that you're a clever bitch, and I'd wager everything I own on the fact that you've been filling Sara's head with lies and this little scene we just played out was totally your doing!"

"Oh, but that's simply not true!" Ann cried indignantly, her eyes darting to the doorway, where she suddenly caught a glimpse of Sara's yellow skirts. "I am very fond of Sara—I would do *nothing* to hurt her!"

"Oh, wouldn't you?" He laughed bitterly. "If it benefited you, you wouldn't think twice about who you would hurt!"

Unaware that Sara had returned and was hovering in the doorway, gathering her courage to confront them, Yancy walked over to Ann. His back was to the door, and tipping up Ann's face with one lean finger, he murmured, "I'll tell you something else, dear, *sweet* Ann— stay away from Sara! And if you want me to continue to be *kind* to you, you'll do as I say. Come near her again or try to *explain* anything else to her, and I swear I'll break your lovely neck—or throw you off the rancho and Tom's welfare be damned!"

The triumphant gleam in Ann's blue eyes should have warned him, but it was Sara's horrified gasp that made him spin around. He caught just the flash of Sara's yellow gown as she raced away once again. Throwing a virulent look at Ann and cursing under his breath, he flung himself out of the room, in swift pursuit of his fleeing bride.

Yancy had no idea where Sara could have run to, and it took him several fruitless moments before he found her in the stables, her arms around Locuela's neck, her face buried in the glossy hide. The sound of her soft weeping tore at his heart, and his thoughts toward Ann at that moment were nothing short of murderous. Instinct had driven him to find Sara immediately, but now that he had, he wasn't certain how to handle the situation. His steps slowed and he approached her almost hesitantly. Standing behind her, he stared at the back of her honey-gold head in helpless anguish. After what Sara had seen and heard, she wasn't about to believe any denial he offered, and he cursed Ann and her machinations again. But no matter what Ann had done, it didn't *change* anything, he thought bitterly; they were *still* getting married today.

Gently Yancy laid a hand on Sara's shoulders and muttered, "Sara, come away. Come back to the hacienda and let Maria tend to you."

"Don't *touch* me!" Sara cried, whipping around and knocking aside his hand. "Get away from me! I never want to see you again!"

Yancy's face tightened. "Rather difficult to do, wouldn't you say, since we're getting married in just a few hours."

"I wouldn't marry you if you were the last man on earth!" she exclaimed with loathing.

His own temper flaring, Yancy gripped her shoulders firmly and shook her lightly. "You damned little fool!" he growled. "Why in the hell I'm determined to marry you is beyond me, but hear this, sweet Sara, you *are* going to marry me! Ann is every bit the lying, conniving bitch her sister was, and I'll be hanged if I'm going to let her ruin my life! I don't give a good goddamn what you think about me right now—all I care about is that you're standing up in front of Padre Quintero with me two hours from now and saying your vows! We'll deal with Ann and her little plots later!"

"I won't marry you! I *won't*! I hate you!" Sara said furiously, her cheeks rosily flushed, her eyes bright with tears.

Yancy swore viciously and jerked her up against him. The eagle-gold eyes glittering fiercely down into hers, he said grimly, "You might hate me, *amiga*, but that sweet little body of yours doesn't! Not if last night was anything to go by, and before you throw away my offer of respectability, think about this—you might already be carrying my child." Deliberately he added, "And, Sara, you're sleeping in my bed and in my arms from now on—whether we're married or not! If you choose to simply be my mistress and bear my bastard children, instead of being my wife, the choice is yours, but you *will* share my bed—even if I have to chain you to it!"

Sara believed him. It was there in the savage promise of his eyes, the inexorable slant to his chiseled mouth and the taut line of his jaw. He meant it.

If anyone thought that the bride seemed particularly pale and remote or that there was a distinctly grim air about the groom, he was much too polite to make mention of it. On that warm, sunny afternoon of June twenty-sixth, in the year of our Lord 1867, with all of the excited population of Rancho del Sol looking on, Yancy Cantrell took as his wife Sara Cantrell nee Rawlings. Despite their seeming lack of enthusiasm, the newlyweds played their parts well, smiling and accepting the warm congratulations that were rained upon them after they had left the church. The exuberant guests more than made up for any lack of outward rejoicing on the part of the newly joined couple, the sound of laughter, guitars and even the occasional gunshot ringing through the air as the festivities progressed.

At the hacienda, in the front courtyard, the revelers merrily helped themselves to the food and drink from the many long tables that had been heaped with all manner of delicacies—enormous trays of turkey tamales and *mole*, piping-hot *carnitas*, huge piles of warm tortillas, bowls of fiery *salsa de chipotle*, plates of rich, sweet *pastel de nuez* and jam-filled *fruta de horno*. Wine and tequila, as well as dark, potent beer brewed at the rancho itself, were liberally offered. As the hour grew late and darkness fell, the hacienda and the front courtyard were ablaze with the lights of many candles and lanterns, the boisterous celebration showing no sign of ending. Long after the bride had modestly disappeared inside, her bridegroom remained behind to drink several glasses of tequila and accept the congratulations of his people, the rhythmic strum of the guitars and the click of castanets carrying on the cooling night air.

Sara was alone in her new rooms. Smiling and clucking happily, Maria had accompanied her to the quarters she would now share with Yancy. Eager to return to the celebration and certain that Sara's impatient new bridegroom would be following close on her heels, Maria quickly divested Sara of her wedding finery and helped her into a soft, delicate nightgown of white muslin, lavishly trimmed with lace and embroidered around the demure neckline and down the front with pale yellow rosebuds. There was a matching robe that went with the nightgown, and lethargically, Sara allowed Maria to coax her into it.

A sly smile on her face, the Mexican woman urged her into Yancy's room and toward a wide door, which Sara assumed led to another room. It didn't. The door opened to reveal an exceedingly private courtyard encased by high adobe walls that were adorned with cascading streamers of fragrant jasmine. The scent of orange blossoms and roses overlaid with jasmine drifted sweetly on the night air as Sara's eyes rested on the iron table and chairs in the center of the small courtyard. A cart laden with several covered dishes, which Sara guessed contained their wedding meal, had been placed just inside the courtyard. In the middle of the table was a bowl of huge white roses; a silver candelabra, the candles burning brightly in the darkness, sat nearby. The table had been lovingly set with crystal and china and the finest silver, and gazing at it, Sara felt a lump rise in her throat.

It was a *very* intimate setting, the soft, evocative thrum of the distant guitars only increasing the almost overpowering romantic appeal of the place, and Sara wished for perhaps the millionth time today that she could have recaptured the mood of sweet anticipation with which she had first greeted the day. Her wedding day. The lump in her throat grew and she fought back the tears that scalded her eyes.

"Is very nice, *sí*?" Maria asked anxiously, her dark eyes expressing her worry at Sara's silence. "*Mi madre* and I fixed it for you and Senor Yancy. We wanted to surprise you."

Sara cleared her throat and murmured, "It is a wonderful surprise, Maria! So very kind and thoughtful of you and your mother. I'm sure that my h-h-husband will think so, too!"

Maria giggled. "I think Senor Yancy will not even notice! Not when he has such a beautiful bride waiting for him! And now I must go before he comes and finds me here!"

Maria was gone in a moment and Sara was left alone with her unhappy thoughts. How could everything have gone so wrong? she wondered bitterly. It seemed that she had been overcoming obstacle after obstacle from the moment she had first met Yancy Cantrell! Repeatedly she had made excuses for his behavior, convinced herself that those who spoke against him were wrong about him or his motives, but she was having a very hard time convincing herself that Ann had *entirely* manipulated this morning's denouement. Ann was crafty and Ann was sly, but . . .

Dispiritedly Sara turned away, refusing to speculate any more on a subject that caused her so much pain. She was halfway across Yancy's bedroom, intending to seek out her own chaste bed, when the outer door to their suite of rooms was flung open. Her lips parted in surprise, several strands of honey-gold hair curling fetchingly over one breast, she faced the dark figure of her very new husband in the doorway.

Yancy was a sight to stir any woman's heart as he lounged there, staring across the distance that separated him from Sara. His hair was carelessly rumpled, one black lock tumbling across his forehead, and there was a glitter in his thickly lashed amber-gold eyes that, despite all the reasons that it shouldn't, made Sara's unreliable heart beat faster. He was still wearing his wedding finery and he looked, she thought bitterly, far too handsome and virile in the short black jacket lavishly trimmed with gold lace and the black velvet *calzoneras*. The outer legs of the *calzoneras* were liberally trimmed with gold lace and small golden bells, and except where the garment flared gently out from his knees to his gleaming black boots, it fit his body like a glove, clearly defining his flat stomach and long, muscular thighs. His face was very dark above the pristine white, ruffled shirt, and the scarlet silk sash at his waist lent an attractive barbaric air to his appearance.

There was a reckless slant to his arrogantly chiseled mouth, the golden glitter in his eyes even more intense as he lazily pushed himself away from the doorjamb and, with that animalistic grace particularly his own, strolled toward Sara. The small golden bells of the *calzoneras* tinkled softly with every step he took, and when he stopped in front of her, the silence in the room was deafening.

Buffeted by the nearly palpable air of barely leashed sexuality that radiated from his tall, broad-shouldered body, Sara would not look at him. She kept her eyes stubbornly on a point somewhere over his left shoulder, hating him and hating even more the treacherous shimmer of excitement that had run through her the instant she had spied him in the doorway.

Sara was concentrating so much on not looking at him that the touch of his hand on her chin as he tipped her face upward startled her, bringing her gaze instantly to his. The raw passion burning in the depths of his eyes brought a flush to her cheeks and made her shamefully aware of the sudden swelling of her nipples.

Leisurely his gaze traveled over her rebellious features, a wry smile quirking at the corners of his mouth at her not-entirely-*un*anticipated manner. "And what," he asked silkily, his words slightly slurred from the generous amounts of tequila he had consumed throughout the afternoon and evening, "have I done to displease my bride so early in our marriage?"

Sara's eyes flashed dangerously. "I didn't want to marry you!" she got out stiffly. "You forced me into this situation, but don't expect me to be happy about it!"

His mouth thinned, his genial mood ebbing slightly. His fingers tightened on her chin and he drawled, "I'm sorry you feel that way, sweetheart, but as long as you're in my bed, at least *one* of us will be happy!"

"You insufferable bastard!" Her resentment at his treatment boiled over and she punctuated her words with a ringing slap against his hard cheek. "I hate you! I don't *want* to be in your bed!" The sound of the crack of her hand against his skin seemed to reverberate through the room.

Appalled by her violent action and trembling with anger, Sara glared at him. The expression on his dark, handsome face suddenly frightened her and she made an abortive attempt to flee from him.

It was no use—she had barely begun to whirl away before his long arm reached and curled around her slim waist. The next instant she was snatched up next to him, their bodies crushed together, and she became instantly, shockingly, aware that he was hard and erect.

Yancy's eyes were pure molten gold and filled with masculine knowledge as he stared down into her upturned face. "Oh, yes, sweet Sara, did you doubt for a moment that I haven't been ready and aching to consummate our marriage since we walked out of that damned church? That I haven't been imagining this night for weeks?" He smiled grimly. "And do you think that after all I have gone through to make you my bride, I am going to be denied your charms?"

Sara struggled in his arms. "I don't *want* you!" she exclaimed breathlessly. "I hate you! Let me go!"

Yancy laughed, but there was a bitter sound to it. "I'm afraid that's impossible—you're my *wife*! And as for not wanting me . . ." He smiled without amusement. "Believe me, *chica*, by the time I'm through with you, you *will* want me!"

Frantic to escape the implacable promise she read in his face, Sara fought wildly to free herself from his hold. It was useless. One arm keeping her anchored against him, he captured her thrashing head with his other hand and held her still as his mouth descended.

The scent of tobacco and tequila was on his lips, the taste of the mingled flavors on his tongue, as he kissed her with blatant demand. Yancy seemed oblivious of her struggles to escape him, his lips and tongue taking precisely what he wanted, his total concentration fixed on the sheer pleasure of kissing her, of exploring the sweet darkness of her mouth, the scent and taste of her far more intoxicating than anything he had ever known in his life.

Sara fought desperately against the treacherous sensations that exploded into life within her as he wreaked his potent black magic against her. She didn't want to feel that warm, giddy rush of desire that began deep in her belly and surged up through her entire body, nor did she want to feel her heart begin to race, her pulse start to pound in erotic demand or her breasts become heavy and aching for the feel of his mouth against them. She wanted none of those feelings to overtake her; she wanted only to remember that she was *supposed* to hate him, but, oh, God! It was so *damned* hard when she pressed against his lean, exciting length, her unruly flesh melting into him, his hungry mouth wooing hers, the memory of his lovemaking, the knowledge that he could give her another glimpse of heaven, fighting with the cool logic of her brain.

She was drowning in his kiss, her young body responding avidly to the carnal demands he made upon her, and with a sudden burst of frantic strength, she managed to tear herself out of his arms. Her breathing labored, her eyes dark with unwanted desire, she stared at him from a safe distance across the room.

Like a man awakening from a drugged sleep, Yancy stared back at her, his golden eyes never moving from her passion-flushed features. They stared at each other for a long time and then Yancy sighed faintly and, terrifying Sara, slowly began to undress. With graceful, economical movements, he took off his boots, threw aside the short jacket and, after unbuttoning the white, ruffled shirt, pulled it free of the scarlet sash and the *calzoneras*. Like that of a great, black-maned predator, his unblinking gaze never left Sara, and as the moments passed, her heart began to beat with such fierce power that she feared it would burst from her breast.

"Are you certain," he asked carefully, "that it has to be this way?"

Sara nodded, not quite certain what she was agreeing to.

He sighed again faintly and then, before she had even guessed what he was about, he was across the room after her. She let out a frightened cry and tried to run for her own room, but Yancy gave her no quarter, his arms closing powerfully around her, lifting her struggling body off the floor and tossing her over his shoulder.

Sara's fists beat wildly against his broad back, her feet drumming furiously as he carried her swiftly to his bed. Unfazed by her punitive actions, he dumped her down onto the welcoming softness of the big feather bed. Fright and a crazy excitement robbed her of breath for one tiny second as he shrugged out of his shirt; then, as he fell on the bed beside her, the scarlet sash held in one of his hands, she recovered her senses long enough to make a frantic lunge away from him.

With a smothered curse, he captured her once more and there was a brief, violent tussle between them. It ended only when Sara's wrists were neatly tied together over her head with the scarlet silk sash and bound to the carved mahogany headboard of the bed. They were both breathing heavily, Yancy's hair even more tousled than before; his naked, hair-roughened, muscular chest rose and fell rapidly, his thighs locked on either side of her hips as he sat lightly on top of her. Sara's gown and robe were all askew, the garments rumpled beneath her body, her long, shapely legs totally naked, her bosom heaving as she glared furiously up into his dark face.

Yancy could not seem to take his eyes off the rhythmic rise and fall of her breasts, and Sara was all too aware of her vulnerable position, far too warmly aware of his potent masculinity as he loomed over her. She would have died with shame to admit it, but she was strangely excited by their battle, by the sensation of being helpless to stop him from doing anything he wanted to her; even the feel of the scarlet sash around her wrists was arousing rather than terrifying, and she wondered how she had become such an utterly depraved woman. It's all *his* fault, she thought hysterically; he's made me this way and I hate him for it. I hate him! I really do!

Almost as if he guessed the tumult raging inside her, Yancy smiled darkly and slowly levered himself down on top of her. His mouth teasingly brushed hers and against her lips he murmured, "And now then, sweet, *sweet* wife, I shall prove to you that you don't know what you're talking about when you say you don't want me!"

Her protest was smothered beneath his lips as his mouth covered hers in a deep, timeless kiss. He kissed her with a quiet intensity, all his attention focused on forcing a response from her. As the moments passed and Sara stubbornly ignored the provocative blandishments of his tongue, fought against the inexorable rise of passion within herself, Yancy nearly gave up; and then, just when he thought he had lost a desperate gamble, her lips softened, her tongue suddenly meeting the thrust of his.

A shudder went through him, a shudder made up of equal parts of desire and exultation. She was *his*! His wife. His woman. And before this night had ended, she would know it, too!

He made no attempt to loosen her bonds, but continued to kiss her passionately, his hands gently framing her face, his body pressing down into hers. Sara helplessly responded to him like a spring flower to the sun, her mouth desperately seeking his when his lips slid along the edge of her jaw and he nibbled gently on her earlobe, his breath warm, his teeth arousing against her flesh. But the sweet promise of her kiss drew him back and he crushed her lips beneath his, a second later plunging his tongue once more into the wine darkness of her mouth.

It wasn't enough to merely kiss her, and Yancy gathered her to him, groaning low in his throat as her body arched up in frank appeal next to his. Sara had been completely snared by him and the wants of her own body and she had abandoned the fight against his mesmerizing presence. She had forgotten why she had been so intent upon resisting him; she only knew now that she ached for him—her lips hungry for his kiss, her limbs eager to feel his hands upon them, her body avid for his possession.

Becoming aware of the fabric of her gown rubbing against his naked chest, Yancy suddenly raised himself up and stared down at the line of yellow rosebuds that hid what he most definitely needed to feel and see. His hands fastened unerringly on the demure neckline, and a moment later, there was the shocking sound of the gown ripping. He smiled with great satisfaction as he brushed aside the torn fabric and stared dazedly at the stimulating expanse of soft white flesh that had been hidden from his gaze.

Her gown lying in tatters on either side of her, Sara's slender body was laid out before him like a feast for a starving man, and realizing that he *was* starving, Yancy bent his dark head and bit with exquisite gentleness at the temptingly upstanding pink nipple of one breast. He had never, he decided hazily as he pulled the hard nub deeper into his mouth, tasted anything so sweet in his life.

Half stunned by the wanton destruction of her gown, Sara moaned softly, delight spearing through her at the touch of his teeth and tongue at her breast. As he suckled her eager flesh, she twisted wildly in her bonds, wanting to caress him, wanting to arouse him as much as he was arousing her.

The demanding ache in her belly had spread and grown until the appeasement of it was the only thing on her mind. She was burning up for him, her lower body moist and throbbing, wanting the glorious sensation of his hard flesh sinking into hers.

But Yancy seemed in no hurry to join their bodies together, his mouth lazily returning time and again to hers, deliberately stoking the fire that raged within them both, all the while his hands warmly and leisurely exploring the soft curves and valleys of her slim form. It was ecstasy merely to touch her, to savor the heady sensation of his fingers gliding over the silken texture of her skin, to linger where he would, caressing and stroking her.

Yancy's languid caresses were an exquisitely sweet torment for Sara, feeling the touch of his knowing hands upon her and yet being unable to satisfy her own sharp desire to touch his body. Beyond hungrily returning his kisses when his mouth found hers, she had to endure his starkly arousing explorations, the binding of his scarlet sash preventing her from partaking of the same liberties that Yancy took with increasing boldness and urgency.

When his lips moved lower, sliding with excruciating slowness down her chest, dropping soft, stinging kisses between her breasts, continuing ever downward across her flat stomach to her abdomen, Sara's breath caught in her throat and she stiffened in stunned astonishment, hardly daring to believe that his mouth was traveling even farther down her body. Her breathing suspended, her thoughts jostling incredulously through her brain, she froze as he pressed an openmouthed kiss against her abdomen, his tongue flicking the warm flesh as his hands fastened on her thighs and, despite a burst of frantic resistance from Sara, easily parted them. With his

body firmly lodged between her legs, he bent his head
and his lips sank into the tight little curls at the apex of
her thighs.

A soft scream of astonished delight erupted from
Sara's throat when Yancy's mouth finally touched her
there between her thighs, his lips and tongue moving
hotly over her. She had never dreamed . . . never imagined . . . The erotic sensations of his mouth touching her,
openly tasting her, were so powerful, so intense, that she
surged up against her bonds, crying out again at the fierce
pleasure that racked her slender body.

Totally enmeshed in his own carnal dream, Yancy was
barely aware of the soft sounds Sara made as she twisted
helplessly beneath his hungry explorations. She was so
sweet, he thought fuzzily, so *damned* sweet! Drunk on
the fragrance and taste of her, he feasted deeply, his
marauding tongue probing and rubbing against the tender flesh that gave him such pleasure.

Lost in the same lascivious dream that dominated
Yancy, her breathing ragged, Sara thrashed wildly
beneath the brazenly sensuous ministrations of his
mouth and tongue, frantically seeking some barely
guessed-at summit. Suddenly she was giddily aware
of a tightening of her body, an instant tensing of the
flesh beneath his tongue, and then, without warning,
the most intense pleasure she had ever felt in her life
exploded through her and she cried out in shaken wonder and ecstasy.

When Sara dazedly became aware of her surroundings
again, it was to find herself in Yancy's arms, his lips gently caressing the soft hair at her temples. As the moments
passed and the aftershocks of her violent release faded,
blunt reality washed over her and she became aware of
other things—her wrists were still bound and he had
clearly made a mockery out of her vehement statement
that she didn't want him! He always wins, she decided

wearily. *Always*! And when she thought of the way he had dominated her, the way she had responded so wildly to his shockingly depraved caresses, a wave of humiliation swept over her. It didn't help her state of mind when she realized that he was still wearing his *calzoneras* as he lay there beside her on the bed. Somehow that made what had happened even worse; that he had done all those wantonly wonderful things to her, had brought to life the passionate, half-maddened, eager creature she became in his arms while still half clothed, was deeply embarrassing, especially since she was increasingly aware of her own state of undress. She suddenly wanted to get as far away from him as possible, and in a small, defeated voice, she said, "You've proved your point . . . would you please let me go now?"

Yancy stirred, and propping himself up on one elbow, he stared intently down into her unhappy face. His own expression unreadable, he asked, "Is that what I did— prove my point?"

Not meeting his eyes, Sara gave a little nod. "Please, could I go to my own room now?"

He sighed. "Sara, I didn't prove anything just now . . . except, perhaps, that I can give you pleasure."

Sara shook her head. "No. You said you would make me want you and you did. There. I've admitted it. *Now* will you let me go?"

"No," he said very deliberately, his fingers trailing down to cup her breast. "I'll never let you go!" His hand closed possessively around her breast, and bending close to her mouth, he said fiercely, "*Never!*"

"And do you intend to keep me bound to your bed for the rest of my life?" Sara demanded furiously, her green eyes bitter and angry. "A slave to your disgusting lusts?"

Yancy smiled. "No, sweetheart, although I have to admit that the idea has its merits!" He rolled away from her and, standing beside the bed, unhurriedly began to undo the *calzoneras*. "What I intend," he said, "is to make love to my very new bride . . . and if the only way I can accomplish that is to tie her up, well, then so be it!"

Despite her fury at him, as the *calzoneras* slipped to the floor, Sara could not take her eyes off his darkly magnificent body; the broad shoulders, lean stomach, strong, muscular legs and, in particular, the rampantly bulging manhood. She swallowed. Oh, Lord, but he was beautiful! As proud as a pagan and certainly as breathtaking. And she loved him! Hated him! Wanted him . . .

He moved to the bed, coming down beside her once more. He hovered over her, his hard, warm chest tantalizingly brushing against the tips of her suddenly tingling breasts, his hands sliding upward along her arms, his mouth pressing teasing little kisses at the corners of her lips. "Last time I simply gave you pleasure," he said huskily. "This time I'll show you precisely how very much you *do* want me."

And all through the long night that followed he did just that, making slow, sensual love to her, time and again denying her the sweet release her body clamored for until, all inhibitions driven from her, she would demand succor, her desperate pleas for his possession hanging softly in the air between them. Only then would he take her, thrusting himself deeply within her, giving them both the voluptuous ecstasy they craved. Exactly when Yancy released her wrists Sara never remembered; she only knew that at last her hands were free to roam where they would, that her fingers could clench in the thick dark hair of his head, that her arms could wrap tightly around his neck as he took her to heaven and back again. He had loosed her bonds, but by then it really didn't matter anymore.

❦ 18

As she had done the previous morning, although considerably later, Sara woke alone in Yancy's bed. But unlike yesterday, there was no feeling of sweet anticipation within her; instead, she was filled with an odd mixture of well-being, embarrassment, hope and resignation. The first two emotions were the most easily explained—Yancy was, she admitted as she stretched languorously, a most inventive and satisfying lover, even if his blatantly carnal demands *had* shocked and embarrassed her! A catlike smile curved her mouth. She *might* hate him, but she could never deny that Yancy Cantrell had given her a wedding night that she would never forget as long as she lived—that she would never *want* to forget. . . .

Sara could also explain why she felt resigned to her situation; what else could she feel? She passionately loved the man who had forced her to marry him and to accept his fierce possession, and there was no denying that Yancy exerted some dark power over her, that he had only to touch her and her common sense, logic, even sanity disappeared in a blinding flash. But hope?

She sat up in bed, wincing in surprise at the protest of certain parts of her anatomy. Yancy was a demanding lover and he had not been gentle with her last night. A curiously tender expression lit her eyes. Not gentle,

no. Exciting. Frankly carnal. Passionate. Deeply sensual
and yet . . . and yet . . . There had been something about
him, some powerful emotion that had fleetingly revealed
itself to her in the sweetness of the kisses he had rained
upon her, some elemental force that had vibrated from
him as he had cried aloud his shaken joy each time
he had emptied himself into her eager body. And that
explained the last emotion she was feeling this morning—she *hoped* those brief moments when the close
guard he kept around his deepest feelings was utterly
destroyed indicated that their marriage had not been
solely to create a child for Casa Paloma! Perhaps he
loved her . . . just a little?

Realizing that if she intended to dissect the many
contradictory facets of her arrogant, infuriating new husband she would never leave her bed, Sara got up, and
picking up her torn garments from the floor where Yancy
had thrown them last night, she scampered into her own
set of rooms. Hastily finding her old chintz robe in the
back of the wardrobe, she shrugged it on and tied the
sash tightly around her waist. Feeling decently covered,
she rang for Maria.

Maria arrived a few minutes later, a twinkle dancing in the depths of her dark eyes. She was carrying
a silver tray set with various pieces of china. The two
women exchanged greetings and then, indicating the tray
she held in her hands, Maria said, "It is such a lovely
morning today that perhaps you would like to enjoy this
outside, *sí*?"

Sara smiled and nodded, pleased at the idea. It was
only when they walked out to the private courtyard off
Yancy's room and the untouched food and drink prepared by Maria and her mother caught Sara's eye that
a flush of embarrassment swept over her.

Maria seemed not the least bit put out that her offering had not been accepted. Chuckling, she said, "That

Yancy! Didn't I tell you he would not even notice our little surprise?" She sent a sly glance in Sara's direction. "He is *muy hombre, sí?*"

Her face bright red, Sara looked everywhere but at the other woman, wishing that Maria was not quite so blunt about Yancy's undoubted masculinity. Maria laughed at her expression and, putting the tray down, poured her a cup of creamy hot chocolate. "Here. You sit and drink this and I shall clear everything else away. And then I shall see that your bath is prepared."

An hour later, freshly bathed and demurely gowned in a morning dress of apple-green ombré muslin, Sara was feeling sufficiently in command of herself to face the knowing glances of the other inhabitants of del Sol. Taking a last look in the cheval glass in her room, she wondered if she looked any different, if anyone could tell from her face the intimate things that Yancy had done to her . . . that she had done to him. A becoming blush stained her cheeks, and before her courage could fail, she walked rapidly to the outer door.

She stepped into the deserted walkway and breathed a sigh of relief that no one seemed to be around. She quickly decided to take a walk away from the vicinity of the hacienda. Despite the lateness of the hour, it was still very pleasant outside, especially in the patches of shade that dotted the area, but remembering all the lectures she had been given on the subject, Sara dashed back into her room to get her wide-brimmed, chipped straw hat, which was essential to wear in the strong Texas sunlight. Her hat firmly on her head, she left the hacienda and began to stroll in no particular direction.

Thinking it would be cooler by the little creek that wandered through a corner of the hacienda grounds, she slowly walked toward that area, her thoughts, not surprisingly, on Yancy. Unaware of the dreamy smile that tugged at the corners of her mouth, Sara instinctively picked out the patches of shade made by the various trees.

A short distance from the creek, she stopped and leaned against the trunk of a gracefully spreading pecan tree. Staring hazily off into space, she wondered if there had ever been a man quite as handsome and passionately exciting as her new husband, Yancy Cantrell. Of course, he was also aggravating, enraging and quite, quite the most odiously arrogant creature she had ever had the misfortune to meet! Oh, but she could live with all of those deplorable traits, she thought tremulously, even glory in them, if only he loved her!

Some of her dreamy glow vanishing, Sara grimaced. Might as well wish for the moon! She had started to leave the shade of the pecan tree when she suddenly became aware of the man and woman half hidden by the small thicket of trees which lined part of the creek. They were not ten feet away from her and, oblivious of their surroundings, they were locked in an ardent embrace, their bodies pressed close together, the woman's hands moving sensually through the man's fair hair, his arms crushed around her waist.

Embarrassed to intrude on the intimate scene, Sara shrank closer to her tree, her apple-green gown blending with the cool shadows. She was on the point of silently slipping away when the man lifted his head. Her mouth fell open in astonishment as she recognized the desire-flushed features of Hyrum Burnell. And when she realized who the woman in his embrace was, she was positively certain that she gaped like a gigged fish. *Ann Shelldrake had been kissing Hyrum Burnell*! And there had been *nothing* platonic about the kiss either, she thought dazedly, hardly believing the proof of her own eyes.

Wishing herself a thousand miles away, afraid to move and bring attention to herself, Sara edged deeper into the shadows, hoping the couple would leave before they discovered her presence. That she had interrupted a clandestine meeting was clearly apparent and she only hoped that they would not continue to the obvious conclusion. They didn't. But Sara became the unwilling witness to a very private scene.

"Oh, Hyrum, what are we going to do? She *married* him!" Ann cried despairingly, her voice carrying with embarrassing clarity to Sara. "Knowing what a virile beast Yancy probably is, she could be pregnant already!"

"It doesn't matter! We'll just have to forget our plans about Casa Paloma." Hyrum kissed Ann again, then implored passionately, "Come away with me, Ann, *now*! I know I can't give you the life you were used to, but I'll take care of you—I swear it!"

"And how will you do that? The South has been destroyed. There aren't many jobs." Ann sighed. "Oh, I know you'll think of something, darling! You won't fail me!"

"For the time being, perhaps it won't be so bad, here at del Sol," Hyrum said slowly. "After all, didn't you say that Yancy has agreed to give you and your husband a small place in the village? That could be a start."

Ann pouted. "And will you be happy with that arrangement?"

"Probably not for long, but we'll just have to see how things go."

They kissed each other again, moving further into the concealing thicket. From the way their hands were roaming over each other, it was obvious that they were going to make love, and deciding that she'd rather be discovered right now rather than be forced to remain here and witness their intimate joining, Sara took a chance that they were too involved in each other to notice anything else and began a stealthy retreat from the area. The far-

ther away from them she got, the swifter she moved, and
by the time she had reached the edge of the orange grove,
she was fairly running.

Once in the sanctuary of the hacienda courtyard, she
sank down breathlessly on the rim of the fountain and
stared sightlessly at the red-and-golden flashes of the
fish. *Ann and Hyrum were lovers*! But how could that
be, she wondered blankly, if Yancy had been Ann's
lover? At least wasn't that what the other woman had
intimated only yesterday, before she had gone to great
pains to make certain that Yancy had been found in
a compromising position? Was Ann involved intimately with two men? Three, counting her husband, Tom
Shelldrake?

Agitated and deeply disturbed by what she had discovered, Sara tried to get her tumbled thoughts into some
sort of order. Nothing made sense! Not Ann's supposed
involvement with Yancy, nor Hyrum's previous actions.
Why would Hyrum ask *her* to marry him if he were in
love with Ann Shelldrake? Did he know about Yancy
and Ann? Or were Ann's implications about Yancy a
total lie? Sara sincerely hoped so! And for how long
was Ann willing to make a cuckold of her husband?
Had she and Hyrum been planning, if events moved to
their liking, for him to marry her and thus to gain a certain control of Casa Paloma, and *she* and Tom Shelldrake
would be duped together? The entire notion left a decidedly nasty taste in Sara's mouth.

She wasn't so surprised by Ann's part in the adulterous liaison—after all, wasn't Ann Margaret's sister? But
Hyrum! He had claimed to *love* her! Had begged her to
marry him! And she had believed him and felt sorry for
him! Lying bastard!

Sara had often prided herself on being a good judge
of character, and now it seemed that two people with
whom she had lived in close proximity for quite some

time had totally deceived her. If she had not seen them together, she would never have believed that there was anything going on between them. They had totally fooled her. Her confidence in herself shaken, she sat there staring dully at nothing. Who else, she wondered uneasily, had she misjudged? Bartholomew? Tansy? Yancy?

"Ah, here you are, my dear," said Tom Shelldrake as he walked over to where she sat.

With the memory of how they had last parted fresh in her mind and with the knowledge of what his wife was doing right now with Hyrum, Sara was distinctly uncomfortable greeting Tom. She forced herself to smile and said politely, "Good morning. How are you today?"

Tom settled himself carefully on the rim of the fountain and absently rubbed his bad arm through the sling in which it rested. "Feeling very guilty and remorseful, my child," he said heavily. "I had no right to speak to you the way I did the other day and I apologize." He sent her a wry look. "I'm afraid that my dependent state has made me rather defensive and inclined to view any changes with a jaundiced eye. I should never have said the things that I did or made such wild accusations. As you said, anyone could have killed Margaret—I should never have vented my unfounded suspicions on Yancy. I hope you will forgive me."

It was a handsome apology, and since Tom Shelldrake had always been a favorite of hers, Sara was suddenly glad not to be on the outs with him. She flashed him a warm smile. "Oh, Tom! I am so relieved—we have been through a lot together, and I didn't like to think that we had finally come to a parting of the ways."

Tom smiled bitterly. "Hardly, my dear, when I am dependent upon you and your husband for every morsel of food I eat."

"Oh, please, don't feel that way! If positions were reversed, I'm sure you would do the same for us."

"Perhaps so. Perhaps so. But come, now, don't let us talk about unpleasant things. Let me instead congratulate you on your marriage and tell you that I thought you made an exceedingly lovely bride yesterday." Tom got a faraway look in his eyes. "You know," he said slowly, "I can't help but feel that this is exactly what Sam planned to happen. Why else would he have left you Casa Paloma in such a ridiculous manner?"

Sara grimaced. "Could we please not talk about *that* either?"

Tom laughed. "Of course! What shall we talk about? Did your husband tell you about the house? The one for Ann and me?"

Before Sara had seen Hyrum and Ann locked in their torrid embrace, the mention of the house for the Shelldrakes would have caused her much pain, recalling as it did the unpleasant scene yesterday in Ann's room, but now Sara was almost certain that what she had seen yesterday was precisely what it had appeared to be: Ann, rather effusively, she would admit, thanking Yancy for his kindness. That Ann had also been gambling on Sara's interpreting the scene differently and reacting as she had was also probably part of Ann's conniving. Once again Sara hoped fervently that it was so. It was still a touchy subject with her, though, but she was grateful to Tom for trying to ease the constraint between them, and she said easily, "No. Tell me about it!"

They chatted amiably for several minutes and by the time Maria appeared to inquire if they wished to eat a light luncheon here or in the dining room, Tom and Sara were once again on the friendliest of terms. Ann joined them shortly in the dining room and Sara wondered if she was the only one who noticed that Ann's hair was slightly rumpled and that her gown was creased more than it should have been. Listening to Ann talk sweetly to her husband made Sara's stomach roil with distaste, and just as soon as she could, she escaped from their presence.

It was siesta time, and having grown used to the quiet hours of rest and repose during the heat of the day, Sara returned eagerly to her rooms. Shutting the door behind her, mulling over what she had learned this morning, she had almost reached the bed before she was brought up short by the sight of Yancy lying there supine. His hands were behind his head, his feet were bare and crossed at the ankles and his bright blue chambray shirt was half open above his breeches. He looked like a big, deceptively lazy cat lounging there, and there was an expression on that darkly handsome face that made her heart begin to pound.

"And did you enjoy your meal with the Shelldrakes?" he asked lightly.

Flustered by his unexpected presence—he'd never returned to the hacienda in the middle of the day before— Sara replied inanely, "Oh, yes. It was quite tasty. Maria's mother is an excellent cook."

Yancy smiled and something in that smile made Sara's heart beat even faster. His gaze roaming warmly over her face and slender body, he said softly, "And did you miss me this morning, sweet bride?"

Sara's little nose went up in the air. "Should I have missed you this morning more than any other?" she asked loftily, wishing he didn't look so very appealing lying there on the bed with his black hair all tousled and a lazy gleam in his eyes.

Yancy laughed and, catching her off guard—something he seemed to do with infuriating regularity— reached over and caught hold of her arm and jerked her onto the bed. Pulling her thrashing form half beneath him, he held her prisoner, and brushing a teasing kiss across her lips, he asked softly, "Have you forgotten that it was only yesterday that we were married? That this is our first morning as man and wife?"

"N-n-no," Sara stammered, cursing her body for responding so instantly and violently to his. Already, with just his barest touch, her nipples were hard and the beguiling heat of desire was stirring deep in her loins. "I didn't expect to see you until tonight."

He kissed her with leisurely enjoyment, his hands framing her face. When his mouth finally left her throbbing lips, he said thickly, "Mmm, I would be a very poor bridegroom if I deserted you so summarily . . . and you haven't answered my question. Did you miss me?"

His mouth was too temptingly close and Sara was drowning in the sensual emotions he had stirred to a fiery pitch by his long, drugging kiss. Before she could prevent herself, her arms closed around his neck and she whispered against his warm lips, "You're an arrogant, overbearing wretch and you don't deserve to be missed . . . but *yes*, I did miss you!"

"And I, *preciosa*, I missed you like the very devil!" Yancy confessed fiercely and kissed her again with a blatant hunger he did nothing to hide or control, his hands impatiently seeking her soft breasts, his body moving more intimately into hers. Possessed by the same carnal demon that rode him, Sara joined him in the frantic disposal of their clothing, and their combined sighs of satisfaction hung on the air when at last they lay naked in each other's arms. All through the long, drowsy hours of the siesta, Yancy made love to his bride, teaching her that passion once loosed was an insatiable beast, one that needed frequent feeding. . . .

It was late in the afternoon when Yancy finally rose from their bed. Oblivious of his nakedness, he walked over to a marble-topped washstand, then, returning with a china bowl of water and a soft rag, proceeded to wash away all traces of his lovemaking from Sara's achingly satisfied body. Her heart melting with love for him, Sara stared at his dark, arrogantly chiseled features as he concentrated intently on his task, long, curling lashes brushing against his lean cheeks, a frankly sensual smile curving his mouth.

Only when she was tingling from his tender ministrations did he rise and, after a brief wash of his own, shrug into his discarded clothing. Thumbs hooked in the gun belt around his waist, he regarded Sara, a savagely possessive emotion gleamed in the depths of his eyes and Sara was instantly aware of her nakedness. Suddenly shy, she grabbed at the sheet and pulled it up over her body.

"There is much that I have to do before the fall, and I can't give you the traditional honeymoon trip," he said abruptly, "but I've thought of a way that I can combine my work with something that you might like also. Since you seem so enamored of Casa Paloma, I've wondered if you might like to spend some time there."

Sara's eyes grew very big and her lips parted in surprise. Remembering how he had been so determined for her *not* to go to Casa Paloma and had told her hideous tales of its probable condition, she regarded him with suspicion. "Why should I? Won't it fall down around my ears? Isn't that what you claimed just a short while ago?"

"No, I said that it would take a great deal of capital to put it in order—money that you didn't have and don't have now," he said gently. A smug look crossed his face. "*I*, on the other hand, have a lot of money and if I wish to spend it refurbishing the place for my bride, don't you think that's vastly different from your goose-brained scheme?"

Her mouth tightened with temper. "And how do you know my schemes were so goose-brained? You never knew what I planned to do!"

His eyebrows rose. "All right, *chica*, I'm asking you

now—what precisely *did* you plan to do to make the place pay?"

For just a moment Sara's confidence in her original plans faltered and she glanced uncertainly at him. If he laughed at her or made fun of her plans, she'd kill him! Her chin held at a pugnacious angle, she said stoutly, "I intended to raise cattle," and at Yancy's derisive smile, she added quickly, "*Not* just *any* cattle—not just for hides and tallow, as is done now, but for *beef*! The East is meat-hungry, and I had planned to supply it with a source of cheap, plentiful beef."

His smile not quite so derisive anymore, Yancy stared intently at her. "And just how did you plan to do that?"

Emboldened by his not-*un*encouraging manner, she said breathlessly, "I was going to import a good blooded Durham bull, maybe two if I could afford it, and cross them with the wild longhorns! And, I had planned to buy a blooded stallion, too! A thoroughbred to cross with the mustangs, to breed a horse with some size and more refinement, yet keep the best qualities of the mustang—toughness and stamina. I had it all planned, and Hyrum was going to run the place for me and help with the breeding programs." Her green eyes bright with enthusiasm, she stated brashly, "It would have worked, too! I know it! I might not have made a fortune at once, but eventually, in four or five years, I'd have started to get a return on my investment." Her hands curled into formidable little fists, she said vehemently, "I *wouldn't* have failed—I would have succeeded!"

An arrested expression in his eyes, Yancy looked at her for several excruciatingly long seconds. Angry at herself for desperately wanting his approval, yet unable to help herself, Sara stared back at him, willing him to at least consider the idea. From the look on his face, it was obvious that he wasn't going to dismiss her plans outright; it appeared that, while she had presented him with something he had never thought of, he was actually mulling the idea over in his mind, and a bubble of excitement welled up in her chest.

Thoughtfully rubbing his chin with his hand, Yancy murmured, "A Durham bull . . . and a thoroughbred stallion." Something perilously close to respect glittering in the depths of his eyes, he drawled, "Well, well, it seems that I have acquired not only a sweet bedmate, but perhaps a hardheaded business partner as well."

Sara gasped with pleasure and her eyes were huge with dazed delight as she stared at his dark face, hardly daring to believe what she thought he was implying. Yancy smiled at her and said gently, "You shall have your Durham bulls—a half dozen, I think, to start with, if we are going to do this on a grand scale. I shall have my business man in New Orleans start making inquiries, but you shall make the final selection, and as for the stallion . . ." He grinned at Sara's dazzled expression. "Shall we start with three? I trust that you will allow *me* to make those choices?"

Sara licked her lips. "Black," she said firmly. "They have to be black, but other than that . . ."

Yancy bowed gallantly, a half smile quirking his lips. "Of course. Black. Anything else?"

A smile on her face which made him blink at its blinding jubilation, she slowly shook her head. "No—other than that you'll have to start culling and castrating as many of the wild bulls as we can catch right away." Tapping a finger thoughtfully on her lips, she added, "And, of course, you'll have to start planning the trail drive for later this summer. We should be able to sell enough of the wild cattle to offset at least some of the costs of the Durham bulls."

He blinked again. His demure bride certainly *had* thought this out! "Of course. Cull and castrate. Plan trail drive."

She frowned slightly. "And you'll have to start gathering suitable mustang mares for breeding next year. We'll have to corral them now, before they are rebred by the wild stallions, then next spring start breeding them to the thoroughbred stallions."

"Of course," he agreed dazedly. "Corral mustang mares."

Sara smiled sunnily up into his bemused features. "I think that ought to cover just about everything for now, don't you?"

He nodded his head. "Oh, yes, I think you've thought of just about everything—you *will*, however, let me make arrangements for the trip to Casa Paloma?" At Sara's gracious assent, he said, "I'll send a group ahead with most of the supplies and have them clean out several rooms for our use." He grinned at her. "And have them make certain that no walls come tumbling down around your sweet ears!"

They smiled at each other idiotically for several minutes and then gradually their smiles faded and some powerful, fierce emotion seemed to brew between them. Yancy took a step toward her; Sara leaned in his direction—

The rap on the door shattered the intensity of the moment, and Sara jumped. Yancy shook himself as if surfacing from a deep enchantment. Never taking his gaze off Sara, he called out, "Who is it?"

"Bartholomew," came the reply, and at Yancy's command to enter, Bartholomew walked in, several men's garments folded over his arm.

Seeing Sara lying on the bed, a sheet her only covering and her hair tumbling in wild disarray around her flushed features, he stopped uncertainly and cleared his throat. "Ah, I didn't realize . . . I can return with these things later."

Yancy shook his head. "You didn't interrupt anything." He smiled wickedly, his white teeth flashing in his bronzed face. "At least not this time." He saw Sara sink deeper into the bed with mortification, and amusement danced in his eyes as he laughed out loud. "Ignore my shy bride and go ahead and put those things away."

Sending Sara a commiserating glance, Bartholomew said with affectionate censure in his voice, "Madam, there is no need to be embarrassed by his vulgarity. You will soon learn that Mr. Yancy takes great delight in saying the most shameful things!"

Yancy only grinned, a mocking light in his eyes as he surveyed the pair of them. "At least, at the moment I'm only *saying* them!"

Bartholomew threw him a reproving look and proceeded to walk over to the huge mahogany wardrobe that sat against one wall. Opening the doors, he began to carefully hang the various garments, as if his chore were the most fascinating task in the world.

Sara watched him, her thoughts jostling themselves merrily through her brain. She would have her Durham bull. And the thoroughbred stallion. And Yancy was taking her to Paloma!

His eyes on Sara's expressive face, Yancy smiled and said over his shoulder to Bartholomew, "I know that you and Tansy just arrived here, but we are planning on removing to Paloma for the summer and I wonder if you would care to accompany us." He shot Sara a mocking look before turning back to Bartholomew and saying, "I have a great many cattle to gather up and bulls to castrate, as well as mustangs to run down and capture—my bride intends that I shall work hard during the next few months. I'm sending some of the men and their families over there tomorrow morning. You could go with them or wait and travel with us later in the week."

Bartholomew clucked his tongue reprovingly. "If that isn't just like you! Always rushing here and there, and now you're dragging your bride along with you! Shocking!" He suddenly grinned. "Tansy always had a soft spot for Paloma, and I shall look forward to seeing the place again myself—especially if you will allow me to leave the running of the household to the others and let me help with the roundup."

"I had planned to asked you to do just that," Yancy said dryly. "You are, if I remember correctly, an expert horseman, and there are vaqueros from my grandfather's day who still talk of your roping skills."

"Then Tansy and I shall be delighted to accompany you and Madam Sara when you leave for Paloma! I shall just finish putting these things away and go tell her of the change in plans."

In his haste to finish his task, Bartholomew moved with rare clumsiness and inadvertently knocked down an object which had been lying on the shelf of the wardrobe. Startled, he stared at the Spanish dagger lying on the floor. Sara recognized it instantly; it was the same dagger she had found so recently in Yancy's possession, the same dagger that had been used to kill Margaret. . . .

Picking up the weapon, Bartholomew glanced across at Yancy, who had gone curiously still. He asked slowly, "What are you doing with this? It's the same dagger, isn't it?"

Yancy's features were unrevealing. "Yes, I believe it's the same one my grandfather gave you."

Dismayed and horrified, staring at Bartholomew as if she had never seen him before, Sara squeaked, "Bartholomew! That isn't *your* dagger, is it?"

Bartholomew shrugged. "Why, yes, it is. As Yancy just mentioned, Don Armando gave it to me, oh, years ago. It is very distinctive—I would know it anywhere." His dark eyes inscrutable, Bartholomew looked at Yancy and asked tightly, "How did it come to be here and in your possession?"

⚭ 19

An ominous stillness filled the room, the three inhabitants frozen in place, Bartholomew's words hanging in the air. Where before there had been lightness
and laughter, there was now only suspicion and ugly accusations that were yet unspoken.

Gripped by a terrible feeling of dread and denial,
Sara stared at Bartholomew, unwilling to believe that
he had been the one who had murdered Margaret. It
occurred to her that she was having a harder time believing Bartholomew capable of having murdered Margaret
than she had Yancy, and on far more damning evidence.
Margaret had threatened Bartholomew's position in the
Cantrell household, had threatened to destroy the very
fabric of his life, and Bartholomew had just admitted that
the Spanish dagger, the dagger that had killed Margaret,
was *his*!

It seemed to Sara as if the three of them remained
unmoving, their eyes locked on the slim, deadly blade
in Bartholomew's hand, for hours, yet it must have
been only a second or two. Then, shattering the tension, Yancy turned away and said idly, "I'm not quite
certain how it got here, but I think it must have been
inadvertently packed with my things one of the last times
I was at Magnolia Grove." He seated himself casually on
the bed and added, "I know how much you treasure it,

but I'm afraid that when I found it, I just stuck it away, intending to return it to you the next time I saw you." He grinned wryly. "I hadn't meant for there to be such a long time between our meetings, but the war made visits to Magnolia Grove somewhat difficult!"

Bartholomew smiled, shaking his head. "I'd wondered where it had disappeared to. I just never thought to ask you about it."

"Well, you'd better take the blasted thing and keep better care of it in the future—you never know *where* a weapon like that will turn up!"

Bartholomew chuckled and, taking the dagger with him, walked out of the room.

There was a thunderous silence after his departure. A second or two later, Sara said tautly, "You knew all along that it was his dagger—that it wasn't yours!"

Yancy stretched himself out beside her on the bed, his hands locked behind his head. "Hmm, yeah, I knew it was Bartholomew's dagger." Dryly, he added, "As he said—it *is* distinctive and not easily mistaken for another knife."

Anger kindling in her eyes, Sara snapped, "Didn't it occur to you that I would have liked to know such a thing? You lied to me that morning I found Margaret's body, when you claimed there was no sign of a dagger! You wanted me to doubt what I had seen!" Her anger growing, she was unaware of the precarious slide of the sheet down her body and said hotly, "You deliberately misled me! You deliberately let me think that the dagger was yours! Oh, but you're sly! You never once admitted that the dagger wasn't yours! Never once hinted that you knew to whom it belonged!" Another thought occurred to her. "Sam recognized it, too! *That's* why you both pretended it wasn't there—you and Sam didn't want suspicion falling on Bartholomew!"

"Something like that," Yancy admitted with exasperating calm, and Sara was so furious she could have hit him. Glaring at his dark face, her bosom heaving, she said tightly, "The dagger is Bartholomew's—he *could* have killed her, and you and Sam decided to play God!"

"Not exactly," Yancy murmured, a mocking gleam dancing in his eyes. "We just didn't want to watch a member of the family, even a member from the wrong side of the blanket, hang!"

Thoroughly outraged and incensed, Sara stared speechlessly at him for a moment. "But you knew that everyone was going to think that you had done it!" she finally exclaimed incredulously. "You might have hanged instead, you bloody fool!"

Yancy looked very pleased at her reaction. "Not likely, sweetheart! There would have had to be a lot more evidence than just my oft-stated aversion to Margaret in order to convict me of murder! I know I'd threatened to kill her, but that didn't mean that I *had* killed her! Besides, my father was a prominent member of the community, and while not everyone thinks of me as a model of decorum, the sheriff would have been very uncomfortable arresting me with nothing more than hot-tempered threats to incriminate me. And don't forget, Sam gave me an impeccable alibi." The mocking light died from his eyes and he added somberly. "But the sheriff wouldn't have hesitated a second to arrest Bartholomew if he'd seen the dagger and discovered that the murder weapon was the property of a black man. Bartholomew's relationship to us wouldn't have mattered. All the sheriff would have seen was an 'uppity nigger' with a knife and that would have been the end of that! Trust me—Bartholomew would have hanged, and neither Sam nor I wanted to see that happen."

What Yancy had said made sense, but Sara just had to ask the obvious question. "But what if he did it? What if he's guilty?"

Yancy regarded her for a long moment, the expression in his eyes chilling Sara. "She deserved killing," he said flatly. "And quite frankly, I don't particularly care who did the deed. She's dead, and who killed her or why doesn't interest me—it never did!"

"You can't mean that!" Sara burst out, aghast. "Everyone thinks that *you* did it?"

"That bothers you?" he inquired dryly.

Sara was suddenly aware that a lot depended upon her answer, and tucking the sheet modestly under her arms, she looked down at her hands and said carefully, "Not exactly. It's not that I'm ashamed or embarrassed by what people think, but it's not fair for you to be painted a blackhearted murderer . . . if you didn't do it."

Yancy lifted up her chin. His eyes boring into hers, he asked gently, "And what do you think, sweet wife? Did I do it? Did I kill her?"

A lump rose in Sara's throat. It always came back to this: Yancy would not defend himself, would not offer any explanations, would not refute any of the evidence against him . . . and yet by his very manner he demanded that she believe him innocent. She gazed intently at his dark, beloved features and the pain in her heart was nearly intolerable. Yancy Cantrell was a complex man. He could be both cruel and kind, arrogant and yet so very tenderly considerate of others, but he could also be inexorable in chasing after what he wanted, allowing nothing and no one to stand in his way. He brooked no interference and was used to arranging his life just as he saw fit. He was capable of killing—in war, to protect his family, to save his own life; she didn't doubt that. She also didn't doubt that he wouldn't hesitate to kill for revenge, but outright murder?

"Is it such a hard question to answer, Sara?" he inquired with an edge to his voice. "You cannot sit on the fence forever, you know—you believe that either I killed Margaret or I didn't. Which is it?"

She had never *wanted* to believe that he had killed Margaret, but every path had seemed to lead right to him. Miserable and uncertain, she stared at him, trying to compile everything she knew about the murder, about Yancy and about her own instincts. Suddenly, with an almost blinding burst of clarity, the truth lay before her. She smiled ruefully. In all her considerations, she had forgotten two very important facets of Yancy's personality: he was a strong man and an intelligent man. An intelligent man would *never* have allowed someone like Margaret to goad him to murder. Neither would a strong man. A strong man would have been able to rise above the petty aggravations and spiteful acts of Margaret Cantrell. Yancy might have thought about killing her, but such an act was beneath him. Sara was positive that in his own mind, Margaret hadn't been *worth* killing!

The tight knot in her chest slowly eased. Of course Yancy hadn't killed Margaret! He'd had no need to! And something else, something she should have realized years ago, occurred to her: Yancy could have destroyed Margaret anytime he chose to. He *was* an intelligent man; he knew Margaret, knew about her infidelities; and despite Sam's besottedness over his young wife and the bitter chasm that existed between father and son, if Yancy had even once intimated to his father what he knew of her blatant disregard of her marriage vows, Margaret would have been a ruined woman. *And Margaret had known it*! Known it and tried her best to seduce Yancy, and when he would have none of it, she had tried another tack.

It was obvious to Sara now, even if it hadn't been at the time, that Margaret had been recklessly skirmishing with Yancy all along, trying desperately to find some

leverage of her own. She had found it in Casa Paloma.
Yancy held the best cards—he could have gone to Sam
at any time with the truth of Margaret's infidelities, but
he hadn't because he loved his father. And Margaret
had decided to exploit that fact. She had never wanted
Casa Paloma, she had merely wanted to strike at Yancy
and she had been gambling on the fact that in order
to save his father pain, Yancy would have let Casa
Paloma slip through his fingers, rather than reveal what
he knew about her. Margaret had been taking a dangerous chance; Yancy might have eventually gone to Sam
and she would have lost everything, but if she won . . .
if she had won, she would have had the satisfaction of
knowing she had wrested something of great value from
her most implacable enemy, and *that* would have made
it worth the risk!

Intent upon her own speculations, Sara suddenly asked
out loud, "Would you have told him?"

Yancy frowned. Not being privy to her thoughts, he
had absolutely no idea what she was referring to, and
while he was not a mind reader, as Sara had surmised,
he *was* an intelligent man and quick-witted to boot! A
second later, enlightenment dawned and he said warily,
"I presume you're asking about Margaret and Sam?"

Sara nodded. "Would you have? Told him about her
infidelities, rather than let her walk away with Casa
Paloma?"

Not wishing to get sidetracked into the past, Yancy
irritably tried to turn the path of the conversation. "I
thought I was the one asking the questions—and you
haven't answered me yet." His frown growing blacker,
he muttered, "I don't see how whether I would have told
Sam has any bearing on what we *were* talking about!"

Sara smiled tenderly at him and, reaching over, cupped
his face between her hands, oblivious of the fact that
the sheet had fallen and had left her naked from the

waist up. Brushing her lips against his, she murmured, "You're right, it doesn't have anything to do with us or your question."

Yancy had waited with incredible patience for her answer, but the waiting had stretched his nerves to the breaking point, and the tension that coiled in his big body was almost palpable. It didn't help his frame of mind to be suddenly confronted by the sight of her temptingly jutting little breasts. Despite his best intentions, he was *extremely* aware of her nakedness, his body responding resoundingly to the nearness of her, his flesh straining against his breeches, his blood thundering in his veins. But her answer to his question was of far more interest to him at the moment, and he gamely fought down the urge to simply take her in his arms and say to hell with the past! Yet even more than needing to slake his passion for her, he *needed* to know, once and for all, if she really believed that he had killed Margaret. "Well? Did I? Or didn't I?" he demanded harshly.

Sara's heart went out to him. She had never realized until this moment how *very* much her answer meant to him. Her green eyes clear and luminous, a breathtakingly lovely smile on her rosy lips, she wrapped her arms around his neck and kissed him soundly.

Helplessly Yancy returned her kiss, his arms automatically crushing her to him. He was shaking with hunger for her when she finally lifted her sweetly tormenting mouth from his. As if from a great distance, he heard her say softly, "Of course you didn't kill her! You're far too smart to have done anything so silly!"

The blood rushed in his ears, her words a balm and a benediction to his tortured soul. Almost violently his arms closed tighter around her, his mouth blindly seeking hers, a hint of tears, unnoticed by either of them, trembling behind his closed lids. With something close to frenzy they moved together, their hands reaching and

caressing, clothes once more flying in all directions as
they lost themselves in the ecstasy to be found in each
other's arms. It was quite some time before Yancy left
his wife's arms and dressed himself for the *second* time
that afternoon.

The room was in shadows, and for a long time after
he had slid silently from the bed and garbed himself, he
stood there staring down at the sleep-softened features
of his bride. She looked very sweet and vulnerable as
she lay there, her slender, well-loved form outlined by
the sheet, her lips still flushed and rosy from their latest
lovemaking. As the minutes passed and he stared at her,
all the intensely powerful emotions that he usually kept
hidden deep within himself were clear for anyone to see
in the depths of his amber-gold eyes. Then the shutter
fell, hiding the fierce secrets of his heart, and he walked
quietly from the room.

When Sara woke a half hour later, she wasn't surprised to find Yancy gone; in fact, she thought with a
rueful smile, she was growing quite used to going to
sleep in his arms and then waking alone. Humming to
herself, her heart very light, she rang for Maria.

Sometime later, freshly bathed and wearing a new
gown, sewn by one of the women in the village, of
lime-green muslin trimmed around the neck, the elbow-
length ruffled sleeves and the hem with a darker green
silk ribbon, Sara walked slowly to the rear courtyard.
It was early evening by now, dusk just starting to fall,
one of her favorite times of day. Automatically, she
wandered to the fountain and idly watched the goldfish
swimming in the cool blue-green depths. The lanterns
which adorned the various archways had been lit, fuzzy
golden pools of light spilling out into the courtyard, and
the scents of jasmine and damask rose drifted on the
cooling air. Dreamily Sara breathed in the heavy fragrance of the flowers, thinking that no matter where in

the world she might ever find herself, she would never again smell that particular mixture of scents without thinking of evenings at del Sol.

For the first time since she had found Margaret's body over seven years ago, Sara was at peace about the murder. She still didn't know who had killed Sam's second wife, but like Yancy, right now, at this exact moment, she wasn't even certain that she *cared* who had killed Margaret. *At least it hadn't been Yancy*! It was amazing, after all her doubts and reservations about his guilt or innocence, how bone-deep sure she was in that belief, and she wondered how she could have thought even for a second that Yancy had killed Margaret.

She would have been lying if she hadn't admitted to herself that she was greatly disturbed to have discovered that the dagger which had killed Margaret belonged to Bartholomew. She didn't want Bartholomew to be the killer—whether the killing was justified or not! She sighed. Perhaps Yancy was right about that, too! Perhaps it would just be best to put the murder behind her and forget about it. But even with her newfound confidence that Yancy had *not* done the crime, Sara could not shake a feeling of unease . . . a feeling that *none* of them were safe until whoever had killed Margaret was caught.

She had entered the courtyard in a lighthearted mood, but as the moments passed and she stared with increasing vagueness at the goldfish, she became pensive. Nothing had been settled between her and Yancy. She grimaced ruefully. Nothing except that their bodies responded wildly to each other. They were married; they had made love, but as yet, not one word of love had passed between them. Sara knew her own heart; she just wished Yancy would tell her what was in his heart. She knew he cared for her—she would have had to have been both blind and deaf not to have realized that, while he might not love her, she certainly aroused deep feelings within him. She wrinkled her straight little nose disgustedly. Knowing your husband had deep feelings for you was not quite the same as knowing he loved you. Some men had great feelings for their horses and dogs, but that didn't mean that they *loved* them!

She sighed. Life certainly would have been much less complicated if Sam hadn't left Casa Paloma to her in such an archaic fashion. With a sinking heart, she realized that until the question of Casa Paloma was settled, even *if* Yancy were to declare his lasting, undying love for her, she would always wonder if he were telling the truth, or if he had been motivated to marry her simply to get his hands on the lands of his forefathers.

Annoyed at her train of thought, she turned away, only to be brought up short by the sight of her husband leaning negligently against one of the archways, watching her.

His arms were folded across his chest, his legs crossed at the ankles, one shoulder braced against the stone of the archway. In the falling shadows, his chambray shirt had deepened to an indigo blue that was very attractive against the duskiness of his skin and his black hair. It really wasn't fair, Sara thought with giddy fondness, for any one man to be quite so attractive.

The expression in his eyes hidden, a faint smile curling his mouth, Yancy pushed himself away from the archway and sauntered over to where she stood. "You look unhappy," he said huskily. "Are you?"

Sara smiled at him and shook her head. "No, I'm not *un*happy—I was just thinking about Margaret and Casa Paloma."

"Don't!" he growled and bent his head and kissed her hard. "Don't think about her anymore. You're a bride of only twenty-four hours—you're *supposed* to think of nothing but your husband!"

Sara put her arms around his neck, a twinkle in her

green eyes. "And, of course, all you've been thinking about is your bride!"

He laughed and lifted her off the ground and swung her gently around, her skirts and long hair flying out behind her. His white teeth flashing, his dark face laughing up at hers, he said frankly, "*Sí*! I have found of late that no matter what task I undertake, your bewitching image has the most damnable habit of appearing in my mind, making me forget instantly what it was that I intended to do!"

It was a very satisfying answer and Sara showed him just how pleased she was at his words by impetuously kissing him. It was absolutely astonishing, she decided dizzyingly as his tongue brazenly met the thrust of hers, how extremely bold she was growing!

Lost in their own world, they were oblivious of a third party entering the courtyard, until Esteban coughed delicately and brought them back to the present. Jerking her lips from Yancy's, Sara looked in the direction of the sound and felt her cheeks flush at the sight of Maria's husband standing there politely, not three feet from them, with his big sombrero held in his hands.

As if it were the most natural thing in the world to be caught kissing his wife by his head vaquero, Yancy unhurriedly lowered Sara down his body, letting her feel how precisely aroused he had become during their embrace. Once her feet were firmly on the ground, and after dropping a brief, warm kiss on her mouth, Yancy glanced at Esteban.

"Ah, good! Maria did find you," Yancy said easily. "I want you to send some people to Casa Paloma. My bride and I are thinking of removing there for the summer. Send along the necessary supplies and house servants to clean and prepare the place for us. We shall arrive there sometime Tuesday afternoon." He grinned at Sara, then looked back at Esteban. "We shall have a busy summer, *mi amigo*—my bride has informed me that we are to start raising cattle for the hungry bellies of the Eastern gringos. She is quite anxious for me to start rounding up cattle to breed to the fine blooded bulls I am to buy, and to begin constructing corrals in which to capture wild horses—the best mares to be bred to the black thoroughbred stallions I am to select for her." His amber-gold eyes full of pride and something else that Sara could not name, Yancy pulled her next to him and, ignoring Esteban, briefly kissed her again. Watching with interest as the embarrassed color rushed up into her cheeks, he said softly, "I am to be doubly congratulated, Esteban, on my choice of a bride. Not only is she lovely and kind, but she is also a hardheaded businesswoman . . . and extremely clever."

Not certain that he would like to be married to a clever woman, but satisfied that his patron was pleased with his bride, Esteban beamed at them. "*Sí*, senor! She is indeed *muy bella*! As for the people for Casa Paloma—it shall be done!"

As soon as Esteban had departed, Sara scolded, "What were you thinking, kissing me that way in front of him! Have you no shame?"

Yancy grinned at her and then kissed her leisurely. Only when her head was spinning did he murmur, "Where you are concerned, *chica*, absolutely *none*!"

Sara made a face at him and stepped demurely out of his arms. "Is Casa Paloma really in terrible condition?" she asked abruptly.

Yancy shrugged. "No one has lived in the place for well over twenty-five years, and quite frankly, I have no idea what we will find. It has simply been left to go to rack and ruin, and while adobe is built to last, it could simply be a pile of rubble. Casa Paloma is a very old rancho. It is where my ancestors first settled in Texas almost a hundred and fifty years ago."

Sara looked surprised. "Not del Sol?"

Yancy shook his head. "No. First came Casa Paloma and then, about eighty years or so ago, my great-grandfather built del Sol."

Ann's tinkling laugh rang out across the courtyard and Yancy and Sara both turned in that direction. Tom and Ann Shelldrake were strolling toward them. As they came closer, Ann said easily, "And what were you two talking about so seriously?" She looked arch. "Or is it something that is none of our business—perhaps a secret between newlyweds?"

Yancy saw that Sara was seated on the rim of the fountain before he turned back to Ann. "Nothing quite so exciting, I'm afraid. We were simply discussing Casa Paloma. I intend to stay there for most of the summer while gathering cattle and horses." He glanced at Sara and smiled. "Sara is coming with me."

Both the Shelldrakes appeared disturbed by this news. Tom looked faintly concerned, but Ann's face was the picture of dismay and she exclaimed, "Oh, but you can't! I mean, why would you want to take her to that ram-shackle place?"

"And how do you know that Paloma is a 'ramshackle place'?" Yancy asked quietly, his eyes fixed on Ann's face.

"Oh, I don't *know* what condition the place is in, but surely Sara would be more comfortable here while you are gone."

Yancy shrugged his broad shoulders. "I'm certain that the place can be made quite habitable. Besides, I don't wish to be separated from my bride for the entire summer."

Ann flushed angrily and snapped, "Of course! I forgot! There is the heir for Casa Paloma—naturally you'd want her with you!"

Yancy's eyes darkened and his mouth tightened. But

it was Tom who muttered, "*Ann*! I think you presume too much! You forget that we are Yancy's guests and that we owe him a great deal."

Sulkily settling herself in one of the courtyard chairs, the skirts and petticoats of her blue silk gown billowing out around her feet, Ann said with a pout, "Oh, I know! I shouldn't have said such a thing. But why should we all pretend that we don't know why they got married in such a hurly-burly fashion?" Ignoring the taut silence that had fallen, Ann rattled on disagreeably. "Everyone knows their marriage is simply to fulfill that wretched requirement of Sam's will! As soon as Sara is pregnant, they won't have to bother about each other!"

Ann's cruel words went through Sara like a knife and she waited desperately for Yancy to refute Ann's statements. To her great pain, he did not. Leaning negligently against one of the archways, he said coolly, "How amazing! Have you always had this gift? The ability to see right into my thoughts and to understand precisely what is in my mind?"

Ann grimaced. "Oh, stop! Don't tease me! You know what I mean and you know that I believe in plain speaking."

It was Tom who surprised them all by saying dryly, "Ah, but only when it suits you, my dear. Only when it suits you."

Ann sent him an uncertain glance and laughed a little nervously. "Well, since I seem to have put my foot wrong, allow me to apologize. I'm sorry, and I'll try not to let my tongue run away with me in the future." She smiled sunnily at Yancy. "There! Have I redeemed myself?"

Yancy murmured something polite and Tom hurriedly injected a different subject for conversation, commenting jovially on his pleasure in the new quarters which they would be moving into within the next few days. Perhaps realizing that she had overstepped herself, Ann ably joined him, and the unpleasant topic of the reason for Yancy's marriage to Sara was left behind.

Sara smiled and contributed to the conversation, but she could not get Ann's words out of her mind. Or Yancy's reply to them. She hadn't actually expected him to suddenly declare that their marriage had had *nothing* to do with the need for an heir for Casa Paloma, but she wished miserably that he had said something that would have disclosed what he really felt about her. She and Yancy had come so far in the brief twenty-four hours they had been married, but Sara was realizing unhappily that not a great deal had changed. She *still* didn't know if he had married her simply to get his hands on Casa Paloma, and there was a growing ache in the region of her heart and many of the doubts she had held about him came rushing back. Oh, not about the murder—she would *never* again have any doubts about *that*—but she couldn't help wondering if she hadn't let her feelings for him and her body's blatantly joyous response to his blind her to cold reality.

Just because he was kind to her, just because his very touch sent her spinning into near ecstasy, didn't mean a damn thing! she admitted hollowly. He could be kind to her, make wildly passionate love to her and yet feel nothing but a solicitous *fondness* for her. Sara felt slightly sick just thinking about it and she wondered how her earlier happiness could have vanished so swiftly.

If Yancy noticed that Sara seemed rather quiet during their evening meal, he kept it to himself, but there was a thoughtful expression in his eyes every time they rested on her face, which was often. Occasionally his cool glance would fall on Ann. He was going to have to do something about Ann. Her cruelty and conniving couldn't continue unchecked, and if he didn't want her to cause irreparable harm, he was going to have to see that she and Tom were removed as far away from him and Sara as possible. With all his holdings, surely there was a suitable house somewhere within miles, weeks, *months* of travel from his and Sara's vicinity? It was a pleasant idea, one he would have to look into more thoroughly. . . .

After Ann and Tom had departed, Yancy noted grimly that Sara was quick to take her own leave of him, and somehow he doubted it was because she was so eager to seek out their marriage bed! His mouth thinned. Surely she hadn't taken Ann's spiteful words to heart! Surely she knew that he— He stopped abruptly. That he what? Loved her? He shook his head vehemently, denying it. He had loved Margaret. During those first heady months, he would have given Margaret everything that was his to give, and look where that had gotten him! How did he know that Sara wasn't the same? After all, like Margaret, she had married his father, hadn't she? In what other ways was she like Margaret? Suddenly furious with the situation and the train of his thoughts, he finished off his brandy in one gulp. *Women!* he thought disgustedly as he got to his feet and walked to their rooms. They wanted a man to lay bare his soul, and then when they held his heart in their soft little hands, they'd gleefully rip it apart! Well, he'd had that done to him once—he'd be damned if he was going to let it happen again, no matter how beguiling and enchanting he found his bride! He was not ever going to be fooled by another woman again. Not *ever*!

PART FOUR

BY THE LIGHT OF DAY

*Time's glory is to calm contending kings,
To unmask falsehood, and bring truth to
light.*

> *THE RAPE OF LUCRECE*
> —WILLIAM SHAKESPEARE

ᘓ 20

Yancy's black mood was not lessened when he discovered, upon entering their rooms, that his bride was sleeping in her own quarters . . . with the connecting doors between their bedrooms firmly closed and *locked*! For a long moment he scowled at the door and then, cursing under his breath, he flung himself down on his bed—his very *empty* bed. Of course, he could smash down the door that separated them, but he was in no mood for a confrontation.

His mouth set in a hard, grim line, he quickly shed his clothes and climbed into bed. Lying there naked on the cool sheets, the scent of their lovemaking mingling with the remnant of Sara's own sweet perfume evoked vivid memories of the previous night and he wasn't surprised that his body instantly hardened and began to ache in obvious places. No, he wasn't in the mood for a confrontation, but he was in the mood to make love to his wife, his very *new* wife, dammit!

It didn't take a lot of sleuthing on Yancy's part to discover what was behind Sara's actions—that damned, prattling, troublemaking bitch Ann! He could have throttled her with her ugly reading of the situation and he didn't doubt that it was all her fault that he was lying here alone and not in the arms of his bride. He grimaced. Well, perhaps it wasn't *all* Ann's fault—he certainly hadn't helped his cause by replying as he had, but what the devil was he supposed to have done? Told Ann that she was so far wrong that it was laughable—that Casa Paloma had *nothing* to do with his marriage to Sara, that he had simply seized it as a convenient excuse to force her to marry him? And whether he and Sara ever had any children didn't concern him in the least; as long as she was his wife, and in his arms and in his bed, he didn't give a damn about anything else? Hell no!

He smiled mirthlessly in the darkness. *Jesus!* Sara already befuddled him, enchanted him, drove him half mad and tied him in knots as it was—she certainly didn't need to be handed any more weapons to use against him!

At least, he decided coolly, at Paloma, except for his own people, there would just be the two of them, and without Ann around to stir up trouble, he was positive that he could smooth things over with Sara. And as for Ann . . .

He scowled blackly as he considered Ann Shelldrake. The news of the affair between Ann and Hyrum Burnell had come as a decidedly unpleasant shock, and he was doubly glad that he had had Esteban set someone to watch over Sara—otherwise he would never have known of it. He knew Sara well enough to know that she would never reveal what she had seen down by the creek. Fortunately, the young boy who had been assigned to watch over the senora while she was on the hacienda grounds had had no scruples about relating all that he had seen to Yancy. The affair was a complication that Yancy didn't want or need, and he sighed.

He wondered if Tom had any idea what was going on right under his nose. From Tom's comments tonight, one could surmise that he had a good understanding of his wife . . . perhaps even of her adulterous proclivities?

Yancy had always found Tom Shelldrake to be a pleasant and genial companion, but for various reasons, he didn't know the man all that well. Perhaps Tom *did* know about the affair and condoned it. That seemed unlikely, but it was possible. It was also possible that the war had left more scars and wounds on Tom than just his bad arm—it could be that he was no longer capable of physically satisfying his wife and, consequently, turned a blind eye to her discreet liaison with Hyrum.

The situation troubled Yancy, not so much because of Ann's infidelity as because of the danger it represented.

He had told Sara that he didn't give a damn about who had murdered Margaret, but that wasn't strictly true. He wanted to know who was capable of such violence so he could prevent others from falling victim to it. And though he had never thought a great deal about *why* Margaret had been killed, the notion that her infidelities had played a large part in her death couldn't be ignored. And if Ann was following the same path as her sister . . . He frowned. He sure as hell didn't want to be confronted by *another* murdered woman!

Knowing he wasn't going to fall asleep any time soon, he got up and fumbled to light the lamp by his bed. The flame of the lamp glowing golden, he shrugged into his breeches and, grabbing a cheroot, lit one and ambled bad-temperedly out into the private courtyard off his rooms.

Settling himself in one of the chairs, he smoked his thin black cheroot, letting the silence of the night, broken only by the brassy croaks of frogs and the high-pitched chirps of insects, flow around his body. The darkness enfolded him and the scent of jasmine surrounded him, but Yancy was in no mood to appreciate either the sounds or the scents of the night.

He took a deep drag of his cheroot, not even enjoying the rich taste of the fine tobacco in his mouth. What he wanted, he decided grimly, was the taste of Sara on his tongue and the feel of himself tightly buried within her body! And since that wasn't going to happen tonight, he had better set his mind to figuring out what he was going to do about Ann and Hyrum. The situation could get explosive, and he sure as hell didn't want it blowing up in *his* face!

Hyrum would just have to accompany them to Casa Paloma, he decided sourly. With Ann at del Sol and Hyrum at Casa Paloma, at least they wouldn't be sharing any more intimate rendezvous any time soon. It wasn't the best solution, but Yancy wasn't quite ready to lay down an ultimatum to the pair, nor was he particularly eager to reveal to them that he knew about their relationship.

What he found most disquieting about the affair was the fact that only weeks ago, Hyrum had been begging Sara to marry him. When had the affair started and for how long had it been going on? Yancy wondered uneasily. It seemed to him that there was more here than met the eye, and before he charged in and started issuing nonnegotiable demands, it seemed only logical that he find out a whole lot more than he knew right now.

He briefly considered ordering Hyrum off the place, but that action might precipitate the very thing he was hoping to avoid. He scowled. He had been looking forward to having Sara all to himself at Paloma—all the more so after Ann's vicious words this evening—and he wasn't at all happy about Hyrum's accompanying them. Yancy smiled nastily. He'd just keep Hyrum so damned busy that the other man wouldn't have time for anything but eating and sleeping—and *that* would be in the quarters with the vaqueros! No special treatment for Mr. Burnell!

Satisfied that he had come up with a temporary solution to the Ann-Hyrum affair, Yancy ground out his cheroot and wandered back inside. Feeling slightly pleased with himself, he sought out his bed in a much better frame of mind. Now, if he could only come up with a quick way to get himself back into his bride's good graces, and bed, definitely her bed, he'd be a happy man!

His bride, lying equally awake and restless in the next room, would have been extremely joyful if he had come up with the most obvious way to insinuate himself back into her arms and bed: tell her that their marriage had *nothing* to do with Casa Paloma! Her green eyes dry and aching, Sara stared up miserably at the silk bed hanging. He wouldn't, she admitted honestly, even have to say that he loved her, only that his obsessive desire to reclaim the land of his ancestors hadn't been behind his forcing her to marry him. She sighed and changed position for the hundredth time since she had come to bed.

Sara had heard Yancy enter his rooms hours ago and she had held her breath as she had listened to his footsteps move toward the locked door of her bedroom. Sitting up in bed hopefully, she had waited for his reaction when she discovered that the door was locked. A suspiciously short time later, when she heard him moving away, she had been both relieved and crushed—relieved that she hadn't had to face him and utterly crushed that he had so tamely accepted her action. Ironically, if anything confirmed that there was more than a little truth to Ann's words, it was his calm resignation to his ouster from her bed. She had bitten back a sob and buried her face in her pillow as his footsteps had faded. Obviously, she had thought wretchedly, he hoped that last night and this afternoon had accomplished his task and that he didn't have to bother himself with the chore of making love to her anymore!

Bitter and unhappy, Sara lay there planning all sorts of impractical means of revenge, and only when she realized that there was very little that she *could* do to Yancy that would rattle or greatly disturb him—except prove to be barren, she thought spitefully—did she give up her unprofitable plans. Miserably she twisted and turned in her bed yearning for the oblivion that sleep would give her.

Eventually sleep did come to Sara, and she was startled awake at dawn by a loud, imperious pounding on her door. Rubbing her eyes and throwing back the tangle of hair that fell across her face, she hastily got out of bed and stumbled to the door. Not even fully awake, she had completely forgotten last's night events. Certain that the rapid banging was imperative, that there was some great urgency behind it, she hurriedly fumbled with the lock and threw open the door.

In the faint rays of the rising sun which permeated the room, she stared uncomprehendingly at the sight of her tall, darkly garbed husband looming in the doorway. The hard gleam in his eyes and the taut line of his lips suddenly brought her very wide awake. With a faint rush of uneasiness, she also suddenly and rather unpleasantly remembered the reason behind the locked door.

A militant sparkle in her green eyes, she asked, "Yes? What is it?"

Yancy stood there staring at her, enraged that after his lonely night—his lonely, *sleepless* night, endured because of her—it was obvious that she had been awakened from a sound sleep. It also didn't help his frame of mind that she looked almost irresistible to him as she stood there in a demure nightgown of soft, rose-sprigged cambric, her green eyes ablaze, her honey-gold hair all sleep-tousled and tumbling down her shoulders. Her breasts were temptingly outlined by the drape of the worn material, and it was all Yancy could do to prevent himself from reaching out and caressing those hard little breasts.

His sleepless night, however, had given him a great deal of time to think and he had realized that one way to defang Ann would be to reassure Sara that his marriage to her had nothing to do with getting his hands on Casa Paloma. . . . But that conversation, he admitted uneasily, once started, was bound to go into sensitive areas, areas that he wasn't quite certain he was ready to explore—or to discuss. Still, he felt the urge to try to set things right between them, but as he stood there hesitating, he was suddenly filled with a painful feeling of vulnerability. With an effort he shook off the unwelcome sensation. *Dios*! If he did not get himself under control, he would be blurting out his deepest feelings like a lovesick fool!

In order to prevent himself from doing just that and a great deal more, he took refuge in cold anger. A sardonic expression on his lean features, he growled, "I'm leaving for the day—and since I don't think you want the state of affairs between us to be common knowledge among the servants, I wanted that damned door unlocked before I left." Not trusting himself to remain in her presence without doing something they would both regret, although he didn't really believe that he would ever regret making love to her, Yancy spun on his heels and stalked swiftly away.

Devastated, Sara stared bleakly after him, hardly able to believe that he had nothing more to say to her. Nothing. Not even a demand to know why she had locked the door! Perhaps he didn't even care! If she had needed irrefutable proof of how little she mattered to him, he had just given it to her, and she wondered bitterly how things could have gone so *very* wrong between them.

Unhappy and dispirited, she wandered into his room and impulsively, driven to reestablish some degree of contact with him, she snuggled down into the imprint left by his body on the bed. There was still a faint, lingering warmth from his body on the sheets and a comforting trace of his scent, and Sara reveled in it, even as she scolded herself for being a fool. A mawkish, stupid, *stupid* little fool at that!

In the next few days, the situation between Sara and Yancy did not change appreciably. In front of the others they were cordial and polite, but alone in their rooms, Sara would immediately seek out her own quarters and shut the door with a decided snap, the sound of the lock turning reverberating endlessly in the silence that followed. Exerting every savage impulse to the contrary, Yancy made absolutely no attempt to cross the lines she had drawn, nor did he ask Sara what had prompted her actions. He simply ignored the problem as if it didn't exist . . . or didn't matter to him, Sara thought painfully on more than one occasion.

She tried to view the situation impartially. Had she been wrong to lock the door? Should she have just boldly asked him outright to refute Ann's statements? Was it *her* fault that they were at this terrible impasse?

Sitting alone in the private courtyard off their rooms late Monday afternoon, she wondered wearily if there was some other way that she should have handled the situation. It had begun to occur to her with depressing regularity that she hadn't been exactly fair to Yancy—one minute she had been yielding and eager in his arms and the next she had, without explanation, locked the door practically in his face. Her lips twisted wryly. Perhaps she had overreacted to Ann's words.

Oh, *damn*! she thought wretchedly. If Yancy weren't such a closemouthed devil, none of this would have happened! If she had been secure in the knowledge that he loved her, that he *hadn't* married her simply to gain Casa Paloma, Ann's words wouldn't have had the power to hurt her so deeply and she wouldn't have reacted as she had. He had to take some of the blame for the situation, she decided stubbornly. And if the damned locked door bothered him, he could say something! If it *mattered* to him, he could do something about it! And if it didn't . . .

As if her thoughts had conjured him up, Yancy strolled out into their courtyard, his dark face set in enigmatic lines. Eyeing her impersonally, he asked coolly, "All packed?"

Puzzled, Sara stared at him, wishing her pulse wouldn't pound so crazily at the very sight of him. "Packed?" she echoed. "What are you talking about?"

His eyes never leaving her features, he replied carelessly, "Our trip to Paloma. Have you forgotten about it?"

"Oh! I don't think that's such a good idea anymore, do you?" she replied uncertainly, her expressive face revealing her confusion. Paloma? He couldn't possible want to go there with her under the circumstances!

"Why not? You're *still* my wife, aren't you?" he inquired silkily. "And if memory serves me, we're to leave tomorrow, aren't we?"

Sara nodded helplessly, unable to tear her fascinated gaze away from the glittering depths of his eyes. At her nod, he smiled, not a particularly reassuring smile, and said briskly, "Good! If you're not packed already, I suggest that you ring for Maria and start getting your things ready. We're leaving just after dawn tomorrow—I don't want you to be traveling in the heat."

He started to turn away and leave the courtyard, but suddenly, gathering up all her courage, Sara blurted out, "Why did you marry me?"

Yancy froze. Slowly he pivoted around to stare at her. His features revealing nothing, he looked at her for a long time, saying nothing. Sara was cursing her unruly tongue and wishing she were a million miles away from this embarrassingly painful interview, when he finally drawled, "Why did I marry you? Why, darlin', I thought you had that all figured out!"

Daunted by the expression on his face, but persevering bravely, Sara replied, "No, I don't have it all figured out—that's why I'm asking you! Why did you marry me?"

All of his angry frustration over the situation between them suddenly exploded within him and, more furious than he could ever remember being in his life, he grabbed her shoulders and shook her soundly. "Suppose," he growled, "you tell me why I married you?"

Sara swallowed. "I can't! I don't know! You hide what you feel. You never reveal what's going on in your mind."

His face darkened, and dropping his hands to her hips, he jerked her tightly against his loins. Sara gasped when she felt the aroused length of him and he smiled grimly. "I don't think I'm hiding what I'm feeling right now, sweetheart. And, as for what's going on in my mind— I'd like nothing better than to take up where we left off before you locked that damned door! I'd like to rip off your clothes and discover if your flesh is as sweet and warm as I remember it."

Sara twisted angrily out of his grip. Fists clenched, she faced him. "That's not what I'm talking about and you know it!"

He folded his arms over his chest and leaned against the doorway. "But what else is there to talk about? Haven't you already decided that it's only for your delectable little body that I pursue you? Or rather," he added cruelly, "what your soft, tempting body can give me? An heir for Paloma? Isn't *that* the only reason I married you? What other reason could I have had?"

Stricken, Sara stared at him, her green eyes enormous in her white face, and Yancy very nearly called back the ugly words, his pain at her pain slashing through him like a sword thrust. But he was far too angry and hurt to deviate from the path he had chosen, far too enraged that she could so easily belittle what lay between them to think rationally. He *wanted* to hurt her, to make her feel at least half of the pain he had suffered these torturous past few days, and while there was a part of him that was thoroughly ashamed of his savage instincts, he was much too stubborn to retreat.

To hear him say the words out loud, to hear him utter all her repellent suspicions, was almost more than she could bear. Her heart twisted agonizingly and the nauseating, bitter taste of defeat rose in her throat. Sara's gaze dropped from his harsh features and she said dully, "I guess there is really no reason to discuss it, is there?" Turning away, she added with chilling politeness, "Will you excuse me now? If you insist upon the trip to Paloma, I must ring for Maria and begin packing."

Like a whiplash, his arm struck out and he grabbed her. Jerking her next to him, he kissed her with all the pent-up fury and anguish that was within him. Only when they were both breathless did he raise his ravaging mouth from hers. His amber-gold eyes glittering fiercely, he snarled softly, "Oh, believe me, I *do* insist! And, Sara, at Paloma . . . you *will* share my bed! There will be, trust me, no more locked doors between us again—ever!"

Glowering darkly at him, Sara said tightly, "Do you intend to gather up all the keys and lock them away?"

"If need be!" he snapped.

"Oh, I think you'll need to, believe me—on *that* we can at least agree!"

They stood there glaring at each other for a long moment, neither willing to concede to the other. Then, releasing her with a rough movement, Yancy spun away and disappeared into the hacienda.

Her emotions blessedly numb, Sara watched him go. Gradually, as her feelings returned, she felt oddly lightheaded, a strange tranquility seeping through her. It was as if, having faced her worst fears, she could now move forward—she was no longer banished to a limbo of uncertainty. She knew the truth now—he had married her for an heir for Paloma. Very well. Despite her proud words, she would give him an heir and *nothing* else, she vowed furiously, and walking inside, she yanked savagely on the bell rope which would bring Maria. She would go to Paloma; she would give him a child and, at the first opportunity, *she'd cut out his liver and fry it before his very eyes*! Suddenly feeling much better, Sara began dragging clothing out of her wardrobe with a vengeance.

At the moment, Sara was not the only person who wished to do violent things to Yancy Cantrell. Ann Shelldrake not only would cut out his liver and fry it— she was furious enough to also feed it to the dogs!

Ann and Hyrum had arranged to meet at dusk at a clump of cottonwoods and willows that grew near the creek which ran some distance behind the pleasant little house Yancy had indicated she and Tom could use as their own. Casting several nervous glances over her shoulder toward the house, Ann ran to the appointed meeting place.

Hyrum's note, delivered surreptitiously just an hour ago by a young vaquero he thought they could trust, had already informed Ann that Yancy had ordered him to Paloma, and so her first burst of fury had already abated. Still, there was a dangerous gleam in her blue eyes when she spied Hyrum's form, almost entirely concealed by the trees and the falling shadows. She went into his arms immediately and they kissed hungrily. Lifting her mouth from his a moment later, Ann cried angrily, "What are we to do? I cannot bear for you to leave me behind! That *damned* Yancy! Why does he want you with him?"

Absently caressing her shoulders, Hyrum replied softly, "I don't know, but I suspect that he may know about us."

Ann looked frightened. "But how? We have been so careful!"

Hyrum shrugged. "This is his land, his people—I'm fairly confident that *nothing* goes on that he doesn't know about. As for what we're going to do, I've been thinking. . . ." He paused, obviously gathering his thoughts, and in that moment of silence the snap of a twig nearby rang out clearly. They both jumped and peered warily in the direction of the sound. There was nothing. No further sound. No movement. Nothing but increasing darkness.

A second later, another twig snapped farther away, and they both released their pent-up breath when one of the many mongrels that roamed the village ambled away from the creek, heading toward the flickering lights of the houses. Hyrum open his mouth to speak, but Ann's hand pressed across his lips silenced him. Despite the sight of the dog, she had the curious impression that someone was *there*, that someone was watching them. She waited tensely, and as the minutes passed and nothing untoward occurred, she gradually relaxed.

A nervous little laugh came from her. "I'm sorry. It's just that Tom has been acting strange lately. I wonder if he . . ."

"You think he suspects?" Hyrum asked in open alarm. He hesitated, then inquired softly, "Are you going to have to get rid of him sooner than we planned?"

Ann shook her blond head decisively and made a face. "I don't really believe he has any idea what is going on, and there is no reason for me to become a grieving widow just yet, but he *has* been acting very strange lately." She shrugged dismissingly. "Forget about my husband for now and tell me you've come up with a way to wrest Sara from Yancy before he makes her pregnant and ruins all our plans."

"Perhaps it doesn't matter anymore whether Yancy is the father of her child or I am," he said slowly.

"What do you mean?" Ann snapped, clearly angry. "We need *you* to be Sara's husband and the father of her child if we are to get our hands on Casa Paloma!"

In the deepening darkness, Hyrum smiled slightly. "If you stop to think about it, we don't need me to be the father of her child—of any of her children. All we need is for me to be Sara's husband."

Ann frowned, staring hard at him. "But if there is no child, what good would your being Sara's husband do? And besides," she added spitefully, "you're not ever going to be her husband as long as Yancy is alive! She has to be a widow before you can marry her!"

In the darkness, Hyrum saw the moment that enlightenment dawned on Ann. Her beautiful face suddenly glowed and she looked at him with warm admiration. "Of course! He *married* her—Sara is Yancy's heir!" She crowed delightedly. "Del Sol, the silver mines in Mexico, *everything* would be hers. We wouldn't need Paloma!" She kissed him fully. "How clever of you, my darling! How very, very clever of you!"

"I'm glad you think so," Hyrum murmured and kissed her lingeringly. "It should be a damn sight easier to kill Yancy than to keep him out of Sara's bed! And once he's dead, I'll be right there to console the mourning little widow." He kissed Ann again and swung her around. "Just think, in less than a year from now, if everything goes as I'm damn sure it will—*I'll* be the *patrón* of del Sol."

Ann giggled merrily then sobered a moment later. An avid look in her gaze, she asked him, "Tell me about what you plan for Yancy. When and how will you kill him?"

Hyrum rubbed his face thoughtfully. "Haven't figured that out yet, but there's no need to rush. Without having to worry about Yancy getting Sara pregnant, I can spend more time figuring out the least suspicious way to make her an unexpected widow." He grinned. "I've decided that being ordered to Paloma may be the best stroke of luck we've had in a long time. While I'm gone, you can start planning on how Tom is to meet his untimely death. As for me . . . at Paloma I can work on repairing my relationship with Sara." His mouth thinned. "I can also figure out the best way to kill that bastard Yancy Cantrell!"

꩜ 21

It was before dawn when they left the hacienda for Casa Paloma. Since Paloma was only a pleasant half day's ride from del Sol, and except for keeping an eye out for any stray Indians, Yancy had looked forward to a leisurely, intimate ride with his bride. The constraint between them, as well as Hyrum's sullen presence, put an end to whatever dalliance along the way Yancy might have considered.

Astride one of his favorite mounts, a stout dark bay, Yancy had watched in grim-faced silence as Sara had lithely mounted Locuela and Hyrum, riding a bald-faced sorrel, had fallen in alongside her. The friendly smile Hyrum flashed Sara made Yancy feel a strong urge to knock the other man out of his saddle, but muttering under his breath, he kicked his horse into motion and led them away from the hacienda. It was planned for Bartholomew and Tansy and a few other servants, along with Sara's personal items and extra supplies, to follow behind in a couple of hours.

Despite her best intentions not to take pleasure in anything that Yancy had planned, Sara couldn't help feeling a rising enthusiasm as they rode away from del Sol. Yancy kept the horses at an easy pace, and as the hacienda and the village gradually disappeared, her sense of adventure grew.

At first, the three of them rode in stiff silence, only the creak of leather and the muted thud of the horses' hooves breaking the vast quiet of predawn. Once the hacienda had been left behind, Yancy dropped back to bring his horse alongside Sara's mount, and though she ignored him, she was tinglingly aware of his glances in her direction.

The mournful cry of a wolf drifted on the cool air, distracting her, and instinctively her eyes met Yancy's steady gaze. As long as she lived she would never hear the howl of a wolf without remembering her terrible ordeal, which would have ended far more tragically if Yancy, her dark rider, had not appeared on the horizon. In spite of herself, as she stared into the shadowed depths of his eyes, Sara was suddenly aware of a breathlessness and a helpless yearning to feel his arms around her, his mouth against her lips. . . .

Furious with herself, she jerked her gaze from his and presented him with an icily lovely profile. His soft chuckle did nothing to make her feel more kindly toward him and determinedly she turned to Hyrum and said, "Well, Hyrum, it appears that we are at last going to Casa Paloma. Are you looking forward to it as much as I am?"

Hyrum gave her a twisted smile. "We had such plans, didn't we? Together, the two of us were going to turn an old, ruined rancho into a grand cattle ranch." He looked wistful. "I had such hopes that we would be partners in other ways, that things would be different, that you would . . ." His voice trailed off and, aware of the thunderous black scowl on Yancy's face, he added hastily, "Uh, while this isn't quite the way I pictured us going to Paloma, I am very eager for my first sight of the place."

It had been a calculated gamble on Hyrum's part to remind Sara of their original plans, and considering that last, acrimonious exchange between them prior to her marriage to Yancy, he wasn't certain how she—or her husband, for that matter—was going to receive his comment. But he'd had to take the risk; it was vital that he reestablish some sort of rapport with Sara, and recalling to mind happier times, times when he and Sara had been full of ideas for Paloma, didn't seem like such a bad start.

Sara could hardly believe that he had dared to refer to the past in such a way and she stiffened, staring at him in outraged disbelief. The image of him passionately kissing Ann Shelldrake flashed through her mind, and knowing that every tender emotion he had professed to feel for her had to have been an unscrupulous falsehood, she bit her tongue to keep from naming him the unprincipled cad she knew him to be. Her eyes were open now to his despicable deviousness and she wasn't about to be taken in by his ingratiating manners ever again! Hyrum was luckier than he could ever guess—only because she was bent on showing her unfeeling, arrogant, overbearing husband that he meant absolutely nothing to her did Hyrum avoid a blunt tongue-lashing.

She smiled mendaciously at him and said, "I'm glad you've discovered that it does no good to repine on the past and that whatever disappointments you may have suffered in regard to Paloma, you haven't allowed them to ruin your basic enthusiasm for the place." She sent her husband a dark look from underneath her long lashes. "Life is far too short for us to dwell on certain unpleasant aspects—especially those we cannot change!"

Through gritted teeth, Yancy growled, "Sweetheart, I think I should warn you that if this conversation doesn't change right now, you're going to have a lot more 'unpleasant aspects' to dwell upon!"

Sara was gratified by Yancy's reaction, and as dawn gradually spread its pink-and-gold light over the purple horizon, at least one of the three riders was feeling very satisfied. For a moment she considered turning the knife just a bit more, but a swift look at her husband's face convinced her that tweaking the tiger's tail, while a heady experience, could also be very dangerous!

Silence fell among the three of them for several miles, but when the darkness vanished and warm, golden sunlight covered the prairies, so did their moods seem to lighten, and eventually they began to converse among themselves. Yancy could be charming when he chose to be, and not wanting to stay in his wife's bad graces—or to give any advantages to Hyrum—he set himself out to be as utterly charming as he knew how. As the miles passed, he beguiled Sara with stories and information about the area, and particularly about Casa Paloma.

At first glance, the land seemed level and boundless, the nearly waist-high grass extending endlessly toward the horizon, broken here and there only by large stretches of almost impenetrable chaparral, mesquite trees and towering prickly-pear cactus. Sara was surprised by the several streams lined with cottonwood, locust and willow trees that they crossed, the horses splashing easily through the clear water. The longer they rode, the more aware she became of the gentle undulations that characterized the land, small gullies and draws that cut across its vast expanse and the gentle rises that broke the utter flatness of the terrain. Like much of this part of Texas, the area abounded with game—antelope, deer, quail and wild turkeys—and with countless numbers of wild long-horned cattle and fleet-footed mustangs that whirled away and raced for the horizon at the first sight of the riders.

Unconsciously basking in the warmth of her husband's attention, listening raptly to his tales of the early days of Spanish settlement in Texas while observing the sheer untamed beauty of the land, made the time fly for Sara and she was astonished when Yancy pulled his horse to a stop and said softly, "There it is, sweetheart. Casa Paloma!"

In the distance, on a slight rise, a small cluster of buildings met Sara's eager gaze. This far away there wasn't much to discern, but as they rode nearer, her heart began to sink at the painfully obvious sad state of disrepair.

There were few resemblances between Casa Paloma and del Sol beyond both being situated along a winding, tree-lined stream and both being constructed of adobe. Like at del Sol, the main house was enclosed by stout walls, the slits for guns and rifles in the smooth surface of the walls reminding Sara forcibly that this was still a wild and fierce land. Comanches still raided and Texans still died in alarming numbers from Indian attacks.

More than a dozen or so small buildings crowded close to the walls which encompassed the hacienda, but there was such a desolate air about them, despite their newly thatched roofs, that Sara's dismay deepened. No well-tended patches of cultivated land and fruit trees greeted her here; Paloma was just a small, lonely spot scratched out from the vast prairies surrounding it, and while there were many encouraging signs that Yancy's people had been very busy in the short time they had been in residence, it was obvious that Paloma had been allowed to go to rack and ruin.

Cactus and mesquite had invaded the area, and though much of the thorny brush had been hastily cleared from near the houses and piled for burning, everywhere Sara looked she could see where more work desperately needed to be done—broken corrals and remnants of old barns and rotting sheds dotting the area. As they rode through the usual assortment of squawking chickens and bleating goats which had accompanied Yancy's people to the site, she acknowledged bleakly that it would take a great deal of money, a fortune, to restore the place to even part of its former productiveness. Certainly far more money than she possessed, and she smiled crookedly. *Damn* Yancy for being right again!

After they had ridden through the gates into the grounds of the hacienda, it was apparent to Sara that Casa Paloma had been an early settlement, the main house appearing far more like a fort than a house. Yancy's men and their families had worked hard to make the place presentable, and seeing the expectant looks on their faces as they jostled one another to press nearer to the senor and senora, Sara smiled warmly at them, her heavy mood vanishing. She told herself that she *should* be happy with the way things had turned out. After all, she reasoned rationally, if she had arrived at Paloma and found it in the depressing, dilapidated state it must have been in before Yancy's people had gone to work on it, wouldn't she have been completely crushed by the sheer enormity of her task? A task made doubly burdensome by the knowledge that if she failed, not only would she have been thrown penniless on the world, but every member of the entire household of Magnolia Grove would have had to bear the same perilous future?

Sara shuddered at the picture that presented itself. Suddenly she felt very glad that she hadn't arrived here with nothing more than wild dreams and everything she owned in the world crammed into a wagon, and her smile became almost blinding in its warmth and beauty.

In the act of helping her dismount her horse, Yancy was stunned by the sheer loveliness of her smile, and his hands tightened around her slim waist. "You're not disappointed?" he asked huskily, allowing himself the pleasure of slowly sliding her slim body down the length of his.

Sara's breath caught when her eyes met his and she saw the naked desire in his gaze. Slowly she shook her head. "No," she answered softly. "I'm not disappointed."

Yancy became oblivious of everything but the woman in his arms. Unaware and uncaring of their audience, giving her every chance to escape, he gently drew her into his arms and kissed her.

It was the lighthearted cheers of the onlookers that brought Yancy and Sara abruptly back to the present. Recalling where they were and the intensely interested audience that watched them, Yancy reluctantly raised his lips from hers. A twisted smile on his handsome face, he murmured, "Welcome to Casa Paloma, *mi esposa* . . . I hope you will be very happy here."

The next several moments were busy as greetings were exchanged and Yancy was informed of the progress of the various tasks that had been undertaken on his orders. Gradually, though, the people dispersed to continue with their many chores. Esteban was among the last to depart, and after exchanging pleasantries, Yancy made arrangements to meet with him later. It was only as Esteban put on his sombrero and started to walk away that Yancy remembered Hyrum.

A hard gleam in his eyes, his arm still anchored firmly around Sara's waist, Yancy turned slowly to gaze at Hyrum, who had remained mounted during the commotion their arrival had caused. "Esteban," he called, "*un momento*." And when Esteban stopped and came back, Yancy said bluntly, "Take Hyrum out to where the men are building the holding pens and put him to work."

He looked coldly at Hyrum. "There is no need for you to unpack—you'll be working out on the range with the other men, and you might as well sleep out there with them, too." He smiled, not a nice smile. "It is a rough camp. Your bed, I'm afraid, will be the ground, but since there is nothing here to interest you, I'm sure you'll agree that it is the best plan."

Hyrum's mouth tightened in anger, but he nodded curtly and, without a word, swung his horse around to follow Esteban. Yancy watched him ride away, wondering just how much of a problem Hyrum Burnell might become.

A sharp pinch on his arm brought his wandering attention back to focus on the far more agreeable prospect of insinuating himself into his bride's good graces. The kisses they had exchanged upon arriving had given him great encouragement, but when his eyes met hers, the militant gleam in that sparkling green gaze informed him that his treatment of Hyrum had lost him some ground.

"That was very bad of you!" she said indignantly. "You should not treat him so cavalierly! He was your father's overseer for years—he followed him into war! He certainly deserves much more consideration than you have shown him thus far. Making him sleep on the ground like a peon! You ought to be ashamed of yourself!" Warming to her theme, she finished heatedly, "Hyrum is not just some vagabond you took pity on, for heaven's sake! He's almost like family."

"Not," Yancy said levelly, "*my* family! I haven't forgotten that he once had amorous designs on you." He gave her a hard look. "With him constantly underfoot, I wouldn't want you to wonder what you might have missed!"

Sara drew in an outraged breath. "How *dare* you! As if I would . . . !" Words failed her. Fairly shimmering with righteous displeasure, her nose up in the air, she said frostily, "Please show me my room! I have nothing further to say to you!"

To her great astonishment, he replied softly, "Sweetheart, I'm sorry! I shouldn't have implied that you would do anything to besmirch your wedding vows—you are far too loyal and honest for that!" A warm glow in his eyes, a whimsical smile on his mouth, he asked huskily, "Forgive me?"

It just wasn't fair! Sara thought despairingly. She was angry at him, yet all he had to do was smile at her, look at her with those thickly lashed golden-brown eyes, and her insides simply turned into custard! But he did apologize, she reminded herself. Hanging on to her indignation by a slender thread, she said weakly, "You don't deserve it."

Yancy grinned and swept her up into his arms. He kissed her soundly and then, while Sara was still recovering her senses, swiftly carried her to the cool interior of the hacienda. Once inside, he set her on her feet and spread his arms expansively. "Your home awaits you, madam!"

Despite its not-so-appealing exterior, the hacienda at Paloma was actually quite comfortable and spacious. There were considerably fewer rooms than at del Sol, and most of them were much smaller, yet the place had a rough charm that immediately caught Sara's attention. It helped, she admitted candidly, that the entire house had been thoroughly swept and scrubbed and that several tasteful items from the storehouses at del Sol had been brought along to furnish the inside. A woven rug of brilliant blues and golds had been placed upon the stone floor; an old-fashioned, beautifully worked tapestry hung on one wall; several comfortable russet leather chairs were scattered about the main *sala*.

Very conscious of Yancy at her side, his arm once more around her waist, Sara was given a tour of her new domain and she decided that she liked it very much. The rooms were uncluttered and the furnishings far more plain and rustic than at the main rancho, and she was aware that while she admired and loved the house at del Sol, there was something about Paloma . . . There was a coziness here, a refreshing lack of grandeur about the place. She felt freer here, less conscious of the wealth and elegance of the long line of Spanish grandees who had lived at del Sol. The first of Yancy's Spanish ancestors who had settled here, who had built this house, had been intrepid adventurers, hard-working men and women of action and vision. Sara identified strongly with them and with the house that stood in mute testament to their victory against the hostile elements and the ravaging bands of Comanches who roamed the area in great numbers.

The small, open courtyard in the center of the house came as a delightful surprise, as did the graceful weeping willow which shaded almost half the area and the tiny, tinkling fountain. An ancient yellow rose clung tenaciously to one side of the hacienda, its sweet perfume carrying on the warm air, and Sara spied several clay pots, newly planted with scarlet and white geraniums, which had been set in a sunny spot at the base of the wall opposite the rose. A small black, filigreed iron table and two chairs with scarlet cushions had been placed invitingly under the cooling shade of the weeping willow, and Sara felt a desire to linger and let the quiet beauty and serenity of the setting wash over her.

Unlike at del Sol, there were no graceful arched, covered walkways, nearly every room of the hacienda opening directly onto the central courtyard. The courtyard was typical of most Spanish houses, and it was here that families gathered and spent much of their free time. Sara could understand why—the setting was utterly beguiling!

Smiling down at her expressive face, Yancy asked, "Does it meet with your approval?"

"Oh, yes!" Sara said happily. "It's like an oasis of tranquility—as if the outside world had simply vanished."

Yancy smiled faintly, taking a second look around the courtyard. His eyes held a faraway expression as he said slowly, "I remember that my mother loved this place.

She and my father spent hours sitting at the same table, laughing and talking while I played at their feet. And when he was gone, she would sit and write him long letters, or read aloud to me the letters he had written to her—at least *most* of the letters he had written to her. I'm sure that she censored some parts for my innocent ears!"

"It sounds like they were very much in love, your mother and Sam," Sara began uncertainly. Yancy seldom talked about his parents and she didn't want to break the flow of his memories, but his words had called out for comment.

Yancy flashed her a cynical glance. "Oh, in the beginning I'm sure they were—before Andy and my grandfather drove them apart."

"But how could your grandfathers have done that?" Sara protested. "Not if Sam and your mother had really *loved* each other."

Yancy snorted. "Andy despised my mother, and while *her* lineage would stand up far better to close inspection than his, he always thought of her as 'that greaser whore' my father had defied him with by marrying!" He looked grim. "I'll give the old bastard credit for one thing— he never made any attempt to hide how he felt about my mother and the marriage! It galled him unbearably and I'm sure he died cursing my mother, perhaps even me."

"But why didn't Sam *do* something? How could he just stand by and let Andy drive him and your mother apart?"

Yancy sighed and impatiently rubbed the back of his neck. He didn't like talking about his parents or *any* of the past, for that matter, and normally he would have cut the conversation short. But he had the feeling that it was important for Sara to understand how it was, important for her to understand how he had felt about Sam

and love. . . . Reluctantly he said, "Sam didn't stand a
chance against his father. Andy had raised him to obey
without question, and I think that the only time Sam
ever defied Andy was when he ran away with my mother. Sometimes I wonder how he found the courage—
it was so totally out of character for him." He stared
blindly over at the tiny fountain, the soothing sound of
splashing water flowing across the courtyard. Abruptly he said, "Sam was a gentle, easygoing man and, as
you know, not at all strong-willed. As far back as I
can remember, he always took the path of least resistance, and with Andy constantly undermining my mother
and making demands that Sam couldn't ignore, it really
isn't surprising that my parents became estranged—no
matter how much they may have loved each other in
the beginning." Yancy grimaced and said bluntly, "Old
Andy Cantrell was a selfish, bullheaded despot—even if
he was my grandfather! And he was well used to getting his own way and bending or breaking people to his
will. It would have taken a far stronger man than Sam to
stand up to someone as determined to have his own way
as Andy. The old devil was clever, too—he played on
Sam's loyalty to him, always calling him back to Magnolia Grove, always claiming that there was some vital task
that only Sam could do. After a while, Sam just found it
easier to go along with whatever Andy wanted."

Sara stared at Yancy, horrified. "But couldn't your
mother have . . . ?"

"Have what?" Yancy asked coolly. "Fought her father-
in-law for the love of her husband?" A hard cast to his
face, he growled, "If Sam had been a man, a *real* man,
and hadn't allowed himself to be manipulated by Andy,
she wouldn't have had to fight for his love! She *shouldn't*
have had to!" The hardness left his face and he admitted
wearily, "But it wasn't just Sam and Andy—she had her
demons, too. *Her* father was never very happy about the

marriage, and even though he eventually became resigned to it, in his own way he did his best to turn her heart against Sam and to belittle her feelings for him. They were both vulnerable, and with Andy working on Sam and Armando working on Madelina, they never stood a chance. What happened between them was inevitable, and I doubt that things would have improved even if my mother had outlived Andy—the damage had been done."

Sara's features were pensive as she looked around the charming courtyard, trying to imagine what Madelina must have felt, loving a man, married to a man, yet always losing the battle to his father and being constantly beleaguered by her own father. And Sam, too—what must he have felt? He had loved Yancy's mother, of that Sara was positive; loved Madelina as he had loved no other woman . . . but Yancy didn't believe that. . . .

Looking back at him, she said suddenly, "You blame Sam for everything, don't you?"

Yancy discarded his hat on the iron table and ran his hands wearily through his hair. "No, and I don't hate him—I never did. Maybe when I was younger I *resented* him for not being stronger, for not standing up for my mother and me, but hate never entered my thoughts. He loved me, in his own fashion, and as I grew older I realized that he simply couldn't help being weak." His fine mouth twisted. "Even after Margaret, I didn't hate him. He hurt me badly—I can't deny it—and there was a time when I was so full of wounded fury that I thought I hated him, but I didn't. He was my father, and when all was said and done . . . I loved him."

Sara's eyes searched his, and what she saw in them convinced her that he spoke the truth—he had loved Sam. Then she asked quietly, "If you loved him, why didn't you answer any of his letters?" She couldn't help the note of accusation that crept into her voice. "When he was dying he begged you to come and see him and you never did! You claim to have loved him, but you denied him the one thing, the *only* thing, he wanted—you by his side as he lay dying!"

Yancy frowned. "What the hell are you talking about? Except for that damned messenger sent by his lawyer, I never received any letters from him—not one!"

Sara looked confused. "But—but he wrote—several times." At Yancy's skeptical expression, she said hotly, "I *saw* the letters, I tell you! I even wrote some of them for him!"

"Well, I never got any of them!" He grabbed her arm and gave her a shake. "Do you honestly believe that if I had received a letter from Sam, if I had known he was *dying* and wanted to see me, I would have ignored it? *Jesus!* You really hold me in high esteem, don't you?"

She glanced at him uncertainly. There was such outrage, such anguish, in his words that she didn't know what she believed anymore.

Hearing her sigh, Yancy tipped up her chin and stared down into the emerald depths of her eyes. "I never received any letters from Sam," he said deliberately. "If I had, I would have ridden through hell to get to his side. And before we leave the unpleasant subject of my parents' marriage—rest assured that I am not my father. I am neither weak nor easily swayed, and I would *never* allow anyone to drive a wedge between us!"

The memory of Ann's words still stinging her, Sara took a deep breath and replied coolly, "No, I don't believe that you would . . . but then, our situation is vastly different, isn't it? We're not in love and you had very practical reasons for marrying me, didn't you? *Love* had nothing to do with it!"

Yancy's nostrils flared with temper and his eyes glittered fiercely. "You are such a blind little fool!" he said thickly. "Women are supposed to be so damned clever about these things, but you're so obsessed with that blasted clause in Sam's will that you can't see what's right under your nose." He shook her roughly. "You know, there are times when I definitely would like to wring your lovely neck!" Spitting the words out like bullets, he snarled, "*Practical* reasons had *nothing* to do with our marriage! If I were a practical man, I'd have left you for the wolves and considered myself damned lucky for having had such a narrow escape!"

Sara stared at him openmouthed, something in his eyes, something in the tone of his voice, sending a dizzying ray of hope flooding through her body. Never taking her gaze from his dark face, gathering up all her courage, she asked breathlessly, "Are you saying that you *didn't* marry me because of Casa Paloma?" She swallowed nervously. "That you had *other* reasons for having married me?"

He smiled and pulled her against him. He kissed her, and only when the blood was pounding wildly in her veins, only when she could not think clearly, only when all of her senses were full of him, her arms locked around his neck, her body pressing eagerly into his, did he raise his head and stare down with satisfaction into her dazed features. Brushing his mouth tantalizingly across hers, he growled, "Now, what the hell do you think?"

∞ 22

Thoroughly bemused, Sara made no demur when he swept her up into his arms and carried her into a nearby room. She had the impression of white walls; a blanket woven in brilliant tones of burgundy, sapphire blue and yellow hung on the wall, breaking the monotony; a heavy, dark, old-fashioned Spanish bed; and the welcoming softness of a feather-filled mattress as Yancy laid her down. He followed her onto the bed, his big body half lying on hers, his hands caressing her even as he stripped the clothing from her.

He kissed her numerous times, hungry, almost violent kisses that took her breath away and made her desperate for more of his demanding lovemaking. Her mind cloudy with desire, she fumbled with clumsy haste and tore at his clothing, sighing with satisfaction when at last her hands were free to roam over his body. She could not seem to get enough of him, her fingers caressing first his face, then his broad back and hard buttocks, finally exploring the smoothly muscled contours of his chest.

When her teasing fingers lightly brushed against his nipples, Yancy jerked and groaned his pleasure, his hands tightening on her hips. He was aching for her, so hard and ready for release that he was certain he would die if he could not find immediate succor in her sweet body. All the powerful desire he'd suppressed these past days was riding him unmercifully and the feel of her silken flesh beneath his hands, the taste of her when his tongue mated with hers, the evocative scent of her filling his nostrils and the soft sounds of delight she made as he explored and caressed her, drove him nearly to the edge.

Sara was not far behind him. If the locked door of her room had denied Yancy the pleasures of the marriage bed, she had been denied, too, and the moment he had swept her up into his arms and carried her to the room, treacherous, unruly desire had dominated her. She wanted him. Wanted to feel him moving within her. Wanted his hands at her breast, his mouth buried on hers and his swollen shaft driven deep within her. She burned with the need to find again the rapture that only Yancy's lovemaking could give her, and when his hand slid between her legs and his fingers began to part the damp, aching flesh he found there, she moaned and her thighs fell apart as she arched up into his probing caress.

Hearing her moan and feeling her readiness, Yancy, already painfully erect, rolled over onto his back, taking Sara with him. Slightly startled, half lying on him, she gazed down at him, and he said thickly, his eyes blazing with primitive desire, "Ride me, sweetheart—you decide how swiftly we reach paradise. . . ."

Sara's eyes widened as he lifted her, placed her thighs on either side of his hips, then slowly, tantalizingly, brought her down upon his upraised shaft. It was a delicious sensation, all the more so as she watched his expression when he began to slide within her tight sheath, all the excitement and pleasure he felt as her flesh parted for his invasion clear to see on his dark, intent face. Eager to help, she pushed downward, marveling that her small body could take all of his magnificent bulk. A guttural sound broke from Yancy when she finally sank down to the hilt of his shaft and he was completely embedded in her narrow, silken passage. She was full of him and he was so big, so hard and tightly lodged inside her that she was almost afraid to move. She wiggled experimentally, her lips parting in wonder at the soft shocks of pleasure that rippled through her. When his hands clasped her hips and urged her upward and then downward upon him, she shuddered wildly at the piercing delight those simple movements caused within her.

Dazedly she stared at him and he smiled tightly. "You do it now . . . take us there, take us to heaven."

Her hands resting on either side of his big body, Sara did as he commanded, her slender hips rising slightly and then pushing downward again, burying his warm shaft deeply inside her once more. It was an incredible feeling, both powerful and vulnerable at the same time, and her eyes glistened with carnal excitement as she did it again and again, the spiraling pleasure within her intensifying, the demanding instinct to find release becoming almost more than she could stand.

Yancy's hands were at her breasts, his thumbs rubbing sensuously across her swollen nipples, making her movements more wild, more frantic, as she brought them closer to the pinnacle they sought. Sara was not alone in her increasingly desperate desire for fulfillment; his hips were rising to meet hers and he groaned aloud his delight with every thrust he made into her slick warmth. He reared up suddenly and found her mouth, kissing her with a fierce hunger. His hand cupped the back of her head and when he lay back down, he pulled her with him, the tips of her breasts swaying against his chest, his lips clinging to hers so that he could mimic with his tongue the urgent motions of his lower body.

Sara needed no urging to tip forward, no urging to return his demanding kisses, her tongue, like a flame, dancing with his as they remained locked together, the frantic pumping of his body into hers making her tremble with all the love and passion she felt for him. The warm touch of his hand gliding up and down her back, the sensation of his hard hips between her thighs, the heady experience of riding *him* making her wish for this moment never to end. It was torture, this frantic, elemental race for fulfillment, the sweetest torture in the world, and together, they reveled in it until rapture found them. . . .

Yancy's hands were suddenly on her hips, guiding her movements, and as the first powerful storm of pleasure burst through her body, Sara flung her head back, her breasts outthrust as she cried aloud her ecstasy. And it was then and only then that Yancy allowed the savage restraint he had held on himself free rein, and almost instantly he found the same explosive rapture that had claimed Sara.

Stunned by the force of her release, Sara collapsed onto Yancy's heaving chest, the thunder of his heart making her release all the sweeter. As the minutes passed, they lay there together, each one unwilling to break the warm intimacy of the moment, Sara's cheek resting upon his chest, Yancy's hand lightly caressing her narrow back and hips, his lips absently brushing against the honey-gold curls of her hair. Eventually, though, Sara moved, slipping down to lie beside him, her fingers toying with the short, crisp black hair of his chest.

Yancy's arm cradled her close to him, and though there was much that Sara wanted to talk about, she found herself succumbing to a languid drowsiness. In less than five minutes she was deeply asleep.

For several minutes after she had fallen asleep, Yancy stared down into her lovely face, realizing suddenly that he was oddly glad that his father *had* married Sara. If Sam hadn't taken such drastic action to protect her, some other man might have won her heart and she wouldn't now be lying so peacefully by his side. He frowned, the queer notion occurring to him that Sam might not have married her just to ensure her future—Sam might have had another reason for marrying Sara, such as to keep her untouched and her heart free until his son returned. . . .

Yancy scowled. The idea was hopelessly convoluted and utterly ridiculous and, he admitted grimly, *exactly* the sort of thing someone as foolishly romantic and guilt-ridden as his father would have conceived! A huge yawn took him and his eyes closed, his arm tightening around Sara. Ridiculous, he thought sleepily. Completely ridiculous even to believe for a second that Sam had married Sara to save her for *him*! . . .

Sara woke first sometime later and for several moments she just lay there savoring the closeness and warmth of Yancy's lax body. Even in sleep his arm was still curled protectively around her and she smiled mistily. Oh, but she did love him! Even if he was the most aggravating male alive!

Refreshed from her nap and with her mind no longer clouded with passion, Sara began to think about the tantalizing words Yancy had uttered in the courtyard. She wanted to wake him and ask him to explain precisely what he had meant, but she was uncertain and just a little shy. He had never mentioned one word of love to her, had never said why he had insisted upon marrying her; and while she couldn't deny that his *actions* indicated some powerful feelings for her, she needed desperately to hear those three simple words "I love you."

Even if she could totally convince herself that his desire for Casa Paloma had not been the *only* motive behind their marriage, and she hadn't quite gotten that far in her beliefs, Sara wasn't quite confident enough to believe that Yancy was in love with her. She knew without a shadow of doubt that he *desired* her—what had happened so recently in this very bed was certainly proof of *that*! But she didn't know for sure that she aroused any sort of *lasting* emotion within him. He was kind to her, indulgent with her, protective of her, concerned about her safety and well-being—but so would be the owner of an expensive broodmare!

Sara moved her head slightly and gazed up at his arrogant profile. She sighed. Even in sleep his expression revealed nothing and *would* reveal nothing, she thought darkly, unless he deemed otherwise. Yancy hid so much of himself, only now and then giving intriguing little hints of what he thought and felt, and Sara wondered bleakly if she would ever really know what went on behind that infuriatingly enigmatic gaze of his. She glanced at him again, desperately wanting to shake him awake and ask him what he felt about her, but she hesitated, afraid she might not like the answer. Her mouth twisted. *If* she even got an answer! Yancy had the irritating habit of answering all her questions with questions of his own—*damn* him!

A clock suddenly chimed in the room, ringing out the hour of three o'clock, and Yancy sat upright with a jerk. "*Cristo*! I didn't realize it was that late!" Springing up from the bed, he swiftly pulled on his clothes and, dropping a hard kiss on Sara's mouth, said huskily, "I don't want to leave you, sweetheart, but I promised Esteban that I would meet him at two o'clock and I'm an hour late!"

He was gone from the room before Sara could even ask him when he would return. Since she was no longer sleepy and there was no *other* reason to remain in bed, she searched around for her clothes, grumbling to herself about *some* men. She found her clothes on the floor where Yancy had tossed them earlier, a silly little smile touching her lips as she grabbed them and quickly dressed.

There had been no time to take in the details of the room when she had first entered it, but now, without Yancy's distracting presence to deter her, Sara glanced around curiously. The room was large and pleasantly furnished. Only one door opened into it, and thoughtfully examining the lockless entryway, Sara grimaced ruefully. She had little doubt that she was standing in the master's chamber, or that at Casa Paloma there was no discreet suite of rooms, no other bedroom to which the mistress of the hacienda could retreat—or lock her husband out of! . . .

Yancy was dwelling on that agreeable fact as he strolled to his meeting with Esteban, and there was a distinctly satisfied grin on his handsome face. Even when he entered the small *sala* at the rear of the hacienda, where they had agreed to meet, his grin was still firmly in place; and when he saw that, despite his tardiness, Esteban was still waiting patiently for him, his feeling of good humor increased. The two men exchanged greetings, Yancy apologizing for his lateness. It was only when they were both seated in the dark green leather chairs in front of the massive, intricately carved desk of mahogany that they began to discuss the reason for the meeting.

Esteban's black eyes fixed on Yancy's face, he said bluntly, "I have discovered where the snake came from, senor—at least, I am convinced that it is the same snake."

"*Where?*" The word was shot out like a bullet.

"You know Guillermo, Maria's cousin Lupe's boy?" Esteban began quietly, and at Yancy's curt nod, he continued. "About two weeks ago, Guillermo and several other boys were out playing when they found the big snake—it was, as you will remember, very large, larger than any of them had ever seen before, and being boys, they captured it and brought it home with them in a bag."

"It was Guillermo's snake?" Yancy demanded incredulously, not believing for a second that any one of his people would have endangered Sara's life. "*Guillermo* put the damn thing in Sara's bed?"

Esteban shook his head vehemently. "*Senor*! To think such a thing! No! No! Guillermo would never harm you or your senora! Never!"

Yancy had the grace to look shamefaced. "I know—I should never even have allowed something like that to cross my mind—forgive me. Tell me what happened."

"I do not know exactly what happened, and the reason I did not immediately seek out Guillermo to see if he still had his snake was because, though I had heard of it from Maria the day he brought it home, I had forgotten about it. And not even thinking of Guillermo's snake, I made inquiries as you had ordered me to do and I could discover nothing. I talked to all the hacienda servants and some of the other people in the village, but no one had seen any of the three gringos leave the area of the village, and since I had forgotten about Guillermo's snake, I had nothing to report to you." Esteban sighed. "I was certain I had failed you, and then, just yesterday, when I returned to del Sol for some extra supplies for Paloma, I stopped by to see Lupe. Guillermo was there and looking rather downcast. I asked him what was wrong and he told me that his snake was gone—that someone had thrown off the lid to the pit and had either stolen his snake or let it go." Esteban's mouth twisted. "Forgive me, senor. I should not have forgotten about Guillermo's snake—I should have remembered it and seen for myself if the creature was still in the pit, but I did not." He glanced worriedly at Yancy. "I would have told you all this yesterday, but you were gone from the hacienda and I had to return to Paloma with the supplies. I am deeply sorry for the delay."

Yancy dismissed Esteban's apology. "Don't worry about it—you've done a very good job. Did you learn anything else?"

Esteban hunched a shoulder. "Not much, senor. I know that Guillermo discovered the snake missing the morning of your marriage to Senora Sara—he remembers it well because he was so excited about all the wedding festivities."

Yancy looked thoughtful, the dangerous glitter in his eyes more pronounced. "Did you find out if the gringos knew about the snake?"

Esteban nodded. "They did, senor, all three of them." He hesitated and then added candidly, "Including Bartholomew and Tansy. Shortly after they arrived, everyone was given a tour of the village, and I asked Guillermo particularly if they had been shown his snake. He said that they *all* had seen the creature." He grinned for a second. "He said that the blond gringa screamed and jumped when he lifted the lid."

"Do Lupe and her family still live in the same house? The one right outside the hacienda gates?"

"*Sí!*" And finishing Yancy's thought, Esteban said, "It would have been a simple matter for any one of them to slip outside the hacienda walls and, after stunning the snake, to put it in a bag or a box and bring it back inside the hacienda. It would have taken only a few moments. . . ."

"And from there just a few moments longer to put it in Sara's bed!"

Esteban nodded and said merely, "*Sí*, senor, just a few minutes."

Yancy swore virulently under his breath, and springing up from his chair, he took several agitated steps around the room. His back to Esteban, he said finally, "I cannot imagine anyone wanting Sara dead or even wanting to harm her, for that matter." He looked over his shoulder at Esteban. "Do you have someone watching her here at Paloma?"

Esteban nodded. "A boy in the hacienda itself and two men outside the hacienda walls."

"*Bueno*! At least here we don't have the Shelldrakes underfoot and I only have to worry about Hyrum!" Yancy said with satisfaction as he reseated himself.

Esteban looked extremely uneasy and Yancy's gaze narrowed. "What?" he asked sharply.

Esteban moved warily in his chair, and rubbing the back of his neck, he said nervously, "I did not want to be the one to tell you this, but the Shelldrakes are *here*!"

With openmouthed awe and admiration, Esteban listened to the varied and inventive curses that rent the air when he had finished speaking. It was some time before Yancy ran out of invectives, but eventually even his fertile mind could think of no more vituperative comments about the Shelldrakes' parentage, their very *being*, or terrible, grisly fates to rain down upon them. When he started to repeat himself, he stopped. Wearily, he asked, "When did they arrive?"

"Just a half hour ago with all the others from del Sol. The blond gringa said that she was going to be bored at del Sol all by herself with no other white woman to talk to. She said she wanted to see Paloma again—she wanted to see if you had made as many changes here as at del Sol." Esteban grinned for just a moment. "She was not happy to discover that work is just *starting* at Paloma or that she would have to share a small and sparsely furnished room with her husband." His grin widened. "Tansy told her that if she didn't like her quarters, she could return to del Sol—that no one had *invited* her along! Tansy does not like her very much, does she?"

Yancy's mouth twisted ruefully. "I doubt that anyone actually *likes* Ann Shelldrake! Most people, myself included, wouldn't mind if she joined her sister in hell!"

Returning to his room a few minutes later, Yancy still wasn't quite certain how he was going to handle the sudden intrusion of the Shelldrakes. He was so furious that his first instinct was to forcefully put Ann and Tom on a pair of horses and send them as far away from him as they could get, along with Hyrum Burnell, too, for that matter, but he didn't know if that would accomplish anything.

Tansy was with Sara and they were busily unpacking several of the trunks that had come with the new arrivals when he entered his room. Sara looked up from her task at the sound of the door opening, and the expression on her face told him that she had already heard the unpleasant news.

That his expression was equally clear was obvious when Sara wrinkled her nose at him and said, "You've heard about our guests?"

Yancy grimaced. "Yes, I've heard about our *guests* and I'm not certain which one I'd like to strangle first!"

Tansy chuckled. "I wouldn't have no such trouble—*that* woman is just about the most overbearing, selfish, greedy, trouble-making, conniving creature I've ever seen!" She looked thoughtful. "Except, of course, for her sister! But I feel sorry for Mr. Tom—she rules him and he just doesn't seem to be able to do anything about it." She glanced at Yancy. "He didn't want to come—he was very embarrassed when she insisted and he tried to talk her out of it. I wouldn't be too hard on *him*!"

"Are you going to send them back?" Sara asked hopefully, her big green eyes fixed on his face.

Thumbs hooked in his gun belt, legs apart, he regarded her, curious about the way she would handle the situation. "What do you want me to do?" he finally asked softly.

Sara made a face. "I *want* to send them back to del Sol immediately, but I don't think it's going to be that easy. I know that the journey here, however short, has probably tired Tom. And as Tansy just mentioned, he came reluctantly and is already feeling embarrassed about the situation—I wouldn't want to cause him more humiliation."

Yancy quirked an eyebrow. "You want them to stay?"

Sara shook her head. "No. At least not for very long." She looked unhappy. "Perhaps we can wait a day or two and then politely suggest that they would be far happier at del Sol."

Tansy snorted and, gathering up a few more items of Sara's clothing, laid them in a drawer in the bureau. Slamming the drawer shut with far more force than necessary, she looked back at Sara. "You listen to me, missy! That wicked hussy is up to something! She's here for some reason of her own, and you can't tell me that it's just because she's so fond of you!"

Sara started to argue, but Yancy broke in, saying coolly, "I agree with Tansy. I think Ann *is* up to something and I think that until we find out what it is, we should allow them to stay longer than just a few days."

"How long?" Sara asked, clearly not liking the idea of being saddled with the Shelldrakes for very long.

"Only until I can figure out what schemes Ann might be fomenting." He hesitated and then said softly, "Sara, Paloma is *your* house—if you want them gone, we can throw them out this very minute."

Yancy's observation seemed to take Sara by surprise, and she suddenly grinned. "Yes, it is, isn't it, and we could, couldn't we?" Meeting Yancy's steady gaze, she grimaced wryly. "But we're not going to, are we?"

"It's your house."

She paused and then shrugged. "Oh, very well. They can stay for a while." A pleasant thought occurred to her and she said happily, "I'll just have to console myself with the knowledge that I can have them leave anytime I want!"

Despite the intrusion of the Shelldrakes and the not-*precisely*-understood situation between herself and Yancy, Sara remained happy during the ensuing days. She loved her husband! She loved Paloma! And she was delighted with all the changes and improvements that were occurring right before her very eyes.

During the day she was everywhere—watching the new roof being put on one of the barns, observing the corrals near the hacienda being repaired, riding out to watch the bulls and mustangs being gathered, listening to Maria and Tansy as they cooked in the big old-fashioned kitchen and told tales of other trips and visits to Paloma. Everywhere Sara went, much to her delight and excitement, there was new life being constantly breathed into the old rancho. And then there was Yancy. . . .

She spent several hours each day in the saddle as she accompanied her darkly fascinating husband on his daily trips to the mustang- and cattle-gathering site to oversee the work of the vaqueros. Sometimes they would be gone nearly the entire day, riding back to the hacienda in the purple shadows of dusk. Some evenings, long after the Shelldrakes had mercifully retired for the night, they sat at the table where his parents had sat so many years before and conversed softly, not about anything important, just the rancho, the work that was being undertaken and what they hoped would be the outcome. Best of all, Sara admitted with a flush, were the nights . . . nights that were spent locked in Yancy's arms as she learned to give full rein to her own sensuality and began to plumb the fathomless depths of her husband's excitingly inventive, definitely addictive lovemaking.

Sara's heart was so full of love for him that a dozen times a day she almost blurted it out; a dozen times at night when he brought her to shuddering ecstasy, she almost screamed it aloud, but the words "I love you" remained unspoken between them. Yancy never mentioned the word "love"; he never brought up the subject of why he had married her or gave any more hints about his true feelings for her, but Sara was oddly content.

She might not be an expert in matters of the heart, but she had a certain amount of that uncommon commodity, common sense. Common sense told her plainly that Yancy could not make such sweet, passionate love to her night after night; could not take such open pleasure in her company or send her those bone-melting glances with such exciting frequency; could not treat her with such heartwarming consideration, or tease her so unmercifully, if there was not a great depth of feeling behind his actions.

He had not told her that he loved her, but she sensed that it was only a matter of time. It'll happen, she told herself confidently. Soon.

There were very few clouds on Sara's horizon these days. Bartholomew and Tansy were happily adapting to life at Paloma, and even Ann and Tom Shelldrake seemed to be making an effort to be agreeable. Yancy had even relented and treated Hyrum with stiff cordiality, assigning one of the newly constructed houses in the village that was growing outside the hacienda walls for his own use when he was not at the cattle camp. To Sara's astonishment, Yancy had even gone so far as to invite the man to join them for the occasional meal at the hacienda. It was a wonderful time for her and she greeted each day with a smile and an excited sparkle in her eyes. By the time they had been at Paloma for five weeks, she was so thrilled by everything that was happening that she fairly floated about the place, a gleam in her eyes and a dreamy smile never very far away from her soft mouth.

July had been full of blistering heat, and when August began and the heat seared across the land with a vengeance, Yancy had dictated that he didn't want her riding out with him when he was going to be gone most of the day. He had promised that there were still some mornings that she could come with him, and he had lessened the blow further with a passionate kiss and had made certain that there were few days that he was away from sunup to sundown.

This particular Wednesday at the end of the second week of August happened to be one of those days, and after moping around the hacienda until late afternoon, Sara wandered over to the pleasant house where Bartholomew and Tansy were currently living. Like Yancy, Bartholomew was out working with the cattle and the mustangs, so when Sara peered around the open doorway, it was to find Tansy sitting in a comfortable wooden rocking chair enjoying a tall glass of lemonade.

The heat and humidity were intense this time of day, and after Tansy motioned her inside and indicated that she should sit in the softly cushioned chair near the rocker, she pressed a glass of lemonade on her. Sara wasn't at all loath to accept either. The two women sat in silence for a while, simply savoring the tart flavor of the lemonade and the blessed coolness inside the small house.

Thinking of all that they had shared together over the years, Sara remarked idly, "This is quite different from Magnolia Grove, isn't it?"

Rocking lazily, Tansy grinned and murmured, "My, my! Indeed it is! Bartholomew and I were saying just the other night that who would have guessed, only two months ago, that you'd be married to Master Yancy and that we'd all be here at Paloma!" Tansy shook her dark head. "Life sure is strange, that's for sure!"

The two women reminisced for several moments, laughing sometimes at happy memories of Magnolia

Grove, other times sobering as they recalled some of the unpleasant times at the plantation—and there had been a lot of those. More unhappy times, Sara admitted sadly, than happy ones. Margaret's murder. The long, terrible years of the war. Sam's horrible wounds. Sam's death.

Sipping her lemonade, she tried to push aside the dark memories that crowded close, but she couldn't help wondering what her life would have been like if Margaret *hadn't* died. She moved restively and blurted out impulsively, "Do you ever wonder what would have happened if Margaret hadn't been murdered?"

Tansy took a long swallow of her lemonade. "Don't think about that woman at all! She deserved what she got! Imagine trying to get my Bartholomew sent to the fields!" Tansy took another drink of her lemonade and, her hazel eyes bright with anger, she said fiercely, "Except for that trouble-causing sister of hers, I never in my whole life met anyone who liked to stir up so much aggravation and heartache as that woman! And enjoyed every moment of it—no matter who got hurt or how much pain she caused! I'm *glad* she's dead, and that sister of hers is no better! There are times that I wish someone would take a fine Spanish dagger and stab Ann to death, too! Just as they did Margaret!"

Sara froze, the air suddenly very cold against her skin. Her eyes slid away from Tansy's gaze. She felt sick and dizzy at the same time. Everyone knew that Margaret had been stabbed. Everyone. But not everyone had known that the weapon that had been used to kill Margaret all those years ago had been a *fine Spanish* dagger! A dagger that had belonged to Bartholomew and that would have been easily accessible to Tansy . . . Tansy, who adored her husband. . . . Had she, Sara wondered uneasily, adored her husband enough to murder for him?

∞ 23

Long after Sara had made her polite good-byes and returned to the hacienda, Tansy's words kept echoing in her head. She didn't, *couldn't*, believe that Tansy had killed Margaret, yet how had Tansy known of the Spanish dagger? Unless Bartholomew had killed Margaret and Tansy had seen it happen?

Sara didn't like either premise, but she realized that she was gradually, because of the great affection she bore them, eliminating suspects. Pretty soon, she thought glumly, I'll have convinced myself that it had to have been a wandering vagrant who just happened to pilfer Bartholomew's knife and just happened to find Margaret alone and just happened to have murdered her!

She sighed, her lovely face revealing her unhappy introspection, and just entering the courtyard, Yancy saw it and frowned. What the devil had happened? He had left a smiling, happy bride this morning, and he came home to a woman who looked absolutely miserable. If Ann Shelldrake had done anything to upset her . . . ! His mind full of unpleasant fates for the hapless Ann, he quickly crossed the courtyard and planted his big, lean body right in front of Sara.

"If you like, I'll stake her out for the Comanches to find," he growled by way of greeting.

Sara had been so involved with her own thoughts

that she had neither seen nor heard his approach, and she jumped at his words. Tansy's statement was still uppermost in her mind, so she gazed at Yancy in some astonishment. "You want to stake out Tansy for the Comanches?" she asked bewilderedly.

"*Tansy!*" Yancy ejaculated, looking as bewildered as Sara. "Good God, no! But what has Tansy done to make you look so unhappy?"

Sara didn't see any reason for prevaricating and she said simply, "It isn't anything that Tansy has done—" She stopped, thinking that if Tansy *had* killed Margaret, then Tansy had indeed *done* something. She began again. "Well, perhaps Tansy might have done something, but at this moment it is more what Tansy has *said* that has disturbed me." She flashed Yancy an uncertain look, took a deep breath and said in a rush, "Tansy knows that Margaret was murdered with Bartholomew's dagger!" But that wasn't strictly true, she realized instantly and added with painstaking honesty, "I mean, she didn't say that it was *Bartholomew's* dagger, but she did say a 'fine Spanish dagger,' and what else could she be talking about but Bartholomew's dagger?"

His dark face revealing neither surprise nor dismay at her words, Yancy took the chair across from Sara and stretched his long legs out in front of him. His wide-brimmed black hat pushed back off his forehead, he suggested calmly, "Suppose you start at the beginning, hmm? And tell me exactly what Tansy said."

And so Sara told of her visit to Tansy and what she had learned. When she finished speaking she looked expectantly at Yancy and was disappointed that he seemed just as relaxed and composed as when she had started speaking. "Doesn't that sound rather incriminating to you?" she asked anxiously. "I mean, how could she know about the knife unless she had seen it—in Margaret's breast, I might add!"

"Just because she saw the knife doesn't necessarily mean anything particularly incriminating," he replied easily. At Sara's incredulous expression, he continued. "Tansy could have seen the knife and yet not have had anything to do with Margaret's murder, you know. The servants were always up and about much earlier than the rest of the household, and she could have discovered the body before you did and simply kept her mouth shut." Yancy's face darkened. "Knowing Margaret's penchant for holding her liaisons in the gazebo, Tansy might have gone there first thing in the morning to start straightening up and might have found the body."

Sara's face brightened. "Oh!" she exclaimed eagerly. "I never thought of *that*!"

Yancy sent her a look. "And now that you have," he drawled, "I suggest you forget about Tansy *and* Margaret's murder and think only of your husband." His lips quirked into a sensual smile. "Do you realize that it's been nearly twelve hours since I last kissed you?"

Instantly diverted, Sara grinned and sprang up from her chair. Standing beside him, she pushed his hat the rest of the way off his head and, as it fell to the floor of the courtyard, dropped a chaste kiss on his brow. "There!" she murmured dulcetly. "Does that satisfy you?"

Yancy's eyes darkened, and with something between a growl and a groan he dragged her onto his lap. Her arms went around his neck as his mouth found hers, and for several minutes there were no sounds in the courtyard except the gurgle of the fountain and the soft sighs of the lovers. Yancy's face was tight with raw desire and Sara's mouth was rosy and swollen when he finally finished kissing her. "I'll never be satisfied," he muttered. "Never!" One arm went around her shoulders, the other under her knees, and standing up with her in his arms, he asked bluntly, "Has your flow stopped? It's been five days . . . and, sweetheart, I am famished for you!"

Despite the intimacies between them, and despite already having had to stammer out her condition to him the previous month, Sara was still a little shy with him. She was particularly embarrassed about discussing her bodily functions with him, but with only a hint of a blush on her cheeks, she muttered, "Yes, it's stopped. We don't have to sleep chastely tonight."

Yancy grinned at her discomfort. But dropping a kiss on her nose, he said, "*Bueno*! Now, before anyone comes and interrupts us, I think I most definitely need to show you just how much I've missed loving that sweet little body of yours these past endless nights!" Once the door to their room had closed behind them, he proceeded, to Sara's great enjoyment, to do just that. . . .

Sometime later, lying naked and satiated in the arms of her husband, her fingers absently toying with crisp curls on his chest, Sara said softly, "It was lonely today without you around. Are you certain you won't change your mind and let me come out to the cattle camp with you?" She raised herself up on one elbow and smiled at him. "I promise I will not melt, and if I become too miserable from the heat, I will say something immediately."

Yancy's mouth twisted ruefully. "Bartholomew has informed me several times recently that my concentration would probably improve miraculously if I could bring it to bear fully on the task at hand, instead of dwelling almost exclusively on a certain green-eyed little wench at the hacienda. In view of that fact, I was going to suggest that no matter how hot it gets or how long I am to be gone from the hacienda, you come with me."

Sara beamed at him and kissed him fully on his mouth. Since Yancy returned her kiss with great enthusiasm, it was several moments before she could speak.

"Bartholomew is very wise, isn't he?" she asked breathlessly when she could.

Through slitted eyes Yancy regarded her lazily. "Hmm, yes, but not quite as wise as I was to marry you!"

Sara sent him an old-fashioned look, and Yancy laughed, pulled her back into his arms and kissed her. Kissing led to fondling and fondling to another sweet journey to the ecstasy that their bodies created together.

That Yancy and Sara never left their room that evening, not even to eat a final meal, didn't come as any surprise to the inhabitants of the hacienda, although an openly envious expression crossed Ann's face. However, Maria's dark eyes as she served the Shelldrakes were full of satisfaction and delight. After the Shelldrakes had retired for the night, Maria smiled to herself as she placed a small tray filled with tempting food and drink near the door to Yancy and Sara's room. By this time next year, she was quite confident, the hacienda would ring with the joyous sounds of a newborn baby. The first of many, if she was any judge!

The next morning as Sara rode Locuela out to the cattle camp with Yancy, who was on another favorite mount of his, a big black gelding, her thoughts were fixed on the possible arrival of a baby, too—but she viewed the idea with mixed emotions and wasn't quite as confident as Maria that it would happen any time soon. The fact that she had just experienced her second monthly flow since her marriage to Yancy preyed on her mind, and with a terrible feeling of foreboding, she had begun to wonder if she wasn't barren. And then there were still the annoying problems of Sam's will and Yancy's reasons for marrying her. . . . Her heart ached at the notion that it was his desire for a child for Paloma that drove him to make love to her so often and so thoroughly. She loved him and she believed that he loved her—despite his not-encouraging silence on the subject! She *had* to believe that he loved her and that one day very soon he would tell her so. She just hoped it was *before* she became pregnant. *If* she became pregnant.

Sara must have made some small sound, for Yancy glanced inquiringly over at her, one black brow cocked in question. She smiled at him and, banishing her moody thoughts, said brightly, "Isn't it a glorious morning? Don't you just love this time of morning, when it is still cool and there is the entire day in front of you?"

"And is it your pleasure in the morning that made you sigh so heavily and look so pensive?" he asked dryly.

Sara made a face. Trust her discerning husband to notice everything, and especially everything that she didn't want him to notice! Not meeting his gaze, she muttered, "Of course not! I was just thinking of something else."

"What?"

A feeling of resentment welled up inside her. She might be married to him, which gave him certain rights, to be sure, but she didn't think it gave him the right to be privy to the workings of her mind. She was entitled to *some* privacy! Tartly, she said, "It couldn't have been anything very important, I'm sure—I've already forgotten what it was!"

From beneath the brim of his black hat, Yancy sent her an unreadable glance. "Secrets, Sara?" he asked quietly after a long moment.

She started to state exasperatedly that she didn't have any secrets—*he* was the one who kept things to himself!—when she remembered Hyrum and Ann. She had wrestled for weeks now whether to tell him what she had seen, and she had come to no clear answer. Sara took a deep breath and said in a rush, "I'm sure that it is none of my business, none of *our* business, but did you know that Hyrum is in love with Ann Shelldrake? That they're having an affair?"

To Sara's astonishment, Yancy looked very pleased at her words. He'd desperately wanted her to tell him about Ann and Hyrum, wanted proof that she trusted him implicitly—wanted fiercely for there to be no secrets between them. At her words, that faint gnawing in his gut vanished and he was aware of a warm wash of pleasure. "I've wondered," he merely said out loud, "how long it would take you to tell me about their affair."

"You *know* about them?" Sara exclaimed incredulously.

Yancy grimaced, suddenly realizing that the next few moments might be a bit rocky—especially if Sara took umbrage at the revelation that he had assigned someone to discreetly watch over her every move since the rattlesnake had been discovered in her bed. He hoped she understood the subtle difference between "watch over" and "spy."

Clearing his throat uneasily, he muttered, "Uh, well, ever since that blasted rattlesnake was found in your bed, I've had Esteban assign someone—" He cleared his throat again at the gathering comprehension on her face. "Uh, several someones, in fact, to keep an eye on you." His voice hardened. "I didn't want you getting any more unpleasant *surprises*, and in the course of your being watched, the affair between Ann and Hyrum was discovered."

Sara drew in an outraged breath. "You set someone to spy on me?" she demanded furiously.

"Not *spy*, sweetheart, watch over," Yancy replied doggedly, his jaw set.

"Well! You'll excuse me if I view the situation in a vastly different manner!" she snapped, green eyes dancing with suppressed emotion, none of it gentle or mirthful. Her hands tightened on the reins and just before she kicked Locuela into a gallop, she said angrily, "When a person is set to 'watch over' someone, the someone knows about it—anything else is just plain *spying*!"

A wry expression on his face, Yancy watched her gallop away toward the cattle camp, which was just coming into view. Glumly he admitted to himself the truth of Sara's angry statement. He rubbed his jaw thoughtfully. It seemed like he owed his bride an apology, and if he wanted to be back in her good graces, he had the distinct impression that he was going to have to do an awful lot of groveling and sweet-talking! He grinned. He might have to grovel, but he didn't mind the sweet-talking at all, and to have his Sara smiling and happy with him, he decided, was worth all the groveling in the world!

Despite scattered areas of chaparral, the cattle camp was easily spotted on the wide plains. The place had been chosen not only for the winding, tree-lined creek that meandered through the area, but also for a series of deep, steep-sided washes which crisscrossed the grassy prairies and which, when blocked at one end, became natural pens. Harassed and harried by the vaqueros, the unsuspecting cattle and mustangs were ruthlessly herded into these washes, and before the frantic creatures found their race to freedom blocked at the other end, hidden gates were suddenly swung shut behind them, effectively trapping them. Beyond the pens, stout working corrals made of rough wooden rails had been constructed in which to drive the cattle or mustangs for culling and castrating. Several wagons in varying shapes and sizes were parked in the shade of the willow and locust trees near the creek, as were quite a few tents. Not far away, a strong rawhide line had been stretched between two trees and about a dozen saddle horses had been tied there.

As Sara rode up, she was assaulted by an overpowering array of sights and scents. Men were briskly moving around, their voices carrying clearly; cattle bawled and horses neighed and the pleasing scents of woodsmoke, freshly brewed coffee and frying bacon drifted on the morning air.

Sara took in a deep breath. She loved the cattle camp! And, she thought grimly as she dismounted from Locuela and tied her to the line with the other horses, she wasn't going to let Yancy ruin her enjoyment of it! Someone to watch over her, indeed!

Ignoring her husband as he rode up behind her, Sara glanced around and spotted Hyrum near one of the fires, drinking a cup of coffee. Shooting Yancy a dark look, she strode off in that direction, a determinedly friendly smile on her face.

If Hyrum was surprised to be the object of Sara's beguiling smile, since she normally treated him to little more than a cool nod these days, he gave no indication, his own face creasing into a grin at her approach.

"Good morning, Hyrum," Sara said warmly when she came within speaking range. "How are you today?"

Hyrum returned her greeting, and nodding to a large pot of coffee sitting on the coals of the fire, he asked, "Would you care for some? It's strong, but fresh."

A cup of hot black coffee in her hands, Sara blew on the steam that rose from the cup and said lightly. "We haven't had much time to talk lately—how are you liking your work here at Paloma?"

"I find that I'm enjoying it much more than I thought possible," Hyrum returned earnestly. "It's very different from raising cotton, and I've been surprised to discover just how very much I enjoy the constant variety of chores that must be done."

Sara nodded eagerly. "Oh, I know! It seemed so simple when we used to talk about it, didn't it? I don't think either one of us ever envisioned the amount of just plain backbreaking work that would be involved."

From the corner of her eye Sara was aware of her husband's approach, so she turned the full force of her charm on Hyrum and sent him a wide, dazzling smile. "But everything is coming along marvelously, don't you think?" she fairly gushed. "Just as we planned at Magnolia Grove!"

Hyrum blinked at the blinding charm of her smile. What the hell was going on? he wondered suspiciously. Sara had been treating him like he'd contracted the plague lately, yet this morning . . . He spied Yancy and, seeing the scowl on the other man's face, realized instantly what must have occurred. There was, it would seem, trouble in paradise for the lovers. Well, well. His luck seemed to have changed. Perhaps he would be granted a chance to get back into Sara's good graces, and from there . . . Smiling back at Sara, Hyrum said casually, "I'm going to go out and help with the gathering of a new bunch of cattle this morning. Would you like to accompany me?"

As Yancy came closer to the pair and heard Hyrum's invitation, his scowl deepened. Sara was smiling too damned happily at that bastard Burnell and responding just too damn enthusiastically to Hyrum's words, as far as he was concerned! The pair of them were standing a little apart from the rest of the men, obviously deeply involved in their own private conversation, and Yancy was conscious of a blaze of displeasure burning within him.

He didn't like it at all that Sara and Hyrum were chatting in such a friendly, intimate manner, especially when Sara was angry with *him*, and he realized with a start that the savage emotion that suddenly roiled in his gut was just plain old jealousy! She was *his* wife, dammit! And he sure as hell wasn't going to meekly stand by and let her work her considerable wiles on someone else. Particularly not Hyrum Burnell!

Before Sara could reply to Hyrum's invitation, Yancy

said sourly, "That's very thoughtful of you, Burnell, and while I'm sure my wife would enjoy rounding up cattle with you, I think she'd enjoy it far more with me! I plan to take her out with me in just a little while, so I'm afraid she'll have to decline your kind offer."

Blandly ignoring Sara's outraged gasp and the fulminating look she flashed him, Yancy grabbed a tin cup sitting near the fire and poured himself a cup of coffee. Glancing over the rim of the cup, he stared at Sara and said grimly, "Isn't that so, sweetheart?"

Sara would have liked nothing better than to throw her coffee in his arrogant face and shout aloud a vociferous denial, but she was suddenly aware of the vaqueros moving around who were covertly watching the scene unfold, and she knew that she would not defy Yancy in such a public manner. Choking back her indignation, she muttered, "Yes, that's right, *darling*!" Then determined not to let him have the last word, she beamed a smile across to Hyrum and said huskily, "But that doesn't mean that we can't do it some other time, Hyrum. Perhaps when I am next at the camp?"

Hyrum tipped his hat, and catching sight of the dangerous glitter in Yancy's eyes, he put down his cup and said hastily, "Whatever you say, ma'am. Be happy to oblige, but right now I think I'd better be going." It was one thing to encourage Sara and another to push her husband into violence! He beat a swift retreat.

Over the rim of his tin cup, Yancy watched him mount one of the horses and ride off with several other vaqueros who were just leaving camp. He and Sara were alone for the moment, and glancing over at her, he growled, "I wouldn't encourage that relationship if I were you. Remember, he's *already* committing adultery with one woman! I doubt he'd have the stamina for two!"

Sara took a deep, outraged breath. Glaring at him, she snapped, "You are the most overbearing, arrogant, *enraging* person it has ever been my misfortune to meet!" Driven by temper, she added rashly, "You can't know how often I wish I had never laid eyes on you, much less married you! I sometimes wonder why I *did* marry you!"

Her words stung and he shot back, "You didn't have much choice, as I recall!" While he had spoken the literal truth, it was not the wisest thing to have said, and Yancy knew it the moment the words had left his mouth. Now was not the time to remind Sara of the way he had forced her into marriage. He cursed his unruly tongue, admitting that *never* would have been too soon to have brought up the less-than-gentlemanly manner in which he had compelled her to marry him!

Her emerald gaze bright with temper, Sara drew herself up and said wrathfully, "Well, thank you very much for reminding me of that unpleasant fact! You know, I'd *almost* forgotten what an unscrupulous, insensitive beast you can be! I won't," she finished hotly, "make *that* mistake again!"

Appalled at how quickly the gentle intimacy that had been growing between them these past weeks had vanished, Yancy was searching desperately for a way to recapture the happy moments that had been theirs before the topic of the affair between Hyrum and Ann had come up—particularly the topic of how he had known about it! Helplessly, he muttered, "Jesus! Sara, what happened to us? I never . . . I . . ."

"Nothing happened that should have come as a surprise to either one of us. After all, we know why you forced me to marry you." Sara's voice thickened with unshed tears. "I just made the mistake of forgetting about it for a while!"

Her words smote like a sword thrust in his heart, and he was on the point of stepping forward, the need to take her in his arms and convince her of the folly of what she was saying overriding every other thought in his head, when Bartholomew, utterly oblivious of the tense scene he was interrupting, strolled up and exclaimed happily, "Oh, hello! I didn't see you two arrive! We're about ready to start working on some of the bulls and we could certainly use your help, Yancy."

Looking very different in his breeches and boots and dusty black hat, Bartholomew smiled teasingly at Sara and asked, "Did you come to watch your handsome husband work today, Sara?"

Both Yancy and Sara turned to glare at him and simultaneously snapped, "*No!*"

Realizing that he had just stepped into a hornet's nest, Bartholomew muttered, "Uh, well, uh, sorry." And turned on his heel and walked rapidly toward one of the bigger pens, which was now filled with bellowing cattle.

Still angry and hurt, Sara said spitefully to Yancy, "Please don't let *me* keep you! I'm sure that they could use your help, and as for me—I don't care if I ever see you again!"

It was apparent that nothing could be settled between them now, and hoping that Sara's temper would cool as the day progressed, Yancy decided that perhaps the best thing for the present was to leave her alone. His face grim, he said tightly, "Fine! I'll do just that! Amuse yourself!"

Through her tears Sara watched her husband stride off in the direction that Bartholomew had taken. She bit back a sob, wishing bitterly that she had not let her temper drive her to say such ugly things to him. Now that the damage was done, she would have given anything to call back her hurtful words, but it was too late. With a heavy heart and lagging steps, she began to follow Yancy.

The cattle camp was almost deserted now, except for a few old men who acted as cooks. Everyone else was either at the pens or out gathering more cattle. She didn't, Sara told herself morosely, have much choice but to wander over to the working pens and watch the men work.

Sara was hardly aware of the dangerous, bloody, dusty work that was taking place in the pen before her, the sudden angry rift with Yancy consuming most of her thoughts. With hindsight, she understood that she had overreacted to the news that he had set someone to watch over her. She should have been pleased by his concern for her, and while she would have preferred to know about the men watching her, she could appreciate Yancy's reasons for doing as he had—he was used to giving orders and running things without consulting with anyone! Flirting with Hyrum, she admitted glumly, hadn't helped matters, and she had known the moment she had smiled so winningly at Hyrum that Yancy would react very much as he had. She'd been deliberately baiting him and so she shouldn't have been at all surprised by his words. But his words had hurt, arousing all her old feelings of resentment and helplessness, and not unnaturally, she had struck out at him.

One foot resting on the bottom rail of the corral, she stared blindly into space and sighed. She had certainly put herself on a very high horse, and she had the disturbing feeling that she was going to have to climb down all by herself. She sighed again. My wretched, *wretched* tongue! Will I ever learn to control it?

It was a miserable day for both Yancy and Sara. Each one was feeling decidedly bruised and guilty at the same time. They avoided each other—which was precisely what neither one wanted. Surreptitiously, each kept an eye on the other, but neither made the first move to heal the breach, although both longed most desperately to do just that!

It was late afternoon when Yancy decided to ride out

and help flush several more longhorns from the chaparral, and he had all he could do not to stop his horse beside Sara and steal a kiss for luck. Watching him ride away, Sara swallowed back the urge to call out for him to be careful.

She continued to observe the men working the bulls in the corrals for quite some time, but eventually, without Yancy's riveting presence to hold her attention, she grew bored and restless. She wandered dispiritedly through the nearly deserted camp, her thoughts on her absent husband, the knowledge that *she* would have to be the one to break the impasse between them uppermost in her mind. Her lips twisted wryly. Yancy certainly wouldn't retreat from his position, and since she *had* lost her temper and uttered those bitterly regretted, hurtful words, it was up to her to extend the olive branch—and hope that he didn't break it in two and throw it back in her face!

She glanced at the sun hanging low on the horizon and realized that Yancy should be returning soon and that before too much more time had elapsed, she would have her chance to make amends. She smiled impishly. Tonight, alone in their room, she would show him just how very contrite she was! A little shiver of excitement went through her and she immediately decided to ride out and meet him. Quickly mounting Locuela, she rode out onto the prairie, halting her horse a short distance from the edge of the brush to wait for his appearance. She hadn't long to wait. Not five minutes later, she heard the whoops and cries of the men and the crashing of several heavy bodies through the brush, and her hands tightened nervously on Locuela's reins.

Sara's breath caught in her throat a second later when more than a dozen unpredictable longhorns suddenly exploded from the brush not fifty feet from where she sat waiting on Locuela. They were huge, rangy, fierce-looking creatures, mostly dun-colored, but the occasional roan or black could be seen, the sunlight glinting on their long, curved, deadly horns as they thundered out onto the plains. Immediately, she urged Locuela into motion, intending to help keep the cattle running toward the trap in the arroyo. She glanced around for Yancy and spied him riding hard on the heels of the herd, his lariat whirling through the air above the backs and horns of the rushing animals. Esteban and Bartholomew were ahead of him, on either side of the herd, but she spared them not a glance, all of her attention on the tall, dark rider astride the big black horse.

For a second across the tossing horns and heaving backs, Sara's eyes met Yancy's and her heart swelled when he flashed her a heart-stopping grin. Her spirits lifted, and with a silly little smile on her face, she turned her concentration to the task at hand. She loved this part of the gathering, loved to race along at a breakneck speed across the prairies, the cattle bawling and plunging as they were ruthlessly herded into the arroyo and the trap that awaited them.

Suddenly a gigantic black bull with crazed eyes and wildly flaring nostrils broke away from the group and bolted back toward the brush. Yancy spun his horse around and, his lariat singing through the air, raced after the renegade, intent upon stopping the animal before it could disappear into the chaparral once more.

Heart in her mouth, Sara jerked Locuela to a stop and watched as the big black gelding and the black bull sped recklessly across the uneven ground. His body at one with his horse, Yancy looked like a centaur, his lariat whistling through the air when he loosed the rawhide rope. His aim was true, the rawhide landing right across the wide, curving horns.

Instantly the black gelding slid to a halt, and the lariat sang taut. The escaping bull hit the end of the rope and hurtled to the ground in a cloud of dust and thrashing hooves and horns. Almost immediately the creature sprang up and, with a great earthshaking bellow, swung around and charged its tormentor. Yancy had already kicked his horse into motion and as the big gelding galloped away, the enraged bull gave chase, those terrible curving horns, in Sara's imagination, flashing malevolently.

She had no rope, no clear idea of what she could do, but frantically she spurred Locuela forward. As the mare leaped into motion, Sara could see Yancy astride the racing horse swiftly working to untie the lariat from his saddle horn, the bull in swift, deadly pursuit. . . .

Esteban and Bartholomew had become aware of the situation, but they were, as yet, too far away to distract the bull, and Sara urged Locuela into a mad pace. The big gelding was running cleanly, easily outdistancing the bull, but suddenly, above the pounding of her horse's hooves, she heard a high-pitched whine and then, before her horrified gaze, she saw Yancy's horse stumble and crash to the ground. Billowing dust erupted into the air, obscuring her view, and when it began to lift, her heart clenched at the sight that met her eyes. Yancy was helplessly trapped beneath the body of his fallen horse.

One leg crushed by the weight of his mount, Yancy frantically spurred his gelding with his free leg, but inexplicably the horse remained still and unmoving. The bull, presented with a different-looking target, halted for a moment, pawing the ground and snorting fiercely a short distance away. Bartholomew and Esteban, on swifter, more powerful mounts than Sara's, intersected her path and, pulling ahead of her, pushed their horses to greater speed, closing swiftly on the bull. But they were too late.

Even as a scream of denial erupted from her throat and she feverishly urged Locuela into a killing run, the bull lowered its massive head and charged. Sara wanted to look away, wanted not to see what was happening, but she could not tear her eyes away from Yancy's trapped form or the huge black beast that was bearing inexorably down on him. Oh, God! she prayed fervently as Locuela closed the distance between them. Oh, God, don't let him die!

There was nothing Yancy could do, she thought frantically; pinned to the ground by his own horse, he was helpless to protect himself, unable to do anything but lie there and wait for the deadly horns of the bull to rip him apart. It will not happen, Sara vowed fiercely. *Yancy cannot die this way*!

But not even Sara's prayers or vows, or Locuela's desperate pace across the prairie, could stop the deadly charge of the bull. Yancy's pistol, however, could, the pistol he always wore strapped to his side. . . . With a choked cry of joy, Sara saw him suddenly reach down, as if he had just remembered the weapon at his hip, and with the gun firmly in his hand, he coolly took aim at the enraged bull. A shot rang out, and though obviously hit, the huge black beast merely shook its great head and still kept coming. Another shot. Another angry toss of its head. And then, when Sara was certain that the bull possessed magical powers, that nothing could stop it, with the animal less than six feet away, Yancy shot once again. The bull gave an angry roar and, with one last burst of life, drove its shuddering bulk onto the fallen horse and rider.

Everything had happened so quickly—it had been only minutes since the bull had first broken from the herd—and it now seemed to Sara as she desperately spurred Locuela onward that time had stopped, that it took her hours to reach Yancy's side. Esteban and Bartholomew reached him first. They were already on the ground and bending over Yancy's still form when Sara pulled Locuela to a rearing stop. She leaped down from her horse and ran toward Yancy, but Esteban intercepted her. "Senora! No—wait!"

The grief and pity in his eyes made her heart stand still, and then, with a cry of rage, she tore herself from his clasp. "No!" she shouted. "No! He is *not* dead!"

Oblivious of the horns of the dead bull, Sara flung herself on the ground beside Yancy, tenderly cradling his head in her lap. Her shaking hands caressed his beloved features; her lips kissed his brow, but there was no response. Choking back tears, she looked into his dark face, staring numbly at the thin line of blood that trickled from his temple, where in its dying throes the bull had struck him.

∽ 24

"**D**on't you *dare* die on me!" she burst out furiously, tears streaming down her cheeks, her hands frantically clutching him to her breast. Trembling lips pressed against his cheek, she exclaimed huskily, "You don't deserve it, you arrogant devil, but I love you! You *have* to live, you can't die!" But her words fell on deaf ears and Yancy remained terrifyingly still in her arms. Crazed by fear, she shook him violently and half tearfully, half wrathfully, she cried, "Oh, Yancy, you simply can't die! I love you! *I love you*! Oh, God! Please, please don't let him be dead!" Oblivious of Bartholomew and Esteban standing helplessly beside her, she kissed Yancy's pale face. "Oh, Yancy, please, *please* don't be dead! I love you! I love you!" Those last words became a litany and she could not stop saying them. Over and over again the phrase rang out— "I love you! I love you!"—as if those words alone had the miraculous power to restore vibrancy and life to the motionless form in her arms. Neither Esteban nor Bartholomew made any move to intrude upon her pain, both of them standing by her side, both so stunned and shaken by what had happened so suddenly that neither could speak or move.

It was Bartholomew, staring in grief-stricken disbelief at Yancy's pale face, who saw the first flutter of the long black eyelashes. His breath caught and his fingers closed like steel talons around Esteban's arm. At Esteban's startled look, he pointed, hardly daring to believe what he saw. The lashes flickered again, the movement stronger this time.

Trapped in some dark labyrinth of horror, Sara was completely unaware of what was happening. She continued to rock Yancy, her lips gently kissing his beloved features as she chanted her passionate invocation. "I love you! I love you! *I love you!*"

Sara was so wrapped up in her own anguish-filled world that she didn't notice Yancy's eyes opening and one hand slowly moving upward to touch a braid of honey-gold hair which had come loose from her usual neat cornet and hung down her chest. It was only when he gave a soft tug on her braid that she stared down into his amber-gold gaze, to see the powerful emotion glittering brightly in their depths.

He smiled crookedly and murmured, "Sweetheart, if I'd known that all it would take to get you to admit you loved me was to get half killed by a wild longhorn, I'd have done it a hell of a lot sooner!"

Irrationally, overriding the ecstatic joy that was flooding through her body, still deeply shaken by what had so nearly happened, Sara was suddenly furious with him. She thrust him away from her and sprang to her feet.

Not expecting his soft, yielding pillow to disappear so precipitously, Yancy hit the ground with a decided thud—or rather, his head did. "Ouch!" he yelped, gingerly rubbing the offending spot as he half sat up. "What's the matter with you?"

"You scared me to death!" she fairly shouted, her emerald eyes flashing, her hands clenched into fists as she glared down at him. "I thought you were dead! Don't you *ever* do that to me again! Do you hear me? Not ever!

You do something like this again and I swear, I'll kill you!"

Apparently not the least bit disturbed by this unlover-like tirade, Yancy nodded and said meekly, "*Sí, querida*, you have my word. I will never try to get myself killed again."

Tears overcame Sara and she sank down onto the ground again. "Oh, Yancy," she wailed, kissing him frantically, "I was *so* frightened. I couldn't bear for anything to happen to you! *I love you*, you miserable beast!"

A wave of dizziness hit Yancy, and sinking back down to the ground, he muttered, "And I you, sweetheart, more than you know. . . ." And having uttered that tantalizing statement, he promptly passed out.

Sara gave a horrified shriek and grabbed him, but this time, as she anxiously cradled his body next to hers, she realized immediately that he was not dead, merely unconscious. But that was little comfort and she raised wide, worried eyes to the two men who stood beside her.

Kneeling swiftly at her side, Bartholomew examined Yancy and then said softly, "Don't worry, my dear, I think it's only a mild concussion. The bull just struck him a glancing blow—he should be fine once we get him home and comfortable." He smiled into her anxious face. "He'll have a hellish headache, I have no doubt, but I don't think you'll become a widow any time soon."

The men from the cattle camp had become aware that something serious had happened and began arriving, their faces anxious and worried. Coincidentally, the group of riders Hyrum had been with suddenly appeared, driving several longhorns from the chaparral. Seeing the small crowd gathered at the edge of the brush, they promptly abandoned the cattle and galloped over to join the others, expressions of concern on their faces. Hyrum rode out of the brush just a moment later and quickly joined the group clustered around Yancy and Sara, the expression on his face unreadable. Assured that the *patrón* would recover without ill effect, the men set to work with a will to get Yancy free of the weight of the bull and of his downed horse, too. It was then that the reason for the fleet and sure-footed black's stumble was discovered.

A thunderous scowl on his dark face, Bartholomew rose from where he had been squatting in front of the horse and growled, "This was no accident! The horse was *shot*! Someone put a bullet hole right in the middle of the black's head."

Sara blanched and a horrified, outraged murmur swept through the gathered men. "Who would do such a thing? El Patrón was beloved! No one would harm a hair on his head!"

His scowl not lessening, Bartholomew muttered, "Beloved or not, *someone* damn sure wanted Yancy to have an accident! A *fatal* accident, from the look of things."

Her features strained, Sara fixed her eyes on Bartholomew as she asked thickly, "But who? Who would want him dead, and why?"

Bartholomew's gaze swept the faces nearest him, seeming to linger on Hyrum's handsome features. Then, shrugging his shoulders, he murmured, "Now's not the time to talk about it. Let's get him home."

Sara didn't disagree. A crude travois was hastily assembled from the materials at hand and before long Yancy was gently placed on it and the journey to Paloma began. Sara was certain that the trip to the hacienda was the longest she had ever undertaken in her life, each yard traveled seeming a mile. Because no one wished to cause Yancy any more discomfort than necessary, the horse pulling the travois was held at a slow, plodding pace as the travois bumped and jerked across the uneven ground.

Too worried about Yancy to dwell even for a moment on his last, sweetly tantalizing statement, Sara kept her anxious gaze on his still features, her spirits soaring when he would wake and stare around him with obvious comprehension, her heart becoming an icy lump of lead in her chest when he would close his eyes and lie on the travois like a dead man.

It seemed like hours to Sara, but eventually the hacienda came into view, and soon enough Yancy was lying naked beneath the covers on his bed, his wound freshly cleansed and a wide swathe of clean white linen wrapped rakishly about his head. At the moment, he seemed to be sleeping normally, and sitting in a chair by his side, Sara watched him anxiously as he slept. He had been awake and extremely vocal throughout the entire process of getting him settled and comfortable, and she smiled faintly as she recalled his pithy comments when he was stripped by Bartholomew and Esteban and hustled into bed, only to be instantly overwhelmed by Maria and Tansy as they fussed over his wound. Her strong, arrogant husband had not liked being so helpless one little bit!

The sleepiness worried Sara, but it did seem that he was awake far more than he slept, and when he was conscious, his gaze was clear and intelligent. Most of her fear that he would die had receded, but she would not be totally at ease until he was once again his usual infuriating, overbearing and oh-so-beloved self! She had known for a long time that she loved him, but she had not realized the depth of her feelings for him until he had lain so still and unmoving on the ground. She would never forget that awful moment. *Never*! Unable to help herself, she reached out and tenderly caressed his brow where the linen bandage covered his wound.

Yancy's dark hand came up suddenly and captured hers. Dragging her fingers to his mouth, he kissed their tips and, with his eyes still closed, murmured, "Are they all gone now? Is it safe for me to wake up?"

A scandalous expression on her face, Sara stared at him as his eyes flickered open. He grinned at her and, his amber-gold eyes dancing with tender amusement, said softly, "Sweetheart, how were we ever to have a moment alone? Only by feigning a feeble state could I ensure that they would leave us alone."

Despite the joyous thunder in her heart, Sara scolded him. "They were worried about you! You frightened all of us! Pretending to be hurt worse than you are! Shame on you!"

His eyes glittering mockingly beneath their thick black lashes, he asked in an injured tone, "Are you saying that you *didn't* want to be alone with me? That you don't love me?"

"Yes! No!" she blurted out, adorably flustered. Snatching her hand away from his, she glared at him. Fiercely she said, "You don't *deserve* to be loved! I'm sure that I will never understand what you do to inspire such devotion and loyalty in your people that you do! They have no idea what an arrogant monster you are!"

Her words didn't perturb him in the least. A crooked smile on his face, he reached out and his hands closed firmly around her upper arms. He gave a swift jerk and Sara tumbled onto his chest, her lower legs dangling off the edge of the bed. His mouth inches from hers, he muttered, "Sara, you little fool! I adore you—even when you are being a shrew!" He kissed her then, a hard, passionate kiss that sent her already befuddled senses swimming.

The universe whirled away, and for Sara there was only Yancy, Yancy's warm lips against hers, Yancy's hands on her body and Yancy's heart beating rhythmically beneath hers. She gave herself up mindlessly to his kiss, to his touch, and when at last their lips parted, she whispered, "Oh, Yancy, I *do* love you!"

He brushed back a lock of her hair that had fallen across her forehead, and a tender smile on his face, he said, "Do you know, there were times I feared that I would never hear you say those words. Times when I was certain that I was the greatest fool in nature to have taken one more look at your sweet little face that first night when I returned to Magnolia Grove and fell helplessly in love with you! You've led me a merry chase, sweetheart—never once giving me a clue to how you felt, constantly throwing Paloma up in my face, refusing to marry me . . . forcing me to act in a manner that I found abominable, but never giving me any chance to do otherwise." He sent her a stern look, which was at definite variance with the tenderness in his eyes. "You have much to answer for, wife!"

Sara smiled dreamily. Her finger outlining his hard mouth, she murmured, "And what about you? You never once explained yourself! You just ordered me around and took blatant advantage of me!"

He kissed her lightly and grinned. "I did, didn't I?" His grin faded and his eyes searched hers. "You're not sorry, are you? It did work out all right in the end, didn't it?"

His sudden uncertainty touched her. Arranging herself more comfortably beside him on the bed, she cuddled nearer and said against his mouth, "I could never be sorry for having married you. *Never!* Nor for loving you."

"*Sweetheart!*" he said thickly. "I *adore* you!"

Yancy's arms tightened around her and his urgent mouth found hers. The silence that descended was broken only now and then by soft sighs and gentle murmurings, and there was little said during the next several moments that would have made any sense to anyone but the two lovers. It was a sweet, precious time, and though there was desire between them, powerful, barely leashed desire, they did not give in to it, preferring instead to experience the indescribable pleasure of knowing simply that they loved and were loved by the other. Their kisses and caresses were almost chaste, Sara fully clothed, lying on top of the covers that blanketed Yancy's naked body, but there was such deep emotion between them that it mattered not. Mistily she decided that being in love with one's husband, *particularly* knowing that he loved her back, was absolutely divine!

Sara's cheek rested against his heart, Yancy's arm possessively cradled her next to his long body, and they lay like that for a long time, savoring this magical moment of utter contentment, this rare and wonderful moment when all was right in their world, when there was perfect harmony between them. All doubts, misunderstandings and troubles were banished and they basked unashamedly in the mystical wonder of their love. Eventually, though, the world intruded, and it was a soft knock on the door which brought them back to reality.

Bartholomew's head appeared around the edge of the door and he smiled, seeing the pair of them lying together on the bed, noticing especially Yancy's miraculous recovery. Entering the room with a twinkle in his eyes, he approached the bed. "I wondered," he said by way of greeting, "just how severe that injury was and just how much was blatant malingering on your part!"

Yancy grinned. "I'm sorry if I caused you any distress, but"—he glanced down at Sara, who had not moved—"I wanted some time alone with my bride!" A gleam lit his amber-gold eyes. "We had *much* to talk about!"

Open affection on his café-au-lait features, Bartholomew looked from one to the other, noting the happiness that shone from both faces. "I take it that you two have discovered what has been obvious to the rest of us for months?"

Sara giggled. Sitting upright, she said saucily, "You know, we might have discovered this fascinating state of affairs much sooner if only someone had kindly pointed it out to us!"

"And missed the fun of watching you two discover it for yourselves?" Bartholomew asked teasingly.

There were several more minutes of easy banter between them; then, his face sobering, Bartholomew asked quietly of Yancy, "How seriously are you hurt?"

Sara had by this time removed herself to the chair by Yancy's bed, and at Bartholomew's question, an anxious expression crossed her lovely face. One of her hands was still entwined with Yancy's—neither being able not to touch the other—and Yancy's fingers tightened reassuringly on hers. "Don't worry, sweetheart, I really *am* all right," he said softly. He glanced across at Bartholomew. "And that goes for you, too. I took a bad knock, but I'm fine. I have a slight headache, but that's all."

Bartholomew nodded as if Yancy's words confirmed his own diagnosis. Grabbing another chair and dragging it nearer to the bed, he sat down, his features worried and intent. "That was no accident today," he said bluntly. "Your horse was deliberately shot out from underneath you. Someone wanted you to die or, at the very least, have a *serious* accident!"

Yancy had been unconscious when the reason for his horse's tumble had been discovered, but he didn't seem surprised by what Bartholomew had just revealed. "I wondered," he said thoughtfully, "what had caused him to go down like that—it didn't *feel* like a stumble in a prairie dog hole. It felt like he just stopped and went down in a heap."

Bartholomew's mouth twisted. "A bullet in the brain has a way of doing just that—dropping an animal in an instant!"

"But who?" Sara asked worriedly, her wide green eyes moving from one face to the other. "And why?"

Bartholomew and Yancy exchanged glances. "I think," Yancy said slowly, "that the answer to that is fairly obvious. . . ."

Sara stared at Yancy, wondering what he knew that she didn't. Surely he didn't believe that one of his men had done such a thing! There was no question that, to a man, the vaqueros—or even Bartholomew, for that matter—would gladly die for him. They certainly would never endanger his life! And except for Hyrum, there had been no one else around. *Except for Hyrum.* Sara gasped as the implication hit her and blurted out, "You think Hyrum did it!"

Neither man made any attempt to deny her statement and Sara felt sick. She had liked Hyrum, had counted him as a friend, and there was a time when she would have found it inconceivable to suspect him of attempting cold-blooded murder. But that, of course, had been before she had discovered that he had been carrying on a torrid, clandestine affair with Ann Shelldrake, all the while claiming to love *her*! She didn't want to believe that he had tried to kill her husband this afternoon, but she certainly didn't trust him anymore, and there was no denying that he *was* the likeliest suspect.

Into the heavy silence that had fallen, she asked abruptly, "But why? I thought things were going well between you. You've been treating him very fairly these days—you didn't turn him off as you could have—you've given him a job, almost the same one he would have had if my original plans had been carried out. He couldn't have any cause for complaint and he certainly has seemed resigned and content with his role here. What would he have to gain by killing you?"

Bartholomew looked at the floor, and it was Yancy who said calmly, "What he's been after all along—*you!*"

"Me!" she squeaked, her astonishment obvious. "What the devil do you mean by *that!*"

Yancy's eyes locked with hers. "Merely that if I were to die, you would become a very lovely, very *wealthy* young widow. If I were to die, you would inherit everything I own—the vast acres of Rancho del Sol, the countless herds of wild cattle and horses, the silver mines in Mexico, everything." He smiled mirthlessly. "Your lovely face and sweet body would be enough to tempt most men, but coupled with a great fortune . . ." Yancy paused, watching the horrified comprehension spread across her face. Quietly he continued. "Coupled with a great fortune, you would become irresistible— especially to a man who has nothing."

"But I would never . . . I've *already* turned down his offer of marriage. Besides," she said desperately, "he's in love with Ann Shelldrake. Even if he *could* convince me to marry him, he couldn't possibly want to tie himself to me for the rest of his life."

Yancy's eyes were hooded. "Who said it would be for the rest of *your* life? If he is capable of one murder, who's to say that after a period of time you wouldn't suffer a fatal accident? Leaving him a rich man, free to marry the woman of his own choice."

"Merciful heavens! Do you really think he is that wicked? To plan not only your murder, but mine as well?"

It was Bartholomew who answered. "I don't know if he plans on your demise or not, but there is no doubt in my mind that he did try to kill Yancy this afternoon and that the motive for his actions was to make you a widow.

A widow he plans on marrying himself. You won't convince me otherwise." He sent Sara an apologetic look. "I know you liked him, but after Sam died, it was obvious to Tansy and me that he was buttering you up, fawning over you for his own means. Maybe you didn't see it, but we did and we worried a great deal about it. He saw you as his hope for the future, and I don't think even your marriage has changed his point of view. That is just another obstacle in his way now."

It all made a terrible kind of sense, and with the sick feeling in the pit of her stomach growing, Sara realized that she agreed with Bartholomew's reading of the situation. She wasn't quite ready to accept Yancy's premise that at some distant time her own death was planned by Hyrum, but she had difficulty discounting it entirely.

"Do you think he killed Margaret?" Sara demanded suddenly.

Bartholomew shrugged and Yancy said slowly, "I don't know. He could have—as well as half a dozen other people!"

Sara rubbed her temple with one hand. "It would certainly be simpler if he had! It is disconcerting, to say the least, to think that we may have a household comprised of not only Margaret's murderer but also someone else entirely who, except for your handiness with a gun, might have arranged your murder this afternoon!"

Yancy grinned at her. "Don't you worry, sweetheart— I am much harder to kill than Margaret!"

Sara glared at him. "This is *not* amusing! He tried to *kill* you!"

Yancy grimaced and kissed the fingers of the hand he was still holding. "I know, sweetheart, I know, but I don't think we have to worry that he will make another attempt so soon. He certainly wouldn't want to arouse suspicion, nor would he want there to be any signs that point in his direction. I don't believe this afternoon's attempt was planned—he simply saw an opportunity and took it. If it had worked, well, then he was successful, but if it failed, he hadn't lost anything by it. At least that's how I see the situation."

Bartholomew nodded. "Esteban and I have already talked about it and we're inclined to agree. Hyrum couldn't have known you'd be at that particular spot or that there would be trouble with the bull. We think he was riding far enough ahead of the others to be hidden by the brush and saw what was going on. Realizing that no one could see him, he seized the opportunity, figuring that when the horse went down you stood a good chance of breaking your neck, and if not that, then there was the bull. . . . He had nothing to lose by trying."

Sara swallowed. "What do we do now? All we know for sure is that someone shot the horse. Everything else is just speculation on our part. We have no proof that Hyrum did it, much less that he even thought about doing it! So what do we do—send him away?"

"I don't know," Yancy began slowly. "I'm not fond of the idea of Hyrum running loose out there with the thought of murdering me foremost on his mind. I'd rather we kept him here, where we can keep an eye on him until we can come up with a better solution—or proof of what he is up to."

Sara nodded reluctantly, unable to offer another suggestion.

Looking at Bartholomew, Yancy quirked an eyebrow. "Well? Do you have any other ideas?"

Bartholomew shook his head disgustedly. "No, I'm afraid not. I don't like the idea of that bastard thinking he got away with something, but I don't see how we can do anything different than what you proposed. Sara's right—we have only suspicions." Grimly Bartholomew added, "But in the meantime, Esteban and I will see to it that he is watched closely. *Very* closely!"

Sara tried to take comfort from Bartholomew's words, but it was cold comfort indeed. Just knowing that Hyrum was even in the same vicinity as Yancy sent icy tendrils of fear racing through her body, and she barely waited for Bartholomew to shut the door behind him as he left before she flung her arms around Yancy's neck and said fiercely, "Don't you *dare* let him kill you! Do you hear me? Don't you dare!"

Yancy smiled and pulled her even closer. Kissing her cheek, he said softly, "Sara, I love you, more than I thought I could ever love anyone. You are my life, and I have no intention of letting Hyrum Burnell kill me. I intend for us to have a long and rapturously happy marriage and I'm looking forward to having you in my arms and in my bed for the rest of my life! Since I've just discovered the glorious fact that you love me, do you think I would let anything, any*one*, stand in my way of reveling in your love? I've waited too long and suffered too many anxieties over the state of your heart to allow Hyrum to cut short the *decades* of loving I expect from you!"

What could she do but kiss him after that? She did so with great enthusiasm and she discovered shortly just how little his wound had incapacitated him. She was never certain how it happened, but in a few brief seconds, she found herself lying naked on the bed with him, her clothes scattered wildly about the floor and his warm, hard body pressed intimately next to hers. He had always had the power to drive coherent thought from her mind, had always had the power to arouse her with a look, a touch, a kiss, but this was different; this time she knew that there was love behind every caress, every brush of his lips, every muttered word that came from him as he explored her body, and her heart rejoiced. *He loved her*!

Compulsively her hands wandered over his lean body, and she smiled to herself at his groans of pleasure when her fingers found a particularly responsive area of his flesh. She took a new, wondrous delight in him, delight in his muscled strength, delight in the increasingly hungry demand of his kisses, knowing that when he claimed her, when at last he slid deeply within her body and began the fierce movements that would bring them ecstasy, the same emotion which was driving her was driving him; that this was not lust, *this* was *loving*!

And afterward, when passion was spent, there was the indescribable bliss of lying beside him, sharing the sweet exhaustion that claimed them both and hearing him whisper softly against her ear, "I love you, *querida*, never doubt it. You are my heart!"

There was, however, just one tiny, *tiny* cloud on her bright, glowing horizon, and knowing that she was a fool for having to ask, but desperately needing that one final doubt banished forever, Sara raised herself up beside him and gazed into his face. "And Paloma? How much did it have to do with our marriage?" She murmured tremulously.

Yancy's eyes darkened and his lips tightened. "I knew I should never have seized upon that damned clause in Sam's will to make you marry me, but at the time, it seemed so convenient!" he admitted baldly. "It was a ready-made excuse to hide behind, a public reason that could cloak my private desires. . . ." His gaze locked on hers, and absently tracing the outline of her soft mouth, he said huskily, "Sara, I wanted you, but I didn't want to love you, I can't deny it. I certainly didn't want to admit, even to myself, that my heart was involved." He swallowed uncomfortably. "After Margaret, I swore that no woman was *ever* going to touch my deepest emotions, that I would never allow myself to care greatly for another female—or show her much consideration!"

He smiled with incredible tenderness at her. "And then there was you . . . after one look, one sight of your lovely little face, all my grimly sworn vows went flying. I wanted you in the worst possible way—I could think of little else—but I wasn't worried—lust is a passing fancy—until I realized that it wasn't *just* your body that I wanted, it was *you*! I *loved* you." He searched her features slowly and then said quietly, "Once I returned to Magnolia Grove and saw you that first night in Sam's office, it was as if we had never been parted, almost as if we were picking up from the time we had kissed on the staircase, the night before Margaret was murdered. I was filled with the same elation, the same feelings of possessiveness and protectiveness I'd had then, and that enraged and terrified me and I was absolutely furious with you for having married Sam—for not having waited for me!" His mouth curved ruefully. "I'm afraid I haven't been acting precisely rational since that moment—you became everything to me and nothing else mattered—certainly not Paloma! Paloma had nothing to do with our marriage, sweetheart, *nothing* to do with what happened between us . . ." He grinned mockingly. "Except that it was damned convenient for me to hide behind! Without Paloma, I might have had to court you in the traditional manner and confess my love a long time ago!"

"You should be ashamed of yourself—you treated me quite wickedly! Seducing me and then forcing me to marry you. You, sir, were a vile, underhanded scoundrel!" Sara said severely, the sweet curve of her lips and the dreamy expression in her emerald eyes taking any sting out of her words.

Yancy smiled smugly and pulled her unresisting body nearer to him. "But you love me, don't you, sweetheart?" he murmured against her eager mouth. "You love me and will until the day you die. . . ."

Kissing him back as passionately as he kissed her, Sara gave herself up to the magic that was Yancy, her heart soaring, happiness welling up through her entire body. "Oh, I do indeed," she whispered some minutes later, when she was able to. "I *do* love you more than life itself—you wretched beast!"

25

The days following Yancy's brush with death were deliriously happy for Sara, and no one who saw the lovers had any doubts about the strength or durability of the powerful emotions that bound them together. The love they shared was nearly tangible, and one had only to see the way that Yancy looked at Sara, or the way her face would soften at just the mere mention of his name, to know precisely how deep and lasting was their love.

It was a joyful time for them, and their joy became even greater that day in late September when Sara shyly told her husband that there would indeed be an heir to Paloma. With a great shout, Yancy caught her up in his arms, his own delight in the prospect of becoming a father clear in the unspeakably tender expression on his dark face.

The news, of course, went through the little hamlet at Paloma like wildfire and there was much rejoicing and excitement among the inhabitants. Nonetheless, not *all* who heard the news of Sara's impending motherhood were pleased. . . .

Risking a meeting with Hyrum in one of the newly restored barns some distance from the hacienda that same evening, Ann wore a tight and sullen expression on her face. "Have you heard?" she demanded as Hyrum slipped in between the big double doors to join her in the cool gloom of the barn. "The little bitch is breeding!"

Hyrum nodded curtly. "It doesn't matter, I told you that! Let her child inherit Paloma! *We* will have del Sol!"

Ann snorted. "When? You missed the only opportunity to kill Yancy that presented itself so far, and you've told me that you think he's set his men to watch you. We can't even meet each other without great risk— and I'm sure that every time you manage to give your keepers the slip, they report back immediately to that bastard Yancy!" She took an angry turn around the middle of the barn. "I feel like a prisoner! Something has to happen soon, or I will go mad, I tell you! I hate this wretched place! I have no one to talk to, and except for dinners with the lovers"—she made the word sound like a curse—"there are no social engagements, no shops, nothing for me to do in order to pass the day. I am so *bored*!" She cast him a fulminating look. "Do you know, I was so desperate to break the deadly monotony that the other day I actually accompanied Sara to those horrid cattle pens!" She shuddered, then fluttered her lashes at him. "Since nearly your every move is watched, I don't even have the pleasure of your lovemaking to take my mind off our troubles. If I am forced to remain here much longer, I will probably begin to look at my husband with fondness!"

Everything she said was true; they'd had precious few moments together these past weeks, and despite the dangerousness of it, Hyrum was starving for her. Reaching for her, he pushed her down into a stack of hay and muttered, "Let me see what I can do to change your mind about that!"

It was an urgent coupling, with few preliminaries, clothing flung aside only enough to allow them access to each other's bodies. Desperation and danger combined with lust was a powerful mixture and rapidly brought them both to a shattering release. The last tremors of pleasure still rippling through them, they lay there for a few moments on the hay, breathing heavily, their bodies still locked together.

Her arms around his neck, Ann asked mournfully, "Oh, Hyrum, what are we going to do? If Yancy really has put his men to watch you, he must know of your plans—you'll never get a chance to kill him! And as for Tom . . ." She bit her lip. "I think he suspects something. He watches me when he thinks I am not looking and he questions everything I do. He is so strange and odd these days. I hate him! I can't wait until he is dead!"

There was a soft, furtive noise nearby and Hyrum stiffened, listening intently.

"Oh, my God!" Ann muttered softly. "Are you certain you weren't followed?"

Hyrum nodded tautly. "You?" he asked tightly.

"Tom was resting in his room when I left. He probably doesn't even know I'm gone from the house."

"Are you sure? You just said he's been watching you lately."

"I was careful, I tell you!"

But the sound had alarmed them and they lay there frozen, straining to hear. Nothing except the nightly chorus of insects came to them. The minutes passed with agonizing slowness, and when nothing else untoward occurred, Ann sighed with relief and moved impatiently. Even though everything seemed normal, Hyrum was uneasy, and he silently disentangled himself from Ann and stood up in the darkness. No sound out of the ordinary carried on the cooling air, and gradually he relaxed.

Helping Ann to her feet a second later and pulling a few wisps of hay from her hair, Hyrum said carefully,

"Perhaps it's time we did do something about your husband. If he were to die, at least one of our obstacles would be gone."

Ann smiled sunnily, her blue eyes sparkling. "Oh, Hyrum, I was hoping you'd say something like that! How shall we do it? And when? Please, please make it soon!"

He frowned at her. "As soon as I can, but don't forget, I am somewhat hampered these days. I am not free to move around as I once was, and it has to look like an accident—we can't have Yancy getting any more suspicious than he is already."

Ann nodded and they spent a few more minutes discussing the situation, but eventually they had to part.

Not five minutes after Hyrum had returned to his house, Juan Mendoza, leaving Rogerio Duran to continue the watch, was standing in front of Yancy in the small *sala* in the hacienda and giving his report.

"He met the blond gringa at the big barn, just beyond the horse corrals. I did not see her arrive—she was already inside waiting for him." Uneasily turning his large sombrero in his hands, Juan said earnestly, "Senor, I think there is going to be very bad trouble soon. The blond gringa's husband was there, too, watching and listening to them."

"*What*?" Yancy asked, startled. "Tom Shelldrake was there?"

"*Sí*, senor! I did not see him at first, but he was hidden in the shed which leans against the barn, and I only discovered him when I thought to go in there myself to get nearer to them so I could hear more clearly what they were saying. His face was pressed to one of the gaps in the boards."

"Did he see you?" Yancy inquired sharply.

Juan smiled, his black eyes dancing in his smooth young face. "No, senor. I was *muy* careful!" His smile faded and he said, "It is not good that the blond gringa's husband knows what she is doing, is it?"

"No, by damn, it's not!" Yancy said forcefully. Frowning he stared at the floor for several seconds before saying grimly, "Well, there is nothing I can do about it tonight, but I think the time has finally come to get rid of that nest of vipers!" He smiled at Juan. "You did well—I'm very pleased with all of you. After you get Diego and Gil to relieve you and Rogerio, go home for the night."

After Juan had left, Yancy paced the small *sala*, his brow furrowed in thought. He didn't like the situation one damn bit, the news that Tom was spying on Ann and Hyrum making him distinctly uneasy.

The door to the *sala* opened just then and Sara walked in. Seeing his frown, she asked, "What's wrong? You look like you'd like to strangle someone."

Yancy's mouth twisted ruefully, and resting his hips back against the desk, he pulled her easily into his arms. Dropping a kiss on her upturned mouth, he murmured, "Ah, but that was before you came into the room. Now I find that I would far rather make love to my lovely wife."

Sara smiled demurely and leaned into his warm, hard length. Kissing him back, she said softly, "Which you can do, just as soon as you tell me why you were frowning so blackly."

He grimaced, but keeping her in his arms, he quickly told her of Juan's unsettling report.

"Tom *knows* about them?" Sara gasped. "He *spies* on them? How appalling! What are you going to do?"

Releasing her, he reached over the desk and picked up a piece of paper. Handing it to her, he said, "This arrived today. I think it is a partial solution to our problem."

Swiftly Sara read the letter. Looking up at Yancy when she had finished, she asked, "How long have you been planning this? You had to write your friend weeks ago to have received a reply this soon."

Yancy nodded. "I wrote to John the day after the incident with the bull. I've just been waiting to hear from him."

Again Sara perused the letter. "California," she said thoughtfully. "Yes, that would do. It's far enough away from us, and the job and the money sound like something that Hyrum would find suitable." She looked at Yancy. "He's not going to like it, you know. He might refuse to take it."

"He might . . . but if he does, I'll just have to explain to him that I have no intention of keeping him working for *me*. It's either the job in California or nothing. Hyrum's a smart man. I think he'll take it, particularly when I say that I've written letters to the local sheriff and to my attorneys both here and in Mexico, explaining that should I suffer an untimely death, Hyrum Burnell should be questioned closely about his movements and whereabouts at the time of my demise."

Sara's face clouded and she clutched him tightly. "Oh, Yancy! Don't talk about dying—I can't bear it!"

He hugged her and said softly, "I'm not going to die, sweetheart, at least not any time soon. I intend to be around when that babe of ours is born, and all the others I hope we will be blessed with! And *their* children! And their children's children! You won't be rid of me for years and years!"

They kissed tenderly and it was quite some time later before there was any more conversation in the *sala*. Eventually, though, the unpleasant subject had to be discussed, and resting her head on his chest, Sara asked, "What about Ann and Tom? Have you decided what to do about them?"

Yancy nodded. "I've come to the conclusion that the Shelldrakes can just as well live off me *away* from me as they can underfoot! It took me a while to come up with the idea, but it suddenly hit me. I own a small rancho, just outside San Antonio, that belonged to an old aunt of mine. In the past, from time to time I've wondered what to do with the place, and it occurred to me that it would suit Ann and Tom perfectly. The hacienda should be in good repair and there are several hundred acres of land. Tom can raise cattle or horses or do whatever he chooses." Yancy grinned at Sara. "And to make certain they never land on *my* doorstep again, I'll settle enough money for Tom, in trust, so that he and Ann should be able to live comfortably at Rancho Domingo for the rest of their lives. It is not a grand place, but my memory of it is that it is sizable and quite pleasant. He won't be a tenth as rich as he once was, but he'll be his own master again and won't have to look to me for the food in his belly and the clothes on his back!"

"What an excellent idea!" Sara exclaimed happily. "And perhaps, with Hyrum gone to California and Tom no longer dependent on your kindness, Ann will realize that Tom is not such a bad husband, after all!"

Yancy sent her a look. "And pigs will fly!"

Sara made a face. "Well, you never know. . . . I just hope that they are all satisfied with what you are doing for them!"

"Satisfied" wasn't precisely the word Yancy would have used to describe the various reactions of the recipients of his generosity. Hyrum was downright surly, but realizing that his hand had been called, he had no choice but to accept the offer of employment at a ranch in California and take the money Yancy gave him to cover his travel expenses. Dropping several gold coins on the corner of his desk, Yancy said levelly, "I'll want you gone by tomorrow morning—early! There is nothing for you here, and the sooner you reach John Westlund's place outside Chico, the sooner you'll be building your own future."

"You think you're so damned clever, don't you?" Hyrum grated, his mouth thin and unpleasant.

"Only when I hold the winning hand! And remember, anything happens to me and the sheriff is going to be very interested in you—and as for marrying my grieving widow, you can forget that! She knows you for what you are!" Yancy smiled grimly. "If I die, *pray* the sheriff finds you before Sara does!"

Hyrum grabbed the gold and stormed out of the room, and Yancy shrugged his shoulders. Now for the Shelldrakes. After a great deal of thought and discussion with Sara, it had been decided that he would meet Tom alone. He damn sure didn't need Ann around creating God knew what sort of scenes and distractions when he explained to the other man what was planned.

Yancy had not expected there to be any great reaction from Tom when he presented his plan to him, and he was right. For several long seconds Tom sat there staring at Yancy dumbfounded. Finally, his voice thick with emotion, he exclaimed, "Thank you! I always believed that you were a good man, Yancy. Sam would have been proud of you!" He bent his head and fiddled with the sling which cradled his bad arm. "I cannot tell you," he mumbled huskily, "what your unexpected generosity means to me. I owe you a great deal."

Distinctly uncomfortable, Yancy muttered, "You don't owe me anything, Tom. I don't need the damned place, and as for the money . . . If Sam had lived, I'm sure he would have arranged something similar for you."

Tom looked at him, his brown eyes curiously remote. "You've had a great deal to contend with since you first returned to Magnolia Grove, haven't you? It couldn't have been easy for you to find yourself suddenly saddled with a whole houseful of people who looked to you for their welfare. I wonder, if I had found myself in your shoes, whether I would have . . ." Tom sighed. "Ah, well, it really doesn't matter, does it? You and Sara have been most kind to me and it seems a shame that I—" Tom stopped and shook his head sadly. "You know, things just never work out the way you think they will. There are always regrets . . . times when you can let nothing stand in your way. . . ."

Yancy cleared his throat uneasily and, seeking to change the gloomy atmosphere that seemed to have fallen, said lightly, "Of course one always has some regrets, but there is no use repining over what you can't change." He smiled faintly. "I will always regret I didn't marry Sara out of hand when Sam first brought her to Magnolia Grove, but in the end, things worked out just fine!"

Tom smiled oddly. "Yes, they did in the end, didn't they? And that's all that counts, isn't it? That things work out in the end? No matter what has to be done . . ."

Eyeing him keenly, Yancy asked, "Are you all right? You seem . . . distracted."

"I imagine that I am a little distracted. I have so much to plan. . . ." Tom seem to shake himself. Rising to his feet from the chair in which he had been sitting, he said heartily, "Well, now, I won't keep you any longer—I'm sure you have other things to do." He hesitated for a moment, then fixed his gaze speculatively on Yancy. "I suppose that you would like Ann and me to leave fairly soon—within the week?"

Yancy saw no reason to pretend otherwise. "As soon as you find it convenient. I can have Tansy and Maria help you pack your belongings, and it goes without saying that some of my people will accompany you and Ann to Domingo and see that you are settled."

There were a few more minutes of conversation and then Tom left the *sala*. Yancy was surprisingly glad to see the last of the older man, but he couldn't have said why. Impatient to tell Sara the results of his morning's work, he shook off the strange feeling of unease and hurried to find his wife.

He found her sitting in the shade of the large willow tree in the courtyard, a pitcher of sangria and some glasses resting in the center of the table, along with several pieces of fruit. After greeting Sara with a kiss, he poured himself some of the sangria and, taking a chair across from her, stretched his long legs out before him. Grinning at her over the rim of his glass, he said, "You'll be happy to know that before the week is ended, we should be rid of our, um, guests!"

Her eyes soft with love as she gazed at him, she inquired, "So it went well?"

He nodded. "As well as I expected, but there was something about Tom . . ." He shrugged and said, "Enough about them—tell me of your morning." And Sara proceeded to do just that.

Several hours later, as he sat alone in the courtyard, waiting for Sara to appear from their afternoon siesta, Yancy was still mulling over Tom's manner. It had made him uneasy but he couldn't say why, and *that* made him even more uneasy! And the envelope that Maria delivered to him just a few minutes later only increased his feeling that there was something afoot . . . something he wasn't going to like very much!

A scowl between his brows, he glanced at the small sheet of paper the envelope had contained. Why the devil did Ann want to meet him secretly in the small barn tonight? What was she up to now? He studied a phrase from her note—"you are to tell no one—it is too *dangerous*!" What the hell did she mean by that? He read the message again, his mind racing. Was it just Ann being melodramatic, or did she really have "something of the utmost importance" to tell him? His scowl deepened. There were several things he could do about the note, but it really narrowed down to only two options: he could toss it over his shoulder and ignore it, or he could meet with the damned woman and find out what was so blasted important that she couldn't just walk up to the hacienda and tell him. He was sorely tempted to follow the first option, but sighing resignedly, he knew he wasn't going to. Like a lamb to the slaughter, he was going to be at the meeting place at the stated time. But unlike the lamb—he smiled savagely—he wouldn't be walking blindly into a trap.

Shortly thereafter, when he sought out Sara in the privacy of their bedroom and apprised her of his plan to follow Ann's instructions, Sara was furious with him. "How can you be so stupid?" she asked, springing up from the dressing stool, where she had been sitting brushing her hair. "It has to be a trap! She and Hyrum are going to try to kill you. They're probably furious with the way you've arranged to split them up! She can't be happy with Hyrum leaving for California while she's to go with Tom to San Antonio. She means to harm you, I just know it!"

"I thought you said she might decide that Tom was not such a bad husband, after all, and mend her ways," Yancy commented innocently, his amber-gold eyes gleaming with laughter.

"And pigs might fly!" Sara retorted wrathfully, her green eyes flashing as, arms akimbo, she glared at him. "You will *not* meet that dreadful woman alone! I forbid it!"

The laughter fled from his gaze, and catching her up in his arms, he murmured against her ear, "*Querida*, I have to meet her! Suppose the note is genuine? Suppose she really does know something of the utmost importance? Something that is so dangerous that she dared not approach me directly? What then?"

Sara made a little fist and hit him in the shoulder. A hint of tears in her voice, she muttered, "I don't care! I just don't want anything to happen to you!"

He caressed her hair. "Nothing is going to happen to me. It is not as if I am walking into her web without warning."

Her features resolute, Sara looked up at him. "I'm going with you!"

"No, you're not," he said gently, his eyes warm and tender as they roamed over her lovely face. "You're going to wait here for me. If it *is* a trap, I don't want to be worrying about saving your lovely neck as well as my far-less-fragile one!"

Sara argued at length and with great vehemence, but in the end, she remained where she was and it was Yancy who glided out of the hacienda sometime later into the murky shadows of dusk. A knife hidden in his boot, the ever-present pistol hanging from his gun belt, every nerve alert for danger, he stealthily made his way to the barn where Ann had indicated she would be waiting for him. It was a small one, located some distance from the rest of the other outbuildings, nestled in the middle of several sprawling pecan and willow trees. As he approached it, Yancy glanced around carefully one more time, and seeing nothing to alarm him, he slowly pushed open one of the doors and silently entered the building. Only gloomy shadows met his gaze and, his hand resting on the butt of his gun, he walked in farther. By now full dusk had fallen and it was even darker inside the barn, but there was just enough light left for him to make out the motionless form lying on the floor near the ladder which led to the loft twenty feet above.

He cursed under his breath, but before rushing to the aid of the fallen figure before him, he took another slow and thorough inventory of the area. The barn had been used to store various odds and ends, and a jumble of barely discernible shapes met his gaze. Again he saw nothing to cause alarm, but he was extremely uneasy. He listened intently for any abnormal sound, yet still there was nothing.

Not liking the situation, but having no choice but to play the cards dealt him, he cautiously approached the dark shape on the barn floor. To his astonishment, he discovered that it was Hyrum lying there! A very *dead* Hyrum, he learned a second later when he crouched and sought for a pulse. His hand came away wet and sticky, and though he could not see its color, he knew that his hand was covered in blood. From his quick inspection of the body, it appeared that someone had struck a fatal blow to the back of Hyrum's head.

The violent rush of air behind him was the only warning Yancy had, and he was already rising and turning, the gun in his hand, when a powerful blow caught him on the temple. With a soft groan, he fell to the floor beside Hyrum's body. It was only his quick reaction that had saved him from sharing Hyrum's fate, but the blow had been forceful enough to render him unconscious for a precious few minutes—minutes in which his hands and feet were swiftly bound.

When consciousness returned, the faint, deadly scent of smoke was in his nostrils, and it was then that he discovered his helpless and dangerous state. Rolling quickly over onto his back, he stared toward the shadowy figure busily adding small bits of wood and straw to the as-yet-tiny fire that flickered near the base of the ladder which led up to the loft. With every second that passed, with every piece of added fuel, the fire grew brighter and stronger, and a thrill of horror went through Yancy when the figure turned and in the dancing light of the yellow-and-red flames he recognized Tom Shelldrake's features.

"*Por Dios!*" he exclaimed. "What the hell is going on? What are you doing?"

In the fiery light, Tom looked at him queerly, the expression in his brown eyes making Yancy's flesh crawl. "Oh, I *am* sorry," Tom said regretfully. "I had hoped that I'd hit you hard enough so that you wouldn't have to suffer. After all, you have been so kind to me." He sighed. "I really am sorry for this, you know, but a little rancho outside San Antonio just wouldn't *do*, you see— not when I can have del Sol and all that bountiful silver from your mines." Momentarily heedless of the growing flames near his feet, Tom went on gently. "It was actually Hyrum who gave me the idea for it—did you know that he planned to kill you and marry your widow? And, of course, he and that slut of a wife of mine intended for me to die, too. I overheard them planning it one night at del Sol. They thought they were so damned clever. But not as clever as I am!" A high-pitched giggle came from him, a chilling sound that made Yancy realize in that tense moment that he was totally in the power of a madman, and he carefully began to test the strength of the bonds that held him. "It won't do any good," Tom said as he watched Yancy's actions. "I tied them very tight. . . . Of course, I didn't have to worry about Hyrum." He giggled again. "Nor my sweet wife, now that I think of it."

Yancy's head snapped up at that and he demanded, "What the hell do you mean by that? Where is Ann?"

Tom smiled and glanced upward. "My dear, *dear* wife is up there—after all, it won't do any good if I get rid of you and I am still chained to that little slut! Besides," he continued conversationally, "she deserves to die! Planning with her lover to kill me! The very idea!"

Hoping to keep him distracted, and stalling for time, Yancy asked, "Why kill Hyrum? He was leaving in the morning."

Tom absently stroked his chin. "The bastard planned to kill me, which should be reason enough for me to kill him, and don't forget, he *was* enjoying my wife's favors. Can you blame me?" He looked accusingly at Yancy. "You know you precipitated all of this, don't you? You brought it on yourself. If you hadn't decided to finally get rid of all of us, who knows how much longer you might have lived? But once Hyrum got his marching orders and you made it clear that Ann and I were also being ejected from your household, everything changed!"

"How?" Yancy asked tightly. "I thought I had been rather generous to all of you."

"Oh, but you had, my dear boy! Very generous. But your generosity paled to nothing when compared to your great fortune. Why should I settle for Domingo when I can have it all—once, of course, I marry your widow." Tom looked pleased. "Sara seems to like older men, doesn't she? She married Sam, didn't she? With Hyrum gone and you gone, I don't think I shall have much trouble convincing her to marry me. After all, I will be a grieving spouse also—just think how we can console each other!"

Yancy's teeth gritted together and he took advantage of the shadows that hid most of his body from Tom's view, inching his fingers desperately toward the knife hidden in his boot. His wary gaze flicking between Tom and the glowing fire, Yancy said dryly, "It would appear that you have it all thought out."

"Well, I actually can't take all the credit—I told you Hyrum and Ann came up with the idea first. I merely refined it and shaped it to my advantage." He glanced at Hyrum's still form. "I enjoyed killing him, you know. Oh, and by the way, the men you had watching him? You'll be happy to learn that I didn't kill them; someone will eventually find them tied up in Hyrum's house—I was careful not to let them see me, and it'll be just one more little mystery for the others to ponder over."

Something suddenly dawned on Yancy. "Your arm," he said slowly. "You're using it!"

Tom smiled slyly. "Oh, yes. I have been for some time, but it seemed so convenient to have everyone think of me as a cripple. People look at you differently when you are crippled—they think you're harmless." He glanced up toward the loft. "It made my wife grow careless and allowed me to spy on her and her lover whenever it suited me. I knew everything they planned! *Everything*! They were such fools! Acting as if a crippled arm had turned me into some sort of doddering idiot! She'd been quite brazen lately, letting her true feelings show a little too much. But in the end, I fooled her!" Tom's mouth twisted. "Her and that sister of hers, thinking they could manipulate me any way they wanted. Well, I showed Margaret the folly of *her* ways, and now I've shown Ann that I am not the simple lapdog she thought I was!"

"Margaret?" Yancy said carefully, an arrested expression on his face. "What do you mean, you showed Margaret?"

That bone-chilling giggle drifted on the smoke-scented air. "Why, only that the silly little bitch thought that she could force me to divorce Ann and marry her!" Tom looked petulant. "She knew that I wanted to be the next judge—tried to tell me that the scandal wouldn't make any difference. Stupid slut! As if I ever could have been elected judge after doing such an outrageous thing. Divorce my wife to marry her sister—who divorced *her* husband to marry me! It was ludicrous! It wasn't to be considered, not even for a moment! I tried to explain all that to her, but she just wouldn't listen!" He turned to the fire and dropped a few more pieces of wood on the flames, saying idly, "She was so beautiful. I'd never met anyone like her in my life and she utterly dazzled me. I was mad for her, even though I suspected that it was only my money she wanted." He glanced back at Yancy. "I was *much* richer than Sam in those days, maybe even richer than you are! Much more affluent and more socially active than your father, and I think Margaret had decided that I would be a better bargain, even if she had to cause a terrible scandal to get what she wanted. She was determined to let nothing stand in her way." He giggled again. "I didn't let anything stand in my way either. When she realized that I wasn't about to fall in with her schemes, she threatened to tell Sam that it was my baby and that she would cause a scandal anyway, just to spite me. I couldn't let that happen, so I stole Bartholomew's dagger and I killed her."

As he listened to Tom's careless confession, Yancy was uneasily aware that the barn was steadily filling with smoke and that the fire was now burning merrily on its own, fiery tendrils licking out greedily to consume whatever it touched. The air was still fairly fresh near the ground where he lay, but it wasn't going to stay that way for very long, not with the fire spreading with every second that passed. He tested his bonds again, to no avail, and with a careful eye on his captor, strained to get his fingers on the knife concealed in his boot top.

At the moment, Tom wasn't paying attention to him; he was far too busy watching the fire and bragging about his exploits, and Yancy prayed that he stayed that way long enough for him to reach the knife. Suddenly Tom swung around and looked directly at him and Yancy froze.

Somewhat proudly, Tom said, "I was the one who put the snake in Sara's bed. I thought she knew that I had killed Margaret, and I wanted to prevent her from saying anything." He shook his head. "What a mistake that would have been! I nearly got bitten myself transporting it to her room, and it was only later that I perceived that Sara had not understood the significance of the conversation she had overheard between Ann and Margaret that night at Magnolia Grove." A moody expression on his face, he continued softly, almost to himself. "I was so frightened at first that I could think of nothing but shutting Sara's mouth, and the snake seemed like a good idea. I realize now that it would have been terrible if my plan had worked and she had died." He smiled. "If I don't marry Sara, how else can I get my hands on your fortune?"

"How else indeed," Yancy replied dryly, wondering that none of them had ever suspected how dangerously ill Tom had become. Probably, he decided grimly, because everyone had looked upon him as a broken, pitiful man, never seeing what was lurking beneath the surface.

"I *am* sorry, you know, that you have to die this way," Tom muttered. "I always liked you, Yancy. You're a fine man, and Sam was good to me after I lost everything. Granted, since I saved his life during the war, he should have been, but still . . ."

"You don't have to kill me, you know—you could let me go," Yancy suggested blandly.

"Oh, no, I can't change my plans now," Tom replied earnestly. "I've already killed Hyrum and Ann, and you know about Margaret, so I simply have *no* choice but to arrange your death, too, now that you know everything."

Tom looked around him, obviously satisfied with the way events were going, and Yancy took a chance and began to struggle away from the fire, towards the doors of the barn. The fire was beginning to crackle ominously, the smoke becoming thicker and more rank, voracious gold-and-scarlet tongues curling around the posts of the loft, the inside of the barn eerily illuminated by the growing flames. In a scant few moments more, the place would be an inferno; no one would get out alive. . . .

Tom suddenly glanced over at Yancy and, seeing him wiggling toward the barn doors, cried out in a scolding tone, "No, no, you must not escape!" Rushing after him, he grabbed Yancy's feet and dragged his protesting body back toward the fire. Nearly breathless from his exertions, he complained, "I planned this too well for you to ruin it! It will be so tragic, all three of you killed in the fire." He gave another of those chilling giggles. "I have to tell you—I'm afraid I pilfered another one of Hyrum's plans. He and Ann had a most interesting meeting this afternoon, and I'm afraid that *we* were to die in the fire! That's why Ann wrote you that note—to lure you here so that Hyrum could kill you. Ann was supposed to get me to go for a walk with her in this direction, where Hyrum would be lying in wait for *me*! Once they had rendered me dead or unconscious, Hyrum was to start the fire, which would burn up all traces of the crime."

Almost oblivious of Tom's aimless chatter, Yancy risked a glance in the direction of the blaze and his blood ran cold. The fire was nearly in full fury, leaping wildly toward the ceiling, wicked whips of red and gold lashing in all directions. The heat was intense and Yancy's skin felt as if it had been scorched; the smoke burned his eyes and lungs and he knew there was not a moment to lose. Unless he got out in the next few seconds, he wasn't *going* to get out!

Lost in his own thoughts, Tom Shelldrake seemed to be completely heedless of the growing danger. Nearly pleading for Yancy's approval, he explained, "I couldn't let that happen, could I? Don't you agree it really was very clever of me to figure out a way to get rid of all three of you at once?"

"Not as clever as you think, you crazy son of a bitch!" Yancy growled, and putting all his power behind it, he angled his body upward and aimed both his feet at Tom's chest. Tom went down with an astonished grunt, and, all his energies focused once more on escape, Yancy snaked and rolled himself toward the barn doors as swiftly as he could. A sigh of satisfaction went through him when at last he bumped into the solid bulk of the doors. Frantic now to get out, terrified that he would never see Sara again, never see his child born, he struggled clumsily to get the doors open with his feet, only realizing after futile seconds that Tom must have lodged them shut from the inside. Dragging in deep gulps of air from the small crack between the doors, his body pressed tightly along their wooden length, Yancy strained to get his hands on the knife.

A sound, a shriek, a moan, he didn't know what it was, spun his head around and to his horror, amidst the leaping flames beneath the loft, he saw Ann suddenly appear, stumbling awkwardly toward the ladder. Fire was all around her, her figure clearly outlined against the flames, but she seemed to be as yet untouched as she staggered erratically along the edge of the loft, clutching her head and trying desperately to escape.

It was her cry that had caught Yancy's attention, her terrified cry that had also alerted Tom, who was just rising from the ground, the ladder next to him. He stood there uncertainly for a moment, his maniacal gaze swinging undecidedly back and forth between Yancy and Ann. Then with a bellowed "*No*! No! You will *not* escape!" he flung himself against the ladder and scurried up into the loft.

Transfixed by the ghastly scene that was playing itself out before him, Yancy lay motionless by the base of the barn doors, the smoke swirling in ghostly tendrils around him, his gaze locked on the two figures illuminated by the fire. Dimly he was aware of Sara's voice, of the voices of Bartholomew and Esteban and the others carrying through the night, and he knew that help was on

the way . . . for him, but not for Ann and Tom . . . never
for Ann and Tom. . . .

Cursing her, Tom finally reached his wife, pushing
her backward toward the flames. Ann fought him with
the fear-driven strength of a wild woman and, their
bodies locked together in a deadly struggle, they swayed
from side to side, utterly oblivious of their surroundings.
The back third of the barn was in flames; the posts
which supported the loft high above the ground began
to list dangerously as the voracious fire weakened and
consumed them. Even when the floor of the loft tilted
drunkenly as post after post gave way and crumpled
into the raging fire beneath them, Ann and Tom were
still bound together in their lethal battle, neither able to
overcome the other. Suddenly, with a shriek of splitting
wood and a thunderous boom, the loft collapsed into the
pitiless inferno below, great tongues of flames shooting
high into the air, glowing embers streaking in all directions, and the two figures were seen no more.

Held totally mesmerized by the horrific scene before
him, Yancy stared numbly at the spot where the
Shelldrakes had disappeared, hardly aware of the shouts
coming from outside the barn. It was only when, with a
solid thud, the doors were rammed from outside did he
realize what was happening. He had just enough time to
roll out of the way before the doors burst open with a
great crash, and blessed, cool, life-giving air rushed into
the barn. Groggy from the blow to his head and the smoke
he had inhaled, Yancy was only partially conscious of
what was going on around him, but almost immediately
Sara's voice, the most loving sound in the world to him,
drifted to him and he breathed in her sweet scent. And
then there were hands, many strong, eager hands, pulling
him from the barn, pulling him from death into life—life
that was all the more precious because Sara was beside
him, her breast against his cheek, her lips on his brow.

EPILOGUE

HEART'S EASE

Make channels for the stream of love
Where they may broadly run,
And love has overflowing streams
To fill them every one.

THE LAW OF LOVE
—RICHARD CHENEVIX TRENCH

⧜ 26

Despite the bucket brigade that Bartholomew organized the instant they had determined that Yancy would survive his ordeal, the barn could not be saved and the night sky was lit with scarlet tongues of fire. His head cradled against Sara's warm breast, from his position lying on the ground under one of large pecan trees a prudent distance from the blaze, Yancy grimly watched the leaping flames, the leaping flames that were to have formed his funeral pyre.

Her skirts spread out around her, her arms wound tightly around him, Sara watched the fire, too, reliving those chilling moments when they had all realized that the barn doors were securely barred on the inside and that Yancy was trapped amid that blazing inferno. She hadn't known then if he was dead or alive, but as long as she lived, she would never forget that jubilant second when they had found him and dragged him coughing and wheezing from the barn, cheating the fire out of one last victim.

Yancy stirred in her arms, and catching up one of her hands, he pressed an ardent kiss onto the palm. "You didn't do as I said, did you, sweetheart?"

Sara smiled faintly, not taking her eyes off the fire, but her fingers moved gently near his mouth. "No, I'm afraid I didn't. You hadn't been gone from the hacienda more than a minute before I went racing to find Bartholomew and Esteban and explained the situation. I was firmly convinced that you were in grave danger and that, no matter how prepared you were, things could go wrong. *I* wasn't willing to take any chances with your life!"

His gaze never leaving the blazing barn, watching as with a great shower of flames and sparks the roof finally collapsed, he murmured, "I'm glad that at least one of us was thinking clearly! Otherwise . . ."

Sara's arms tightened around him. "Don't say it! Oh, God, Yancy, I was so scared—I just *knew* that Hyrum and Ann planned to kill you and that there wasn't a moment to lose!" Her voice thickened. "Esteban and I wasted precious seconds trying to determine Hyrum's whereabouts, and when we discovered Juan and Rogerio gagged and tied up in his house, I was frantic to get to the barn!" She hesitated, then asked in hard tones, "Were *they* in there?"

Yancy nodded slowly. "All of them. They're all dead."

"What do you mean by *all* of them?"

Wearily he said, "Hyrum and Ann did intend to kill me, but Tom thwarted their plans and decided to adapt Hyrum's original plans to murder me and marry you for his own designs. He was in there with them."

Sara gasped and pushed him away so that she could look into his face. "Are you telling me that *Tom* was behind all this?"

Seeing Bartholomew and Esteban start their way and feeling more in command of himself, Yancy rose slowly to his feet and reached out a hand for Sara. "Yes, he was. He killed Hyrum—and planned for Ann and me to die in the barn fire, thereby accomplishing several things at once."

As Sara stared at him in horrified astonishment, Yancy turned to the two men who had approached them and said casually, "Well, gentlemen, it appears that is one barn we don't have to worry about repairing, wouldn't you say?"

In the dying light of the fire, they nodded, their somber expressions fading a little at his easy tone. It was Bartholomew who said, "You know, I hadn't thought of it exactly that way, but I believe you're right!" He cast Yancy a long look and asked quietly, "You okay?"

Yancy nodded and, his arm around Sara's waist, he replied, "I'm fine. Get someone to take charge of everything here and you and Esteban come to the hacienda. I have a long and complicated tale to tell you."

A half hour later, they were all gathered in the courtyard of the hacienda, the smell of smoke clinging to their clothes, their faces still streaked with soot. Sara and Yancy, Bartholomew and Tansy, and Maria and Esteban were seated comfortably around the table, and the others listened in thunderstruck horror as Yancy revealed all that he had learned during those perilous moments in the barn with Tom. There was a shocked, stunned silence when he finished speaking.

"It was Tom Shelldrake who put the rattlesnake in my bed?" Sara finally asked in incredulous tones.

Yancy nodded. "You apparently had mentioned to him a conversation you overheard the night before Margaret died, and something you said made him believe that you knew he had killed Margaret. His first thought was to shut you up as soon as possible, without, I might add, drawing attention to himself. It was only when that failed and he'd had time to think about it that he realized that killing you was the *last* thing he wanted to do. And I guess, in the meantime, your manner had reassured him that you were unaware of the importance of what you had overheard."

"And the incident with the bull?" Bartholomew asked grimly. "Who was responsible for that? Surely not Shelldrake?"

Yancy's mouth twisted. "No, I think we can safely assume that it was Hyrum who shot my horse out from underneath me. It's possible, since Tom wasn't the cripple we all thought he was, that he *had* concealed himself in the brush and taken advantage of the situation, but I doubt it—and he never alluded to it, despite being very eager to tell me everything else!"

In the early hours of the morning the small group finally broke up, and by the time they all sought out their various beds, the subject of Ann and Hyrum's dastardly plots, as well as Tom Shelldrake's confession of murdering Margaret and opportunistic schemes, had been minutely dissected and thoroughly discussed. Despite their best intentions to put the distasteful incident behind them, it was days before they could stop talking about it, weeks before Sara stopped waking up suddenly in the middle of the night and desperately reaching out to touch Yancy and reassure herself that he was alive and well and lying at her side. There was, however, one unpleasant task that had to be dealt with before the entire topic could be put away forever— someone had to go through the personal effects of Hyrum and the Shelldrakes and dispose of them.

Yancy volunteered to tackle Hyrum's few belongings, and Tom's as well, if Sara would see to the disposal of Ann's things. Although her first inclination was to let someone else do it, Sara made a face at her husband and reluctantly agreed. And so it was, one morning a few weeks later, that Yancy discovered Sara sitting on a chair in the house where Tom and Ann had lived, a small, locked iron box on her lap.

"What's in that?" Yancy asked as he walked up to her.

"I don't know," Sara replied with a frown. "I've looked and looked, but I can't find a key among her belongings that will unlock it." She looked across at her husband. "Why in the world would she keep it locked anyway?"

Yancy quirked a brow. "Love letters from Hyrum, maybe?"

Sara wrinkled her nose. "I suppose."

At first, after Yancy had made short work of the lock, it appeared that he had been right—there *were* several letters neatly folded in envelopes crammed inside the iron box. Distaste clear on her expressive features, Sara picked up one of the envelopes and, turning it over in her hand, said, "I have no intention of reading these!" She started to pitch the offending item into the fireplace, to be burned later, when something about the writing caught her eye. Puzzled, she looked at the envelope again and suddenly gasped. "This is one of Sam's letters to *you*! How in the world . . . ?" Her eyes widened and in shocked comprehension she stared at Yancy. "Oh! Of course! Ann or Hyrum must have intercepted them, not wanting you to appear and disrupt their original scheme until Hyrum was sure of me."

His brows snapped together and wordlessly he took the envelope from Sara, his name, written in his father's hand, leaping out at him from the front of the envelope. "More than likely, that's exactly what happened," Yancy muttered as, his face revealing nothing, he removed the letter inside and began to read it. When he finished, he looked away from Sara for a second and said gruffly, "You're right. It is one of Sam's letters to me."

With dawning enlightenment Sara stared down at the half-dozen or so envelopes now lying in her lap. "You never received even *one* of his letters, did you?" she asked in low, remorseful tones.

Yancy shook his head, and glancing over at her, his emotions once more under control, he said dryly, "If you'll remember, I *told* you that I hadn't."

Sara looked uncomfortable and admitted unhappily, "I didn't believe you—I thought you were lying for your own ends."

"Considering your appalling opinion of me, I wonder you ever married me," he retorted with a slight edge to his voice.

Springing up from her chair, the letters flying, Sara flung her arms around his neck and kissed him at the corner of his mouth. A beguiling twinkle in her green eyes, she said softly, "But that was before you took my innocence and blackmailed me into marriage and I learned to love you!"

Yancy laughed reluctantly and pulled her close. "I guess," he admitted huskily, "that we both acted badly at times."

"Mmm, that we did," Sara said against his mouth. "But that's all behind us now, isn't it?"

"*Por Dios*, yes!" Yancy said forcefully as his lips found hers, the letter falling from his hand as he lost himself in the heady magic that they created between themselves.

In early October, Yancy and Sara, along with Esteban and Maria, prepared to return to del Sol, leaving Paloma in Bartholomew's capable hands. The trail drive to the new railhead at Abilene, Kansas, would commence the following week and Sara was inordinately pleased with the way her plans had been implemented by Yancy. As they rode away from Paloma toward del Sol, she was surprised to discover how little regret she felt at leaving Paloma, despite its quaint charm; how eager she was to return to del Sol; how she longed for the first sight of the gracious walled hacienda with its magnificent grounds; how deeply she yearned to return *home*! She didn't know when it had happened, when she had stopped thinking of Paloma as the only thing that was really hers, had stopped thinking of it as a place of refuge and had come to think of del Sol as home. . . . So much had changed in the few months they had been at Paloma: these days she openly adored her tall, mesmerizing husband and knew without a doubt that he returned her feelings; her fears that he had married her to gain Paloma had been thoroughly banished; and she could now look forward to the birth of their first child next year, in late May, with joyful anticipation—no shadows or suspicions to cloud the now-longed-for event.

Some hours later, as del Sol came into view, she was smiling softly to herself, and glancing across at her, Yancy inquired lightly, "And why are you looking like such a satisfied little cat?"

She flashed him a dazzling look that left him nearly breathless. "Oh, I'm just so happy to be home!"

Almost as one, they pulled their horses to a stop and let the others ride on ahead. His eyes fixed intently on her lovely face, Yancy asked quietly, "Are you really, Sara? Is del Sol really your home? No regrets?"

She leaned over to him and brushed her lips against his. "Wherever you are is my home, and as for regrets . . . I have none, my dear husband. Not *one!*"

Heedless of the dancing horses, he dragged her into his arms, pulling her from Locuela onto his horse. Draped across his thighs, held securely in his embrace, Sara gave herself up to his hungry kiss. Her slender body was pressed ardently next to his, her arms tightly clasped around his neck, and as the heady, passionate emotions he could arouse so effortlessly began to rise in her body, she blessed again the fates that had brought this arrogant, outrageous and oh-so-*beloved* dark rider into her life.

They were both flushed and breathless when Yancy finally lifted his head, and with the sensuous promise of sweet delights to be shared through the years gleaming in his golden gaze, he said softly, "Let's go home, sweetheart. . . ."